# Hurricane Blues

# Hurricane Blues

Reed Bunzel

coffeetownpress

Kenmore, WA

Epicenter Press
6524 NE 181st St.
Suite 2
Kenmore, WA 98028
www. Epicenterpress.com
www. Coffeetownpress.com
www. Camelpress.com

For more information go to: www.coffeetownpress.com or
www.reedbunzel.com



This is a work of fiction. Names, characters, places, brands, media, and
incidents are the product of the author's imagination or are used fictitiously.

Cover Design by Anthony Sands
Interior Design by Rudy Ramos

Hurricane Blues
2020 © Reed Bunzel

Library of Congress Control Number: 2019943858

ISBN: 9781603817745 (trade paper)
ISBN: 9781603817738 (ebook)

Printed in the United States of America

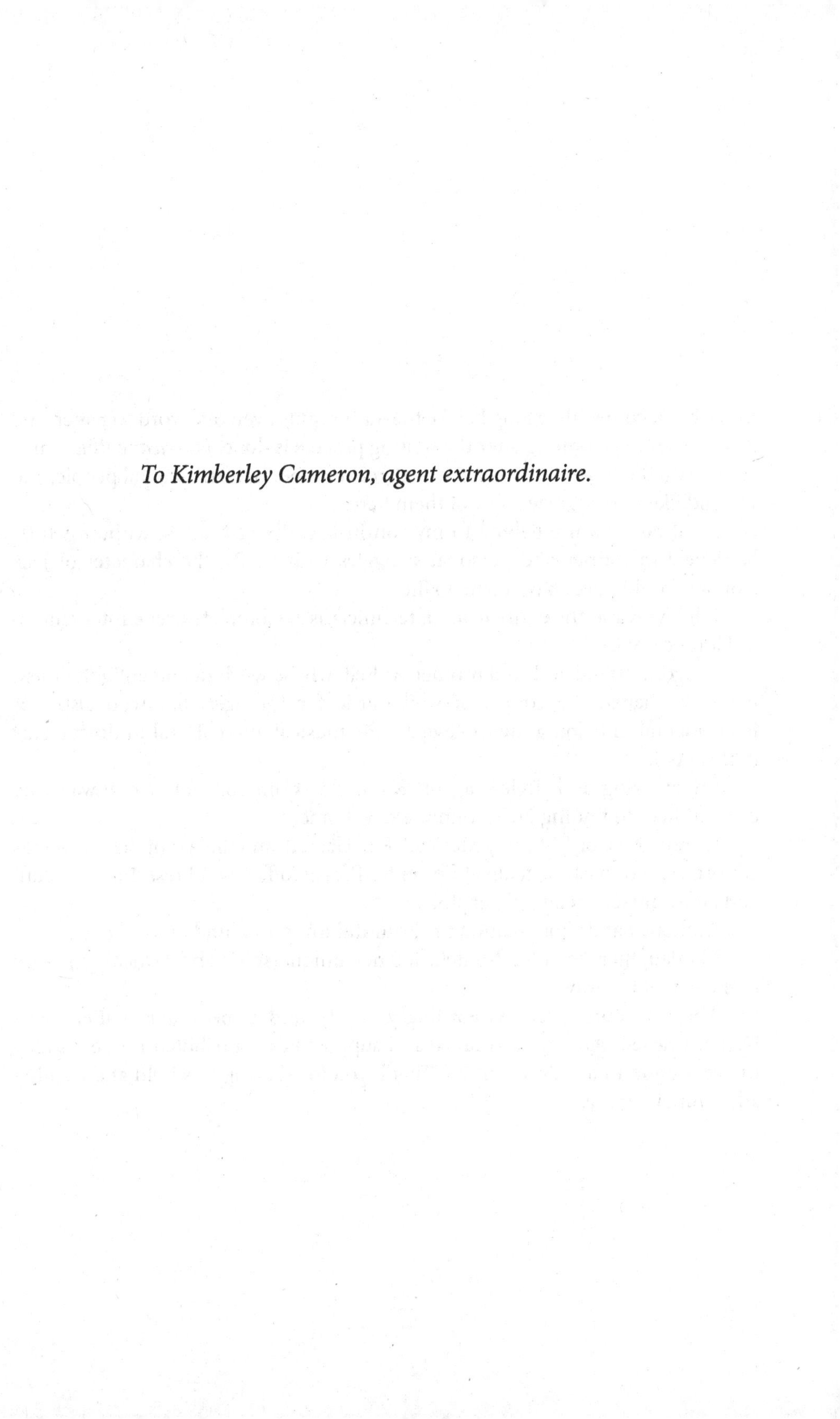

*To Kimberley Cameron, agent extraordinaire.*

Every book comes alive long before the author puts even one word to paper, and it continues to grow long after the writing process is done. *Hurricane Blues* came about with the welcome assistance of a great number of instrumental people, and I would like to recognize a few of them here:

As always, I am indebted to my son-in-law, Pierre Nantell, without whose battlefield memories and personal struggles with PTSD, the character of Jack Connor would never have come to life.

Bill Flynn and the entire team of technicians at Complete Scene Intervention in Florence, SC.

My good friend and soul brother Al Bell, whose wisdom and enlightenment not only shaped the course of soul music for the ages, but who also was instrumental in helping me to navigate the musical and cultural undercurrents in this book.

My amazing and tireless agent, Kimberley Cameron, for her unwavering commitment to finding Jack Connor a new home.

Jennifer McCord, Murray McCord, Phil Garrett, and the rest of the marvelous editorial and publishing team at Epicenter Press/Coffeetown Press, for their faith and belief in Jack's recurring exploits.

Anthony Sands, for creating the beautiful imagery found on the cover.

My daughter, Jennifer Nantell, for her unique spirit and critical guidance every step of the way.

And, of course, my extraordinary, lovely, and unbelievably patient wife Diana, whose ongoing reassurance and support has contributed immeasurably to every book I have ever written. Thank you for sharing this bold and dashing adventure with me.

# Chapter 1

Jack Connor stood in the doorway and stared at the grim scene that lay before him.

Blood had dried in brick-colored pools on the floor, drawing deep lines where linoleum tiles had been pushed together years ago. Crimson spatters streaked the walls, rough slashes that were thick near the floor but tapered to droplets near the ceiling. An almost sweet smell of warm copper hung in the thick air, while light from an aging fluorescent bulb flickered with the hesitation of a lost soul trying to decide whether to leave this world, or maybe hang around just a little longer.

*What the hell happened here?* he thought as bullets of rain slammed hard on the old tin roof. The rapid-fire drops and the scent of blood yanked him back to the streets of Kirkuk, a distant memory that still bit hard at the back of his brain. Just for an instant he was inside a blown-out concrete shell that once had been a corner market. He was holding his M4 and standing over the young man he had just shot at point blank range. Then, just as now, blood was pooling on the tile floor, and Connor heard himself curse as a dusty ray of light sliced through a crack in the fractured wall.

His Army unit had been on routine patrol through a neighborhood that at one time had been teeming with life. He and two of his men had ducked into the store for a quick sweep when the young man—really no more than a teenager— had disturbed a pile of rubble and surprised them. Connor had hesitated at first, not wanting to kill him. Shit—he didn't want to kill *anyone*—and for a second, they locked eyes in a showdown of bravado and fear. Then the kid pulled a gun from his loose-fitting trousers, and the look on his face shifted from surprise to hatred.

In that split-second Connor realized he had no choice, so he had fired.

At that moment a blast of thunder wrenched Connor back to the present. He blinked several times, trying to rid himself of the ancient memory, but the blood was still there. On the floor and walls of this room, and in the cobwebs of his mind.

"Hey, boss…you doin' okay?" came a voice from behind him.

"You never get used to it," Connor said, as the shift in both time and distance momentarily unsettled him. Then it all came together in an instant and he felt the familiar wave of anxiety subside. "All the blood and the life that was spilled in that damned war."

"I hear you, brother," Lionel Hanes agreed. He was standing in the doorway with a bucket of cleaning supplies he'd brought in from the truck. He stared at all the blood and added, "Sweet Jesus, if this don't beat all."

"I don't think Jesus had anything to do with this," Connor said as he slowly walked around the perimeter of the room. "Looks like someone butchered a hog in here."

"I've seen that, and this is worse."

"Don't know how," Connor replied as he glanced up at the ceiling. No blood up there, but plenty of rain hammering the roof. "Sounds like it's getting worse outside."

"It'll blow by in a bit," Hanes replied. He set the bucket down and came over to where Connor was standing. "Any idea what we got here?"

*Here* was the Cavalry A.M.E. church on Salters Hill Road in Ravenel, a rural town located a half hour south of Charleston. It was a simple white cinder block building with a modest steeple and three weathered crosses planted in the brown lawn out front. Connor and Hanes weren't actually standing in the church proper, but rather the vestry, where choir robes and other objects seemed to be stored. The room was about twelve by fifteen, with one window and a sloped roof that so far was keeping the weather out. The linoleum floor was well-worn by a half-century parade of shoes, and a good portion of it had been turned brick red where a body had bled out. The short story was that the victim had been stabbed repeatedly, which had caused the vertical slashes of blood on the walls.

"This just ain't right," Hanes said in a hushed tone. "Bein' it's a church, and all. They give you any idea what this was?"

"Same as it always is," Connor said. "Someone died, we clean it up."

Hanes shot him a look that translated to *give me a break*. "This is a church, man," he said. "You gotta be a little reverent 'bout what happened here."

Connor said nothing for a moment as he studied his friend and team member. Hanes was a few years older than Connor, a full ride Georgia Tech football grad who had played a total of four games in the NFL before an ankle injury ended his career. Now he was employed fulltime as a trainer at a local gym, and the part-time work he picked up at Palmetto BioClean paid for the high-end Nikes on his two sons' feet. Just barely, even at outlet store prices.

"All I know is a woman was killed," Connor told him. "From the look of things, she didn't stand a chance."

"Damn," Hanes said, shaking his head. "Police have any idea who killed her?"

Connor lifted his shoulders in a shrug and said, "County sheriff arrested her husband. Found him with the knife that killed her, guess they figured it was pretty cut and dried. Sorry. And keep that between you and me. When the others get here you don't know anything."

*The others* were D-Dub and Jenn who—along with Connor and Hanes—comprised the front line of Palmetto BioClean. Whenever there was a death scene to clean up, they got the call.

"I was brought up in one of these," Hanes said, using his eyes to emphasize the church itself. "African Methodist Episcopal. Largest black church in America, got started up in Philly and spread through the south after the Civil War. My mama taught Sunday school, but my old man rarely set foot inside. He figured if it was a day of rest for the Lord, it was a day of rest for him."

"I've seen these churches all over down here, but I didn't know what the A.M.E. thing was all about," Connor said.

"Who made the call about this job?"

"The pastor. His name is Parker, said he'd meet us here."

Connor had been walking out of the Citadel Mall when the call had come in on his cell, and he'd driven right down. He'd arrived about fifteen minutes before Hanes, who was just wrapping up a boxing drill at the gym when Connor had alerted him about the job. Since Hanes was closer to the BioClean facility where the truck was parked, he'd driven it down here.

"You mean you broke in?" Hanes said, his eyes wide with disbelief.

"Of course not. Reverend Parker said he left the back door open and to go on in if we got here ahead of him. Especially if it started raining. The cops had already cleared the scene, so here we are."

"And I'm sorry I'm late," came a voice from the doorway. The rain hammering on the roof had masked the pastor's footfalls as he'd come up the wooden steps outside, and now he moved into the vestry with the authority of a man of God. His eyes darted from Lionel Hanes to Jack Connor and he made an informed guess about the hierarchy here. He offered his hand to Connor and said, "Leon Parker…I think we spoke on the phone."

"Jack Connor, sir. I got here as fast as I could. And this is Lionel Hanes, my right-hand man."

Introductions and hand-shaking out of the way, Rev. Parker couldn't help but give Connor a thorough assessment. "You have a lot of tattoos, young man," observed.

"Sort of a work in progress," Connor said, managing a grin.

"Aren't we all," the pastor said.

Connor figured him to be in his late fifties, maybe sixty, a thin bristle of ash-colored hair covering his head. He was thin, almost lanky, dressed in jeans and a T-shirt that seemed odd on a man of the cloth. His dark skin had an almost purplish tint and carried the deep lines of a life that began in the era of separate washrooms and civil rights sit-ins. His eyes—large and deep-set and yellowed around the edges—spoke volumes about what he had witnessed through the years.

"I'm sorry for what happened here," Connor told him. "I had my office run a brief background as I was driving down."

"Ruby was a magnificent woman and a pillar of this church," Rev. Parker said, slowly nodding his head in painful reflection. "Ruby Freeman, that was her name before she got married. Grew up just south of here, in Hollywood. Sleepy little town, quite the opposite of the one out in California. The finest woman you ever met. As a girl she attended Sunday school in the old church, before this one was built. Got married right here. I performed her wedding. The second one, I mean."

That begged a question that Connor did not intend to ask. In fact, he said nothing for a moment, so Hanes filled in the silence by inquiring, "If I might ask, sir, how long ago did this happen?"

Reverend Parker though on this a moment, then said, "Thirty-five years ago this December."

"No…I mean, when did her death occur?" Hanes clarified. "I'm asking because it may help us determine the extent of what we have to do."

"Oh…right…of course," Rev. Parker said. "My mind does that sometimes, drifting back to other times, so you'll have to forgive me. What happened was, last Sunday we had regular church services, and then there was a potluck supper after that. Oysters, chicken, mac and cheese. Ruby stayed behind with a few others to help clean up afterwards, and then everyone went home. Except it seems that Ruby…well, the next morning Alicia James came in to mop the floor and…well, that's when she found her."

The mention of the name *James* raised Connor's attention. It was very common around the Charleston lowcountry, with a number of streets and even an island bearing the name. It also was the name of Connor's immediate boss and the owner of Palmetto BioClean. Jordan James. He parked a question in the back of his mind and said, "That was Monday—"

"That's right. Alicia called me immediately, right after she called the police."

"And they arrested her husband," Connor probed.

"Damned fools," Rev. Parker said as he rolled his eyes. He tipped his head skyward as if he was begging forgiveness for passing supreme judgment. "Everyone knows ol' Hurricane couldn't hurt a fly, let alone his wife."

"Hurricane?" Connor repeated.

"Lester plays a mean sax, blows it like a wild typhoon. Ruby was his entire life. He adored her."

"Right," Connor said. He didn't want to sound impatient or uncaring, but his real concern was how long the blood had remained pooled on the linoleum. "And that was the day before yesterday?"

"The police said time of death was likely around eleven Sunday night," the pastor said. "Maybe midnight. Why do you ask?"

"Blood has a way of soaking into everything, sir. And when it does it's almost impossible to get it out without total remediation."

"Whatever that is, it sounds pretty extensive. And expensive."

"Usually a bit of both, unfortunately," Connor said with a pensive nod. "Blood's a lot like water, except there can be a lot more nasty stuff in it. And just like when a water pipe breaks, blood can cause a lot of damage if it's left unchecked. Since this happened Sunday night we're probably looking at sixty hours, which means it likely penetrated through to the subfloor."

Rev. Parker pursed his lips and gave a resolute nod. "Just do what you need to. As I said, Mrs. Rollins was a magnificent woman and a cherished presence in this church. We want to do what's right. Whatever the insurance won't cover, the kind hearts of our church family will provide. How long do you think this will take?"

"About eight hours, give or take," said a voice from the doorway. "Unless there's termite damage or something else hidden under the surface."

Connor had seen D-Dub arrive and now took the opportunity to introduce him to the pastor. "Reverend Parker, meet D'Wayne Davis," he said. "He's our carpentry expert, and he'll be able to give you a better idea of what we're looking at once we take the floor off."

"Any chance you might know how many layers of linoleum there are?" D-Dub asked, nodding at the ancient tiles. "These old floors often were re-covered a number of times without removing the old stuff first."

In a previous life D-Dub— a.k.a. D'wayne Davis—had earned a respectable living doing drywall work, until the housing downturn had busted him almost flat. In the post-recession building boom he was back to hanging drywall, but his expertise was useful whenever the BioClean team had to deconstruct walls in order to remove the blood that had found its way into the deepest cracks and crevasses. His construction work was earning him a good paycheck again, but cleaning death scenes paid for his new home theater system, complete with widescreen TV and 7.1 surround sound.

"This is the third layer since I've been here," Rev. Parker said with a shrug. "I don't know what else might be under it."

"Well, we'll know that in just a few minutes—if we're good to go."

D-Dub looked at Connor, who glanced over at the pastor. Rev. Parker gave it about three seconds' thought, then said, "Do what you have to do."

As it turned out there were five layers of linoleum, dating all the way back to the 1970s. Glued one on top of the other, the entire mass was about a half-inch thick, which made the removal process more tedious and time-consuming than D-Dub had originally anticipated. But the additional substrata of linoleum also provided greater protection for the subfloor, and when the BioClean team had pulled it all up the old wood only showed a few dark lines where slight traces of blood had managed to seep through the seams.

An hour into the job the fourth and final member of the crew came charging through the door, a trademark can of diet Cheerwine in her hand. She studied her teammates for about half a second, then picked up a crowbar that was leaning against the wall and started scraping through the layers of linoleum.

"Sorry I'm late," she apologized without looking up from her work. "All the bridges were open, slowed me down."

"Luck of the draw," D-Dub said. "Get it? Draw bridge?"

She groaned and shot him a look that said *really?* Her name was Jenn, but she also was known as Jennifer, Jenna, Jenster, and The Jenmeister, depending who was talking to—or about—her. She was the rookie member of the BioClean team, and when she wasn't mopping up dried blood and other body fluids she taught yoga at a studio in downtown Charleston. She'd learned about Palmetto BioClean from an ad on Craigslist, and when she'd explained to Connor that she'd grown up embalming dead folks at her family's funeral home, he figured she had the stomach for the job. After a year without one episode of vomiting it appeared she did.

The rest of the team either ignored D-Dub's quip or hadn't heard it. Jenn caught Connor eyeing her yoga outfit and realized it wasn't quite proper attire for church. Or for cleaning up a room full of dried blood.

"I just finished teaching a class and didn't have time to change," she explained with an apologetic smile. "Where do you want me to start?"

"Put on a hazmat suit and see what you can do with the drywall," Connor suggested.

"I'll grab one out of the truck," she said. "Be right back."

Company regulations required that each team member wear an OSHA biohazard suit over his or her street clothes, as well as masks covering their faces and protective booties on their feet. Depending on the time of year and the presence of air conditioning this could become hot and stifling, but Rev. Parker had offered to turn up the AC in the vestry. The ancient unit was cranking as hard as it could but was barely churning out enough cold air to overcome the August humidity. The heavy rain didn't help matters much.

• • •

Nine hours later they were done. The entire room had been stripped of a half-century of cheap flooring, revealing that all but one small patch of the subfloor had been spared any blood seepage. D-Dub assured Rev. Parker he would come back the following day to replace it, and then the church could hire a carpenter to finish it up. Jenn had been able to scrub the blood out of the walls, except for one spot where she'd had to cut out a section of sheetrock. Fortunately, there was a small piece left in Moby Dick, the big white trailer that was towed behind the BioClean truck. D-Dub screwed the drywall scrap to the old studs, so all it needed was mud, sanding, and a fresh coat of paint.

Meanwhile Lionel Hanes had done most of the heavy lifting. He'd cut down the chunks of linoleum and disposable cleaning materials and packed them into sterile biohazard boxes, which then were loaded into the trailer. At the same time Connor had wriggled into the crawlspace under the vestry to inspect the subfloor and support trusses for contaminants. Once everything had been removed from the room he used one of the heavy-duty vacuums from the truck to thoroughly clean it.

It was more night than day when Rev. Parker returned, giving the job a nod of approval. "You folks are very thorough," he said with a sigh as he took one last look and closed the door. "I assume you have some paperwork for me."

"In the truck," Connor told him. "I just need your signature on a few forms and we'll take care of the rest."

"Even the insurance company?"

"That's a hassle no one needs at a time like this."

The horizon burned like a giant wedge of orange through the pines, and the underbellies of the parting clouds glowed with a violet hue. The rain that had pounded down earlier had long since cleared out, leaving behind a clean but earthy scent that a former girlfriend had once described to Connor as *petrichor*. She was all about helping him build his working-class vocabulary, and they hadn't dated very long.

Connor had already prepared the paperwork, which was affixed to a metal clipboard in the cab of the truck. It was a converted Ford E350 ambulance that had been refurbished to accommodate the needs of the work crew. All the emergency lights and markings had been removed from the vehicle, which now bore the words "Palmetto BioClean Services," along with the company logo that incorporated the international symbol for a biological hazard.

Lionel Hanes had driven the truck down to the site by himself, and he waited patiently while the pastor studied each page before signing off. When Rev. Parker finally finished he handed the clipboard over and again shook hands with Connor.

"Don't take this the wrong way, but I hope I don't have to do business with you again," he said.

"No offense taken, sir. And I sincerely hope you and your parish are able to move past this horrible time and think of Mrs. Rollins with only the fondest memories." Connor shuddered at his own words, thinking they sounded as if they'd dripped right out of a sympathy card.

"Blessed are the dead who die in the Lord, that they may rest from their labors, and for their deeds to follow them," the pastor recited from memory.

Connor had not been in a church since his niece's funeral years ago in Michigan. That had not been a pleasant experience for any number of reasons, particularly since his entire family blamed him for what had happened to her. Since then dozens of his buddies had gone home from Iraq in flag-draped coffins, and he still hadn't come any closer to God. Now he was at a loss for words.

"Revelations," Hanes said, filling the silence. "My mama would say that verse when someone in our family transitioned."

"If we live, we live to the Lord, and if we die, we die to the Lord," Rev. Parker said. "So, whether we live or whether we die, we are the Lord's. Romans fourteen eight."

"You're better at this than me," Hanes replied, lifting a shoulder in a shrug. Then he turned to Connor and said, "Mind if I head out? I've gotta pick up my boys before they fall asleep inside some video game."

"Go," Connor told him. "I'm right behind you."

Which would have been the God's honest truth if—at that very moment—a South Carolina state trooper hadn't pulled into the dooryard in front of the church. The flashing blue strobes on the roof bar sliced deep into the glowering woods. A bustle of crows took flight into the dusky sky, and even the wind seemed to stop blowing. The police vehicle was followed moments later by a very long and very black limousine, which skidded to a halt in a whirling dervish of dust.

Connor stared at the two vehicles with all the wonderment and respect that a limo usually commands. Its headlights cast long shadows against the front of the church, and absolutely nothing happened behind its tinted windows for a good fifteen seconds. Then the front door of the police unit opened and a trooper unfolded from the interior, one hand holding a Maglite and the other resting on the butt of a holstered gun. The cop assumed a posture of authority: feet slightly apart, back and neck rigid, tight lips that seemed full of purpose and power.

"Which one of you is Connor?" he demanded, his voice deep and threatening. "Jack Connor?"

# Chapter 2

Connor felt the same anxious hitch that seized him whenever some mucky-muck in Iraq had called his name or summoned him to HQ. No one ever wanted to gain the attention of the brass and, when it happened, nothing good ever came of it.

"That would be me, officer," he admitted now, taking a step forward.

The trooper eyed his tattoo sleeves with prolonged suspicion, then lifted a hand-held radio from his epaulet and mumbled something into it. A few words squawked back at him, and the cop said, "Ten-four." He had not taken his eyes off Connor the whole time, and now he said to him, "Come with me."

"What for?" Connor said. "Did I do something?"

The trooper started to say something, probably an authoritative quip to demonstrate who was in charge here, but his words were cut short when the front door of the limo swung open. A moment later the driver climbed out from behind the wheel. He was young and black and looked uncomfortable in the black suit and white shirt that looked far too big for his lanky frame. He adjusted the matching black cap on his head, then walked back to the rear door and gave the handle a firm tug. He stepped back and waited with a bored look as the occupant took his sweet time getting out.

Eventually a pair of seersucker trousers emerged, followed by a man in a matching summer-weight jacket. His skin was tan and tightly stretched over chiseled cheek bones, his eyes hidden behind dark glasses. A long-bill golf hat was perched on his head, and as he got out of the limo he looked very much like a duffer stepping out of an electric cart, ready to take his second shot on a long par five.

Connor had lived in the Carolina lowcountry for just under two years and paid as little attention as possible to state politics. Still, he recognized this man from the billboards that had greeted Charleston commuters for months during the interminably long election season last year.

"You're Connor?" the seersucker man asked, a fat cigar stuck between his lips bobbing up and down as he spoke.

"Yessir," Connor replied.

The man gave a brusque nod and walked toward him. "Governor Luck," he said, extending his hand to shake. "And a very lucky man I am to make your acquaintance." The words came out as if he'd used the same line thousands of times before.

"Likewise, sir," Connor replied, puzzled by the presence of this politician, and equally suspicious of what it might mean. "Do you mind if I ask—"

But the governor stopped him mid-sentence. "Tell your friends goodbye, then come join me in my car," he said. Then he pivoted on one heel and returned to the limo, where he disappeared into the darkness of the passenger compartment.

"Let's get you something to drink," the governor offered a couple minutes later, after the trooper had frisked Connor and allowed him to slide into the rear of the stretch Lincoln. Luck knocked on the bulletproof partition to signal the driver to get going, then settled into the plush leather seat. Once the car was moving he folded an armrest out of the seat back, exposing a small compartment that held a bottle of Russell's Reserve and two cut-glass tumblers.

"Anything you want as long as it's bourbon," he said with a chuckle.

Connor eyed the glasses and the liquor, wondering what the hell this was all about. He felt a thorn of contempt for the officious trooper who had patted him down before letting him get into the limo, but let it go.

"I'd better not," he said, shaking his head. "It's a long drive back."

"Not your problem," Governor Luck replied as he folded a polished walnut tray out of the wall separating the driver's seat from the rear compartment. He locked it in place, then set the glasses down on the heavily lacquered surface and poured two fingers of whiskey in each. When he was done he handed one to Connor and kept one for himself. "We're driving you home."

Connor had no choice but to accept the glass the governor pressed into his hand. "What about my truck?" he protested, cocking his head toward the POS Toyota parked under an oak tree whose limbs were weeping thick tears of Spanish moss.

"I was told you drove a Camaro. Nineteen sixty-seven with a three-ninety-six under the scooped hood. Orange."

Either the trooper had accessed Connor's DMV data on his computer or the governor had been talking to Jordan James. Either way Connor decided not to get into any of that right now. "It's in the shop," he said. "They gave me a loaner."

"Well, I've got you covered. One of the deputies from my detail will drive it home." Governor Luck touched his glass to Connor's, then said, "Here's to a speedy calm to the tempests of the past, the storms of today, and whatever squalls are yet to come."

Judging by the governor's speech, Connor had the distinct feeling the man had already had a head start on the bourbon. But three years in the military had taught him to keep his observations to himself, so he raised his glass and said, "Yessir."

"Please—my friends call me Howard," the governor told him as he knocked back the contents of his tumbler. "And I like to consider you my friend, considering how you took down my opponent last year."

"That was not my intention, sir," Connor said as he felt a film of moisture form on his bald head. "Mr. Wicke was the root of his own undoing."

Governor Luck waved off Connor's words as if he were brushing away a pesky mosquito, then sloshed some more bourbon into his glass. "Maybe so, Mr. Connor. Jack. Do you mind if I call you by your first name?"

"No, sir."

Governor Luck pounded the shot of Russell's Reserve in one fluid movement and closed his eyes as the liquor flowed down his throat. Then he said, "The way I look at it, if it was Wicke's roots what caused him to put that bullet in his brain, you shook 'em right down to the tips."

Connor reflected on the grisly events of last summer, how his dogged persistence had led to the very public suicide of a politician with a very deep and dark secret. "You reap what you sow," he replied, sipping his bourbon. Then, remembering what Jenn was always saying, he added, "Karma's a bitch."

"You sound like my wife," the governor said. "Anyway, that bastard got what he deserved. And so did the people of South Carolina, through the process of elimination. L-O-L." *El-oh-el.*

Connor glanced at the back of the driver's head through the glass partition. He figured the rear compartment was not only bulletproof but sound proof, as well. Not that it mattered; Connor had very little to say that was of any consequence to the world at large.

"I do my best to keep away from politics, sir," Connor told him. "Especially here in South Carolina."

"Jordan James said you were smarter than all those tats make you look. Seems he's right. Besides, that's not why I'm here. In fact, politics are the last thing on my mind."

Connor doubted that politics were ever far away from this man's thought processes, but he let it ride. "So, what would be the first thing?" he asked.

Governor Luck said nothing for a minute, pondering the empty glass in his hand. Connor could almost see the Tetris pieces falling into place as the man figured out how to proceed here. Eventually he set the tumbler down on the walnut tray and leaned back in his seat.

"Ruby Rollins was a part of our family," he said, his voice no more than a whisper.

"Sir?" Connor asked.

"Well, not by blood, obviously," he said quickly. "But she…well, Ruby worked for us for almost twenty years. Cooked the meals, cleaned the house, did the laundry. She sewed clothes for our kids, patched up their skinned knees, and drove 'em all over God's country to ballet class and baseball games. Shit—she even taught Peter to throw a nasty curve."

"Yessir," Connor said again.

"Anyway, when I heard what happened to Ruby…how someone took a knife to her… well, I can't believe she's gone. And my wife…well, she's a basket case. Curled up in a ball in our bed, can't stop crying."

"My apologies and condolences, sir," said stiffly. "I'm sure it *is* just like losing a relative."

"That it is," the governor said. "My wife thought of Ruby like a sister, or at least a cousin. And then those shit-for-brains cops go and lock up Lester for it. Total idiocracy. That man couldn't hurt a cottonmouth if it was bitin' him on his ass. An' this is just you and me talkin', you hear?"

"Loud and clear," Connor assured him. "But since you put it that way, are you going to tell me what this is all about? Just between us friends?"

The governor looked like he wasn't sure if Connor was being sarcastic, and Connor wasn't sure himself. There was something about Howard Luck that almost demanded impudence, the mix of bourbon and cigars and self-confidence that in many men doubled for narcissism.

"What this is about, Jack, is family. *My* family. My *son*, in fact. Peter, the one who learned to throw a mean curve and pitched for the Gamecocks three years straight. Thanks to Ruby. Thanks to Ruby for a lot of things. And my wife and me…well, we *owe* her."

Connor was sure Mr. and Mrs. Luck owed her for more than a good curveball, so he patiently took another sip of bourbon and waited. He glanced out the window at a mobile home that was illuminated with purple flood lights, like some kind of ghostly nebula framed by the tall coastal pines.

"You see, son," the governor continued, his choice of words indicating just how easy it was to go from being a friend to part of the governor's family. "Ruby Rollins, she not only took care of our children—she brought both of 'em into this world. She was a gifted nurse, and unlike Butterfly McQueen, she knew a whole Goddamn lot about birthin' babies."

Connor was pretty sure Luck was talking about an actress, and he figured the line was out of some famous movie. Guessed it probably something that had to do with the South.

"You mean Mrs. Luck had both of her children—you all's children—at home?"

"Exactly. Even back then Linda was into the natural birth thing, didn't want to go to some sterile delivery room. Karen was the first one to come along, and she was easy. Popped right out like the Pillsbury dough boy. But Peter…he was a little more trouble. Kinda breeched on the way out and got all caught up in the cord. If it wasn't for Ruby he probably wouldn't've made it, or at least had some issues. Soon as she saw what was going on she piled Linda into the car and drove her to the hospital."

"All the way to Charleston?" Connor asked, still wondering what this had to do with him.

"The Medical University," the governor said. "Best place to go. Traffic was heavy because of the July fourth fireworks, but she got there in record time. Plus, she knew the docs. They said the umbilical cord got twisted as Peter moved toward the birth canal, cutting off his supply of oxygen and blood. They have a term for it—anoxic brain injury—but Ruby's quick thinking saved his life."

"I can see why you think you owe her."

"We owe her big time. And now she's dead."

"And you don't think her husband did it."

"Like I said, he couldn't hurt a soul. Not human or otherwise."

Connor gave a slight nod and emptied his glass. Damn, if it wasn't the best bourbon he'd ever washed down his throat. "So why did the cops arrest him?"

"Cuz they found him with the knife that killed her. And he had Ruby's blood on his hands and clothes."

"Slam dunk."

"So they said," Luck said. "But I don't believe it."

"No offense sir, but it's more important what twelve men and women believe."

The governor turned and studied Connor long and hard, as if he were trying to figure out if he might be messing with him. "Can't take that chance," he finally said. "Which brings us to why I'm here. Why *we're* here."

They were somewhere on Highway 17—Old Savannah Highway—passing a farm store that had row upon row of orange Husqvarna tractors on lighted display out front. "I've been wondering when we'd get to that," Connor said.

Governor Luck picked up the bottle of bourbon and poured another splash into both glasses. There was no toast this time; he simply knocked it back, then stuffed his unlit cigar back between his lips.

"As governor of this great state I cannot take sides in a pending legal matter," he said. "It would be unseemly, and probably a violation of a half dozen of our archaic laws. At the same time, I cannot simply let Lester Rollins rot in that hellhole out on Leeds Avenue."

Leeds Avenue was the location of the Charleston County Detention Center, where Connor had spent twelve very unpleasant hours last year while he was tracking down the killer of a former girlfriend. The same killer who had been chasing Governor Luck in the last election, until Connor discovered an old skeleton in the man's closet and put an end to his ambitions.

"And you can't just issue an executive order to release him."

"Now you're seeing it," Luck said. "I need your help."

"I'm not sure what you think I can do."

The governor cut him off by raising the palm of his hand. "Jordan James said you'd be stubborn," he said. "Told me you're modest about your deductive ability, and that you'd try to say no. He also said you have a rational approach to your work, and superior critical thinking skills. Lord knows that's a lost art these days."

"There's no art in cleaning up death scenes, sir," Connor said. "And I think I know where this is going."

"Where it's going is, I need you to find out who did this," Governor Luck told him. "Mr. Rollins just lost his wife and the Sheriff's got him sitting up there at Leeds. The bond judge declined bail, despite the fact that he doesn't have a passport and he's been a pillar of the community for years. He won't last two weeks in that shit hole."

"Like I said, I'm not sure what you think I can do—"

"To hear Jordan James talk, there ain't nothing you can't do, son. Fact is, Lester Rollins did not kill his wife. He was nowhere near that church when she was attacked. But someone was. Someone who stabbed her thirteen times with a hunting knife, one right after the other. You saw the blood; you just cleaned it up. So what does that tell you?"

"What it tells me is whoever did it really wanted her dead," Connor replied.

"A crime of passion," the governor said. "That's what it was. No simple burglary, no one breaking in to steal the cash from the plate or the receipts from an oyster roast. Whoever it was had a grudge against that poor woman—and I want you to find him."

"Him?" Connor asked.

"I saw the crime photos, Jack. Those thirteen stab wounds were not done by a woman. Or Lester Rollins."

"But you said he was found with the knife—"

"Lester Rollins was playing a gig Sunday night, roadhouse in the woods down near Edisto. Sax and trombone. He admits to drinking too much, and he doesn't remember anything after that except waking up on his kitchen floor."

"So, he can't say for sure that he's not guilty—"

"He *isn't* guilty," the governor insisted, his voice growing agitated. "That's what I keep telling you."

"Yessir. He couldn't kill a spider or a skeeter. I'm just trying to draw a sketch here, fill in the colors later."

"This is not about color, son. Doesn't matter if he's white or black or green—he's part of the Luck family."

Connor ignored the governor's racial sensitivity. Memories grew as hard as oak in South Carolina, and there were many areas of the state where time and distance were still measured by the way Jim Crow flies.

"It's just an expression," Connor said. "Anything else I should know about the Rollinses?"

"So, you'll do this?" Governor Luck asked.

Connor stared at his glass. It was empty, and he decided it was best to keep it that way. The limo was stopped at a light in front of a used car lot that featured old American classics. A yellow sixty-nine Plymouth Fury with a black racing stripe seemed to be calling to him, and for a second, he felt guilty for visually cheating on his sixty-seven Camaro. The one that was in the shop, replaced by the POS pick-up he'd been given as a loaner. One more week, the guy at the shop had told him.

"I'll do what I can, sir," he finally said. "But I'll tell you what I told Mr. James when I did that thing for him last year."

"And what's that?"

"I'll take this as far as I can, but I can't make any promises."

"I'm a politician, Jack. I know all about the kind of shit promises can get you into. Just do what you can to find the bastard that killed Ruby."

"I'll do my best," he said, turning his attention back to the car.

"Nice set of wheels," Luck said, nodding at the Plymouth.

"My dad had a sixty-six, but it was a real gasmobile."

"I had myself a Stingray once, sixty-six rally red with a big block 427 V8. Real chick magnet, but it drove like a Conestoga."

Connor's mind flew back to the eighth grade and how his teacher used to tell him that U.S. history might seem like a real waste of time, but you never know when it might come up in real life. He figured this was one of those times. "Guess those pioneers could've used a few more Detroit horses under the hood," he said.

"That where you're from, right? Detroit?"

"Lansing," Connor said. "My dad worked the Cadillac line his whole life, and I did some time there, too."

"Well, now you're working for me," Governor Luck said. "But the thing is, no one can know about this. If it looks like I'm interfering in the Lester Rollins case it might appear..."

"*Unseemly*," Connor finished for him. "Don't worry. This is just between me and you."

Governor Luck detected a hitch of uncertainty in Connor's voice. "Except?" he said.

"Except I don't have a ticket."

"A ticket?"

"An investigator's license. Legally I'm not allowed to go poking around stuff like this."

"So, keep your nose down and it probably won't come up. And if it does there are ways of making things go away."

"Yessir." Connor thought a moment, then said, "I'm going to need to talk to Mr. Rollins up at the jail."

"Of course," the governor assured him. "So, we have a deal, then?"

"Like I said, no promises—"

"Right. Just know that I want you to spare no expense to get Lester out of jail. Save every receipt and I'll take care of everything. And that means you, as well."

"What *about* me?"

"Your compensation," the governor explained. "Like I said, Jack, this whole thing is off the books. It has to be. But when it's all over and done with—whatever the outcome—you'll be taken care of. Very generously."

"I'm not in it for the money—"

"Jordan James said you'd say that. In fact, he had a question or two about why you chase danger when most men leave it alone. He also said you'd change your mind."

Connor cast him a dubious look, just one of several since he'd climbed into the back of the governor's limousine. "Is that a fact?"

Governor Luck looked longingly at the bottle of bourbon, then glanced at his watch and offered a resigned sigh. "The only fact I know is that someone killed Ruby Rollins," he said. "And whoever did it won't think twice about killing again. That includes you, if you get too close."

"I spent sixteen months dodging bullets in Iraq," Connor reminded him. "I can take care of myself."

"I'm sure you can," the governor said. "But just like in war, shit happens. And I can't have any shit on my hands."

"I got that part," Connor said. They were on the Cooper River Bridge now, crossing from Charleston into Mount Pleasant, its suburban neighbor to the north. *Good*, he thought: *only a few more minutes of this*.

"What I want to make sure we're clear on is that I don't get a call from my chief of staff telling me something's happened to you."

"Like I said, sir, I can take care of myself."

"Yes, you did. But just like when you were in Iraq, you've got to look out for those around you, as well."

"Bring it on," Connor said.

Brave words, but the minute they left his mouth he sensed he'd just unleashed the fury of a thousand demons upon the earth.

# Chapter 3

The governor dropped Connor off at the Palmetto BioClean headquarters in Mount Pleasant, near the Wando shipping terminal on Long Point Road. It was a little past nine when the limo and state trooper disappeared into the night, and Governor Luck assured him that his rust-bucket pick-up was on its way. Assuming the transmission didn't fall out or the radiator overheat somewhere along the way.

Connor passed the time filling out the paperwork for the A.M.E. church job. The insurance form was four pages long and required a half dozen digital photos, which Connor had taken with his cell phone at different stages during the afternoon. Palmetto BioClean's policy was to file all work claims as quickly as possible so the client had as little contact with the actual clean-up as possible. The claims process was just another layer of bureaucracy that those who already were grieving didn't need to deal with, and Connor was glad to push it through on his end.

Hanes had already dropped the work truck and trailer off before heading out to pick up his boys, wherever he'd stashed them. Connor checked the gas and oil levels, then restocked it with cleaning supplies so it was ready for the next job. You never knew when the next job would be called in, and the truck had to be ready to roll at a moment's notice.

A few minutes later a state trooper knocked on the office door and peered inside through cupped hands. He was dripping with sweat as he handed Connor the keys to the truck and said, "Where did you get that shit box?"

"It's a loaner," Connor explained. "Hope third gear didn't give you too much trouble."

"What third gear?" the cop asked. He had a nameplate pinned to his shirt that identified him as Deputy Richard Stroble. "Damned thing's only got forward and reverse, the brakes are metal on metal, and the AC is busted. I'm probably breaking half a dozen laws just giving it back to you. "

"Feel free to impound it," Connor told him, halfway meaning it.

The trooper poked his head through the doorway and gave the office a brief once-over. "Palmetto BioClean," Deputy Stroble read from a laminated sign on the wall. "What do you guys do here?"

"We tidy up after people die. Crime scenes, decomps—that sort of thing."

"I get it," he said, nodding as if that it explained everything. "That's what you were doing down at that church."

"Someone's got to do it," Connor said, wondering how much the deputy knew—or thought he knew. "Mind if I ask you something?"

"Long as I can use your bathroom first," the cop said. "Your shock absorbers are busted, threw my bladder out of whack."

Connor showed him where the toilet was, down the hallway and to the right. When the trooper returned a couple minutes later he said, "That's better. You had a question?"

"Spending close to an hour with the governor makes you start thinking," Connor replied. "Are you part of his regular detail?"

Deputy Stroble flexed a shoulder and looked as if he was uncomfortable with the question. "I get called from time to time," he explained. "Security work, mostly. Tonight, it was to return your turdmobile."

"Don't expect me to thank you," Connor replied with a grin. "Anyone tell you what happened inside that church?"

"You probably know more than anyone, since you were saw it up close and personal. Besides, I thought that's what the governor wanted to talk to you about."

"He told me a bit, but I was just wondering what you might've heard. Beyond what's on the news."

Deputy Stroble scratched his chin for a second, then said, "All's I know is that black woman's death was a big deal to the governor. His wife close to had a breakdown when she saw it on the TV. I guess they must've been like sisters, or that yin and yang thing. Black and white, you know."

Connor knew. Black and white were racial bookends here in the South, typically at opposite ends of the shelf. "What can you tell me about Leeds?" he asked.

"You mean the county jail?"

"That's the place." The governor had already indicated he could grease the skids, but Connor wanted to leave his options open. "I need to get in and see the suspect. Lester Rollins."

"Why you want to do that?"

"I hate for the man to stay in that place any longer than he has to."

"Yeah—if he's really innocent," the deputy pointed out, a hitch of skepticism clouding his voice. "My experience, if a man ain't guilty of one thing, Lord knows there's usually something else."

"I guess that goes for all of us," Connor said. "Probably why Jesus said that thing about casting the first stone."

After the deputy took off, Connor ran a Google search on Lester Rollins. He wanted to know more about the murder of Ruby Rollins, and the quickest way to do that was to see what the local media had reported. The local newspaper and television coverage was thin, but at least was a start. The first story he clicked on, from the *Post & Courier*, gave him a thumbnail of what had gone down:

**Ravenel Man Held For Brutal Killing Of Wife**

Charleston County Sheriff's deputies arrested local resident Lester Rollins for the brutal slaying Sunday night of his wife, Ruby, following a potluck supper at the A.M.E. church in the town of Ravenel. Medical Examiner Ivan Mullinax said Mrs. Rollins was fatally stabbed in the church's vestry just before midnight, and a trail of blood led through the woods to the Rollins' home about a quarter mile away.

A spokesperson from the Sheriff's office said Lester Rollins, originally from Memphis, Tennessee, was found in the kitchen of his house, along with the knife that had been used in the attack. Tests showed his wife's blood was on his hands and clothing, and his fingerprints were on the handle of the knife. When questioned, he was unable to account for his whereabouts at the estimated time his wife was killed. The spokesperson indicated Mr. Rollins made statements suggesting he may have killed her.

A bond judge ordered Rollins to be held at the Charleston County Detention Center without bail, pending his formal arraignment.

Ruby Rollins was born and raised in Hollywood, SC, and attended local schools. A registered nurse, she worked as a domestic housekeeper for many years in the Ravenel area, and regularly attended services at the church where she was killed. According to Reverend Leon Parker, Ms. Rollins was known for her unyielding faith, generosity, and dedication to the church where she ironically was killed. "I have never seen anyone more committed to the teachings of the Lord Jesus and helping regular folks in need than Ruby Rollins," Reverend Parker said. "If she had not stayed late to clean up after our summer potluck, she would still be with us."

Lester Rollins moved to Ravenel in the late 1970s from Memphis, where he had established himself as a talented musician featured on a number of blues and soul recordings. He played trombone and saxophone for a variety of well-known artists including Otis Redding, Isaac Hayes, B.B. King, and Bobby Blue Bland. After moving to South Carolina, he was employed at a local painting company and also played with several bands in the area. He met his future wife, Ruby Freeman, at a wedding where they both were working. They were married the following year and lived in the Ravenel area since then.

Curiously, the story made no mention of Mrs. Rollins' connection to the Luck family, which Connor attributed either to professional courtesy of poor journalism. The article did, however, include photographs of both the deceased and the accused. The photo of Ruby Rollins was decades old, taken at the time of the announcement of her wedding to Lester. Connor could see she had been a knock-out in her early years; the black and white picture showed her to be dark-skinned with a thin face, stunning dark eyes, strong cheekbones, and an innate sensuality that reminded him of Lena Horne. There seemed to be an almost otherworldly beauty to her that in another place, another time would have led to a sense of royalty, but here in the South at this point in history she was defined by color, and color alone.

The photo of Lester Rollins appeared to be taken more recently, someplace dark and smoky and crowded. A broad grin showed two rows of white teeth, a broad nose, and deep-set eyes that seemed to be staring at someone—or something—just beyond the camera. A black leather cap was perched on the side of his head, and he was holding a bruised saxophone in one hand. Connor guessed it had been taken a few years ago at a bar or club somewhere in the area. Despite the old adage about not judging a book by its cover, Connor had a hard time thinking this old man could have taken a knife to anyone, much less his wife. But he'd been wrong before.

He found a half dozen more stories on different news sites but they all repeated the same general facts. Only one of them—really more of a blog written by someone who billed herself as an arts journalist for a weekly alternative paper—offered anything of value. The story mentioned that the night of Ruby Rollins' murder, her husband had been playing with his band at a place called The Nest, on Pelican Creek down near Edisto. The short squib did not mention what time Lester had arrived or when he'd left, but it confirmed what Governor Luck had told him earlier: Hurricane Rollins was playing a gig at a local joint but had gone home at some point later in the evening. The sheriff's office would have checked out the timeline to see if Rollins had been at the club at the approximate time of the murder, and since the old man was in jail they clearly believed there was sufficient evidence to hold him.

The governor was of a different mind, however, and Connor was starting to have his own doubts, as well. Blood on a knife did not come close to the reasonable doubt a jury would need to convict, but an even halfway-skilled prosecutor would ratchet it up as if it was the crucifixion. Still, as Miss Benson had hammered into the young minds in Connor's high school physics class, "'if P, then Q' does not necessarily yield the same results as 'if Q, then P.'" It all had to do with P and Q being true or false, true and false, or neither true nor false. Or something like that.

Connor had learned the hard way there was no easy path between true and false. Every time one of his buddies met the blunt force of a bullet or a bomb in Iraq, he grew more aware of the hazy shadows that dwelled between fact and fiction. The fiction was that the people who lived in the dark corners of war would welcome the soldiers that liberated them from the grip of tyranny. Handing out flowers in the streets of Baghdad was political mythology; the fact was they were grieving and angry at what the power of war had brought upon their lives. Many had taken up guns and IEDs to repel the invading forces in a religious battle that Americans back home barely understood.

Likewise, Connor sensed that a whole spectrum of truths and lies was lurking in the ugly darkness of Ruby Rollins' death. The sheriff's story was that Lester had laid down some sax and horn Sunday night at a roadhouse in the middle of the Carolina pines. Then, for reasons not even known to him, he had returned to the church, grabbed a knife, and hacked his wife to death. Whereupon he had trudged a quarter mile through the woods to his own house, where he blacked out and was found the following morning.

It certainly was possible Ruby Rollins' murder could have unfolded in such a simplistic and straightforward way but connecting the dots properly from following a logical and sometimes linear process of deduction. More than a few innocent men and women had ridden a needle because the dots had been connected too hastily, and Connor was worried Lester Rollins could be headed to a similar fate.

Unfortunately, Rollins had been under the influence of great quantities of alcohol at the time of his wife's death. As a result, he did not remember anything that had happened the night before, nor the next morning. Connor's father had been susceptible to the same blackout woes, and there were times that Connor wondered if the syndrome could be lurking in his own DNA. Dr. Pinch at the V.A. kept suggesting his friendship with gin was unhealthy, but so far Connor had no lapses in memory or blackouts. Still, he could certainly imagine how Lester Rollins had no recollection of what happened that night.

Connor had just locked the doors and climbed into the cab of his loaner truck when his cell phone rang. The screen told him it was Jordan James, and for an instant he thought about not answering. It was close to midnight and all he wanted to do was fall into bed as soon as he got home. But James was his boss and at least partially responsible for getting him into this thing with the governor, so he sat there with the engine idling and hit the talk button.

"Jack," the eighth-richest man in Charleston greeted him in a sloppy voice loosened by his nightly dose of martinis. Gin was just about the only thing he and Connor had in common, and tonight he sounded as if he'd indulged freely. "I hope it's...not too late...to call."

Connor knew Mr. James held the number eight spot in personal wealth because the local alternative newspaper had published a ranking of local millionaires, and James had threatened a lawsuit over it. Not because he didn't want the people of Charleston to know how much money he had, but because he didn't want the six men and one woman ahead of him on the list to lord their position over him. It was purely an ego thing.

"No, sir," he said. "I'm just leaving The Plant."

"Then I caught you...at a good time," Mr. James replied, either ignoring or not hearing the weariness in Connor's voice. "I understand you had...a long chat with...the governor."

"Good news travels fast," Connor acknowledged. "Mr. Luck loves his bourbon."

"He who is without vice…would set a real precedent," Jordan James said. "Vice precedent…get it?"

"Yessir."

"I also heard you're…going to help him out."

"Actually, it's Lester Rollins I'm going to help out," Connor corrected him. "Out of jail, I mean. I've been in there and it's no place for a man in his seventies."

A little over a year ago a couple of smug cops had arrested Connor on fabricated charges and dumped him in the county holding pen. He'd endured one sleepless night and a disgusting breakfast before Mr. James had sprung him, and the memory lingered like a stain on a motel sheet. Spending a night at the Charleston County Jail was not something most people put on their bucket lists. Unless Rollins was the cold-blooded killer the Sheriff believed him to be, it was no place for a weathered old black man who liked to crawl inside his blues and booze.

"That's why you have…a meeting with him…in the morning."

"A meeting with who?"

"Rollins. You can't just…walk in there and ask to have coffee…with a prisoner. They have rules…lots of them…so unless you're family or…have official business…with someone, forget it."

Connor said nothing for a moment as he thought this through. Despite being thoroughly inebriated, Mr. James was correct. Rollins was the keystone to this case, and Connor definitely needed to hear his story, told in his own words. The jail was a difficult place to navigate, and a little grease from higher up was always good at getting things moving. But James' A-plus personality often caused him to take charge of everything, and in this case,  he was doing that by cutting some corners with official protocol.

"Thank you, sir," Connor told him. "Still, I need to tell you—"

"I know…stay clear," Jordan James said. "That's what I told the governor… and I'll do the same. From now on I'm watching…from the sidelines."

"No sending in any plays," Connor insisted.

"You're the quarterback." Connor heard a clink of ice cubes on the other end, followed by more gin-induced ragged breathing. Then Jordan James added, "Meantime, when you get to the jail…tomorrow morning, ask for Darryl Powers. He knows you're coming…he'll get you in."

Twenty minutes later Connor was sitting in a cheap plastic chair on the small patch of grass that served as his backyard. He was sipping a glass of tonic water, no gin, gazing at the moon hanging in the thick black sky. According to the TV weatherman it was waxing gibbous, which Connor thought sounded like the name of an alt-rock band from the nineties. Somewhere out in the marsh something made a splash, but Connor had no reason to pay it any mind as he stretched his legs out in front of him and soaked in the warm August evening.

That's when his phone chimed, indicating a new text had just arrived. It was from Danielle, who had an early day tomorrow and should have been in bed hours ago. It read:

Can't sleep. You up?

Connor typed a reply explaining he'd had a long day and had yet to go to bed. Blood and death were still swirling in his head. He waited a minute, and then she texted back:

Sounds like a typical day at the office.

Working at Palmetto BioClean meant there were no typical days, and very few of them were actually spent in the office. In fact, Connor had begun doing some contract work at Citadel Security, another firm owned by Jordan James, who kept urging him to join the company fulltime. Citadel was in charge of security at the downtown shipping port, and goods had a way of disappearing from recently arrived containers. Mr. James had brought Connor on board—no specific title other than "advisor"—to help find out who was responsible, but so far, he hadn't been able to stop the thefts.

Danielle had been supportive of the change but was wary of any work that put him in the path of danger. Such as when James had hired him to find a missing painting a little over a year ago, a case that had almost gotten Connor killed. She'd made it clear she wanted no more of that, which he'd thought was sweet. So he wrote back:

Pretty much. Looking at the moon now, but hard to enjoy it with this empty chair beside me.

To which Danielle responded:

Make sure it stays that way, until I'm up there Friday.

This was Wednesday, which meant Friday was just two days away. Really just over one, considering that it really was Thursday now and Connor had an appointment with Lester Rollins in the morning. The timing was going to be trouble, since the governor of South Carolina expected him to get Lester Rollins sprung as quickly as possible. But he didn't want to go into any of that right now, so he wrote back:

I'm counting the hours

Thirty seconds later her reply came back:

Well, I'm going to go try counting sheep. Love you.

He texted "LU2" back to her, followed by a smiley face emoticon. Then the screen went dark, just at the same moment the moon—waxing gibbous as it was—slipped behind a cloud. Connor remained where he was for a minute, realized the cloud was big and the moon wouldn't be coming back any time soon. He drained his glass of tonic water and swatted away a lone mosquito, then stood up to go back inside.

He'd left the TV on, and as he slipped through the glass slider he found the late-late news was just ending. The station's meteorologist was finishing his long-range forecast, noting that temps were going to be in the low nineties. There was a thirty percent chance of rain the next few days, including when Danielle arrived on Friday. Typical summer weather pattern, with no end in sight.

"What we really need to watch is this tropical depression that moved off the west coast of Africa on Monday," the weatherman was saying. "The National Weather Service is predicting this mass of unsettled air will turn into Tropical Storm Eleanor by noon tomorrow, and if it intensifies as expected, it could become a hurricane by Friday."

Hurricanes were a fact of life in the Carolina lowcountry. The area was visited by one every few years, strong enough to cause wind damage and coastal flooding and jam up the lanes of the interstate heading out of town. The last major storm had been Hugo, which had killed several dozen people and destroyed much of the South Carolina coast back in 1989. Because more than a quarter-century had passed since that disaster, some locals said the area was due for another one at any time. Others insisted so much time had passed that the odds of a major hit in any given year were diminished.

"Let's take a look at the computer models," the meteorologist was saying. "While it's hard to predict these things more than a few days out, many of the long-range forecasts place the southeast U.S. coast inside the cone. That's the path a hurricane is likely to take as it makes its way northward."

Connor dumped the ice out of his glass and set it on the counter. He'd only lived in South Carolina for two years, and so far, Mother Nature had been more than kind. There'd been a couple brushes with tropical storms, but those usually drifted out to sea or fizzled before they got anywhere near Charleston. No reason to think this one would be any different.

"As I said, hurricanes can be wildly unpredictable, especially at this early stage," the weatherman expounded. "But all signs point to this one intensifying and, as Eleanor becomes a major storm, she'll definitely be one to watch."

# Chapter 4

Connor arrived at the Charleston County Detention Center on Leeds Avenue a half hour early. Planning a little extra time was always a smart move whenever the government was involved, and he figured this was especially true when prisoners were added into the mix.

He followed the plastic wall signs down a hallway and eventually found himself in a noisy room crowded with chairs that were not purchased with comfort in mind. Most of them were occupied, and mostly by women. It was a diverse crowd, a melting pot of blacks and whites and young and old. A few rugs rats were tumbling around on the floor, and one of the women—she couldn't have been more than sixteen—was trying to quiet down a toddler she was bouncing on her ample lap.

The woman at the Visitation Desk told him to sign in, then took his photo I.D. and ran a background check to see if he had any outstanding warrants. Connor spent the time trying to discern her name on the official badge she was wearing on a lanyard around her neck. He finally found it just as she looked back at him.

*Rhonda.*

"Who're you here to see?" she asked in a voice devoid of any life.

"Name's Lester Rollins," Connor replied. "He was booked in Monday morning."

"Well, that's going to be a problem," the woman named Rhonda told him. "A prisoner has to be incarcerated for at least seventy-two hours before receiving any visitors."

"Not even his attorney?"

"Lawyers and clergy are exceptions. But I usually have a good eye for people, and you don't seem to fit either category."

"No, ma'am. But this is important—"

"They all say that," she said. "I'm afraid you'll have to come back tomorrow."

Connor thought for a second, then said, "Where can I find Darryl Powers?" He hated taking the path Jordan James had smoothed over for him, but this was neither the time nor place to argue with officialdom.

Rhonda studied him over the rims of glasses that looked like they had either come out of the fifties or a box of used spectacles at the eye doctor's office. Eventually she made a clucking sound and said, "Do you have an appointment?"

"That's what I've been told," he assured her.

She fixed those fifties eyes on him, almost looking disappointed that she couldn't spoil his whole day. "I'll see if Mr. Powers is in," she said.

Mr. Powers *was* in, and five minutes later he came out from behind a locked door and looked around the room at the waiting spouses and girlfriends. He appeared perplexed, until Connor approached him and extended his hand.

"Mr. Powers? I'm Jack Connor. I was told to ask for you if I encountered any challenges getting in to see someone."

Mr. Powers was a short man, thinning gray hair, wire rims with lenses that made his eyes appear huge. His mustache was wooly enough for the Farmer's Almanac to predict the next winter, and his lips were thin and tight, like elastic bands.

"Mr. James said you might ask for me," Powers said. "He didn't say why."

Connor wondered how Mr. James and Mr. Powers knew each other, doubted they belonged to the same country club or social circles. "I'm here to see a detainee, but I'm told he hasn't been here long enough for me to do that."

"Just give me a moment and we'll have you inside," Powers said. "And by the way, we call them inmates here. Even if they're just awaiting trial."

Ten minutes later Connor was seated in a small cubbyhole that looked more like a flight simulator than a visitor's cubicle. The Charleston County Jail was equipped with a closed-circuit video visitation system rather than a face-to-face set-up with glass partitions and phones. It was designed to eliminate the smuggling of contraband and to cut down on having to move prisoners from one area of the jail to another. No direct visual or physical contact was permitted, another reminder that those on the inside were totally cut off from the outside world.

Connor made himself as comfortable as possible in a plastic chair and settled in front of a video monitor. The deputy who brought him in told him to be patient, that the prisoner was being moved from a holding cell and would be online presently. That took a few minutes, during which time Connor was privy to everything from deep sobs and violent cursing coming from the other viewing booths.

Eventually the monitor flickered to life, and the face Connor recognized from the online newspaper photograph was staring at him. He quickly introduced himself and thanked Lester Rollins for taking the time to see him.

"Time's all I got in here," Rollins grumbled, his dark eyes focused just a bit down from where the camera must have been located. "What bidness I got with you?"

Gone was the broad grin and the white teeth from the photo. In their place were an angry scowl and a deeply furrowed brow that reflected the defeat that a couple of nights in jail could bring upon on a man.

"My name is Jack Connor, and I'm here to get you out."

"You a lawyer?"

"Not in a million years," Connor told him. "I just think the cops got the wrong man, and I aim to set you free."

"Well, good luck with that. Why the fuck you care?"

It was a good question, and Connor didn't want to get into the details. Not just yet. "Like I said, I don't think you did it. Killed your wife."

"Well, good for you," Rollins grumbled.

"What about you? Do you think you did it?"

"Shit, man. I may've been drunk to the world, but I know I didn't kill my Ruby."

"Sheriff says you couldn't remember what you did and didn't do."

"Damned whiskey done changed my brain cells."

Connor studied the man on the screen, saw the misery in his tired eyes. "You're not helping yourself with this blackout bullshit."

"Bullshit? You think I like not bein' able to remember what happened that night? Damn—my wife's dead an' I'm lookin' at a needle for it. I'm screwed, so just leave me be."

"How'd you end up with the knife?"

"Damn, boy—you ain't listenin'. If I knew that, you think I'd be in here?"

"So, who did it, then? Drove a knife thirteen times into your wife until she was dead?"

Connor knew he was being rough on Rollins, but he had to jolt the old man out of his despair. Shock the self-pity out of him. He'd seen the symptoms of denial too often in the war, good soldiers who had witnessed or done things that were killing them inside. Way too often pride or vanity or shame pushed it all just below the surface tension of reality.

"Just get out," Rollins hissed. "Now!"

"I told you, I'm here to help—"

"I know why you're here," Rollins snarled at him, spittle bubbling from between his teeth. "You think I'm a drunk and a fool. Ol' nigger blues man can't stay away from the bottle, got sloppy drunk at some juke joint and lost his alkie mind. You know what a juke joint is, young man?"

"I've heard the phrase, sir—"

"It's a southern black thing," the old man said, raising his hand to interrupt him. "Comes from the Gullahs, actually, from around these parts. Slaves from Cape Verde, dragged here centuries ago. The word derives from the word *'joog*,' means to get blow-your-socks-off, down-and-dirty rowdy and disorderly. *Joog* joint."

"Is that what happened Sunday night?" Connor asked him. "Did you get down-and-dirty drunk?"

Lester Rollins leveled him with those large, black eyes and said, "I know what this is. It's that sorry-ass bastard up in Columbia put you up to this. Yeah—I can see it in your eyes. So, listen good to what I've got to say. I don't need you or the governor. My luck's done run out, an' I don't need no one's help."

For a drunk who hadn't had a drink in two days, going on three, Rollins' seemed to be more perceptive than the tired eyes and worry lines on the TV monitor let on. Connor sat there studying the man, looking for any movement in the deep creases, a wary blink of an eye or a nervous twitch of skin. But Lester Rollins had this hostility thing down pretty good, so Connor just rode with it. He knew Rollins could see him too, so he sat back and drew the blank look of indifference across his face. Then he waited.

Ten, fifteen seconds passed, but eventually Rollins spoke: "What you think you got?"

There: an opening. Just a small crack in the ebony veneer, but an opening was an opening. "What I've got is the truth, sir. I don't know what that might be, not just yet. Neither do you. But you give me half a chance I'm going to get you out of this stink hole."

"I got nothing out there, not no more," Rollins told him. "They took my Ruby away from me, and that's just 'bout killed me."

"Yes, sir," Connor said. "But you're in *here*, and whoever took your wife away is out *there*. And you ask me, whoever stole her life is thinking he's home free and clear. Is that all right with you?"

"Course it ain't right," Lester Rollins mumbled, shaking his head. "But what you think you can do 'bout it?"

"Whoever did this wanted more than your wife dead. He wanted her *really* dead. A thief would've beat her once and gotten the hell out of there. What that sick bastard did to your wife, he was full of rage."

Rollins waved off Connor's words with his hand, said, "See, that's the thing. Sheriff's not listening when I tell him I couldn't've done this. Just 'cause I don't remember what happened, don't mean I hurt my precious Ruby. I loved her too much."

"So, you have any ideas who it was? Anyone who was mad enough at her to kill her?"

"Nope," Rollins said, shaking his head. "Ruby, she was the kindest heart in the whole world. She would've given a stranger her last dime if she was asked. Everyone loved her."

"Not everyone," Connor pointed out.

Lester Rollins sat there and stared at the camera, his blank eyes void of life.

"Sunday night you were playing a gig?" Connor pressed him, changing direction.

Rollins nodded and said, "Place called The Nest, down near Edisto. We play there most Fridays and Saturdays. Sundays, too, if the mood strikes."

"Who's 'we'?"

"We got ourselves a band, play us some Chicago blues and Memphis soul. Old men, old style—not the lame-ass crap comes out of those gangsta dirtbags can't sing worth shit."

"Does this band have a name?"

Rollins looked up and cracked a slight grin. "Blacks and Blues," he said. "What it is."

"Do the other guys in the band have names?"

"You're wantin' to talk to them? Prove I was there?"

Connor shook his head and said, "I know you were there. But they might know something, could've seen something you don't remember. No harm talking to 'em, just to make sure."

Rollins thought on this a moment, then said, "I guess not. Talk to Walter. He's our bass man, does most of the vocals. Known him the longest of any of 'em, and my opinion, the brains of the outfit."

"Does Walter have a last name?"

"Hill…Walter Hill. He's been off the sauce for close to twenty years, brain's clear as a Blue Ridge breeze."

Connor made a mental note of the name, then said, "Thanks, Mr. Rollins. You've been a big help."

"Don't see how, but anything you can do's much appreciated. And when you see the governor, give him my best."

Connor narrowed his gaze and stared at Rollins' image on the screen. "How did you know—"

"C'mon, Tattoo. No one in this state's gonna take an interest in an old Memphis horn player except that man. Thinks my Ruby walked on water, and that goes twice for his wife."

"Well, you got me on that one," Connor admitted. "Just so long as it stays between you and me."

Rollins leaned back in his chair and laughed. "You think I'm tellin' anyone in here the governor of South Carolina's got a shine on me? I got me a dimwitted old black man image to protect."

Connor let out his own laugh and said, "I hear you. Look: like I said, I'm going to do my best to get you out of there. No guarantees, no promises. And no bullshit. But I may have other questions to run by you, so if I drop by, you'll know I'm making progress."

"Yeah, well, I ain't keepin' my hopes up," Rollins told him. "Mind if I ask you a favor?"

"Name it."

"I hear Ruby's funeral's tomorrow. Married thirty-one years and they won't even let me go to my wife's burial."

"That stinks."

"I'm tellin' you," Rollins said, letting out a long sigh. "I just was wondering, could you go? Not the graveside, if you don't want to. But the church?"

Connor hadn't been to a funeral since his niece had died up in Michigan. That was before he'd shipped out to Iraq, before several dozen of his buddies had gone down for the big sleep. Now he bit back on the impulse to say "no" and instead replied, "I'd be honored, sir."

The old man pressed his broad lips together and looked down, away from the camera. He was quiet for a long while and then, without looking back up, he muttered, "Thank you kindly."

Connor found Reverend Leon Parker sitting in a tiny office at the back of the A.M.E. church, next to the vestry that Connor's team had cleaned just yesterday. To call it an office was an exaggeration; it actually was a storage closet that had been fitted with a table, several chairs, and a wall cross draped with a purple sash that seemed to flow off the horizontal bar. Shelves that at one time had held paint cans and solvents now were cluttered with mementoes from the pastor's life: carved wooden statuettes that looked as if they came from Africa, old baseball cards embedded in Lucite, trophies from various sporting contests. Connor couldn't tell if they were from a church league or left over from the man's glory days.

The air conditioning didn't seem to be functioning, but a large oscillating fan was churning August steam around the room. Reverend Parker was pecking away on a keyboard when Connor knocked on the doorframe, then wiped the sweat from his brow when he looked up.

"Mr. Connor," he said, rising to shake hands. "I wish I could say it's good to see you again, but under these circumstances…well, you know how it is."

"I do, and I'm glad you could find the time to see me. I only have a couple questions."

"Whatever I can do to help," the pastor told him. He waved Connor toward one of the rickety ladder back chairs and said, "Please, have a seat."

Connor had called ahead to make sure Parker was at the church, then explained what he was up to. He'd left the governor's name out of it, but the pastor was a smart man and had easily heard what Connor wasn't saying.

"Whatever I can do," he replied. "What do you want to know?"

"What can you tell me that might shed some light on whoever really may have killed Mrs. Rollins?" Connor asked.

On the drive down from Charleston he'd run a replay of Sunday night in his head, looking at the murder from all available angles. At first, he placed Lester Rollins at the center of every play, trying to get a handle on whether the old man could have killed his wife. Then he substituted random suspects into the mix to see what motive and opportunity someone might have to stab the poor woman to death. At this stage of his inquiry he hardly knew any of the folks involved with Ruby Rollins' life, but everyone on that very short list was a suspect. Until they weren't.

And that included Reverend Parker.

"Like I mentioned on the phone, I'm trying to get Mr. Rollins a get out of jail card. I sure could use your help."

"Just what do you think I might know?" Reverend Parker asked.

"Everyone who knew Ruby Rollins knows something," Connor told him in an impassive voice. "It's just a matter of whether it means anything in the long run."

"I already told you all I know, yesterday. I admit it's not a whole lot and probably not very helpful."

"Maybe not directly, but it's also probably not all you know. So if you just have a couple minutes—"

"Sure, sure," Reverend Parker said with a sigh. He pushed back from his desk and folded his hands in his lap. "Like I said, whatever you need."

"And like I said, I need to know all I can about Ruby," Connor told him. "Yesterday you mentioned that she grew up around here, and you married her and Lester. But you also said she was married before that."

"Indeed I did. The first time was right after she graduated high school. She was a real sweet girl but fell in with a no-good sonofabitch. Gerald Walker was his name. Couple years older than she was, all he was interested in was finding himself a baby mama."

"I take it that marriage ended badly."

"I wasn't here back then, but a lot of folks thought maybe it would settle Gerald down. Instead it just got him looking around for his next mama. Three months later he was gone—Atlanta's what I hear—and he's never been back."

"And he left Ruby with a child to raise on her own?"

Reverend Parker shook his head sadly and chewed on his lower lip before he answered. "No, in fact, he did not," he said. "The Lord works in mysterious ways and in this instance, he reached down and took that little unborn baby right up into heaven. Ruby cried for months afterwards, but over time she convinced herself that God needed that child more than she did. So she stopped crying and turned her life back around. Changed her name back to Freeman, went to nursing school. Specialized in pediatrics, where she could look after babies who *did* need her. I'm telling you more than I should, but it was the best thing that ever could've happened to her."

Connor scribbled a few thoughts in a notebook, and when he finished he looked up and asked, "And you say this Gerald Walker's never come back?"

"Not that I know of. And since we have a pretty tight community here, I'm pretty sure I would've heard about it."

"Do you recall if he had a temper?" Connor pressed.

"Yeah, I'm told he did," Reverend Parker said. "I didn't know her back then, but the few times his name came up you could see it in her eyes. And I can see where you're going with this."

"It's just one of many places I'm going. What about Lester? Did he have a temper?"

The pastor seemed to think on this for a moment, then said, "He's gotten into a skirmish or two out at The Nest, busted a tooth or two. But I'm a hundred percent positive he never lifted a finger towards Ruby. Or their two girls."

"They had children?"

"Two lovely creatures of God. One's out in California, trying to make it big in the music business. The other one lives down in Yemassee, waits tables six days a week. How Ruby ever found time to raise them the way she did, only He knows."

Connor made a note of that, then said, "Can you think of anyone else who could've held a grudge against her?"

"Not in a million years," Reverend Parker said, almost too quickly. "She had a heart of gold, that woman did. Just ask anyone who knew her."

"I'll get to that," Connor promised him. "What about the governor? He told me Ruby did some work for the Luck family way back when."

"She was their sole household help for close to eighteen years," Parker said with a slow nod. "This was before he got himself elected to anything. Cooked and cleaned for them, delivered and raised both kids. Brought their daughter into this world, and pretty much saved their son when he was born."

"Saved him how?" Connor already knew the answer to this question but wanted to get the pastor's take on it.

"There was a problem during his birth. Something that had to do with his breathing, possibly anoxic brain injury. She rushed Mrs. Luck to the hospital, made sure the baby got the proper help. Sometimes I think Ruby was more of a mother than Mrs. Luck ever was."

Connor sensed deep disapproval in his voice, judgment that also was evident in his piercing eyes. "After eighteen years you end up seeing a lot," he observed.

"That you do. And Ruby had twenty-twenty vision."

Connor let Parker's words hang there a minute, then said, "This place you mentioned. The Nest. That's where Lester Rollins was playing sax the night Ruby was killed?"

"That's right. It's on the bank of Pelican Creek, in the pine woods down near Edisto. It was Lester's home away from home."

"He mentioned it to me this morning," Connor told him.

"You spoke with him?" the pastor asked, looking startled.

"It was more like Skyping, but yeah, we had a few words."

"How did he seem?"

"Like anyone caught up in that place would seem," Connor replied. "Angry, worried, grieving. Lost. So, who would you suggest I talk to about Sunday night?"

"It's not the sort of place I frequented, but talk to J'Neece Taylor. She owns the place, took over after her uncle died. She's there almost all the time."

Connor wrote down the name and thanked him, then said, "Lester told me Ruby's funeral is tomorrow."

The pastor nodded, then said, "There's a service here at the church at two o'clock, with burial immediately afterward. It's unfortunate he won't be able to be here."

"Is it open to anyone, or closed to just family and friends?"

"If you're asking what I think you're asking, you are more than invited, my son," Reverend Parker told him.

"Much appreciated, sir," Connor said. "It could be helpful in getting Lester Rollins out of that hell hole."

"Do you really think whoever did this might actually show up?"

"It's been said that the Lord works in mysterious ways, Reverend Parker. See you tomorrow at two."

# Chapter 5

Connor had parked the truck in the scorched lot to the side of the A.M.E. church, out of view of Reverend Parker's small, windowless office.

He started to pull the door open on its cranky hinges when he spotted an opening at the far edge of the field. He made his way over and found it was the well-worn entrance to a path that cut into the thick scrub of pine and Carolina creeper. Yesterday the pastor had said the police had followed a trail of blood from the church through the woods to the Rollins' house, and he figured this must be where that trail began.

He gently closed the truck door and made his way across the lot. The earth was damp from yesterday's rain, muting his footfalls as he retraced Lester Rollins' steps. The old man probably had come out through the back door of the vestry after finding his wife's bloody body. He'd most likely stumbled down the stairs, still clutching the knife, then somehow staggered toward the path through the woods toward his home. Connor pictured him weaving down the trail on wobbly legs, lurching from one tree to the next.

Why Rollins had gone home rather than remain at the church and call 911 was anyone's guess. Maybe he didn't have a cell phone with him. Maybe he didn't know where the church phone was and was too inebriated to figure it out. A lot of maybes, and not a lot of answers.

Then there was the knife itself: If Lester had not killed Ruby, why would he have picked it up and carried it with him through the dark woods back to his kitchen? The only explanation was that the overindulgence in whiskey wasn't helping Rollins think straight, and the shock of what he had just seen had caused him to black out.

A little further up the trail he spotted a little orange flag that someone had planted in the ground. Probably a detective or a member of the sheriff's Crime Scene Unit, marking a spot where blood had dripped to the ground. Further up the path he found another flag, and then another. It was like Hansel and Gretel marking the way home, but with a different outcome.

The pastor had said the Rollins house was a quarter mile through the woods, and Connor tried to picture the old man staggering all that distance in the middle of the night. The only light would have been that of a partial moon filtering through the pines, and the exposed roots easily would have pulled him to the ground. Especially after a night of drinking and carousing at some rowdy juke joint named The Nest on the bank of a tidal creek.

The path snaked through the dense woods, the edges defined by shallow ditches that were filled with run-off from yesterday's squall. Connor figured the trail had been built up manually through what must have been a waterlogged swamp, part of an old rice plantation that had been fashioned out of wetlands. Most likely plowed and planted and picked by slaves, land that now was overgrown with trees and vines and painful memories that were relegated to history books and local lore.

Eight wire flags later he came to a clearing. A muddy rut was cut through ankle-high grass and led directly to the rear of a small brick house with black shutters and an unpainted back porch. A couple of white plastic chairs were positioned so whoever sat in them could look out over the back yard, and an old oil drum cut lengthwise was set on X-shaped braces. A clothesline was stretched between two metal poles, an array of clothespins marking where Ruby Rollins probably hung her laundry on warm summer days. An old bird bath had a spray of flowers sprouting from it, and an empty birdfeeder dangled from a low branch.

Connor spent a minute absorbing the scene, then made his way toward the house. He took care not to step in the creases of mud and sludge that had formed in the path. A musty fecund odor filled the air, and the screech of a raptor—hawk or turkey vulture, Connor wasn't very good at these things—filled the cloudless sky. He hesitated a moment and gazed at a large bird rising on a thermal. That's when the back-porch door opened and a shotgun appeared, aimed directly at him by the shadow that was standing behind it.

"Who the fuck're you?" a voice called out, followed instantly by the distinct sound of a shell being pumped into the chamber.

Connor stopped in his tracks and raised his hands, palms outward. He hadn't thought this far ahead so he didn't have a good answer. He simply said, "Name's Connor. Jack Connor."

"What the fuck you want?" the man with the gun demanded, jerking it in Connor's direction in emphasis.

"This the Rollins house?"

"Stay put, else I'm gonna blow you're fucking head off."

Except for raising his hands, Connor hadn't moved a muscle. Not an inch. He was studying the man up on the porch, squat and rotund, knit skull cap pulled tight over his head. His skin was dark, almost midnight, and his face seemed flat and wide. He was wearing black jeans that hung low on his waist, and an old shirt with a faded logo was stretched over a pulled pork belly.

"The reverend at the church other side of the woods, there, said there was a path that led to the Rollins place," he replied, skirting the truth and enunciating every word while he was doing it. "Is this it?"

"Why you want to know?" the man barked at him. Trying to sound confident but coming across as nervous. Maybe even afraid.

Connor squinted at him, saw now that he was no more than a kid. Just like so many other scared kids in his platoon over in Iraq. A lot of them barely out of diapers, trying to be brave when they actually were terrified of every little movement or sound. Petrified that some blood-thirsty raghead would plant a bullet in their head, and just as scared to show the rest of the squad the fear that was cinching every inch of their gut. "I'm here about Lester Rollins," Connor called back. "He's a friend."

"You're a friend of Mr. Rollins?" the kid said, shaking his head in disbelief.

"I'm trying to help him."

"I don't believe you," the large kid with the gun snapped.

"It's the truth," Connor insisted, trying to sound patient and non-threatening. "And if you want to know what Lester told me this morning when I spoke with him, put the gun down."

The kid had no immediate response. He just stood there on the back porch staring at this bald white cracker who had come through the woods into the backyard. He probably couldn't see all the tattoos from where he was standing, but Connor's calm demeanor—and the fact that he said he'd spoken with Rollins— seemed to settle him.

Finally, he lowered the gun, just a couple inches, and said, "Get over here. Slowly. And keep your hands in the air."

Connor did as he was told. He was far enough away to turn and make a mad dash into the woods, but he had no doubt the kid would take a shot, sending a load of buckshot into his ass. Besides, he was curious who this guy was, and what he was doing with a gun inside Lester and Ruby Rollin's home. So he made a point of showing that his hands were as high in the air as they would go and walked very slowly across the soggy backyard.

"I'm unarmed," Connor told him as he started up the splintered back steps. Carefully, one step at a time.

He looked the kid right in the eye, trying not to drop his gaze to the gun. Mostly trying not to return in his mind to that day in Kirkuk and the young Iraqi kid he'd shot dead.

"See, no weapon?" Connor said, turning slowly like a music box ballerina doing a pirouette in ultra-slow motion.

"Pockets," the kid said.

"Search 'em," Connor said. "My hands are staying in the air."

The kid seemed uncertain, not knowing what to do next, so Connor took the opportunity to break the ice. "Look, pal. If I were in your shoes I'd be suspicious. Bald white dude coming through the woods, what are you going to think? Especially given the circumstances."

"What circumstances is those?"

"Mrs. Robbins is dead and her husband's in jail because of it," Connor explained. "I don't think he did it. And you don't either."

The kid looked down at the plank deck and Connor saw his finger ease up a notch on the trigger. He could've gone for a flash of surprise, try to grab the gun, but he decided to let this play out. Eventually the young man said, "They was good to me, Mr. and Mrs. Rollins. Better'n most, and believe me, I known a lot."

"How do you mean, they were good to you—"

"I had nowhere else to go."

"So, they took you in?"

"Yeah, an' not for the money. County pays shit. They was good people, 'specially Mrs. Rollins. Not that we didn't have words, an' shit. They kicked me out on my ass more'n a couple times. Thing is, I deserved it. But she didn't deserve this."

The poor kid—Connor now figured him to be nineteen at most—was trying not to let the tears give away his fragile façade. A gun, even if it was loaded, only went so far to provide courage or nerve.

"How 'bout you put that gun down and we go inside?" he asked.

"Not so fast," the kid told him. "You got something says who you are, *Mr. Connor.*"

Connor slowly reached for his back pocket. The kid nodded permission, and Connor took out his wallet, showed him his driver's license and a business card that identified him as an investigator with Citadel Security. It was a bit of a stretch, Jordan James' idea of providing him latitude if he ever needed a way out of a pinch. Like this one.

"Please point that thing somewhere else," he said as he tucked the wallet back in his pocket.

The kid obliged him by aiming the rifle at the deck. But he was still fidgeting, his trigger finger dangerously close to taking a life. "You really saw Lester?" he finally asked, a nervous edge in his voice.

"This morning, like I said," Connor told him. "You got a name?"

"William," he said. "But my friends call me Bacon cuz of my size."

Connor nodded, remembering how cruel kids could be to other kids. "How 'bout a last name?"

"I got two of those. My sperm donor, his name was Reeves, but he was gone before my momma even knew what he done. So I got her name, Truman, and that's who I am today."

"You live around here, William Truman?"

"Hell no. No, my crib's up in North Charleston. Got me a job in a paint store, cleaning the place mostly."

Connor inhaled a deep breath, saw the kid relax a bit. "When was the last time you saw Lester or Ruby?" he asked.

"You think I killed her?" Bacon snapped, suddenly agitated, his hand tightening on the gun.

Connor had seen the edginess before, the glossy eyes and the fidgeting and the paranoia that seemed to lurk in the back of this kid's brain. He figured he either was cruising on some sort of benzo high, or coming down from one.

"Actually, I'm pretty sure you didn't," he said. "Just like Lester didn't. But here you are at the Rollins' house, so what I want to know, is what the fuck are you doing here?"

Bacon jerked his entire body as if Connor had slapped him, then shook his head as if trying to clear it of spiders or bad memories. He glanced down at the gun, then stared off at the woods as if in some kind of measured daze.

"It's all I got," he finally said. "I been smacked, whacked, beat, whipped, slapped, pounded, even locked in the basement for days and nights. People are fucking evil, man, and I seen the depths of it. But none of that happened here. Lester and Ruby, they's decent folk. Gave me food and a place to sleep."

"So, what happened?" Connor asked him.

"I turned eighteen, is what happened," Bacon said, his voice suddenly almost a whisper. "They said I could stay, but the money—what little there was—it all dried up."

Connor nodded instinctively, wondered why Reverend Parker hadn't mentioned that Lester and Ruby had served as foster parents. He'd said they had two daughters of their own but had left out any reference to taking in foster kids.

"And you're what now?" Connor asked.

"Just' turned twenty."

"You've been working in the paint store since you left this place?"

Bacon shook his head slowly and looked down at the floor. "Things happen," he said. "You know how it is."

It was a loaded statement, again something Connor had heard from dozens of fresh recruits who joined the Army as a course of last resort. Fact was, the U.S. military was populated by the same people the Statue of Liberty welcomed into New York harbor: the tired, the poor, the huddled masses yearning to breathe free. Add to that the fatherless, the hopeless, the jobless, and those without a chance for a future and you pretty much filled all those boots that politicians were so hell-bent on putting on the ground in order to let freedom ring.

*You know how it is.*

"Tell me," Connor said. "How was it?"

"Why you give a fuck?"

It was a good question, and Connor didn't have a good answer to it. So he said, "You got me there, Bacon. Why don't you tell me why I should give a fuck, especially if you don't?"

"I still got the gun," the young kid said, placing a firm hand on the polished wood stock.

"You're not going to shoot me," Connor told him. "Not with that gun, which I suspect belongs to Lester."

Bacon blinked rapidly and his eyes began to well up. "It ain't right," he finally said. "Miss Rollins is dead, and they got Mr. Rollins locked up for it. Anyone got any sense know he ain't done this."

"Exactly," Connor said, his gaze shifting from the gun to the kid's dark eyes. "So help me out here. You have any idea who could've murdered that poor woman?"

Bacon spent a minute pinching his skin, his clothing—just about anything that could be pinched. Then he said, "Can't think of one person woulda wanted her dead…she was just too nice to everyone."

"But someone did," Connor reminded him.

The kid chewed on that idea for a few seconds, and Connor let him take his time. "Whole lotta time's gone by since I lived here," he eventually said. "People change, things change. But some things stay pretty much the same, 'specially if you be black."

"You think someone could've killed Mrs. Rollins just because of her skin?"

"Like that never happens no more?" Bacon said.

Connor shrugged, watched as a squirrel shimmied into the crotch of a live oak and made a jump onto the limb of a sweet gum dripping with Spanish moss. "You mind if we go in, take a look around?"

"You really lookin' to spring Mr. Rollins from Leeds?" Bacon asked, a distant hitch in his voice sounding as if he was familiar with the place.

"If he's not guilty, someone else is," Connor told him. "I aim to find that bastard and make a swap."

"Follow me," Bacon said, handing Connor the gun. "Better take this, less I shoot somethin' with it."

They entered the house from the rear porch and stepped into a tidy and very homey kitchen. It had been spared the HGTV touches—no granite countertops, no cabinet upgrades, no center island with six-burner gas range. Just a standard kitchen that an older couple had lived in for years. Floral paper on the walls, cookie and sugar and flour jars on the Formica counter. The fridge and stove were the same green as Connor's mom's up in Michigan—avocado, he remembered—and frilly valences puffed out at the top of the window over the porcelain sink.

Connor surveyed the room carefully. It was a piece of Norman Rockwell Americana, except he didn't remember seeing too many black people in those old pictures. A ceramic bowl still had bananas and pears in it, and a small chalk board on the wall indicated Ruby and Lester had been out of peanut butter and bananas. A pile of plates and bowls was waiting to be dried and put away, but there was no one to bother with that right now. Except maybe Bacon, but he didn't seem to be the homemaker type.

Governor Luck had said the police found Lester Rollins slumped on his kitchen floor, along with the knife that allegedly had been used to kill his wife. Connor again tried to picture the old man staggering through the back door and collapsing against the wall, possibly right there in front of the refrigerator. There were no scuff marks on the linoleum or obvious blood spatters, but that was a detail that at this point didn't matter. All that information would be in the case file, if Connor was able to get his hands on it.

Not very likely, unless the governor was able to pull some serious strings.

"What're you lookin' for, anyway?" the kid named Bacon asked as Connor moved through the doorway into a compact dining area.

"Whatever speaks to me."

"Like, you hear voices and shit?"

"Not so much," Connor said. He glanced out the kitchen window at an old Suburban parked in the driveway, figured it probably was Lester's. "Usually just something out of place, maybe comes to me later when I'm not thinking about it."

"Yeah, I get it."

Right now, nothing in the dining room was doing much talking at all. A table and six matching chairs—dark wood that looked like it had weathered several generations—were the center fixture. A sideboard contained a full set of china decorated in an ornate pattern. Connor assumed it was a wedding gift from long ago. A rogue's gallery of photos hung on one wall, some of them lopsided, and he studied them for a moment to get a sense of family here. All the people in the pictures were black except for one that showed a young woman—Connor assumed it was Ruby—flanked by a smiling white woman and man. He recognized the man as a young Howard Luck, grinning there to Ruby's left, but there seemed to be a blankness to Mrs. Luck's eyes, as if a veil had been pulled down over them.

The rest of the house revealed more of the same. The living room was furnished with a well-worn couch and a couple overstuffed chairs. A coffee table ringed with old stains was set in front of them. More photos cluttered the walls and a book shelf was crammed full of nick-knacks and a few trophies. Singing competitions, mostly, probably the older daughter who was now trying to break into the music biz. But there was one trophy that depicted a pitcher winding up on the mound, causing Connor to recall how the governor had said Ruby had taught his son how to throw a decent curve. A large contemporary print hung over the mantle, an image of an African American musician playing dual keyboards and bearing a signature that said it was by someone named Michael Wallace. Connor didn't know the name but got the sense that he should.

Down the hall he found three bedrooms, one slightly larger than the other two, and they all shared a modest bathroom. The two smaller rooms were decorated in a style that suggested Ruby and Lester Rollins longed for a visit from their kids, either biological or foster. The bedspreads seemed musty, and a thin layer of dust covered almost every flat surface.

"Which one was your room?" he asked Bacon, who was following one step behind him.

"Right there, across from the bathroom. Their girls were gone, so both rooms were used by kids they took in, like me."

"How well did you know these other kids?"

Bacon shook his head, as if it were a dumb question. "There wasn't many, and none of 'em stuck around too long."

"You ever see any of them anymore?"

"It wasn't like we were family or nothin'. They came, they went."

"Any of them have a grudge against Mrs. Rollins?"

"Nothin' that might've caused 'em to kill her," Bacon replied. "And the

Rollinses—it wasn't like they was a foster factory. It was just a couple kids in a bad way. Like me."

Connor nodded as he took a quick look through the master bedroom. It was filled with old furniture refinished to look nice, floral bedspread and curtains that spoke of a woman's touch. In fact, the entire house seemed to have the personality of Ruby Rollins, which caused Connor to stop and think a minute. Something was missing here, and it took a few seconds to figure out what it was. Then it hit him, and he did almost a full turn as he surveyed the bedroom.

"I don't see any instruments," he said to Bacon. "There had to be music."

The kid's mouth turned up in a grin and he said, "Follow me."

They went back to the dining room, where Bacon studied the seventies-style paneling for a second. Then he pressed the heel of his hand on a section and gave a firm push. Part of the wall sprang back an inch and the kid flashed Connor a mouthful of teeth that hadn't seen a dentist in years.

"Mr. Rollins was a fine musician, but Miss Ruby wouldn't let him play in the house," he said as he pulled open a section of the wall. "Not the main part, anyways."

He flicked a light switch, then invited Connor to go up a steep set of rickety stairs. They led up to a musty attic space, a long narrow room smelled that smoky and stale, as if cigars had been lit and puffed for long hours at a time. Probably something else Ruby wouldn't let her husband do downstairs. Connor had to crouch to avoid the sloping rafters, but there was enough headroom in the center to stand up straight and take a good look around.

No doubt about it; this was Lester's man cave, except it was much more an emporium that spoke to the history of music. At one end of the long, narrow space a half dozen saxophones of all sizes rested lazily against metal stands. Next to them several trombones stood on their bells on the floor. A set of black pearl Ludwig drums was set up in the corner, while several Fender guitars were displayed on a hand-crafted rack. A small electronic keyboard was wedged into a corner, and a collection of slide harmonicas rested on a stool beside it.

But the instruments were only part of it. The low vertical walls beneath the sloped ceiling were lined with shelves that held row after row of old vinyl LPs from over a half century of American music. Connor glanced over at Bacon, who seemed to know what he was thinking.

"Go ahead…take a look," the kid said. "Mr. R was proud of his collection."

Connor pulled out one of the albums, the cover of which mostly showed the bald head of soul superstar Isaac Hayes. He grinned at the memory of "Hot Buttered Soul," going all the way back to when his dad would drag him down the street to Tyrelle Liggins' house on a Saturday afternoon. Connor was just a kid then, about six or seven, and Liggins usually had some sort of soul or blues playing on the stereo while he and Mr. Connor drank Schlitz from cans and talked about how they would change things on the GM line if they were put in charge, just for one day.

Connor slipped the album back into its place and slid out another, this one titled "Gerald Albright: Sax For Stax." Next to it was the Memphis Horns' "Flame Out" and "Get Up And Dance." Connor found all of it fitting, considering the array of tarnished brass in the corner.

"This is one helluva collection," he said as he eyed the shelves that ran the length of the narrow attic.

"Just 'bout every blues, soul, and R&B record ever made," Bacon said. "Stax, Motown, Volt, Chess—everything up to when they stopped doing vinyl. That's what Mr. R said, at least."

"I get the feeling he'd know. You ever hear him play?"

"All the time, when I was living here. He'd bring me up here, wail away on that sax until my head hurt. An' he was damned good."

*I'll bet he was*, Connor thought, getting the feeling that playing weekend gigs at The Nest was just a fragment of the entire story. "What about Mrs. Rollins?" he asked.

"Man, she had a beautiful voice," Bacon said with a shrug. "When she let loose in that church her voice would wake the angels. An' when she sang that old song by Beyonce—I forget the name of it—there wasn't a dry eye in the house."

"The house?" Connor repeated. He took one last look at the attic, then turned toward the narrow staircase.

"The Nest," Bacon said, following him. "I mean, she wouldn't let me go there, but what I heard, her and Mr. R, they killed 'em."

*Odd choice of words*, Connor thought. "You mean Ruby—*Mrs. Rollins*—sang when her husband played?"

"Not all the time...Mrs. R didn't much like that place. But sometimes, when the mood struck her, she'd go with him, and when word got out she was on stage the joint got jammed to the roof."

Back downstairs Connor took another good look around the kitchen, snapped a few photos with his phone. Then he opened the back door and stepped back out onto the porch, ejecting two shells from the rifle and pocketing them before handing it back to Bacon.

"Be careful with that thing," he told the kid. "You'll shoot your eye out."

Bacon stared at him with that same blank expression that seemed to be the canvas on which the rest of his life was painted. Then a spark jumped a distant synapse and he brightened for a second.

"'At Last,'" he said.

"At last what?"

"That's the song Miss R used to sing," Bacon said, triumph in his voice. "By Etta James. If she'd been a hittin' woman she would've slapped me upside my head, me thinking it was Beyonce."

# Chapter 6

Connor retraced his steps through the woods to the church parking lot. The afternoon was quiet and hot and carried a fetid aroma like a pot of okra that had been left on the stove too long. The dense canopy of oaks and pines and sweet gums trapped the summer heat, and by the time he'd climbed inside the creaky old pick-up truck his shirt was soaked and his scorched head was throbbing like a baked potato.

He had just swung a wide loop through the lot and was ready to pull onto the two-lane when the door to the church vestry banged open. Connor expected to see Reverend Parker wander down the stairs, maybe remembering one last detail that wouldn't add up to much, so he was surprised when a man with pale skin and long blond hair backed down the steps. From this distance he looked like any kid wasting his life pumping gas or picking up trash on the side of the road for the Department of Corrections. He was gesturing wildly and yelling something at the pastor, who remained standing in the doorway.

The truck engine was too loud for Connor to hear what was being said, but the gestures told him this was not a pleasant social call. At one point the man started back up the stairs but stopped, and Connor slipped the transmission into Park just in case he needed to run interference. But the blond man backed off again, throwing one last gesture at Reverend Parker before storming off toward an F-150 dually that had mud smeared behind its wheels and, Connor noticed, on its rear plate.

Connor waited until the truck disappeared around a bend in the road and the vestry door swung shut. He sat there a moment, the engine idling, wondering whether he should go back inside to speak with Reverend Parker, see what that was all about. Instead he chose to leave it alone and instead go in search of the place called The Nest. He gave one last look at the church, then made a right turn onto the highway and headed east toward the small town of Hollywood.

fter three wrong turns and a few suspicious looks when he asked for directions, he found the place. It was marked on the main road by a hand-painted pallet sign with an arrow that indicated the place was two miles down a gravel road called "Pelican Run." Every twist and turn into the pine woods seemed to take him another decade back in time. The houses here devolved from brick postwar ranches to squat cinder block cottages to rusted trailers, and finally weathered gray shacks that seemed to have sprung from the loins of Reconstruction. Dogs and kids ran freely in the road as he steered the truck further toward the tidal marsh, knowing the place had to be around here somewhere.

One final crease in the road and there it was. Despite what he'd heard about The Nest, Connor hadn't known what to expect, and somehow it was both exactly and nothing as he'd imagined. The main structure was low-slung, weathered board-and-batten walls and an old tin roof that was patched with different shades of rust. A large sign with the words "The Nest" and a silhouette of a robust pelican were hand-painted on the front wall, and the dense limbs of live oaks provided a cooling shade against the afternoon sun. To one side of the parking lot was a lopsided storage shed constructed of ribbed aluminum roofing, and beyond that a dock stretched far out into the water.

A dog of no recognizable breed lifted its head as Connor backed his loaner truck into a spot in the thick canopy of the oaks. Figuring nothing out of the ordinary was about to happen he dropped his head back between his paws as Connor cut the engine. A dozen vehicles were scattered around the lot, mostly old pick-ups of various makes and models.

He sat in the cab of the truck a few seconds as the engine ticked, then got out and slowly made his way to what appeared to be the entrance. A heavy smell of pork barbecue and smoked oysters hung in the air and blended with the smell of pluff mud exposed by the low tide. The house dog gave him only a cursory glance as he passed, his inquisitive instinct giving in to the torpid heat of a steamy summer afternoon in the south. Then the front door flew open, the screen slamming against the weathered siding with enough force to send several crows into the sky. A man and woman stumbled outside on legs softened by booze and driven by the promise of lust that was only a backseat away. They ignored Connor as they staggered toward an old Buick parked at the edge of the trees; the dog didn't lift his head an inch as they scuffed by.

Connor grabbed the screen door on the rebound and stood for a second in the entryway before pushing his way inside. At first glance it seemed like any corner tavern he'd known in Michigan or upstate New York, when he was posted at Fort Drum. A wooden bar stretched the length of the place on the right, and about a third of the dozen stools were occupied by men who were slumped over their drinks. Connor had always figured you could tell a bar by the bottles on display, and if that were the case here this was a bourbon and gin crowd. No designer Cosmopolitans or pear martinis here.

He edged himself onto one of the stools nearest the door and gave a slight nod as one of the slouched men shifted an eye and gave him the once over. Then a woman, maybe early thirties, wandered up and used a balled-up rag to wipe up something off the bar in front of him.

"What can I getcha?" she asked him, fixing him with a pair of deep brown eyes.

"What kind of beer do you have on draft?"

"Whatever we didn't run out of last night," she said.

"Guess I'll have one of those," he said, flashing her a bright smile.

She ran a mug under a tap, letting the beer fill it slowly and then dumping off the small head of foam that had formed. She set it in front of him, no napkin or cork coaster or pretense. "We don't get a lot like you in this place," she said, nodding down the bar at the other drinkers.

Connor took a long sip of beer, the cold liquid feeling good as the brew sizzled down his throat. Then he said, "That going to be a problem?"

"Not here," she said. "Just saying." Then she nodded at his tattoo sleeve and added, "Besides, you got more color on that one arm, there, than anyone in here."

"That's nothing compared to what you can't see."

"Way too much information," she giggled.

Her skin was almost the color of coffee, with a dollop of cream in it. Her face seemed fashioned out of Hollywood stardust, and damn if she didn't have the most beautiful eyes. He found himself thinking *what are you doing in a place like this,* then realized this place was no better or worse a place for someone to build a life. His mind flashed on Ruby Rollins' daughter, living out in California and trying to be discovered, probably working in a place no better or worse than The Nest. And her dreams were probably no better or worse, either.

"Jack Connor," he introduced himself, extending his hand across the bar.

"J'Neece Taylor," she said. "And you don't look the type to just make a wrong turn and walk into a juke joint at the end of a dirt road."

"I heard you had the biggest selection of beer in the state," he told her.

"Evidently you heard wrong."

"Still, it does the trick."

J'Neece folded the dishrag one way, then the other. "What else did you hear about this place?" she asked.

"That you've got some of the best blues and soul going this side of Memphis."

"Place does get jumping some nights," she said with a nod. She unfolded the rag needlessly, then folded it again just as a spark went off in her eyes. "Let me guess: you're here about The Hurricane."

Connor narrowed his eyes and focused on hers, trying to measure what she was talking about. "What hurricane?" he asked her.

"You a reporter?" she quizzed him, her tone suddenly suspicious. "'Cuz if you are, that beer is free and then you're gone."

Connor set the mug down on the bar and sat upright. The lightness in her eyes was clouded by a veil of distrust, almost anger, and he didn't blame her. "You're right. I didn't make a wrong turn and end up here. But I'm not a reporter, and I'm not here to do a number on anyone. And I don't know about any hurricane, except maybe the one the guy on TV is talking about out in the Atlantic. Like I said, I heard this was the place to go to listen to some good ol' fashioned blues. And I also heard no one makes the music rain 'round these parts like when Lester Rollins wailin' on his sax."

J'Neece placed both hands on the bar, the rag under one of them. "Like I said, The Hurricane. No one can touch that man when he's on fire. And right now, he's sittin' up there at Leeds 'cuz the law is blind when it comes to black."

Connor sat on his stool and studied her. And his beer. He picked up his mug and took another long sip, letting a good, long time go by before responding. Then he said, "Maybe we should start this over again," he told her. "Like I said, my name's Jack Connor. But what I didn't say, and maybe I should've, is I'm here to make sure Lester Rollins gets his ass and his sax back down here to Pelican Creek."

"How're you gonna do that?"

"Any way I can."

The young bartender grabbed his mug and ran it full again. She set it back in front of him and said, "Lester was like an uncle to me, 'specially since my real uncle Lou died last year. Left me this place."

Reverend Parker had already mentioned that J'Neece owned The Nest, but Connor didn't want to let on what he knew, or how he knew it. "This is all yours?" he asked, looking around the joint.

"The bank's got a big chunk of it, but yeah. So, what you're sayin' is real? You're here for Lester?"

"I'm here for the truth," Connor told her. "And something tells me the truth and Lester are on the same side in this."

"That's what I told the sheriff, when he came in here with all his questions." J'Neece nodded her head toward the door in emphasis. "But that dickhead, he already got it all played out in his head the way he wants it."

"I know how that goes," Connor said, going on personal experience but also playing up to her. "So, tell me about Sunday night."

J'Neece glanced nervously at the slouches, then lowered her voice a notch. "Sunday's usually pretty quiet, at least compared to Saturday," she said. "But it was Cuzzy Tyler's birthday, so a few of the regulars decided to throw a party. Started early in the day and kep' goin' later, more an' more folks showin' up. 'Fore long the place was spillin' out the door, an' then word got out. Half an hour later Blacks and Blues showed up."

"That would be Lester Rollins' band." It was a statement, not a question.

"Yessir," she said. "He and Walter Hill—he's bass and vocals—they started jammin', and 'fore long Jimmy Stone, he lives jus' up the road, he comes in with his fifty-nine Gibson. That's when the joint truly started jumpin'."

Connor mentally played the image in his mind, then said, "Do you remember what time Lester left?"

"Not exactly, but it would've been 'round the time the music stopped. Eleven or so. Place started to empty out then, folks figuring they still had to get up in the morning. 'Cept I figure there was a lot of work didn't get done till Tuesday."

"Had Lester been drinking?"

"Shit, Mr. Connor," J'Neece said. "No one 'cept Walter comes in here not drinkin', and Mister Rollins kep' up with the best of 'em. Couple guys offered him a ride home, but he said he was good. He was one stubborn old fool, and if he said he was good, he was good."

Connor's great-Uncle Maximillian had been like that, insisted on driving until the day he sideswiped a kid on a bicycle he claimed he didn't see. Fortunately, the kid only broke an arm, and went on to catch three seasons for Michigan State, setting a record for nailing base runners trying to steal second. But great-Uncle Max never drove again and died ten months later from an aneurism.

"He took his own car?" he asked her.

J'Neece thought on that for a bit, then slowly shook her head. "Didn't think much on it," she finally said. "He just slipped out the door there, and like you can see, there's no windows. No tellin' how he got home."

Connor drew his mind back to something Reverend Parker had told him and focused on what had gone down Sunday night: If Lester Rollins had driven the Suburban to the church to check in on his wife, how had it ended up in the driveway? Did someone offered Lester a ride from The Nest to the church, or did he drive himself home first? If that was the case, he probably had realized Ruby had not come home, and he had gone to the church looking for her.

"When I spoke with Lester this morning he suggested I talk to Walter Hill," he told her. "Maybe he knows some things about Sunday night."

"You spoke to Lester?" J'Neece asked, her eyes widening with a touch of newfound respect. "How's he doing?"

"About how you'd expect," Connor replied. "Tired, hopeless, depressed. So, do you know where I can find this Walter Hill?"

She nodded in understanding of Lester's plight, then said, "Home, most likely, watching game shows. Road he lives on's not on any GPS, but I can make you a map."

J'Neece was right: Connor never would have found the place if she hadn't drawn it out for him. And forget GPS: there wasn't a satellite in orbit that could have triangulated an elephant that far up the creek. But eventually he pulled the loaner truck around a final stretch of road and found a steel shipping container set on cinder blocks at the edge of the marsh. It was one of the long ones, brick red with the words "Hamburg Sud" in faded white lettering on the side. Someone had cut an opening in the ribbed steel and inserted a window that looked like it came from the local Habitat store. An old wall AC unit hung from a cut-out at the end of the container, and water was dripping out onto the ground. A clump of wires ran from the corner of the container up to a pole near the road, and a Dish antenna was fixed to the flat roof.

Connor did his usual thing, sat there in the truck a few minutes sizing the place up. He had that odd sensation that someone was watching him, probably through a small gap in whatever was covering the crude glass. Over the past months he'd been spat at, screamed at, and shot at, and just a few hours ago a kid named Bacon had aimed the Remington at him from the back porch of the Rollins' house.

He pulled the tired handle and leaned his weight against the door, then stepped out of the truck. The air was heavy and thick with the moldy odor of low tide, and trickles of heat rippled up from the marsh. Music was playing somewhere, a four-string bass, faint and yearning like the soundtrack of a summer long gone by.

Connor had covered half the distance from the truck to the container when the door swung open and a thin, pale man stepped out onto a narrow wooden porch. Dark mirrored shades were wrapped over his eyes, and a pork pie hat was perched on top of a head that flowed with platinum hair. At first Connor thought the man was wearing some sort of neck brace, then realized the contraption was holding a harmonica in front of his mouth.

"You Connor?" the man asked through a set of teeth that looked too perfect to be real.

"Yeah—that's me," he replied. For logical reasons he'd figured the guy would be black but saw no need to mention it. "You must be Walter Hill."

"J'Neece probably didn't tell you I was white as an egret."

"Just that you play a mean bass, is all," Connor said. "She called ahead, let you know I was coming?"

"Texted, actually. No one talks anymore. Said you were askin' questions about ol' Hurricane, tryin' to get him out of jail."

"Right now, I'm trying to get a handle on what happened Sunday night, get some sort of time line. I heard you were one of the last to see Lester before he headed home."

"Weren't too many of us saw much of anything that night," Walter Hill told him. "Listen, whyn't you come inside, get out of the heat."

Connor wasn't sure the inside of a steel shipping container would be any cooler than the surface of the sun. But the AC unit was humming loudly, so he decided to give it a chance. He followed Walter Hill inside and was instantly hit with a blast of Arctic air.

"Getchoo somethin'?" Hill asked as he waved Connor into a chair. "All's I got is soda pop."

"Sounds good," Connor said as he took a good look around.

Essentially the container was one very long room, with the main living area nearer the rear, which was made up of two massive steel doors. One of them appeared to be welded shut, but the other extended from floor to ceiling, with a nylon screen flap designed to keep the bugs out. A second window had been cut into the side of the container, overlooking the tidal creek and the marsh beyond. A small couch and a couple of old chairs that looked as if they'd come from Goodwill were set on an old carpet remnant, and beyond that was a galley kitchen with a harvest gold range, sink, and fridge. A bed was tucked into a far corner of the box, and the rest of the space was cluttered with instruments. A stand-up bass leaned on a stand, and a half dozen more electric guitars were propped against the wall.

Hill grabbed two cans of Mountain Dew out of the fridge and flipped one to Connor.

"Careful…might've got a bit shaken up," he said as he popped his and took a long gulp.

Connor cautiously opened the can, but the short toss hadn't done much to stir up the contents. He took a hefty gulp, then steered Walter Hill back on course. "Sounds like that party went long and hard," he said.

"That's puttin' it mildly."

"And you saw Lester when he left?"

"Yeah. We had a few words just as he was leaving."

"Words?" Connor repeated.

"Not angry, nothin' like that," Walter Hill said, a little too quickly. "He liked his bourbon, and he'd had his share that night. We all did, and it showed. Whole band was out of tune and out of sync, 'cept no one noticed. Enough booze makes a pig look like a princess. Anyways, we'd just finished a song, I think it was 'Sweet Home Chicago,' and all of a sudden Lester says he's gotta go, didn't realize it was so late."

"And you didn't want the party to stop?"

"No one did, but it wasn't like that. Ruby—Lester's wife—she was supposed to drop by after closing up at the church, but she never showed."

"So, he went looking for her?"

Walter Hill swatted at something that had gotten past the nylon screen and was buzzing around his white hair. "All he said was he had to go. We were just getting' ready to play 'Who's Makin' Love'—you know, the old Johnnie Taylor song—when he just picked up his sax and made for the door. I told him to stick around for just one more, but he wasn't hearing it."

"How did the two of them get along?" he asked, steering the conversation in a different direction. "Lester and Ruby, I mean."

"I'm sure you already know the answer to that one," he said. "But let me make it clear: they were like peas in a pod. Not that they didn't have differences after decades of marriage, but they'd learned to work things out. That's why it just don't make sense."

"Lester killing her, you mean?"

"That's exactly what I mean. Never would have done that, not in a million light years."

Miss Benson, Connor's high school physics teacher, had made it abundantly clear that a light year was a measure of distance, not time, but he decided not to draw the distinction here with Walter Hill. Instead he said, "The cops seem to think he could."

"Cops," Hill sneered. Just one word, but his tone conveyed much more. "That's what chased him out of Memphis, all those years ago."

"Cops?"

"Times were different back then," Hill said. "In some ways, at least. Lot of white folks in Memphis didn't like it that all these black musicians were makin' more money than they were. Didn't help much when Isaac Hayes started driving around in that pimped-out Caddy. Then one of Lester's friends—the drummer for Booker T. and the MGs—got himself shot. Next day Lester packed up his car and headed east."

"That's quite a story," Connor replied.

"No shit," Hill agreed. "But it's true. Least, most of it. It's on Wikipedia."

Wikipedia had more holes than it took to fill the Albert Hall, but Connor decided to let it pass. "So, if it wasn't Lester, do you have any idea who could've killed Ruby?" he asked. "What I hear, she was nothing but an angel."

Walter Hill studied Connor over his bottle of soda with steel-blue eyes that radiated a fierce intensity. "'And his tail drew the third part of the stars of heaven, and did cast them to the earth,'" he blurted out. "'And the dragon stood before the woman which was ready to be delivered, for to devour her child as soon as it was born.'"

Connor had started to raise his can to his lips but paused and stared at Walter Hill. "Excuse me?" he said.

A smile formed on Hill's lips, and he said, "Revelations, I think. I'm not a Biblical man. Not as much as people tell me I should be, living in this wonderful state. But the last few months there's been this guy hangin' 'around, spreading the word of God. *A very white God.*"

Connor nodded; he'd run into such folks in the parking lot at the mall and in Marion Square downtown. Harmless, mostly, but definitely devout and sincere. "So, what does he have to do with Ruby Rollins?" he asked.

"This guy was down to the Quick Stop 'bout a month ago, preaching about the supremacy of the white race to anyone who'd listen. It was mostly shit about how God designed the world for white domination, and anyone less than white was there to serve. So along comes Ruby, who tells him he's got his story wrong. What I heard, she tells him God made this a world of love and compassion, not fear and hatred. He got in her face, telling her God is going to punish man for all His sins, especially the niggers and fags, and she was one dumb nigger bitch, if she believed otherwise."

"He used those words?"

"Close enough."

"Can you describe this guy?"

"You askin' if he was white or black?" Hill asked him. "Cuz these days the word 'nigger' comes in all colors."

"I just want to know what he looked like. So I know him if I see him."

"Folks that seen him said he was a white dude, wore a baseball cap backwards. Some kind of logo in the back. Any hair he had coulda been stuffed up under it. That's all I know."

Connor thought on this for a moment, then said, "This confrontation at the Quick Stop. You remember when this was?"

"About a month ago," Hill told him. "It was a big deal for a while, but then it just blew over. Like most things."

"Anyone seen him around lately?"

Walter Hill scratched his head of thick white hair and said, "Like I told you, it was four weeks ago, maybe longer. You can ask around, see if anyone says different. Me, I spend most of my time down here on the creek."

Connor rose from his chair and walked over to the window that looked out on the marsh. In the distance a skiff trolled a rivulet for red drum or whatever it was they caught out here. Finally, without turning around, he said, "You think this racist douchebag could have killed Ruby?"

"No telling if he did or didn't," Walter Hill replied. "But one thing is certain."

"What's that?"

"Whoever did it took a great disliking to that woman. No one stabs someone that many times without extreme hatred in his soul."

"You know of anyone who fits that description?" Connor asked.

"How could anyone hate an angel?" Hill said. It was an observation, not a question.

"Yet someone did—"

"That is a fact," the old white man grumbled. "Which means whoever did it either didn't really know her or was totally fucked up in the head."

# Chapter 7

By the time Connor got to his small apartment on Sullivan's Island the sun was starting to make its journey toward evening. He'd picked up a pizza on the way home and now was sitting at the edge of the marsh with a slice in one hand and a glass of gin in the other. Dr. Pinch at the V.A. kept trying to steer him away from the juniper berries, and some nights the doctor's advice seemed to be winning. But on other evenings Connor often felt the need to cleanse his brain in an alcoholic bath, and this was one of those nights.

He took a sip of the gin and gazed out at the first strokes of orange that were just beginning to appear on the horizon. The days were getting shorter and the nights were growing longer, but summer still clutched the lowcountry firmly in its grasp. Bugs buzzed in the sweetgrass and the aroma of barbecue and onions and sweet potato fries hung thick in the air. Somewhere close by a screen door slammed, causing a blue heron to take flight from where it was hiding in the marsh. The bird punctuated his displeasure with a loud honk as he lumbered into the sky like one of the C-17a taking flight out at the Air Force base.

Connor studied the twin spires of the Ravenel Bridge in the distance, the sun looking as if it were going to slide right down between them. Then his mind carried him a few miles farther, out to Leeds Avenue where Lester Rollins was likely having a dinner of tasteless beans and franks and something that could hardly pass for cornbread. This would be the start of his third night in jail, and his brain would be buzzing as noisily as the bugs out in the sweet grass.

It was clear Rollins had no memory of what had happened Sunday evening. He'd blacked out either because of the booze or the shock of what he'd seen, and when the cops found him the next morning he remained in a daze. Connor was familiar with that sort of vacuum; he'd had more than his share of dark nights after he'd let his niece get blown away at the Mega Gas C-store when she was only five. Her name was Lily, and she'd been carrying a half-gallon of moose tracks ice cream when she surprised a man in a ski mask at the cash register. Connor had been filling out a Powerball slip in the back of the store and had not seen the gunman come in, and by the time he heard the shot it was too late.

His life had crumbled around him after that. His family blamed him for Lily's death, and his marriage disintegrated. It was his fault that Lily was dead, pure and simple. He was powerless to turn back time, and that realization left him hollow and helpless in the days to come. A few months later Connor signed his recruitment papers and shuffled off to Buffalo. Or, to be more precise, a few miles east of there to Fort Drum.

The shock of seeing his young niece fall at the whim of a man with a gun was nothing compared to the next three years.

For fifty minutes a day—one day a week for a couple a year now—Connor sat in a sterile office at the V.A. fielding questions from Dr. Pinch. The government shrink continually pressed him on why he willingly seemed to throw himself into the path of an oncoming train. Was he some sort of one-man morality play, battling the evils of the world in search of truth, justice, and the American way? Was it lingering remorse or responsibility over Lily's death, or was that just part of a greater excuse? Maybe battlefield guilt played a role, all the death he had seen and some of which he had caused. PTSD was like the chimera of Greek mythology, a multi-headed monster that metaphorically ravaged the war-torn terrain of Connor's mind.

Truth was, after all those sessions he had no concrete answer for why he dived into a case with almost reckless abandon. Nor could he explain why tonight he was thinking about Lester Rollins and what he was enduring up at the Charleston County Correctional Center, most likely huddled in fear and indignity on a bunk surrounded by repeat offenders who had been denied bail or had no chance of being bonded out before their court dates. As a suspected murderer Rollins would have been kept out of the general population of drunks and wife-beaters and PWIs. That stood for Possession With Intent—the intention being to distribute a controlled substance—which was how Connor had spent one night in the place before Jordan James had straightened out a big misunderstanding. That had been over a year ago, but every one of those twenty hours remained fresh in his mind.

He let the rest of the gin slip down his throat, then set the glass on the parched lawn and dug into a slice of pizza. He knew he owed Danielle a call, but right now he just wanted to let the evening settle into him. A power boat was slowly churning up the Intracoastal on a sunset cruise, and Connor thought he heard a Bob Marley song drifting over the incoming tide. For a moment he was carried back to the shipping container at the edge of the creek, what Walter Hill had told him about the religious zealot named Matthew. Connor wondered if it could be the same guy he'd seen shouting at Reverend Parker on the steps of the church. Pasty skin and long blond hair, gravel spewing from the tires of his Ford long-bed as he made good and gone.

Just like Lester Rollins the day after his friend was murdered in Memphis.

*So, what was that about?*

Connor took another bite of pizza, picked up his phone to call Danielle when it started buzzing in his hand. He waited for caller I.D. to do its thing, but all the screen showed was a number with an 803 area code. South Carolina, but upstate. He hesitated a moment, thinking it might just be a call being forwarded from the BioClean line, figured he had to answer it one way or the other. So he punched the "talk" button and said, "This is Jack Connor."

"So, what have you learned?" the voice on the other end asked. *Demanded.*

Connor recognized the voice, and said, "Learned about what?"

"Who killed Ruby Rollins," the voice said. "What did you think I was talking about?"

Three years in the Army had taught Connor to respect and obey his superiors, or those who thought they were. The past eighteen months talking to Dr. Pinch, however, had begun to convince him that civilian life greatly reduced the number of people you felt inclined to salute, much less kiss ass. Despite the fact that a majority of the state's voters had elected the man to office, Connor placed Governor Luck in this second category.

"Look, Governor," he said. "We need to get something straight—"

"And just what might that be?" the governor probed, impatience in his voice.

"If I have information to share, I'll call you. Otherwise—"

"I know, I know. James made it pretty damned clear: I'm to stay clear when you're on a job. All I want to know is whether you've made any progress."

"I've been at this less than a day, sir," Connor said. Adding the last word just to defer to the man's strong sense of ego.

"I know. It's not much time. I just thought you could give me an idea—"

"Let me tell you how this works, Mr. Luck," Connor said impatiently. He switched the phone from his right hand to his left so he could take another bite of pizza. "I ask a lot of questions. I dig around. I make observations and I read people. A lot of it may add up to nothing, and a few things may add up to something. But it's not a linear thing. I don't go straight from A to B to C, and then suddenly I have the guy who killed Ruby Rollins."

"Of course," the governor said. "Deduction and reasoning, and all that."

"And all that is largely intuitive," Connor continued. "It comes from tiny scraps of information and hunches and other shit that the thinking brain sometimes doesn't pick up. The by-the-book, A-B-C sort of guy in this case is the sheriff who put Lester Rollins behind bars. But that's not why you shanghaied me last night and got me to do this. Against my better judgment, in fact. So what I'm going to tell you is that yes, I made some progress today. What sort of progress, I don't have a clue. And tomorrow I'll make more progress, and I probably still won't have a clue. Then, one of these days, all that progress—all that information— will fall into place. Or maybe it won't. But until then, please don't ask me about progress, because I'm not ready to think about any of that shit yet."

There was a long silence on the other end, and Connor thought he heard Governor Luck take a long sip of something. He knew he shouldn't judge the man for his vices; his own empty gin glass was sitting right there beside his chair on the grass. Finally, after a long pause, Luck said, "Okay…I get it. I'll leave you be. Just know that my wife is very anxious about all this, and she's pushing me for closure."

"Please tell her I'm doing my best to make that happen," Connor told him.

"I'll do that," the governor replied. "And I want you to know, I don't mean to meddle—"

"Of course not, sir. I respect your interest in this case, and in Lester Rollins. But now that you've mentioned your wife, I'm going to need to speak with her."

Luck hesitated a second, long enough to take another sip of whatever he was drinking. Then he said, "Do you really think that's necessary? She's actually in quite a state, considering what happened to Ruby. And Lester, of course."

"I just have a few things to ask her," Connor pressed him. "General things, easy questions. If anything starts to cause her any stress, I'll stop."

The governor again hesitated, and Connor could almost hear the gears whirring in his head. And the ice clinking in his glass. "I'd like to sit in on the interview," he eventually replied.

"First, it's not an interview—it's just going to be a conversation," Connor clarified. "And second, it needs to be just your wife and me."

"But—"

"Look, sir. You're the governor. Her husband, and the father of her children. My guess is, you carry a lot of influence in all those roles. I want her to be able to speak freely, without any of that influence weighing in from across the room."

This time a good fifteen, maybe twenty seconds went by before the governor said a word. Connor patiently waited while her made up his mind.

"Fair enough, Jack. But I want to be in the next room, in case anything happens."

Connor wasn't quite sure what Luck expected to happen, but he said. "That works for me. And the sooner the better."

"I agree. Can you be up here in Columbia tomorrow afternoon?"

"Bad time…the funeral's at two o'clock and I need to be there. But morning works fine for me, about ten o'clock—"

"I'll have to clear a few things, but I can make it work," Luck said. "Linda said she wanted to go and pay her respects, her and me. But I told her it would be a distraction, the governor and first lady showing up out of the blue."

*It definitely might raise a few eyebrows,* Connor thought. "I'm sure you're right, sir," he said. "Do you want me to come to the mansion?" He was referring to the governor's mansion on Arsenal Hill in Columbia, where the first family of South Carolina traditionally lived.

"It's hardly a mansion, and we only use it for celebrations," the governor said. "I have another place in mind, a little more discreet."

"Whatever you say. If you give me directions I can punch it into my GPS—"

"Forget that," Luck told him. "I'll send a security detail to get you."

"I'm perfectly capable of driving myself, sir."

"I know you are," Governor Luck replied with a chuckle. "It's that piece of shit truck of yours that I'm worried about."

It was that piece of shit truck that prompted Connor's next call. It had served its purpose just fine, but he was anxious to get the Camaro back with its new modifications in place. He'd heard about shop up in Charlotte that specialized in the work he had in mind, and they finally had a slot open up in their calendar to take care of the changes. They'd even volunteered to provide temporary wheels while the work was being done, so Connor had agreed to the vehicle swap. They'd exchanged cars at a rest stop on I-26 and Connor watched as the guy offloaded the rusty old pick-up and rolled the Camaro onto the flatbed truck.

"Two weeks, three max," is what the guy promised as Connor signed the disclaimers and waivers. His name was Don Wilson, and he'd been in on the plan since Connor's first call last December. "We'll let you know when we're done."

That had been at the beginning of August and Connor was hoping he'd have it back by next weekend. He'd tried to be patient, calling only once to get a status report, but Don Wilson had told him that interruptions only slowed things down. Interruptions like phone calls, he'd emphasized—pretty much the same thing Connor had told the governor just now.

There was a history to the Camaro that brought him back to Iraq every time he drove it. It was a 1967 convertible, bright orange with a 396 V-8 under the hood, and it had belonged to a member of his squad in Kirkuk. Eddie James had been twenty-one years old when he rotated into the desert and not quite twenty-three when an SOB handcuffed to the wheel of an old van loaded with explosives T-boned the Humvee Connor was driving. Both vehicles blew apart instantly, as did a young kid named Danny Benson, who had been in the passenger seat beside him. Eddie James had drawn gunner duty that day, and the blast blew him about sixty feet into the air.

If Connor had been listening during high school physics class instead of eyeing Miss Benson's legs he would have learned that an explosion is a sudden and violent change of potential energy, transferring to its surroundings in the form of a rapidly moving rise in pressure called a blast wave. That's what the doctor in Kuwait had told him, and he later found it on Google, almost word for word.

In any event, somewhere during the expansion of gaseous molecules, Eddie's arm was pulled off at the elbow and, when he landed, his forehead bounced off what was left of the front passenger door. Connor had been blown sideways out the driver's side, and all he recalled was the Iraqi desert spinning beneath him as if he were riding the roller coaster at Michigan's Adventure Park when he was a kid. He came to earth on a heap of rocks with a shard of hot metal protruding from his gut, and as he lay there he wondered if he might be dead. His head was pounding like a jackhammer and his ears were ringing as if it were Sunday morning—something the doctor in Kuwait patiently explained was caused by a punctured ear drum.

But at that instant in the desert, death and destruction were all around him. Finally, the screams of another squad member named Andy Templeton brought him back to the moment. Andy had lost all the toes on his left foot and his leg had been ripped open, but that's not why he was screaming. Eddie James was lying in the roadway, blood gushing not only from the jagged wound where the rest of his arm had been, but also from the indentation in his forehead that made it impossible for him to be alive.

Despite the hammering in his brain Connor managed to tie off Eddie's severed arm with his shirt, then kept him conscious until a chopper arrived to take them out of there. The Army docs quickly realized Eddie needed better treatment than they could provide, so he was airlifted to Germany where a team of surgeons stitched him back together. It was the same story thousands of other U.S. soldiers endured as part of their Iraq experience, but Eddie's chapter was about to affect Connor's life in a profound and lasting way.

His job at Palmetto BioClean was an example of that. So was the '67 Camaro that right now was in the shop. Eddie had received the car when he'd graduated from high school, and he'd parked it in his father's garage the night before he headed off to war. The same car in the faded photo he showed to everyone at the F.O.B. in Iraq who would look, as if it were his first love. The same car he'd signed over to Connor from his bed at Walter Reed Medical Center, when not even his doctors were certain he'd be able to function as a human being again.

As Eddie had put it at the time, "Isabella needs a good man, someone to keep an eye on her and take her out for a dance. An' I ain't never gonna be able to do that no more."

That's how the translation went; the actual words he'd tried to form were much shorter and mangled. The brain damage had been considerable.

Eddie James had managed to beat the odds. Not all of them, of course; he had a severe mental impairment that was most noticeable when he tried to speak. His motor control was compromised and his reaction time had slowed to a snail's pace. But he was aware of the world around him, he could articulate enough words to be able to have a simple conversation, and he was able to steer the three-wheeled electric scooter his father bought him.

That's what gave Connor the idea about the Camaro.

The clang of bells on the swing bridge that spanned the waterway yanked his attention back to the present. The clouds in the west were shifting from tangerine to plum, and a pair of egrets—lowcountry angels—lifted off from the marsh against a sun that was setting in a blaze of orange. Connor watched them a moment as he contemplated his empty glass, deciding whether it was best to keep it that way or pour another splash of gin over the ice that hadn't yet melted.

Laziness dictated his decision, and he just sat there a few minutes, the ice continuing to melt as his monkey mind leaped from one mental branch in his brain to the next. Lester Rollins, his face looking faded and hollow on the video screen at the county jail. J'Neece Taylor, wiping her rag on the polished wood countertop. Bacon Truman, his finger just an inch away from pulling the trigger on Connor's life. Ruby Rollins, who'd had words with a racist freak who maybe had the passion to kill for his convictions.

Then his brain made the leap to Danielle Simmons. She had tumbled into his world a little over a year ago when Connor was investigating the death of her twin sister. Neither of them had expected anything to come of that fleeting interlude; Danielle was a married veterinarian living in Florida and Connor's experience with her twin was more than enough reason to jam the brakes on.

But that was then, and this was now. As Miss Benson had explained to her inattentive physics students, protons and electrons have a significant power to attract. In the case of Connor and Danielle the negatively charged electrons were attracted to the positively charged protons and now, fifteen months later, the two charged particles were inseparable. Her marriage was long since over and his caution had taken flight. The only thing standing between them was distance, and it was Danielle's turn to take the one daily non-stop between Orlando and Charleston tomorrow afternoon.

Which caused the mental monkey to miss his branch and crash to the ground.

Ruby Rollins' funeral was tomorrow afternoon.

"What time does your flight get in?" he asked her twenty seconds later when she answered her phone.

"A little after five. Is that still going to work for you?"

Connor quickly ran the math in his head. He had no idea how an A.M.E. funeral worked, whether it was a quick thing or something dragged out by a high mass of some sort, like his niece's Catholic service that seemed to span days from start to finish. Even if it was two hours he'd have plenty of time to politely slip away and get to the airport on time. As long as he didn't go to the graveside service, if there was one. And *if* he didn't get delayed by someone or something that the church full of mourners might throw at him.

That was a lot of *ifs*, and his experience with them wasn't good.

"Not a problem," he said. "I'll be there. How's Cyrano?"

Cyrano was the prize white rhino at the animal park where Danielle worked. The adolescent animal had been orphaned in Africa the previous winter by poachers harvesting the species' prized horns. As Danielle had explained at the time, rhino horns by weight can fetch as much as gold on the black market, where they are ground to a fine powder for medicinal purposes. Or, as many people believed, to be used as an aphrodisiac.

The surviving calf had not yet begun to show signs of a horn so he was left to starve, and the game warden who discovered the slaughtered animals rescued him from certain death. He eventually made his way to Orlando, and somewhere along the way acquired the name Cyrano, even though his horn was neither a horn nor part of his nose. Lately the animal had shown signs of fever and loss of appetite, and Danielle had been worried.

"We think it was gastrointestinal torsion and impaction," she said. "We started him on medication last night and he seems to be getting better."

"Great news," Connor said, and then they launched into the tales of their respective days, as they did most evenings. Yesterday had been an exception because the clean-up job at the church had gone long, and tomorrow they'd see each other in the flesh. The mention of which caused Connor to giggle into the phone.

"Is that all you have on your mind?" she pressed him, already knowing the answer.

"Absence makes the heart grow fonder," he reminded her. "So what are you wearing?"

"Don't push it, Connor."

He had come to realize that when Danielle called him by his last name she was playing with him in an affectionate, teasing sort of way. When she called him Jack he knew she was asking a direct question, for which she wanted a straightforward answer. And when she used both names he realized he was in trouble for something. So far that hadn't happened too many times.

"I'll see you tomorrow at the airport," he told her. "I'll park in the cell phone lot, so just call me when you land."

"I'm counting the minutes."

"And I'm counting the seconds," he countered. "Love you."

He ended the call and set his phone in the grass. Out in the marsh a wood stork stepped carefully in the mud, while a gentle gust rattled the palmetto fronds at the edge of his small lawn. The aroma of fried onions and fish tacos seemed to light on the same breeze. All seemed right in this little corner of the world.

Meanwhile, out in the Atlantic, the perfect confluence of warm water, warm air, and low pressure was on a track to change all that. Tropical Storm Eleanor had just become a category one hurricane, and she was gathering steam.

# Chapter 8

Governor Luck was full of surprises.

His political opponents had learned that lesson the hard way, all of them going down to defeat one way or the other. Luck had never lost an election, a fact that helped to fuel his unparalleled motivation and unbridled ambition. He openly ridiculed Washington with his unique brand of homespun scorn and made no secret that he was intent on moving there—God and the American voters willing. While such things were yet another election cycle in the future, it was critical that Luck maintain complete control over everything in his public and private life.

This morning that meant sending an unmarked SLED vehicle to intercept Connor and transport him to an undisclosed location. That location was a ninety-two-acre farm on the Ashepoo River in Dorchester County that belonged to—*who else?*—a wealthy donor to the Luck campaign. The governor and his family used the place occasionally to escape the pressures of the state capital, and this was one of those occasions.

The cop who drove Connor turned out to be Deputy Stroble, the same officer who had driven his pick-up home from the church Wednesday night. He had a large cup of steaming coffee and a bag of donuts waiting for Connor on the back seat of the unmarked Escalade. There also was a copy of the Charleston *Post and Courier*, and under that a folder that was marked "Jack Connor: Eyes Only"

It was a thin file that contained no more than ten pages, all of them photocopied from the originals. Since Connor was nowhere close to being a detective he had never read an actual murder file before and did not know what to expect. The off-hand comment he had made to the governor about wanting to see Lester Rollins' arrest report was just a fleeting wish, and he had not expected Howard Luck to come through on his request.

Considering that a woman had been brutally murdered and a man's life was hanging in the balance, he was surprised to find there wasn't much substance in the file. The first two pages consisted of the official Sheriff's Department report, wherein the officer who responded to the call from the cleaning woman at the church described what he'd found. Roby Rollins was lying on the floor of the vestry, pretty much in the exact spot where most of the blood had pooled.

It was clear from the start that Mrs. Rollins had died a horrific death, and the crime scene photos confirmed it in gruesome four-color detail. There were eight photos in the file, shot from various angles around the body, and whoever took them thoroughly captured the sheer horror of the moment. It was obvious that she had fought her attacker, but she had been overwhelmed by his sheer strength and the fact that each of the thirteen blows killed her a little bit more.

The report itself was detailed in its writing but told Connor nothing he didn't already know. After confirming that Ruby was dead, investigators discovered the drops of blood that led out the door and to the Rollins house, where they found Lester lying on the kitchen floor. He was still passed out, presumably from all the drinking and then the horror of killing his wife. Later when he had been questioned by sheriff's detectives he had confirmed that he did not remember what he had done last night and that yes, it was possible he had blocked the death of his wife from his mind. The detectives took this to mean that he did not deny having killed Ruby, but Connor could see that Lester might have just meant that he didn't remember seeing her lying there on the vestry floor.

Connor closed the murder book and set it on the seat beside him. He knew from personal experience that police as a whole were not stupid people, but individually they were under extreme pressure to get results. That often meant cutting a corner here or there and focusing so much on what they considered the obvious that they might overlook the truth. This had been the case in the death of Connor's niece, and because of hasty work and pre-conditioned minds her killer was out there, somewhere.

Same thing here. Connor was sure of it, and that's why the governor had brought him into the fold. The Sheriff's Department had found its man and the case was closed. All that remained was the court case—or a plea bargain, if it could be arranged. South Carolina was a death penalty state, so if Lester Rollins wanted to save his skin he might just plea down to life without parole. That would save a lot of taxpayer dollars, and that's what seemed to matter most in the halls of justice these days.

Neither Connor nor Stroble exchanged a word on the ride down Old Savannah Highway. Eventually the deputy turned off the highway and started up a long oyster shell drive flanked by classic live oaks dripping with Spanish moss. At the end of the drive was a massive wood frame house, white, with ionic columns and a wraparound porch. Outdoor ceiling fans turned lazily to wash away the heat that was just starting to settle in. Stroble said something into the radio that was clipped to his shoulder, and a voice squawked back, "Come around back to the barn."

Stroble did as he was told, and that's when Connor spotted the blue Ford T-bird. It was pulled up against the white-board fence that encircled a large pasture where several horses were grazing and swatting flies with their tails. The governor was leaning on the top rail of the fence, one foot hooked on the lowest board, watching the horses as he talked into his cell phone.

The SLED car edged off the driveway opposite the T-bird and stopped on a patch of freshly mown grass. The governor turned around and lifted a hand to indicate he'd be done with his call soon, then went back to his conversation.

"Just wait, sir," Stroble said. "He'll be finished soon."

Connor didn't see the first lady anywhere and began to wonder if this was all some sort of a complicated ruse. "I'm not here to see the governor," he replied as he opened the door and climbed out. "I'm here to talk to his wife."

"My instructions were to have you wait here—"

But Connor wasn't interested in the governor's instructions. He was on a tight schedule if he was going to finish here and get back home in time to turn around and drive down to Ruby Rollins' funeral in Ravenel. Defying Stroble's command, he walked up to the governor—who still had his phone pressed to his ear—and said, "Where is she?"

The governor said something into his phone that sounded like "just give me a minute," then said to Connor, "Let me just finish this call and I'll take you to her."

"Sorry, sir. This is just between her and me. No interference."

"Interference? She's my wife—"

"Exactly. So, if you'll just please tell me where she is we can get started."

The governor flashed him a look of exasperation, then glanced at the phone in his hand. His call was still waiting. Finally, he uttered an impatient sigh and said, "She's in the tack room in the barn. They have TV in there, full cable. HBO even."

"I'm not here to watch a movie, sir."

The governor appeared taken aback by Connor's abruptness, but let it slide. He had a call on hold, so he said, "Go on in. But try to be quick—she's rather fragile about all this."

"Of course."

"And Connor," Luck continued, holding his arm. "No recording devices allowed, no cameras. This meeting never happened."

Connor found Mrs. Luck seated on a large leather couch, knees together, a cup of coffee clenched in her hands. She'd been staring straight ahead at the blank television, no HBO or premium cable channels for her. He'd surprised her by walking in, but she barely moved a muscle as she stared straight ahead.

"Mrs. Luck?" he said. "I'm Jack Connor. I want to thank you for agreeing to see me, especially considering everything that's gone on this week."

She studied him intently as she slowly sipped her coffee. "Howard said you had a lot of tattoos," she replied with a rigid smile. She was wearing a simple cotton sundress that seemed designed to cover her legs properly, just above her knees. Her hair was dyed light brown and raked up in a tight bun on the top of her head. She remained seated, so the coffee cup barely moved, except when she drew it to her lips. "He's not a man who's drawn to exaggeration."

"No, ma'am," Connor said. "But he does appear to have married the most lovely woman at the prom."

"Why, thank you, young man," she said, the tightness giving way to a more genuine smile. "Seems you did your homework."

Now it was Connor's turn to grin. The Internet was full of stories about how Howard and Linda Luck met at their high school prom. Both had come with different dates, but they had bumped into each other out on the dance floor and ended up going home together. Not in the carnal sense, of course; Howard had walked her the three blocks to her house, whereupon her father had banned him from the premises for life because he'd brought her home ten minutes after curfew.

"It's a good story," he told her.

"And every bit of it true. Except the next morning my dad realized that the boy who brought me home wasn't the same one who picked me up earlier that evening. So he was fine with Howard."

"Probably never figured he'd end up governor," Connor pointed out.

"My father definitely was of a mind that no one was good enough for his little girl," she conceded. "But that's not why we're here, is it?"

"No, ma'am," Connor said. "And like I said, I want to thank you for agreeing to see me this morning."

"It was good to get out of that drab and dusty house, especially considering the events of this past week."

Connor was pretty sure her idea of drab and dusty was miles apart from his, but that was probably true of most things. "Anyway, I appreciate you agreeing to speak with me about Ruby Rollins," he said. "Your husband said you and she were close."

"I don't know if I could have made it without her," she said with a sniff. "When Howard and I got married…well, I was the youngest of four children. I had no idea what it was like to be around babies, much less take care of them."

"Yes, ma'am. Parenting doesn't come with a training manual."

"It certainly does not." She studied him a moment, no doubt considering the array of body art on his arms. "Do you have children, Mr. Connor?"

"No," he told her, shaking his head. "I was married briefly but not long enough for kids to be part of the deal. Your husband said Mrs. Rollins delivered both of yours?"

Mrs. Luck took a sip of coffee, her pinkie finger raised in the air as she lifted the cup to her lips. "She did a lot more than that, I'll tell you. But yes, Ruby was there when both of them were born. I'm sure Howard told you she was like a sister to me."

"In fact, he used those exact words," Connor replied. "Tell me…how did the two of you meet?"

"She answered an ad in the paper," the first lady said simply. Her knees were locked together tight, her facial muscles firm, as if they had just been injected with Botox. "When I was about six months pregnant with Karen I started to get these panic attacks, wondering how on earth I was going to take care of her. Like I said, I never had any experience with young children and Howard was at work all the time. Every day the attacks just got worse, this horrible constricting feeling in my chest like a snake was squeezing me to death."

Connor was familiar with that snake. It had coiled around him on a daily basis when he first had returned from Iraq, squeezing him at the slightest of triggers: a van following him on the road, any sharp sound or bright flash that zapped his brain out of nowhere. Night sweats coupled with unshakeable images of Danny Talbott catching a bullet in his eye, or Sgt. Suarez stepping on a mine, bringing his entire universe to an end. Connor's visits with Dr. Pinch had helped ease some of that, and Danielle's warm grip around his body during those darkest gutters of the night served to ease the roiling nightmares.

"Mrs. Rollins delivered Karen at home?"

Mrs. Luck dipped her head in a slight nod and gave him an embarrassed look. "I know it sounds nutty, but I've always been afraid of hospitals. Probably because my own mother died in one when I was eight. To me they were death factories, and I didn't want to go through that when I was bringing my first child into the world. That's why I hired Ruby: she was a nurse, specialized in pediatrics. And I felt at ease with her from the moment she walked through the door."

"Must have been quite a transition for her, going from nurse to nanny."

In the flash of a second Mrs. Luck's tight forehead was creased with deep lines and her eyes grew a shade darker. "She was *not* a nanny!" she explained sharply. "She was Ruby, and she was the glue I could never provide."

"Yes, ma'am," Connor said. "All I meant was she must have appreciated the transition from nursing to…well, to being everything she was to you and your family."

Mrs. Luck set down her coffee cup and rose to her feet. She wandered over to the window and gazed out at the pasture and the horses and, probably, her husband. Eventually she looked back at Connor and said, "Pediatric nursing is a tough and demanding job, and it took its toll on Ruby. She was glad to find something that took her out of that environment."

"Yes, ma'am—"

"And please…stop calling me ma'am," she told him. "I know it's the polite, southern thing, the way people are raised here in the South. And that goes for me, too. My family goes back before the war. But I am so tired of the hypocrisy that goes with all that politeness and civility. I know my husband is the governor, and you're former Army, but if we're going to have mutual respect and trust here, I want you to call me Linda."

Connor nodded and smiled, thinking the name Linda Luck sounded more fitting for a pole dancer than the first lady. "As you wish," he said. He didn't like sitting when she was standing, but he figured getting out of his chair would appear awkward, so he shifted his position, raising his back a little straighter.

Then he said, "Look—as I'm sure you know, I'm here because your husband doesn't believe Lester Rollins could lay a hand on his wife. Neither do you."

"So, what do *you* think?" she asked.

"The husband is always an obvious suspect. Too obvious in this case."

His answer seemed to satisfy her, so she came back over to the couch and sat down. Again, she locked her knees and carefully tucked her dress tightly beneath her thighs. Tightness seemed to be her stock-in-trade.

"What do you want to know?" she said after a moment.

"You knew Ruby probably better than anybody," he said. "Just tell me what you can about her, why you think someone could have done this to her."

She closed her eyes and dropped her chin a bit, then gently shook her head. "I've been asking myself that same thing ever since I saw it on the news," she told him. "Terrible way to hear about it, that bimbo on TV just reading it off…off one of those things—"

"Teleprompter?" Connor said.

"Right. Ruby Rollins was a real, live person, and that woman rolled her entire life rolled into one short story with a ten-second sound bite."

Connor rarely watched the TV news. Not long after he had moved to Charleston he had hooked up with a beautiful TV reporter, and that had not gone well for either of them. After betraying his secrets on the air, she had been brutally murdered in a case that he ultimately had solved, a case that oddly involved Governor Luck's political foe. The only good thing that had come from that incident was meeting Danielle, the dead reporter's twin sister.

"There's a big difference between reporting and investigating these days," Connor pointed out. "Anything you can tell me about Ruby will be a huge help. Her interaction with you and your family. Her own family, her church. Whatever comes to mind."

Mrs. Luck nodded slowly, and Connor could see her mind retracing the steps of time. She said nothing for an uncomfortably long time, then looked him squarely in the eyes and said, "I'd never met someone who so totally cared for other people. Honestly and genuinely. She had true compassion, not just a means to an end like so many people these days. In yoga we call it 'ahimsa.'"

Connor had heard the Jenster use that word one day after teaching a class. Later she had explained it was derived from the Sanskrit root "hiṃs," which means to cause injury. So "a-himsa" was the opposite: to cause no injury and do no harm.

"Such a very violent way for someone so caring to die," he said.

"Precisely. Somehow it was tied to her karma."

"I thought karma was when you do a bad thing, something bad will happen to you," he replied. "Sort of like what goes around, comes around."

"Karma is a lot more complicated than that," the governor's wife explained. "Again, karma comes from Sanskrit and literally means 'action' or 'doing.' That can be things we consider good or bad, but either way it refers to actions driven by intention and results in consequences. Whatever the consequences, the intentions are the determining factors in the rebirth in samsara. The cycle of rebirth."

Connor said nothing, just nodded and considered what she was telling him. It was more than just her observation about Ruby and the consequences of her murder; Mrs. Luck was actually making an admission, of sorts.

"Is this a Buddhist thing?" he asked, not knowing a better way to put it.

"You mean, am I a follower of the Buddha?" she said with a laugh. "Not in public, not in this state. And certainly not while ambition is my husband's middle name."

"But in the privacy of your own home…and this confidential conversation?"

She again thought for a long moment, then said, "Let me put it this way: we have a crucifix hanging in our dining room, but there's a statue of Buddha in the rose garden out back. I don't eat meat, I believe in a path toward enlightenment, and I know there are many roads to follow on a spiritual journey. And I fail to see what this has to do with Ruby Rollins."

"I guess it just helps define spiritual parameters," Connor told her. "You think her death—or maybe the way she died—has something to do with something that happened in the past?"

She blinked, as if pricked by a sudden reality, but whatever it might have been, she quickly recovered. "As I said, karma is part of the circle of rebirth. That means what happens in this life may be the consequences of something that occurred in a previous life, or could lead to consequences in the next. Ruby was not perfect; none of us is. But the way Ruby died: well, nothing that woman did could explain how someone could have done that to her. Slashing her with a knife, over and over."

Connor pretended to scribble a note in his spiral pad, but it was just a stalling tactic so he could arrange his next thoughts. Eventually he asked, "When was the last time you saw her?"

She glanced up at the ceiling as if the answer were written up there somewhere. "Oh, heavens…it's been forever," she replied. "Five or six years, at least. After Peter went off to college the house was quiet again, and there was nothing for her to do. She suggested it was time she move on, and I had to agree."

"This final time you saw her…was there a special occasion that brought you together?"

"She came to Peter's final game…the college World Series playoffs. She taught him how to throw a great curve."

*Why does everyone feel it's necessary to mention that?* he wondered. "And you lost contact after that?" he asked her.

"We kept in touch—Christmas cards and things like that. Though it was less and less frequent as time went on."

"What did she do after she left you?"

"She went to work for another family, but that didn't last long," Mrs. Luck said with a sigh. "She ended up using her nursing degree again. Got a job at a doctor's office near Charleston. Pediatrics, of course."

Connor got the distinct feeling Linda Luck wasn't telling him something. Maybe it was the tension in her face or the tight body language that made her look as if she were struggling to keep some great truth inside her.

"After all these years...do you have any idea who could have wanted her dead?"

She shook her head rapidly, side to side, then said, "No one. I just don't see how anyone could do that to her."

"Yet someone did."

"Yes, I know that," she said, almost defensively. "All I meant was she was so kind and gentle—"

"What about old history?" he asked her.

"Haven't you been listening?" she said, her voice prickling. "I've told you, she never could have done anything to anyone."

"I'm not talking about Mrs. Rollins' history, ma'am," he told her, coming back to polite formalities. "I'm referring to this state. The South hasn't exactly been kind to black people over the years."

The blank stare in Mrs. Luck's eyes shifted to understanding, and she nodded. "I suppose she could've cut off a pick-up truck on the highway, or looked the wrong way at some bubba in Wal-Mart."

"Those bubbas elected your husband governor," Connor pointed out.

She glanced out the window nervously at her husband, as if he possibly could have heard him. "That's the reality of politics," she said.

"What about the pastor of her church?" Connor asked, quickly shifting the line of questioning. "Reverend Parker."

If he was trying to catch Mrs. Luck off guard, it didn't work. She huffed indignantly and rolled her eyes as if to say *are you really that dumb?* "She adored that man, and he adored her," she said succinctly.

"Precisely my point," he pressed.

"I mean adored as in respected and treasured, not of a romantic nature."

"Unrequited love is a very strange beast, ma'am."

"I told you, cut the 'ma'am' shit."

The last word sneaked out before she could stop it, and she suddenly seemed flushed with embarrassment. "I'm sorry—I shouldn't have said that. It's just—"

He raised a hand to stop her and said, "No, I'm sorry. I pushed you too hard just there. I was just hoping that...well, your husband said you and Mrs. Rollins were so close, so I had this idea you might remember some secret or distant thing that could help me along. Now I feel I've worn out my welcome."

"Nonsense," Linda Luck said. "But I do feel as if I'm being no help at all."

On the surface Connor was thinking the same thing, that this whole trip had been a waste of time. But on another level—a deeper one he had learned to trust with his life—he suspected she had told him more than either of them knew. The trick was just to let it simmer and eventually bubble to the surface.

It was that part he addressed when he said, "You've actually been a tremendous help, ma'am. Linda. And I'm sure I'll have more questions as soon as I leave here."

"The French have a term for that," she said with a smile. "*L'esprit d'escalier*. It means to think of something critical to a discussion only after you've left it, actually at the bottom of the staircase."

"Well, there's no stairs between here and the car I rode in on," he told her. "But I'd sure like to be able to call you if anything else comes to mind."

"Let me give you my phone number," she suggested as she rose to her feet. She found a slip of paper in her purse and scribbled her number on it. "That's my private cell. No one else answers. You can call or text me any time."

# Chapter 9

Officer Stroble got Connor back home in just under ninety minutes. He used his lights only once, when a mystery stoppage caused a back-up on I-26 ten miles west of Charleston. This time the off-duty cop attempted to engage him in conversation, but Connor was focused entirely on his conversation with Linda Luck and what she had told him. Or, to be more precise, what she had not said, and he was trying to coax it out of his memory to figure out what was bugging him.

He eventually scrolled through the contacts in his phone, and when he found the number he was searching for he hit the "call button." Sixty seconds later he had a plan in place, or at least part of a plan.

Seven minutes after Stroble dropped him off at his front door Connor was back out it, this time dressed in a dark jacket and black trousers, and a blue shirt with a tie that looked somber and respectful enough for a funeral. He looked a little incongruous climbing into the loaner truck, but he wasn't doing this for show and he strongly suspected it wouldn't be the worst vehicle parked in the church lot today.

By the time Connor arrived at the A.M.E. church in Ravenel the only parking spaces available were a hundred yards down the road alongside a drainage ditch. He had to pull onto the shoulder carefully, guiding the tires right up to the lip of the deep trench that was filled with rotting leaves and rusting beer cans. He waited for the engine to stop coughing, then climbed out and joined the slow procession of mourners who were trudging silently back up the road toward the church.

Almost all of them were black; men and women and children, even a few teenagers who would rather be doing anything else on their final Friday of summer vacation than going to a funeral. But Roby Rollins clearly was a pillar of the community and people were turning out in the hundreds in a sincere show of respect and admiration. Black and purple seemed to be the colors of the day, suits and starched dresses and broad-brimmed hats that resulted in rivers of perspiration. The sun was unmercifully hot, the air  layered with the smell of pluff mud oozing in from the marsh.

Connor fell in step as the line of mourners filed up the steps. He felt the sting of eyes on him, parishioners wondering what this white man was doing here in this sea of color. Periodically someone would nod at someone or whisper a greeting. There were a few murmurs of greeting from folks who had not seen each other for a long time, but otherwise the parade into the church was a silent one. A refrain of familiar music was coming from a piano up in the front of the church, a hymn that brought Connor back to his childhood when his mother would drag him and his sister down the street on Sundays while his father stayed home and watched football. He only learned later that they were Presbyterians, and he had no idea what that meant or what made them different from the Methodists or Baptists or Lutherans.

• • •

He started to take a seat in the last pew but then realized there wasn't enough room for everyone filing inside. So he slid out the other side and joined a small gathering of men who were packed into a corner, none of them paying him any mind. This was an African American church, but the marquee planted in the dried lawn out front maintained that all were welcome in this house of the Lord, and that included white veterans with shaved heads and a human canvas of body art.

The front pew had been reserved for family, and Connor saw a young woman he figured must have been one of the Rollins' daughters. She was wearing a dark violet dress with a small matching pillbox hat and was holding the hand of the thin young man seated next to her. Positioned on both sides of her were older men and women, probably aunts and uncles and other relatives who were there to pay their last respects to Ruby. Connor felt a momentary jolt of remorse for Lester, who right now was sitting on a hard cot up at the county jail, missing this final farewell to his wife.

Five minutes later the piano stopped and the church fell silent. Reverend Parker mounted a few steps to the pulpit and gazed out at his flock, punctuating the solemn moment with silence. Then he said, in a voice that rumbled with authority that seemed to come from the heavens above, "In the gospel of John, Chapter Fourteen, Verse one, Jesus tells us, 'Do not let your hearts be troubled. You believe in God; believe also in me. In my Father's house there are many dwelling places; if that were not so, would I have told you that I am going there to prepare a place for you? And if I go and prepare a place for you, I will come back and take you to be with me that you also may be where I am. You know the way to the place where I am going."

"Amen!" the overflow congregation called out, almost in perfect unison.

"And thus, the Lord Jesus begins his farewell," the pastor continued. "The cross on which he will die stands before him and he is preparing his disciples to go on without him. He is telling them that he is anticipating his journey to His Father's house, and life must go on without Him."

"Hallelujah!"

"Jesus is urging those disciples to carry on His great deeds, to do the work he has taken upon Himself to do," Reverend Parker boomed out to his flock. "And that is what Ruby Rollins would ask us to do today if she were here among us. She would not want us to weep. She would not want us to grieve. She would not want us to despair. She would want us to live, to hold her spirit deep within our hearts. And, in so doing, help our friends and neighbors the way she helped us all."

The pastor's words were greeted with murmurs of approval and rejoicing, and then he stepped aside from the pulpit. A young woman in the front row rose from her pew and turned toward the gathering. She seemed to be in her late twenties and was wearing a dark charcoal dress that clung to her body in a style that screamed Hollywood. Connor realized she probably was the Rollins' daughter who had moved out to L.A. in search of fame and fortune. There were a few whispers as others in the church recognized her, and then she began to sing.

Her voice sounded like a dove taking flight, gaining altitude as her spirit soared into the rafters and heaven beyond. She sang to the Lord, asking him to take her hand and guide her through the storm and lead her home. Then the dove transformed into the wings of an angel—Connor could think of no other word for it—as she implored God to hear her cry, to listen to her call as she stood by the river in the looming darkness. He did not know the words to the song, which was not surprising for any number of reasons, but every head in the church was nodding in recognition and tears streamed from the weary faces of Ruby Rollins' mourning friends and family.

When the young woman finished the church was filled with cries of "hallelujah!" and she offered them a polite but embarrassed smile. Then she took her seat, and the congregation turned its collective attention back to Reverend Parker, who stepped back to his lectern and said, "How do you follow something as rich and powerful as that?"

But follow he did, again imploring these folks not to let their hearts be troubled, and then he took off on his own path to heaven. He reminded his flock that the first time Jesus uttered the word "troubled" was when he talked about the death of a friend, and again as he faced the cross, grasping the great agony that lay ahead. That's when he said, "My soul is deeply troubled unto death."

More scripture from John and Corinthians and Revelations came next, as Reverend Parker sought to redefine death by helping mourners to view Ruby Rollins' "transition" from her human vessel in a divine perspective. His words were followed by more hymns, this time sung by a congregation that poured its heart and soul into every line, every nuance. Then several women spoke about how Mrs. Rollins made their lives fuller, and her absence would make the world a more empty space.

The service closed with a responsive singing of *The Battle Hymn of the Republic*. Most of the congregation knew their parts in this soaring tribute to Jesus of Nazareth and now, by extension, Ruby Rollins. The singing began with the sopranos and tenors, then was filled in by the booming baritones that provided the power of the lightning and the Lord's swift sword. The voices grew louder and richer as the hymn continued until Connor was certain the ceiling would rain down upon them all which, he figured, was the whole point of it.

Then it was over.

Connor had never seen or heard such a spectacle. As he watched the men and women rise to their feet he began to understand how the word of God had been such a powerful force for a people who had been trampled and oppressed for hundreds of years. The African American religious experience had been born in the cotton fields and rice swamps of the South as a way to rejoice rather than despair, to celebrate rather than live in darkness and gloom. When all else appeared bleak and the horizon was but a distant line on a troubled sea, the Lord was there with hand outstretched to help, not recoiled to whip. That was the message of black churches from the Mississippi delta to the Carolina lowcountry, and on this sweltering afternoon it hit home with all the ferocity of a summer storm.

Connor lingered in the back of the church, watching as the crowd of mourners pressed up to the front to pay their respects to the Rollins' family. He had no way of knowing who they all were or what their relationship to Ruby might have been, but he studied them closely as they shook hands, kissed, hugged, cried, and wiped their eyes. The odds were slim, but any one of these folks could have taken her life, so he wanted to note any interaction they might have with the Rollins' daughters and other relatives.

"That was truly somethin'," the man who had been standing next to Connor said. He looked to be in his fifties, with thin, graying hair and a broad nose. Black suit and a wide tie knotted severely at the throat. "But then, Ruby was somethin' else."

"So I've been told," Connor replied. "I never had the privilege of knowing her."

The man studied Connor a second, summing up the tattoos that extended beyond his cuffs and up the side of his neck. "Well, you clearly ain't with the newspaper, son, so if you didn't know her, do you mind me asking why're you here?"

Connor had no reason to bury the truth. In fact, the more people who knew he was searching for Ruby Rollins' killer, the likelier it would be that someone might speak up about knowing or seeing something. So he said, "I don't think the Sheriff did everything he could before he slammed the door on Mr. Rollins. I'm here to set that straight."

"Shit…you're a cop?" the man asked.

"More like a private investigator," Connor revealed.

"Damn! Tell the truth, I figured you for repo or bail bonds, come here lookin' for someone."

"I am looking for someone," Connor conceded. "Just not for the reasons you might've thought."

"Orson Blaine," the man said then, extending his hand to shake. "Someone payin' you to be here, or are you on your own clock?"

Connor told him his name, then said, "I can't discuss the details of my employment, but maybe you can tell me how you knew her. Mrs. Rollins, I mean."

"You're thinkin' I took that knife to her like that?" Orson Blaine asked him.

"I'm thinking nothing of the kind. I just figure everyone here but me knew Ms. Rollins. I just want to get an idea of what sort of person she was."

"Just what the Reverend said. Kind, compassionate, respectful. And *respected*, by everyone."

"Almost everyone," Connor pointed out.

"Yeah, you're right about that."

"Did you know her well?"

"Everyone around here knows everyone pretty well, Mr. Connor. That's what makes a community. But since you asked, my kids grew up with her and Lester's. My wife and me, we got a daughter too, so we all had day care in grade school, then soccer later on. You have children yourself?"

"Not yet," Connor replied. He suddenly was conscious of the time and stifled an urge to check his watch. The funeral had gone long, and it had to be well after three. Danielle's plane was due a few minutes past five, so he had to make good use of the next hour. "Do you and your wife still live here in town?"

"I do," he said with a nod. "The missus left us three years ago. Said 'goodbye' to her soul right here in this church."

"I'm very sorry—"

"Thank you. Big C got her, so I had time to love her good at the end. Not like what happened to Ruby, and now Lester's up there in that jail."

"A pity and a shame," Connor agreed. "And someone is walking around right now thinking he got away with it. I'm here to change that."

"Anything I can do to help, my brother?"

Connor thought on that a moment, then came up with an idea. "You say your daughter went to school with the Rollins' girls?" he asked.

"K through twelve. They're right up there in front."

Connor nodded and said, "You think you might could introduce me to them?"

Orson Blaine took about a half second to think it through, then said, "Follow me."

Connor did just that, trailing a couple steps behind as Mr. Blaine edged his way up the side of the church, avoiding the throng in the center aisle. When they reached the front they both hung back a bit, waiting for others to finish paying their respects and clamp their arms around the girls with massive hugs. Connor sensed the minutes ticking by but didn't want to miss an opportunity that might not come again.

Eventually Orson Blaine stepped up and took the hand of the older girl, the one who had stirred the church with her voice, and said, "I don't know whether I should tell you how sorry I am, or how beautiful you sounded."

The young woman smiled in embarrassment, and then Blaine kissed her younger sister, the one who was dressed in violet. He offered his condolences and both girls said a polite "thank-you." Then he stepped back half a step and said, "I'd like to introduce you both to a friend of mine. His name is Jack Connor, and he's working to get your papa out of jail."

Both women did solid double-takes as they regarded this bald white man clad in an ill-fitting suit standing in this A.M.E. church. At their mother's funeral, no less. Then the older one extended a gloved hand and said, "I'm Jamaicka, like the island but spelled with a c-k. Whatever you can do to get our poppa out of that dreadful place is a lot more than anyone else is doing."

Connor told her—both of them—that he was doing everything he could, but it might take some time. Then he said, "He's holding up pretty well, considering everything he must be going through."

"You saw him?" the younger one asked, then immediately looked mortified by speaking up. She quickly put a hand to her mouth as if to put the words back in, but it was too late. It was clear she deferred to her older sister, probably always had.

"Not exactly," Connor told her. "They don't allow visitors to actually see the prisoners—it's all done by closed circuit TV. But, yes…I spoke with him."

The younger woman nodded shyly, but her older sister said, "This is Laysha, my little sister. We're both hoping to pay a visit, probably tomorrow. You're really trying to him out of there?"

"Whatever I can do," he assured them. "And anything you can tell me might help."

Jamaicka glanced around the church, saw a few more folks coming up the aisles to offer their condolences. "Not here," she said in a hushed tone. "We can talk later. There's going to be a reception after the graveside service, place called The Nest."

"I know the place," Connor said, realizing he'd just double-booked his evening. *His and Danielle's evening.* "What time?"

"Any time after five," she told him. "It's going to be a long night."

Kat Rattigan had told Connor she'd meet him in the billiard hall next door to her P.I. office in Charleston at three o'clock, and she was true to her word. She was leaning over one of the high-end tables, polished mahogany with mother-of-pearl inlays, lining up a bank shot to put the 8-ball in the side pocket. Her opponent, a young man dressed in cargo shorts and a Guy Harvey fishing shirt, was standing back, a resigned look on his face.

Kat made the shot with ease, the 8-ball landing in the pocket with a resounding *thunk*. "Nice game," she told the guy, then turned and saw Connor standing behind her, watching the action. She nodded her head toward the bar, then told the guy, "Give me a second."

"Take your time," he replied.

Kat sauntered over to the long counter, only a couple of drinkers this time of day. She was wearing a pair of tight jeans and a sleeveless blouse the color of a

Caribbean lagoon. Pink lipstick, just a hint of eye shadow, and blondish hair cut just below her shoulders.

Connor got to the bar the same time she did and extended his hand. "Great to see you, Kat," he said.

"Jack Connor," she greeted him. "How's the leg?"

"Doing fine." Connor had met Kat Rattigan a year ago when she was working a different angle on the same case he was investigating. Despite their competing agendas she had helped him decipher a complex riddle that centered around a young chanteuse whom, he suspected, was now living in some distant banana republic where the threat of extradition was minimal. "I still get a little phantom itch every once in a while."

"I've heard about that," she said. "So, what can I do for you?"

"Right to the point," he said. "I like that."

"I'm kind of in the middle of something," she said, casting a glance at the young guy who now was pulling billiard balls out of the leather pockets and setting them on the table. "What do you need?"

"You still doing background checks?" he asked.

"Ninety percent of my business," she said. "Not including this place."

"I need you to run a report on someone."

"Of course," she said, lifting her shoulder in a slight shrug. "You could've done that online, saved you the trip."

"I'm more of a face-to-face kind of man," he told her.

He thought he saw her blush, but she shrugged it off and said, "So who are you backgrounding this time?"

Connor shook his head at her question and handed her an envelope. "The name's in there. And I don't need to tell you to be as discrete about this as possible."

She stared at him, then opened the envelope and glanced at the slip of paper inside. "Holy shit, Connor. What have you got yourself involved in this time?"

"Can't tell you," he said.

"Don't you do some work for Citadel Security?"

He nodded and said, "Part time…but this thing's too sensitive to go through normal channels."

"You got that right. What are you looking for?"

"Anything you can find—records, warrants, rumors, whatever."

"You got it," she assured him. "Just remember one thing."

"What's that?"

"You know what happened to you last year? That's nothing compared to the kind of hornet's nest you might wander into this time.

Connor got to the airport just three minutes late. Just as he was pulling into the waiting lot his cell phone rang and Danielle was telling him her plane had landed early and she was out at the curb waiting for him. The last time they had seen each other was the weekend before he'd turned over the Camaro, so she didn't recognize the POS Toyota when he pulled up in front of her. Nor did she recognize him in the dark jacket and damp sleeves down to his wrists.

"Connor?" she finally said, using his last name as a term of endearment, as she always did.

"Surprise!" he said as he threw his arms around her and gave her a long kiss. She returned the hug pound for pound, and again he found her body comfortable against his.

She made no effort to pull her lips from his, but when they finally came up for air she took a moment to size him up. "You look like you just came from a funeral," she finally said.

They'd been dating for almost fifteen months now, and sometimes he couldn't tell if she was joking or being serious. So he said, "Guilty as charged."

She took off her sunglasses and studied him, saw the truth in his eyes. "You're not kidding, are you?" she said. Matter-of-fact, not a question.

He said nothing, just kissed her again, a quick one before he picked up her carry-on bag and placed it in the bed of the truck. Then he yanked the door open and ushered her inside the cab with a chivalrous sweep of his hand.

"Your chariot awaits, ma'am," he said.

"You're working on another case." Once again, her words came out as a statement, not a question. "And where did you get this…wreck? Where's Isabella?"

Connor had taken great pains over the last couple of weeks not to reveal his plans for the Camaro. "All your questions will be answered in good time," he told her. "Meanwhile we have a party to go to."

"A party?"

He flashed her a guilty grin, instantly lost in her eyes. They were deep blue, just like the endless ocean that lured ancient mariners in ancient myths. Her face was framed by blonde hair with a few streaks of platinum, and he noticed she was wearing a new shade of lipstick that reminded him of pink azaleas in the spring.

"Well, it's more like a gathering, really. But there will be martinis and music."

She stared at him a moment, and then what he was saying sank in. "You're inviting me to a funeral reception?"

Connor gave her another kiss, this one more apologetic than romantic. "It's not something I planned on," he told her quickly. "And it's not what you think."

"What I think is I'm not wearing any underwear," she said with a wink. "Not one stitch."

"You mean…*on the plane*?"

"Just call me Commando Danielle," she giggled. "I was going to surprise you when we got to your place."

"I'm sure I can find an empty space in the parking garage—"

"No way, buster. You lost your chance." She stared into his eyes again, then added, "A funeral? Really?"

"Like I said, it just sort of came up," he insisted. He shifted into gear and pulled the rusty truck away from the curb. "In fact, I sort of got trapped."

Then he launched into the story of how the governor ambushed him at a crime scene, told him a story of woe about how his wife had depended on the victim of that crime had helped raise her kids and became almost like a sister.

"Almost?" Danielle repeated.

"I forgot to mention that the dead woman—her name is Ruby Rollins—is black."

"And the governor's wife most assuredly is not," Danielle pointed out. "So why you?"

"Take one guess," Connor said.

"The governor is friends with your boss," she replied. "Jordan James. But it's been over a year since…the last time."

In addition to his ongoing investigation at the port there had been a few other small jobs since Jordan James had hired him to find suitcase full of cash. Connor had been seriously wounded at the end of that one, and she took every chance she could to remind him of that fact.

"Don't worry—it's not going to be like last time," he assured her.

"You promised me," Danielle reminded him. "You almost got killed in that garage."

"But I didn't. And no one's going to get killed this time, either."

She said nothing for a while after that. Connor finally pulled to the red light at the airport exit, where he had to make a decision: turn left and go home to his place on the island, or go in the other direction back down to Ravenel. A blast from a horn behind him caused him to make a decision, and he instinctively turned the wheel to the right.

"You're sure this guy is innocent?" she asked him over the wash of air rushing through a crack in the windshield.

"I'm not sure of anything," he said with a shrug. "But everyone tells me Lester Rollins couldn't hurt a fly."

"I didn't know you were in the middle of a thing," she said. "I probably should have stayed home until you were done."

"I promise—this won't get in the way of our time together," he assured her. "I'll wine you and dine you end kiss every inch of your body. You won't even notice an investigation going on. And you might even enjoy this reception I'm taking you to."

She cast a suspicious eye at him but said nothing. They rode in silence a few minutes longer, until well after he'd turned from the I-526 spur onto Old Savannah Highway. Then she said, "Have you been watching the weather?"

He wondered if she were pissed, just making idle chatter until the storm cloud passed. So to speak.

"I've been keeping an eye on the TV," he told her. "It appears there's a hurricane heading this way."

"You don't seem too worried about it."

"It's been years since there was a serious storm around here."

As soon as the words left his mouth he recalled what Miss Benson told her restless physics class about probability: "Probability is quantified as a number between zero and one—zero indicating impossibility and one meaning certainty," she would say. "The higher the probability of an event has of hitting one, the more certain we are that the event will occur."

"Which means the odds of there being a hurricane are going up," Danielle pointed out.

"Or the climate cycle has shifted."

"The computer models show it could hit by the middle of next week," she continued. "Do you have an evacuation plan?"

He considered that a moment, then said, "Haven't really thought about it. I might just stay put, tough it out."

"This is shaping up to be a huge storm, Jack." *Jack* this time, not *Connor*. Ruh-roh. "They're saying it could be as strong as Hugo."

Hurricane Hugo was the category four storm that smacked the coast just a few miles north of Charleston in 1989.While it was busy killing twenty-seven people in South Carolina, its twenty-foot tidal surge swept across Sullivan's Island, taking out most of the houses and the only bridge that connected it to the mainland. Connor's place was built at ground level underneath an elevated home that had replaced one of those houses that did not survive Hugo's fury.

"I'll keep an eye on it," he assured her. "If it looks like it's coming this way I'll head over to The Plant."

"I've seen that place. I don't think that roof will stay put it if a hurricane hits."

"Then I'll hole up in the truck. It's not going to go anywhere."

He could tell she wasn't satisfied by his *ad hoc* plan, but she had said her piece. He reached out and took her hand and was reassured when she squeezed it. He knew this was a bad start to what was supposed to be a romantic weekend, but he'd made his decision when he turned right instead of left back at the airport.

They made small talk after that, Danielle telling him that the antibiotics had worked and Cyrano seemed to be getting better. A lion cub had been born the night before last and the mother at first had rejected it, but eventually came around to accepting it as her own. And a penguin had hatched in the Polar Habitat, something she insisted didn't happen very often in captivity. He listened with genuine attention, and before he knew it they were passing the A.M.E. church on Salters Hill Road. All but a few vehicles remained in the lot, one of them being the car he recognized as belonging to Reverend Parker. Like the captain of a ship, the pastor was the last person to leave his church.

A mile up the road Connor slowed down and pulled the pick-up off the road into the dusty lot of a closed filling station. In fact, it was more than closed; it appeared to have been abandoned years ago. The pumps were long gone, trash littered the overgrown yard, and the front windows covered with aging plywood. He slowed the truck to a crawl, then guided it around the corner of the building toward the back.

"Where are you taking me, Connor?" Danielle asked him.

"It's a surprise," he replied.

"Why does that scare me?"

"Because it should."

"Just what do you have in mind?"

He stopped the truck and shifted into park. "No one around for miles," he said as he turned off the engine.

"What's that supposed to mean?" she asked.

Connor flashed her a lascivious grin and said, "Are you really wearing nothing under that amazingly sexy dress?"

"Like I said, I wasn't planning on going to a funeral."

That's when the grin shifted from lascivious to lewd, and he said, "You mind if I check for myself?"

# Chapter 10

The road leading through the woods to The Nest was lined with cars parked on the shoulder. Connor pulled the truck into the first available space at the edge of the dense woods and cut the engine. He transferred Danielle's carryon bag into the cab of the truck, where she rummaged through it until she found a pair of panties. She slipped them on, then climbed out of the truck and waited for him to lock the door.

"I can't believe we just did that," she told him as she squeezed his hand. "We could have been caught back there."

"That's the point," he said, squeezing back.

"I feel like I'm back in high school."

"And that's a bad thing?"

"You didn't know me in high school."

"One of life's great sorrows," he replied. "And besides, you once told me when that you did a whole lot less than your twin sister back then, but got caught a whole lot more."

She laughed at that, then pecked him on the cheek. "I also told you that's all you need to know," she said. "And that hasn't changed."

Up ahead The Nest was jumping. The lot was packed with folks who were hanging around the maze of cars that had been packed in at every possible angle. Music was throbbing inside the low-slung building, mixed with the rap and hip-hop pounding from car radios outside. Connor could tell these outdoor revelers were mostly on the young side, the boys trying to impress the girls or older boys, the girls hanging with other girls while preening and primping. Just like the church earlier in the day virtually all of the celebrants were black, but they paid no attention as Connor and Danielle wove their way through the tangle of vehicles.

When they pushed their way inside, the celebration of Ruby Rollins' life hit them full force. The place was wall-to-wall people, a fire marshal's dream. The bar where Connor had sat by himself just yesterday was a sea of humanity, and the liquor was flowing freely. He caught a glimpse of J'Neece back there slinging drinks, but tonight she had much-needed help. He felt a momentary panic as he always did when he was caught in the middle of a crowd, the streets of Iraq closing in on him quickly. But coming here had been his idea, so he pushed aside the momentary anxiety and gently steered Danielle through a small gap in the multitude.

The music was louder in here, pulsing from an old-fashioned jukebox in the corner. A shiver iced Connor's spine as he recognized the record that was playing, a particularly haunting gospel-soul song titled "I'll Take You There" performed by the great Mavis Staples. The last time he'd heard it was the night he met the woman who almost got him killed, and later very possibly saved his life.

"I love this song," Danielle said, tugging on his arm. Then she leaned closer and said into his ear, "Tell me again how you're supposed to catch a killer in here—"

The place was so crowded he doubted she saw him grin, but it didn't matter. And she had a point: so many people were packed into the place that he doubted he'd even see the Rollins girls, much less find time to speak with either of them.

"That's not exactly how this works" he explained over the din. "Let's just see how it all plays out."

"You think they can make a dirty martini in here?" she asked. "It looks more like a beer and bourbon sort of place."

"No problem," he told her. She cast him a skeptical look, so he added, "I know the bartender."

Connor almost had to shout his drink order, but J'Neece caught it and set to work. She splashed a healthy dose of cheap gin over some ice and then poured in some of the juice from a jar of olives. She set it on the counter, then poured another solid measure of gin into a jelly jar and dropped in some ice.

"So, remind me again why we're here?" she asked him after taking her first long sip.

"One of the victim's daughters invited me," Connor told her. He clinked his tumbler against her glass and notched a mental reminder that he had a long drive home, and to limit himself to just one. Two, max. "I just have a couple questions, then we can leave."

"I don't want to leave," she replied. "We just got here. Do your thing and I'll just hang over there by the jukebox."

"But—"

"Move your ass, Connor," Danielle insisted. "I'm going to find someone to dance."

He shot her a look that said *really?*, but she gave him a friendly nudge like a mother bird pushing her chick out of the nest. Appropriate, considering the name of this place. She had a mischievous look in her eye, and he could tell that—despite her protests about being taken to a funeral reception—her sense of adventure had kicked into gear. He flashed back to their escapade about twenty minutes ago in the cab of his truck and a warm rush pulsed through his body. Then he launched himself into the crowd.

Connor located Jamaicka Rollins about ten minutes later. She was standing on the back deck at the edge of the marsh, her younger sister at her side. They were talking to a couple of older men that seemed about their father's age. The hot August evening and the gentle breeze easing in off the creek created a comforting duet, a song that the South had been singing since slaves were toiling in the fields.

He didn't want to intrude on their conversation, so he made his way over to the deck rail. The Nest sat on the grassy shore of Pelican Creek, a lazy estuary that fed into the Edisto River, which in turn wound its way from the upstate hill country down to the sea islands. Here in the lowcountry it fed into what was known as the ACE Basin, joining the Ashepoo and Combahee rivers to form one of the largest wetlands along the Atlantic coast. Connor placed both hands on the unfinished wood railing and watched flock of tiny cattle egret poke their way through the sweetgrass. Some distance away a pair of wood storks, with their ugly faces and long, hooked beaks were making one last effort to find a bite to eat before today disappeared forever. A bird of prey—possibly a bald eagle, but more likely a red-tailed hawk—circled lazily overhead.

Connor was not trying to listen in on Jamaicka's conversation, but it was hard not to hear the man who was speaking with her. He had a rich, deep voice and an accent that clearly had its roots in the deep south—possibly Mississippi or Alabama. He spoke clearly and slowly, with a purpose behind every word, and his cadence made it seem that he had a dime balanced on his tongue.

"Your father was one of the best horn players in Memphis," he was telling the Rollins sisters. "The whole river delta, in fact."

"He never spoke of those days before he came to South Carolina," Jamaikca replied. "It was like anything that came before never happened."

"I always figured he left some kind of secret behind," the younger one named Laysha said. "I almost asked him about it a couple times but never did."

"Maybe if Mr. Connor, there, has his way, you'll get a chance." Jamaicka clearly had seen him leaning against the railing, trying not to interrupt in. She looked him in the eye and said, "I'm glad you could come."

Connor took that as his cue to edge over and join the conversation. "I appreciate the invitation, but I don't wish to intrude."

"We were just talking about our poppa and how he should be here. And how you're working to get him out of that place."

"Whatever it takes," Connor said, aware of how lame he sounded. "The more I learn about your parents, the better chance I have of doing just that."

"Joe Turner here was just telling us about Poppa before he moved here from Memphis," Laysha said. "He says our father was kind of famous, played on lots of records back when they were still made of plastic."

"Vinyl," her sister corrected her. Then she said, "Mr. Turner...this is Jack Connor."

The large black man studied Connor—mostly his tattoos—and then extended his hand. "Nice to meet you, sir," he said. "I haven't seen cover art like that since my days at Stax."

It was a comment almost lost on the younger generation who had grown up listening to MP3s or Pandora on an iPhone. But Connor had grown up with his father's Zeppelin and Beatles albums and had spent hours poring over the *Mothership* and *Sgt. Pepper* artwork.

"Life is a canvas upon which the passing years are painted," he said.

"Truer words were never spoken," Joe Turner said in his rich, steady voice.

"Mr. Turner played bass and slide guitar at Stax Records back in the day," Jamaicka told him. "Worked with Isaac Hayes and Otis Redding and the Staple Singers."

"Back when music was still music," Connor said, for lack of anything better to say.

"And soul was still soul," Turner added. "Word about ol' Hurricane's troubles made its way to Memphis, me and Bobby decided to come here and check it out."

Jamaicka turned her attention to the other man, thinner and taller and looking uncomfortable in his ill-fitting suit. "This is Bobby Johnson," she continued. "He was with a group called Soulidify and played on a lot of records with Poppa."

"He was supposed to be on the plane that crashed with Otis Redding," her younger sister added. "But he was in the studio, laying down tracks with Poppa, so he missed the flight."

"I still can't believe he never told us about any of this," Jamaicka added. "It's like he had this whole secret life before he met Momma."

Joe Turner took a handkerchief from his jacket pocket and dabbed a bead of perspiration from his forehead. Despite the lengthening shadows, the August heat was stifling, and a dark funeral suit and tie only made the heat worse.

"I always wondered what became of Lester," he said. "One day he was there in Memphis, and the next day he was gone. No one ever saw him again, but there were lots of questions. I wouldn't have heard about this except for my nephew, who saw it on the web."

"There must have been theories," Connor said. "Stories going around."

"Absolutely. Some folks said he'd died, while others believed he'd disappeared because of what happened to Al Jackson."

The words hung there a moment as Connor glanced from Jamaicka to Laysha. Neither of them seemed to know what Turner was talking about, so he asked, "Who was Al Jackson?"

The man named Bobby Johnson took the lead on this one. "Al was the drummer for Booker T. and the MGs," he said. "'Green Onions' and 'Time Is Tight,' and the Stax house band. He was shot at his home back in seventy-five, and Hurricane Rollins disappeared the next day."

"Did the police think Lester did it?" Connor asked.

"I don't think he was ever a suspect," Johnson said, shaking his head. "Mrs.

Jackson had already shot Al a few months before, so there was something else going on."

"Like maybe she hired someone to kill him?"

"Or she was having an affair. Rumors were circling like buzzards."

"Seems like Mr. Rollins was in the wrong place at the wrong time," Connor pointed out.

"He damned sure wasn't expected to be in Memphis that night," Johnson agreed. "You ask me, he came home unexpectedly from watching that boxing match, walked in on something, and someone popped him."

"They ever catch the guy?"

Johnson shook his head, said, "Nope. Cops found him a year later, took him down. After that the case was supposedly closed."

"*Supposedly* is a pretty strong word," Connor observed.

"There were rumors at the time that the real killer was never caught," Johnson explained. "That maybe there was more to the story than what the police let on. But that was southern justice in the seventies."

"And not a whole lot has changed since then," Jamaicka said. "Seems the cops were damned quick to lock Poppa up for something he didn't do."

"He was holding the knife that was used to kill Momma," Laysha pointed out.

"You can't think Poppa did this—!"

"Of course not. But you know how the po-lice are."

No one said a word to that. Racial overtones or not, the police as an institution had earned a questionable reputation for meting out equal justice for all.

"What about you, Mr. Turner?" Jamaicka finally asked. "Do you think our Poppa could have done this?"

"Not the Lester Rollins I knew, no," he said quickly. "The only thing he could kill was any song got thrown his way."

Connor took a sip of gin, let it trickle slowly down his throat. "You said there were rumors that someone else killed this Al Jackson?" he asked.

"There's been talk over the years of opening up the case again, but that's all it is. Talk."

"So, if someone else besides this mystery intruder did it…well, what if Lester Rollins knew who it was? What if that's why he left Memphis?"

Joe Turner appeared to ponder the question seriously a moment, but Bobby Johnson said, "You're thinking that's what this is? Someone's trying to silence him after all these years?"

"I'm just exploring every angle," Connor told him. "Maybe the real killer found out where Lester lived and came looking for him."

"Then why would they kill his wife and not him?"

Connor had no answer to the question. In fact, he'd asked himself the same thing as soon as it crossed his mind. "I'm not looking to answer the 'why' question here," he said. "Just considering all the possibilities."

"I guess anything is possible," Bobby Johnson agreed. "But if Lester Rollins had knowledge about what happened to Al Jackson forty years ago, why would someone want to kill his wife and not him? Any why now, after all this time?"

"Those are 'why' questions," Connor said. "If anyone has the answer to them, it's probably Mr. Rollins."

"If he's sat on them for forty years, what makes you think he'll say anything now?" Jamaicka asked.

"Because he's missing your Momma as much as anyone in here," Connor said, cocking his head back at the packed roadhouse in emphasis. "If the murder in Memphis had anything to do with what happened, it's a truth that's been stalking him for a long, long time."

# Chapter 11

Connor and Danielle left about an hour after that. The parking lot was still jammed with cars, and the spillover crowd from the party inside, dancing to the music. Johnnie Taylor's old school "Soul Heaven" was cranking on the jukebox and the tearful refrain drifted through the pines and mossy oaks as the sun kissed the edge of the marsh. The smell of Carolina barbecue and fried okra hung thick in the air, weighed down with the odor of ever-present pluff mud.

Connor threaded the needle of cars parked on both sides of the road, sometimes crammed so close together he thought he'd lose a side view mirror. Eventually the gauntlet of vehicles thinned out, and that's when he noticed a dark-colored car backed into the trees, an older-model sedan silhouetted in the growing darkness. The lights of the pick-up swept across the side of the car, the three vent holes in the front fenders telling him it was a Buick. And then, just for a moment, the glare illuminated a person inside, lounging back and staring up at the ceiling. As the headlights fell upon his eyes he turned his head, and in that instant Connor recognized him.

It was the same man he'd seen yesterday, arguing with Reverend Parker outside the A.M.E. church. Pale skin and long blond hair, this time partially stuffed up under a dark baseball cap. Their eyes met, and Connor could feel those penetrating eyes on him as the truck bounced past on the corrugated road.

"Did you see the guy in that car?" Danielle asked him, cranking her head to look back.

"Sure did," Connor told her, feeling the icy fingers of pure evil tickling his spine. He thought about what Walter Hill had said about Ruby Rollins' encounter with the nut job outside the Quick Stop. "Didn't look up to any good, you ask me."

"Straight out of *Breaking Bad*," Danielle said. "You think we should call someone?"

"Like who?"

"Like the cops," she said.

"And tell them what?" he replied. "It's not a crime to sit in a car in the woods. Not until something happens."

"And when something does happen?"

Connor was thinking the same thing, but the last time he got involved with someone lurking in the woods it hadn't gone well. The old truck rocked through a massive rut in the road, jolting both of them down to the base of their spines. He steered out of the pothole, then grabbed his phone out of what at one time had been a cup holder.

"Just a precaution," he said to Danielle as he punched in 9-1-1.

The police dispatcher who answered the phone was peeved that Connor had called about something so mundane as a man sitting in a car. "Your concern has no more substance than my mother's tapioca," was how she put it.

"I'm just telling you what I saw," Connor explained. "There's a white man in a car lurking down the road from a funeral for a black woman."

"Something happens, get back to us. Have a good night."

She hung up, leaving Connor to realize why ordinary citizens don't have more respect for those hired to protect and to serve them. Until after the fact.

The rest of the evening had nothing to do with death or dying. Danielle admitted she'd had a better time at the funeral than she'd expected while Connor was off doing his P.I. thing, dancing with several young boys who also had been dragged to the reception but were getting into the music. The old Seeburg was loaded with lots of Chuck Berry, Little Richard, Bar-Kays, and Kool & The Gang, and she admitted she'd gotten her groove on big time.

They had a late dinner at Poe's on Sullivan's Island, another dirty martini for her and another basic glass of gin for him. They sat at a table out on the patio that was warm from the late summer heat. The sun had long kissed the day farewell, but the block-long downtown section of Sullivan's was swollen with music, beer, barbecue, and the ever-present salt air that merged at this midpoint between the beach and the Intracoastal waterway.

"You're not mad at me?" Connor asked her.

She studied him over the rim of her martini and said, "Mad? How could I be mad?"

"This isn't what you signed up for," he reminded her.

"I signed up for you," she replied. "And let me remind you, whenever you visit me in Orlando you never know if there's a zebra going into labor or a camel with a urinary infection. Our lives go on, no matter where we were."

He nodded, swirled the liquid in his tumbler. "I get that," he said. "But a funeral—"

"It's just another point on the path through life. Happens to all of us."

"You know what I'm saying—"

She reached across the table and touched a finger to his lips. "What *I'm saying* is we finish our lovely meal, then pay the check and go back to your place. We hold each other as if there's no tomorrow, you peel off my clothes, and then we slip quietly into the darkness of your bedroom. Then all there is, is you and me and a long, quiet night. And the moon shimmering across the marsh."

"There is no moon tonight," he said. "Too many clouds."

"There's always a moon, you moron," she laughed. "Just because you can't see it doesn't mean it's not there. And just because you can't always see me, doesn't mean I'm not always *here*." She emphasized her point by touching the same finger to his heart.

And that was the crux of a very big problem. What had begun as a simple—*what, friendship? crush?*—more than a year ago had developed into something much deeper. Connor had never expected to find love again, not after his first marriage crumbled, his niece died, and he traded in those nightmares for another one in Iraq. But then Danielle had plunged into his life with a blast of pepper spray, throwing all bets out the window. Their attraction had been hesitant and tentative at first, forcing them both to color inside the lines of her failing marriage and his past baggage. But when those lines finally were crossed they'd made up for lost time, figuring they'd just see where the whims of life took them.

He gently touched her hand, held it in his for a moment. Then he said, "I know how the moon works, Danielle. And the sun and the stars and the tides. And I'd give all of them for the chance to be able to see you every day and every night."

She made no effort to take her hand back. "Long distance is a bitch," she agreed.

"So, I've been thinking—"

"Uh-oh."

"Just hear me out," he told her. "I did some reading, looked around a little on Google. It seems Orlando has its fair share of homicides and accidental deaths. Per capita it's way ahead of Charleston."

"And you're telling me this why?"

"Because someone has to clean up those death scenes down there just as they do up here," he explained.

"And?"

"And there aren't a lot of people knocking the door down to do what I do. So I did some more checking, and guess what: there are five companies just like Palmetto BioClean in the Orlando area. And three of them are looking for experienced technicians."

Now she took her hand back, used it and her other one to pick up her martini glass. "You're talking about moving down to Orlando?"

"I'm talking about doing anything I can to be with you every day and every night," he told her.

She took a long, slow sip and let the gin wash down her throat. "Does Mr. James know you've been doing all this Googling?" she finally asked him.

"Nope, and I've even deleted the searches from my computer. And you don't have to say anything more—I just thought it was something you should know."

She stared at her plate of fish tacos, then glanced up at him. A smile had crept into her face and was illuminating her eyes the way they had on their first dinner date. "It's very sweet, you know," she told him. "Doing all this research."

"Something's got to give."

In fact, it was something they'd both been thinking about a lot lately, mostly ignoring it during those few hours when every third or fourth weekend allowed them to be together.

"I thought you didn't like Orlando," she reminded him.

"It's better than Kirkuk, and I have great respect for what you do."

She giggled at his words, both sweet and stiff, then said, "That's like saying you'll still respect me in the morning—"

"I'm just saying that I can make anything work as long as I have you."

Danielle picked up a taco and took a bite, chewed it slowly. When she was finished she said, "I was going to tell you this later, but I've been doing some Googling of my own."

"Googling about what? There's no zoos or animal parks anywhere near Charleston."

"No, but there's a horse rescue farm about an hour south of here," she said. "A hundred fifty acres right on the water, thirty-one horses and a dozen old mules. Work animals, mostly, and they've had pretty hard lives. The foundation that runs it just happens to be looking for a large animal veterinarian, and I just happen to know one. A damned good one, if I do say so myself."

"You've already spoken with them?" Connor asked.

"A short discussion on the phone," Danielle told him. "They want to meet with me tomorrow afternoon."

Inwardly Connor was thrilled that she was considering relocating to South Carolina, but he heard himself blurt out, "When were you planning on telling me this?"

"Earlier than now, but I didn't know I was going to be shanghaied to a funeral," she said. "I was hoping you'd be pleased."

Connor leaned forward and fixed her eyes with his. "Pleased? Damn…I'm as happy as a pig in shit. But I'd hate for you to give up your job for me."

"It wouldn't be for you," she explained as she took another bite of taco. "It's for us. And the horses, of course."

"Still—"

"Stills are for moonshiners and deep waters," she told him. "Something my dad used to tell my sister and me."

"What about Cyrano?" Connor pressed. "And the zebras and camels and lions?"

"Look, Connor," she said. "We're just talking things through here. No promises, no guarantees. Like I said, you're sweet to have looked into jobs down in Orlando. But I know you like it here, and so do I. Totally different pace of life, and there's a man up here I'm totally crazy about."

"Crazy is as crazy does," he said, raising his glass in a half-assed toast. "Here's to two crazy-ass people."

"If it's all right with you we can leave my ass out of it," she said as she clinked her glass against his.

"In that case, if I said you had a beautiful body, would you hold it against me?"

"Eighth grade? Really?

"I'm just sayin'…"

She shook her head, as if she couldn't believe she'd actually fallen in love with this tattooed ex-Army grunt who still lived in the halls of his Michigan high school and quoted his dazzlingly gorgeous science teacher. "Pay the check, buster, and let's go see just what I'm ready to hold against you."

He was awakened the next morning by the sound of a train whistle. It sounded faint at first, then grew louder with each blow, until Connor realized it was the new ringtone he'd downloaded into his phone. He glanced over at Danielle, who was tangled in the thin cotton sheets she'd given him for his birthday. She seemed to be asleep, so he punched the "answer" button with a touch of apprehension.

"Is this Jack Connor?" a male voice on the other end said.

"Who's asking?" he replied. He slipped out of the bed and wandered into the kitchen so he wouldn't wake Danielle.

"Sergeant Jim Crane, Charleston County Sheriff," the voice said. "I'll ask you again, are you Connor?"

"I was when I went to bed last night." He realized he was coming across as insolent, but he hadn't had a whole lot of positive interactions with the local authorities. "What's this about?"

"It's about a call you made from this phone last night, around seven thirty," Sgt. Crane said. "Something about a man sitting in a car in the woods?"

"That's right. Just down the road from a bar called The Nest, near Ravenel."

"Do you remember what kind of car it was?"

Connor felt a dark sense of dread pulse through him. "Why…did something happen?" he asked.

"Just answer the question, sir," the sergeant told him.

Connor thought back, remembered the vent holes illuminated in his headlights. "I think it was a Buick, kinda old. Dark, maybe blue but not black. Can you tell me what's going on?"

"Did you get the license plate?" the cop asked him, ignoring his question.

The old sedan had been backed well into the trees, and Connor pointed this out. "I would have if this state wasn't too cheap to put plates on the front bumper. So no, I didn't get the number. Are you going to tell me what happened?"

Sergeant Crane hesitated, then must have figured there was no harm in divulging an outline of the facts. "There was an incident last night, a couple hours after you called," he said.

"An incident?"

"Shots fired. No one was hurt, but there was some shattered glass and people saw a car speeding away from the scene. That juke joint where them blacks was partyin.'"

"This car…was it the Buick?"

"No one was real specific, but it fits your description. Listen…someone might want to talk to you about this later."

"You have my number," Connor said. "It's my cell."

Sergeant Crane thanked him for his help, didn't apologize for calling so early, and then hung up.

Connor set his phone down on the counter and glanced toward the bedroom, hoping he hadn't awakened Danielle. The first light of the new day was washing across the marsh outside, streaks of pink and orange splitting the dawn like giant cracks in some celestial orb. He realized he had zero chance of falling back asleep so he set about making a pot of coffee, with the intention of taking a cup out back and watching the morning spring to life.

That's when he heard, "You coming back to bed?"

He turned and smiled at Danielle, who was peering around the door jamb. "I don't think I can go back to sleep," he told her.

"No one mentioned anything about sleep, silly," she said, giving him a sly wink.

Coffee and the new morning were just going to have to wait.


"You think the guy in that car did the shooting?" she asked him later.

Connor had been instantly distracted when she'd poked her head out of the bedroom, but eventually he'd filled her in on why Sergeant Crane had called him so early.

"He didn't say exactly," he replied. "But it seems there were a few witnesses."

They were sitting out on Connor's small patch of grass, both of them warming their hands with identical mugs of coffee. Danielle had a skimpy silk robe wrapped around her, nothing underneath, but Connor had already thrown on a pair of board shorts and a T-shirt.

"He was just sitting there in the trees," she said, shaking her head with a shudder. "With a loaded gun."

Connor slowly sipped his coffee and dug his toes into the grass. "That's why I've never played the hero," he told her. "First thing I learned in Iraq is the other guy just might be crazy."

"Remember that next time you get shot while you're running around playing detective."

The clang from the swing bridge up the Intracoastal caused him to glance at his watch: eight o'clock on the dot. A clump of purple martins swooped back and forth across the marsh until they were pulled into the brightening sky to the east as if by an unseen net.

"I remember that every time my leg starts to ache," he assured her. It had been over a year since he'd taken a slug in his thigh, and the occasional spasm still caused it to seize up.

"That's what I'm talking about," she said. "Next time you might not be so lucky."

"Is this where I'm supposed to say something about the dangers of hanging around a private dick?"

She kicked his chair playfully with her bare foot, then said "be nice" as she watched a large ketch with an unusually tall mast slip through the open bridge.

Connor realized again just how much he loved this woman, how deeply she had crawled into his heart and taken up residence there. He'd thought he'd been in love before, once at the end of his senior year in high school and again when he married his first wife. But neither of those times had he felt anything that came close to how swollen his chest felt whenever he looked at Danielle, heard her voice, or kissed her lips. He'd made it through his sixteen months in Iraq because he'd had no ties to anyone, no picture to carry in his wallet, no girl back home to try not to die for. But now he had Danielle to think of and to care about, and that was a game-changer.

His mind drifted again to the zealot who had confronted Ruby Rollins outside the Quick Stop down in Ravenel, wondered if there was more to the encounter than just a matter of faith. There was no gun involved with that incident—at least not that Connor was aware of—but that didn't mean the guy hadn't been armed. Or had a gun close by. Either way, if the C-store was equipped with a surveillance camera, the chance that it was slim to none. Still, it was a possible lead to chase down, so he added it to his mental list of things to do today.

He glanced over at Danielle, knew in this very moment that he could build his entire life around mornings like these. Just his girl and him, and the marsh. And a fresh day ready to spring to life.

"What time is your appointment?" he asked her.

"They said two o'clock," Danielle said. "I was thinking we could drive down together, maybe find a nice place to have lunch along the way."

"Whatever the lady wishes."

"That kind of thinking can get you into a lot of trouble," she warned him.

"Trouble is my middle name."

"Well, in that case, care to go back inside and cause a little more?"

"Your wish is my command."

# Chapter 12

Three hours later they were heading south on old Savannah Highway.

The official name of Danielle's prospective employer was the Gregorian Chants Second Chance Ranch. It was hidden at the end of a narrow two-lane hard scrabble road that ran through a maritime pine forest, adjacent to the Edisto River near the Ernest Hollings ACE Basin National Wildlife Refuge. This was one of the last vestiges of pristine wetlands in America, home to untold species of flora and fauna in a setting that hadn't changed much since before humans invaded the shore. There had been some farming here during colonial times, but the low-lying land and high-water table made for poor conditions and meager harvests. As a result, most of the plantation owners settled further inland, away from the marshes and rivulets that coursed through this stretch of shoreline.

The Second Chance Ranch was bordered by a whitewashed board fence erected along the far side of a drainage ditch that ran along the shoulder of the road. The fence went on for about a quarter of a mile before Connor found the entrance, marked by a sign erected across two upright timbers. The sign read "Gregorian Chants Ranch," and a line below that explained, "Giving Horses A Second Chance At Life." A wrought iron gate was closed to through traffic, but an intercom call box was right where Danielle's directions said it would be.

Connor pulled up to it and pressed a button, then said to her, "You want to do this?"

She nodded and leaned across him just as the buzzer buzzed, "Gregorian Ranch," a voice announced. "How may I help you?"

"Danielle Simmons," she called out. "I have an appointment at two o'clock with Ken and Elena Gregory."

"Yes, ma'am," the voice said. "I'll let them know the Clampetts are here."

Danielle gave a deep sigh at the obvious reference to Connor's truck, but said nothing. There was no camera anywhere to be seen, but the voice clearly implied there was one. Probably set in one of the tall pines on the other side of the gate. The gate that now began swinging inward, granting them access to a broad white gravel drive that appeared to disappear into a dark forest ahead of them.

"This truck's just a loaner," Connor explained defensively while Danielle hid her head in her hands. "My Camaro is in the shop."

"Right," the voice replied. "Anyway, just pull that thing around back of the house, if you don't mind."

Connor drove through the gate and followed the gravel road about a quarter mile. It made a lazy turn through the trees and then the Edisto River came into view, the water wide and glistening. A hundred yards offshore a boat was cutting a lazy arc and the spray came off the bow like diamonds in the sun. A few seconds later Connor pulled into a vast open area, the center of which was occupied by a large white house that sprouted from the earth on concrete pilings. A set of stairs led up to a wraparound porch festooned with window boxes awash with colorful annuals. Ceiling fans spun lazily in shade provided by sweeping live oak trees that dripped great gobs of Spanish moss.

A Lincoln SUV was parked in front of the central stairs, but no one appeared to be around. Connor heeded the advice of the voice on the intercom and continued driving, following the road around the side of the house. It narrowed to one lane and wound around a stand of trees, then continued on to a weathered barn that was set at the side of a fenced-in pasture. Several horses glanced up as Connor applied the brakes and the old pick-up rattled to a stop in front of the barn door.

"Smooth, unobtrusive entrance," Danielle said. "First impressions being what they are."

"There's nothing wrong with showing up in a rusty old truck," Connor replied. "It's got a lot more character than that fancy Navigator parked out front."

"That fancy Navigator probably belongs to the people I'm meeting with," she reminded him.

Connor realized she most likely was right, so he let it drop. "So how do you want to do this?" he asked her.

Danielle checked her watch, then said, "I'm sure you could wait, but I have no idea how long I'll be."

"Not a problem," he told her, shaking his head. "There's something I need to take care of, so if it's all right with you I'll leave you here for a bit."

"Something that has to do with this thing you're working on?"

"I'm not sure. I won't be far, so just give me a call and I'll be back for you when you're done here."

She nodded at that, then yanked the handle and gave the door a body slam. It sprang open, and she gave him another mortified look as she climbed out. "The Camaro would have made a much better impression," she said.

"Horse doctors don't drive muscle cars," he replied. "Break a leg."

"Surprised that hasn't happened already," she told him as she got out and pushed the door shut.

"Good luck," he said through the open window. Then, just because he could, he added, "I love you."

"Love you too."

She tapped the roof, then turned to see where she should go. As if on cue a woman emerged from the barn—shorts and T-shirt and a straw hat with a wide brim—and waved at her. Danielle walked over to her and they shook hands, and Connor heard faint introductions over the sputtering engine.

He touched the accelerator and made a tight U-turn in front of the barn, then headed back the same way he'd come. He kept an eye on Danielle in the rear-view mirror, watched as she walked with the woman—probably Mrs. Gregory—back inside the barn. This had all happened so fast that he hadn't really had time to digest it all: Danielle telling him about her job interview, the idea that she might actually give up her position at Animal World down in Orlando and move up here to South Carolina. Working with horses that had spent their years pulling plows and tourist carriages and somehow had been rescued and given a new life here at the Second Chance Ranch. And moving closer to Connor, but still being far enough away so there was room for them to breathe.

He had to admit he liked the idea. Liked it a whole lot more than moving to Orlando .

Connor had been telling the truth when he'd said he had a small matter to take care of. He hadn't mentioned it to Danielle on the drive down because he hadn't wanted to alarm her, but now that she was safely inside the horse ranch it was time to deal with the issue. When he got to the main road he pulled to a rolling stop, then turned left, heading back toward Highway 17.

He figured the van couldn't be more than a half mile up the road, probably backed into the trees or a thicket of Carolina creeper. He drove slowly, scanning both sides of the roadway and slowing down at every driveway or turnaround. About half a mile up the road he found it, backed into the shade of some trees next to a dilapidated storage building whose better days were long gone. The van was an older Ford Econoline, early eighties, like the one his cousin Gilbert had driven up in Michigan. Gil was an electrician and had bought the van from a friend and had driven it until the paint had fried and the chassis was held together by rust.

That seemed to be the case here, but Connor wasn't interested in the rust or the paint. Just the fact that some creep had followed him all the way down here from Sullivan's Island. It had pulled out from a gas station thirty seconds after Connor and Danielle had left his place that morning, and it hovered a hundred yards back all the way through Charleston and down Old Savannah Highway. Whoever was driving waited patiently on the other side of the road while Connor and Danielle had sat at a picnic table outside a place called the Oyster Royster and enjoyed a quiet lunch in the shade of an elm tree. Then the sonofabitch had followed them down here, hanging back while Connor pulled up to the gate and announced their arrival.

Now it was Connor's turn.

He drove past where the Econoline was waiting, giving the driver—

whoever he was—time to either keep sleeping behind the wheel or suddenly engage the engine and kick the transmission into gear. Then Connor pulled an abrupt U-turn and swerved back into the lot, tires sizzling on the loose gravel. He pulled to a stop just inches from the Econoline's front bumper and cranked the gearshift into park.

Before the engine had sputtered out Connor jumped down from the cab of the truck and circled around the front. He squeezed through the small gap that separated the bumpers of the two vehicles and rapped on the window. The driver in the Econoline blinked his eyes open and suddenly realized his lame attempt to follow Connor had failed. The jig was up.

He leaned out the window and yelled, "Hey, fuckah…move your truck!"

Connor paid him no mind, instead eyeing the rust scars on the weathered hood, and the bird shit splattered on the windshield. Then his eye was drawn to the small metal tag fixed to the dashboard where it met the glass, and he committed the last five digits to memory. That would probably be enough.

"I said, you're blocking me in," the scuz ball behind the wheel snarled. Round face, a few tufts of hair on his chin, hair cropped to fit the obtuse shape of his head. Cheap drugstore shades covered his eyes, and his breath stank of Red Bull and corn nuts.

"You've been following me," Connor snapped at him. "Tell me about that."

"Following you? You're out of your fucking mind—"

But Connor was in no mood for playing games. This little shit had been on his tail for the last two hours, which was bad enough. But Danielle had been in the truck, which meant that whatever was going on here—whoever had put this guy on him—had placed her at risk. He reached down and picked up a rock, said, "Tell me who put you up to this or I put this through your windshield."

"Go ahead and try, you pussy—"

Connor had no patience for dumb turds like this, so he slammed the rock down hard on the glass. A jagged crack appeared, like a bolt of lightning on a clear summer afternoon.

"Tell me who put you up to this—"

"You fucking broke it!" the turd screamed at him.

"And I'm going to finish the job, you don't tell me what this is all about."

"Shit, man—this van ain't mine."

It was clear this douchebag was either following Connor on his own or he'd had instructions to do so. Either way he knew where Connor lived, and that pissed him off. He hefted the rock in emphasis and said, "I'm going to ask you one more time—who put you up to this?"

"Go to hell," the scumbag said, dark defiance in his eyes.

Connor slammed the rock down, harder this time. The windshield shattered into a million tiny diamonds, and a big sheet of crumpled of them folded in on the dashboard.

"You fucker!" the guy said. "You gonna pay—"

Connor just shook his head at the threat and said, "Here's where you get to prove how smart you are, you dumb sonofabitch."

"You a dead man—"

Connor kept an eye on both hands, which right now were in plain view. That could change in about two seconds, and he knew it. He leaned his face in so he was only inches from the shithead's. Damned, did his breath smell of Red Bull and corn nuts. "Who sent you?"

"Don't know what you're talking 'bout, asshole," the driver said, a bead of spittle forming on his sneering lips.

Connor had had enough. He pulled out his cell phone and snapped a picture of the guy—along with the broken windshield—and slipped it back into his pocket.

"Wait, you motherfucker—"

But Connor simply ignored him as he walked back to his truck. He climbed inside and yanked the door closed, then started the engine.

"Listen, asshole!" the driver of the van yelled at him. "You don't got nothing. Plate's gone, an' there's hundreds of these old vans on the road." He sounded almost triumphant, leaning back in his seat and grinning through the gap in his windshield.

"Plates don't matter," Connor called back through the open window. "I got your VIN, and that's enough to see who owns that piece of shit."

"Keep your nose out of this, asshole!" the scuz ball yelled back. He keyed his engine to life and gunned the accelerator hard. "That nigger bitch ain't no concern of yours—"

Connor said nothing, just raised his middle finger and let the gesture linger a second. Then he backed off a few yards, leaving just enough room for the Econoline to swerve past him and fishtail as it hit the paved road.

*Nigger bitch.*

Once it had disappeared out of sight, Connor hit speed dial on his phone and waited for the line to connect.

"Citadel Security," a voice greeted him on the other end.

Connor immediately recognized the voice, said, "Good afternoon to the most gorgeous woman in the Lowcountry."

"Tat Man!" Caitlin Thomas cooed to him in a shrill voice that was a mix of a mouse's squeak and fingernails on a chalkboard. He'd first come to know her during the same case that had involved Kat Rattigan, and quickly learned that she was a wizard at digging up dirt on just about anyone and anything. If there was a warrant or a subpoena or rumor hanging in someone's closet, Caitlin knew the who, what, where, and when. "To what do I owe the pleasure…especially on a Saturday?"

"Do I have to have a reason to call a gorgeous woman?"

She laughed at that, mostly because no one except Connor ever called her gorgeous. Pixie-ish, yes. And perky. Pert and bouncy. But not gorgeous.

"No, but you always do," she said. "Give me what you've got and I'll see what I can do."

Connor felt an odd sense of guilt, almost as if he'd cheated on her by going to Kat Rattigan first. But he had a few less-sensitive things he needed Caitlin to check out, and he listed them now by order of priority.

"Did you get the entire number?" she asked when he was done.

"I took a picture, but only the last five digits are visible," he told her. "But it's a Ford van, probably from the eighties. You should be able to find it in the system somewhere."

"Got it, Tat Man. Anything else?"

"I'll let you know," he told her, and rung off.

Danielle didn't walk out with the job, but she earned herself big points because one of the mares in the barn was in labor and the foal ended up being twisted upside down. The mother was a younger horse that had been repeatedly mistreated by its owner up in Greer and eventually was rescued by the Second Chance Ranch. She had been impregnated at her former home and there had been trouble from the start. She had gone into labor early that morning, before the sun was up, but things had begun to look bleak by the time Danielle got there.

Danielle immediately realized the two hind limbs were twisted up underneath the foal and the rear end was caught as it tried to come out first. The only way to correct this problem was to reverse the foal, which meant she had to push the him back into the uterus deep enough so she could turn him around. By the time Connor pulled up outside the barn the foal was out and, while totally exhausted from the past six hours, he actually standing on his tiny legs.

"I'm going to strongly recommend you to our board," he heard Mrs. Gregory gush when they finally emerged from the barn. "You saved that little colt's life."

"It's a delicate procedure, but I've had some practice with zebras," Danielle replied. "And an antelope."

"Well, we don't have a lot of antelopes playing around here," the woman said. "Nor a lot of pregnant mares. But your skills are impeccable, and you'd be a Godsend to the ranch. You already have been."

"Thank you," Danielle said, shaking her hand. "It would be fun and a challenge to be part of this place."

"We'll see what we can do to make that happen," Mrs. Weston assured you. "Meanwhile, have a pleasant trip back."

Danielle climbed back into the truck and yanked the door shut. Connor gave her a quick peck on the cheek, then wrenched the transmission into gear and circled through the dooryard.

"Sounds like your visit went well," he observed once they were on their way.

That's when she told him what had happened, and by the time she had finished with her story he had fallen in love with her all over again.

"She's going to give me a call on Monday, Tuesday at the latest," she explained.

"Do you think you're ready to say 'goodbye' to the happiest place on Earth?"

"I think I could be pretty happy right here," she replied. "I mean here in the lowcountry, not this particular truck."

"How 'bout the guy driving it?"

"Ten four, good buddy," she said.

That was good enough for him.

# Chapter 13

Until three months ago Connor had played congas in a reggae band every Saturday night at a place called Jimmy's Buffet in Folly Beach. Jimmy's was a free-range bar known for build-your-own drinks and live music featuring local bands that had absolutely no chance of ever signing a major record deal. Connor had figured the Caribbean Jerks would continue that grand tradition of anonymity, but it turned out that a promoter had heard them play at a local music festival and was impressed by what he called their "freestyle musicality."

Eventually the Jerks were signed to open for a semi-established band that performed a hundred dates a year, and so far, things had worked well for them. The group played a seven-song set each night, mostly Bob Marley and Peter Tosh, with no opportunity for an encore. Connor had only been an honorary member of the band and had no interest in going out on tour or pursuing a musical career, so he'd wished them well and followed their travels on the web.

That meant he had his nights free again, which was how he and Danielle ended up at a place called Red's, at the edge of Shem Creek. Streaks of crimson and violet were painted across the sky, casting a brilliant glow across the tidal marsh. Live music was playing at the half dozen bars located along the creek, and shrimp were beginning to boil somewhere close by. Out on the boulevard a siren screamed and then faded into the distance. Connor flashed on something about the Doppler Effect he'd learned in high school physics, but he forgot it just as quickly.

The hostess seated them at an outside table right at the edge of the creek. She set menus in front of them and informed them that their server would be along shortly to tell them about the specials of the evening.

"No rush," Connor told her as he nervously fingered the box in his pocket. "We're just enjoying the view."

"Maybe I can get you something to drink while you're waiting?" she asked.

Connor glanced at Danielle, picked up on the wink that said she wanted her usual. "One very dirty gin martini for the lady, and I'll have a gin on the rocks," he told her.

"Coming right up."

They had talked about horses all the way back up from the ranch, Danielle talking herself into accepting an opportunity that hadn't yet been offered to her. But she had a feeling, she said, a sense that things were coming together in her life in a way she hadn't experienced in years.

"I really want this," she finally blurted out as the hostess sauntered off. "All of it. *This*. I know that'll probably jinx it, but this just feels so…right."

"Yes, it does," Connor said as he squeezed her hand.

The box was still in his pocket, waiting for just the right time.

"By the way…I was so excited earlier that I never asked you. What did you do while I was delivering that foal? You said there was something you needed to take care of."

Connor was hoping she'd forgotten what he'd told her. The more they talked about the horse ranch on the ride back up the more he felt convinced it had slipped her mind. But now it was clearly evident that her sharp mind had just tucked it away for later, and this was later. Now he considered trying to cast it aside as if it were nothing, tell her that nothing had come of it. But he had grown to really know this woman—what made her tick and what made her wonderful brain work—so he knew that wouldn't work. Besides, he had promised Danielle that he would never lie to her. He would never mislead or cheat on her. And he would never obfuscate. He had to look that one up in the dictionary, just to make sure.

So he told her.

And after he did she said, "He followed us all the way down there?"

"I picked him up near the bridge," he confirmed. "Kept an eye on him the whole way down."

"And then you went and confronted him while I was in my interview?"

"We had a chat," Connor said. "I don't think we'll be seeing him again."

Danielle glanced around, as if thinking this might be a good time for the waitress to bring her martini. "This has something to do with what you're working on, doesn't it?"

"Maybe. The guy wasn't particularly forthcoming with answers."

She pursed her lips tightly and inhaled a long breath through her nose. Then she closed her eyes as if she were counting backwards from ten to zero, or something. "You know how I feel about this shit," she finally said. "Last time you did something like this you almost got yourself killed."

"So you keep reminding me. Look…nothing happened today, and nothing is going to happen."

"I just don't want you getting hurt again," she said, fixing him with those beautiful blue eyes. "I've kinda gotten used to having you around."

"Me too," Connor assured her. "I promise I'll be careful."

"Just as long as you remember there's a killer running around out there," Danielle reminded him. The tone of her voice suggested she was trying to balance her concern for his life against not being a nag. "And whoever it is won't think twice about doing it again…especially if he started to feel cornered."

"Right…but I don't think the dude in the van was the guy."

"What makes you so sure?" she asked.

"His brain was softer than cheese grits. Whoever killed Ruby Rollins was a sadistic bastard who thought the thing through. But the bubba in the van was a minor leaguer."

"Still, he's involved in it somehow."

The waitress chose that very moment to sidle up to their table with their drinks. She set them on the table, then launched into her spiel about the night's specials. Most of them involved shrimp or oysters, prepared any number of ways, and she reeled them off with a smile trapped in her teeth the whole time.

When she was gone Connor and Danielle stared at each other blankly, both of them having temporarily forgotten what they were talking about. Or maybe just taking the interruption as a chance to change the subject.

Connor raised his glass in a toast and said, "To all the beauty of the Carolina coast, from the surf lapping the edge of the beach to the tangerine sun setting over the marsh." He'd memorized his words up to that point, all twenty-five of them, but now he hesitated as if thinking through the rest. Finally, he added, "And the woman sitting across the table from me at this very moment."

Even in the waning light he could see her blush. And smile. She clinked her glass against his and replied, "Here's to many more evenings just as perfect as this one. And all of them one right after the other."

Connor's hand slipped back into his pocket and touched the box again. *Was this the right time?* he wondered. His mind flashed back to the last time he'd done this years ago, remembered how that had turned out, and felt his gut hitch just a bit. Then he realized Danielle was sitting there patiently, her glass poised in mid-air, waiting for him to take the first sip.

*Now!* a voice screamed in the back of his head, and his fingers tightened around the box.

Then his cell phone chirped and the moment was gone.

She shot him a glance that said *really?* Then she nodded at his phone, which he had habitually set on the table. "Go ahead and answer it," she told him.

He lifted his glass and took a quick sip, then said, "It can wait." Still, his eye drifted to the screen. It read: Citadel Security

Danielle took a long sip from her martini, then told him, "If you don't answer it you'll be thinking about it for the rest of dinner."

She was right, of course, so he gave her an apologetic look and punched the "answer" button. "Tat Man," he said, already knowing who was on the other end.

"Sorry to disrupt your romantic evening," Caitlin Thomas squeaked. "But I just got a hit on those numbers you gave me."

"How would you know about my evening?" he asked her, more abrupt than he should have. But she was right: it was a romantic evening, at least as he'd planned it. And she *was* interrupting it.

"Citadel Security knows everything about everything," she reminded him with her standard but creepy answer to such things. "If you want to call me back, just tell me."

Connor shot another look of apology to Danielle, who nodded a "go-ahead" to him. So, he said, "No, now is fine. What did you turn up?"

"What I turned up is that van belongs to a Mr. Robert E. Lee up in Florence," she said.

"You mean like the Civil War general?"

"No apparent relationship, but yeah. And get this: he's the fourth, as in Robert E. Lee with an IV after his name. Meaning there were three more that came before him."

"Sons and grandsons of the Confederacy?"

"Typical southern pride, is more like it," Caitlin said. "This one's a former high school football coach, got himself fired over some trouble."

Connor thought back to the driver of the van, who looked like he was in his mid-twenties. "Do you have an age on this guy?" he asked.

"Just a date of birth that puts him at fifty-nine next week," she told him.

"How 'bout a mug shot?"

"Sure. You want me to text it to you?"

"That would be great," he said. He flashed a meek smile at Danielle, then added, "And email me anything you have on him, if you can."

"Copy that," Caitlin said like a squeaky Jack Bauer. "And since I know you're going to ask, I'm working on the other thing."

"No rush on that," he told her, and then hung up.

"Work stuff I presume?" Danielle asked after he'd set the phone back on the table.

"Nothing that can't wait until later," he explained. He reached out and took her hands in his, looking her square in the eye. "I can turn it off, if you'd like."

She had a slight grin of—*what, forgiveness? Love?*—on her lips, and she shook her head gently. "It doesn't bother me," she told him. "Really, it doesn't."

"Still, I'm sorry for the interruption."

"It's not a problem," she insisted. "Honestly. And besides—"

"Besides what?"

She gave him a quick wink and squeezed his hands. "Well, I have an orangutan that's set to give birth any day now, and I left instructions for the park to call me as soon as there's any word."

"Work is only a ring tone away," he said.

"No escaping it."

"Truth. But I apologize for the distraction—"

He was going to have to apologize again, because his cell phone was ringing again. Just like last time the screen read Citadel Security, so he answered by saying "Hi, Caitlin."

"Don't shoot me," she pleaded. "I'm just the messenger. Well, not really, since I also came up with the message, but you know what I mean. Anyway, I'm sorry to be a pest, but…"

Her high-pitched voice trailed off, leaving Connor to say, "You're not being a pest at all. What's up?"

"What's up is I forgot to tell you that Coach Lee has a restraining order on him. Can't ever set foot within a hundred yards of any football stadium where his former team plays. Home or away."

"What's that all about?" Connor asked her.

"The records are sealed," she replied. "I can dig into it if you want."

"Not tonight."

"You're the boss," Caitlin said.

"Not in a thousand years," he told her. "Now go home. It's Saturday night."

"I was just heading out the door," she said. "Oh, and Tat Man?"

"Yes?" he asked warily.

"My search on that other guy came in. Gerald Walker."

Gerald Walker was the name of Ruby Rollins' first husband, the one who ran off to Atlanta after leaving his young, pregnant bride. "What did you find out?"

"Just that there are forty-seven men with that name living in South Carolina and Georgia," she said.

"That's quite a lot," he replied.

"Not if you narrow it down. Thirty-three are under the age of fifty, so we strike them."

"That leaves us fourteen," Connor said, doing the quick math.

"Exactly. And six of those fourteen are white, which leaves us with eight."

"See what you can do to find those eight," he said. "Adding "please" just so he wouldn't sound like an asshole.

"Already on it," Caitlin told him.

Connor thanked her for her help, especially on a Saturday night, and ended the call.

"I'm sorry," he said to Danielle as he started to set the phone on the table. But then it rang again, the screen displaying a number that looked familiar but he couldn't quite place.

"Answer it," Danielle said, nodding at the offending phone. Her lips were curled up in a tight grin, but she didn't seem annoyed.

"It can wait—"

"I'm not going anywhere," she insisted. "Please."

Connor hesitated, then sighed and punched the "talk" button again. "Jack Connor," he said in a voice lined with irritation. He'd all but forgotten about the box in his pocket.

"Good evening, Jack," a familiar voice said on the other end. "This is Howard. I know I promised not to call you, Jack, but it's regarding my wife. Linda's in the hospital. Looks like she took an overdose of something. The media doesn't know anything yet, but it's just a matter of time before those crap hounds find out. I just wanted you to hear it from me before you saw it on television."

*The governor. Talk about timing.*

"I'm so sorry, sir," Connor said, flashing an *I'll-tell-you-later* look at Danielle. "Is she going to be okay?"

"The doctors aren't saying anything specific but they're cautiously optimistic," Governor Luck replied. "They pumped her stomach and she's on a one-on-one watch through tonight. They're not taking any chances."

"Any idea what happened?"

"Peter found her on the sofa in the living room," the governor explained. "There was an empty bottle of Ambien on the table next to her. No telling how many pills she may have swallowed, but it looks like the prescription was refilled just last week."

"Do you think it was intentional?" Connor asked, instantly realizing it was a stupid question. "I mean, did she leave any sort of note?"

"No note, no text, no voicemail," Governor Luck said. "Just the empty bottle and a lot of unanswered questions."

Connor took a deep breath and stared at his glass of gin. The rocks were starting to disappear, along with the anticipation of this romantic dinner on the edge of the creek. "If there's anything I can do, sir, please let me know."

There was a long pause on the other end, and Connor instinctively knew he'd just said the magic words. Eventually the governor cleared his throat and said, "Well, Jack. Actually, I'm curious what the two of you talked about yesterday. Whether she mentioned anything that might be bothering her or gave any indication that she might be…depressed."

In fact, she *had* seemed depressed, but Connor didn't want to go into any of that. Not here, and not now.

"Look, sir. Can we talk about this tomorrow morning?"

"Of course, Jack," the governor told him. "I'm just worried to death about Linda and…well, I'm confused about how on earth she would have done this."

"That makes two of us," Connor said. "I'll call you first thing."

"No," Howard Luck said. "I'll call you."

And with that he was gone. Along with any semblance of intimacy that remained of the evening.

On top of that, five minutes later Danielle received a call saying her orangutan had given birth. It was a boy, and the staff had already named him Clyde. Some reference to an old Clint Eastwood movie, when he was going through his country comedy stage.

# Chapter 14

Governor Luck was a man of his word. Connor's phone rang the next morning at six-twelve. And again, at six-thirty-one, six-forty-two, and seven o'clock sharp. Each of those times Connor was indisposed, but he finally answered at seven-eighteen.

"My phone was charging out in the kitchen," he lied to the impatient governor. "I didn't hear it until I got up to go for my run."

Howard Luck grunted an apology, something about calling him so early on a Sunday morning. Then he said, "The doctors say Linda's going to make it. It was a rough couple of hours last night, and she's going to be in la-la-land for a while. All that Ambien—"

The governor's voice trailed off, so Connor said, "I'm glad to hear she's doing well. She was such a warm and welcoming woman." It was another of those Hallmark lines, something that didn't quite sound natural but was better than nothing. "Do you have any more of an idea what made her swallow all those pills?"

"Haven't got a clue. Which is why I'm calling you."

"Like I told you last night, I'm not really sure I can help you—"

"What you told me last night was you were out on a date and to call you tomorrow. That's today. And it's going to be a long one."

The governor was right, and Connor conceded as much on the phone. Then he said, "I don't know what I can tell you that will help you get to the bottom of this."

"That's just it, Jack," Governor Luck said. "I don't have time to get to the bottom of this. But I think it's connected to what happened to Ruby, and I want you to find that connection."

"What makes you think—?"

"I am not a man who believes in coincidence. And Jordan James told me you're not, either. That's why I hired you for this job. It may sound like a cliché, but where there's smoke, there's fire. Always."

"*Almost* always," Connor said.

"So prove me wrong," the governor replied.

Connor inhaled a long breath while he thought about this. There could be any number of reasons why Mrs. Luck swallowed almost a full bottle of prescription knock-out pills. At the top of the list was general depression, and she swallowed them in an attempt to put herself out of her own misery. Maybe it was just an accident, especially if she'd been drinking.

Or maybe she had been forced to put them down her throat.

Connor recalled the words his angry father told him years ago, just before Connor confessed to throwing a baseball through the neighbor's plate glass window. "There are no coincidences in this world," he had said, somehow knowing that his son had done it on purpose because the neighbor had run over his new skateboard. That was just before the man had added, "You really need to get control of that knuckleball. Timing is everything."

But the message was clear, and Governor Luck was saying the same thing now. His wife's overdose somehow was connected to Ruby Rollins' murder, and it was one more set of variables that Connor now needed to work into the overall equation. If she had OD'd six months from now no one would have seen a link, but coming so close on the heels of the church stabbing there was every reason to make that leap of faith.

"How long before she's awake and able to talk?" Connor asked him.

"That's anyone's guess," Governor Luck told him. "Just a single Ambien can turn out your lights for hours, and sometimes there's a heavy fog when you wake up. The doctors really don't know how much got into her system before Peter found her, or what effect it will have on her when it starts to wear off."

"I'll need to talk to him," Connor said. "Your son."

There was a long pause on the other end, the governor clearly thinking this through. "Is that really necessary?" he eventually asked.

"It is if you really want to get to the bottom of this. He was the one who found her unconscious, and there may be something he saw and possibly has forgotten."

Another lengthy silence, and then the governor reluctantly agreed. "I'll have him call you, set up a meeting as soon as possible. It's Sunday, so he may be doing something with his fiancé and her family this morning."

"That's fine," Connor said. Danielle was leaving on the early flight Monday morning, and he was reluctant to spend their last full day together chasing down the governor's son. "Just give him my number and we'll figure out a time and place."

The governor fell silent for a third time, and Connor could tell he was considering something else. He suspected he knew what it was, and he was right. "I hate to ask, but do you have any leads in this whole thing?" he finally said.

"In all honesty, sir, I'm not sure," he replied. "I've discovered a few loose threads, and I'm trying to see how they all tie together. Your son may be able to shed some light on a few things, but I won't know until I speak with him."

It was a brush-off the governor probably expected, but he was resolute about it. "Well, give me a call if you do turn up anything," he said. "I want to close this out as soon as we can."

"You and me both," Connor agreed. "Any progress I make, you'll be the first to know."

"I take it that was your employer?" Danielle asked him a few minutes later when he brought her a cup of coffee in bed. She was snuggled under the thin top sheet, every curve defined by the way the fabric fell across her body. Not much left to the imagination, which was just fine with him.

"The man is a royal pain in the ass," he replied as he set the mug on the nightstand.

"Hard to believe my man has a direct line to the governor."

"I'm not a big fan," Connor said dryly. "Any update on your orangutan?"

"I sent a text while you were chatting it up with the Big Man," she told him. "It appears Clyde made it through the night just fine, and both mother and son are resting peacefully."

Connor took a sip from his own mug and opened the curtain that covered the slider to the back lawn. "Sunday morning in our little corner of the universe and all is right with the world," he observed.

She turned her head and looked out at the Intracoastal Waterway in the distance. The new sun was throwing an amber glow across the sweetgrass and setting fire to the bottoms of a few clouds lumbering across the sky. Connor opened the glass door and instantly the room swelled with a cacophony of bird songs drifting down from the trees that lined the marsh.

"I heard what you said about the governor's son," she said. "Any idea when that face-to-face might take place?"

"Not today, if I can help it," he replied. "Today is just you and me and wherever the day takes us."

He got it mostly right, with just one or two diversions along the way.

They actually had planned to drive down to Botany Bay Plantation, a state preserve carved out of a section of Edisto Island and formed in the 1930s from the merger of two colonial-era plantations. Located less than an hour south of Charleston, the place remains pristine and almost untouched by human development. No resorts on the sand, no litter on the paths, not one shell disturbed for over a hundred years.

"You're sure no one's following us?" Danielle asked as they merged onto the bridge over the Cooper River.

"Absolutely," Connor told her. "No one's going to pull that shit twice."

"What makes you so sure?"

"That asshole already tried it and got burned," he said. "No one's that stupid to do it again."

But even as the words came out of his mouth he doubted the asshole in the Econoline was about to back off. As George Carlin said in one of his old comedy routines, "Think of how stupid the average person is and figure half the population is dumber than that."

The idea didn't bring him much comfort the rest of the day.

Despite the governor's push for answers on Ruby Rollins and his own wife's overdose, Connor was not about to squander a Sunday with the woman he loved. They took a long walk along the beach, kayaked up and down one of the winding tributaries of the Edisto River, and ate lunch at a place just steps from the sand. It was one of those places where the menu was printed on the placemat and the food was served in plastic mesh baskets. Kenny Chesney and Jimmy Buffet were playing on speakers set under the weathered eaves, and handmade mermaids decorated the walls. No vans with missing license plates followed them anywhere, and the governor's son didn't bother them with a phone call.

Not until Connor was helping Danielle back into the truck. She'd just settled onto the lumpy seat when Connor's cell phone rang, and the number on the screen had an 803 area code. He intuitively knew who it was before he hit the "talk" button.

"You're the guy working on Ruby's murder?" Peter Luck said in voice that carried the same Carolina lilt as his father's. Along with a heavy dose of suspicion, because the old man no doubt had instructed him to make this call.

"That would be me," Connor replied. "And you must be the baseball star with the amazing curve."

He heard an embarrassed sigh on the other end, and then Peter Luck said, "My father's obviously been telling stories again. Did he happen to mention I had absolutely no fastball, changeup, or slider?"

"He left that part out," Connor replied. "But he did mention it was you who found your mother yesterday."

"Yeah. It's why I'm calling you. What do you want to know?"

"What I want to know we can't talk about on the phone."

"I can't do it today," the Luck kid said. A quick Google search earlier had told Connor that Peter was twenty-five years old, had a B.A. from U.S.C., and was general sales manager for his old man's used car business. Luck Auto Mart, twelve locations all over the state. Keeping it all in the family.

"Me neither. How 'bout we meet someplace halfway in the morning?" Connor already had signed up to take Danielle to the airport first thing, and he didn't mind tacking on some extra miles so he could talk to this guy. "Just say where and when. The sooner the better."

They settled on a time and place, and Connor hung up. The Toyota truck had difficulty turning over, the starter making a peculiar whining sound that brought him back to the reality of the week ahead. Just a few days until he turned the "loaner" in and got the Camaro back. And then parted with it again.

"Homeward bound?" Danielle asked as they pulled onto Palmetto Boulevard, the main street that ran through Edisto Beach and eventually turned into State Route 174. She shot him a wink and giggled, "Maybe shake the sheets a little?"

"You mean a little bone storming?" Connor said with a chuckle.

Danielle's giggle turned to laughter. "More like a joint session of Congress."

"Assault with a friendly weapon?"

"I'm talking about a good ol' *shaboinking*."

"The old pants-off dance-off."

"Pruning the rose."

Connor turned to her then, said, "Wait a sec—your maiden name is Rose.'"

"Now you're getting it. Or you will be."

And so it went for the next few minutes, until Connor hung an abrupt left and turned down a narrow road that seemed to get swallowed up by the pines and elms and maples. "Hope you don't mind a short detour," he said as the truck thumped through a pothole.

"We're not doing the front-seat foxtrot in this truck again," she said.

"Just humor me," he almost begged. "Then we'll make a beeline for the beehive."

"So where are we—?" she started to ask, but they were already slowing down and pulling into the parking lot, kicking up a cloud of dust in the process. Danielle peered at the sign over the door: The Nest. "What are we doing here?"

"Just five minutes," he told her.

"Connor—"

"I just have a question to ask the bartender," he told her. At this hour on a Sunday afternoon the lot was almost empty, so he pulled into an unmarked space near the front door. "You can wait out here if you want to."

"The AC's busted and there's something dead under the seat," she said, wrinkling her nose. "I'm coming with you."

"Just so you know, it's about the 'thing'—" Using the euphemism that had emerged for "investigation," which she clearly had an issue with.

"Really," she said. "But that sister made one mean martini last time we were here, and it wasn't beginner's luck. Let's go."

J'Neece was standing behind the bar, leaning against the counter and watching something on the flat screen TV mounted on the wall. She glanced over as the bell over the door tinkled, then squinted at Connor and the woman with him.

"Jesus Michael Jackson Christ," she said, shaking her head in dismay. "What're you doing here?"

"Just out for a Sunday drive, thought we'd stop in for a quick brew," he said.

"They don't have beer where you live?"

"Right now, I'm not where I live," he said with a grin. There was almost no one in The Nest, just an old man slouched over an array of empty glasses at the far end of the bar, and a young couple with their heads together at a table in the far corner. An old song by Clarence Carter was playing on the jukebox, a suggestive tune called "Strokin'" that Connor's mother banned from the house for all eternity after hearing the first thirty seconds. The memory caused him to grin a moment before he could regain his bearings.

"Did I introduce you to Danielle the other night when we were here?"

"Yeah, we met. So what do you really want?"

"A martini for the lady, and I'll take whatever you have on draft that's cold."

J'Neece shot him a look that said *cut the bullshit,* then pulled out a steel shaker and sloshed a large dose of cheap gin into it.

"Just a drip of vermouth," Danielle told her. "Just like the other night."

Connor glanced up at the TV, realized it was tuned to the Weather Channel. The volume was off, but the woman on the screen was gesturing at a large red mass superimposed behind her. The mass seemed to be spinning in a counter-clockwise direction, with a very distinct round dot in the middle of it. The caption at the bottom of the screen read:

Hurricane Eleanor now a Category 4 storm with 140 MPH winds

"That thing's gonna rip apart anything in its path," J'Neece said as she capped the steel shaker and began agitating it. "Weatherman's saying it's almost as strong at Katrina, and about four days out."

As if on cue the image on the screen changed and now showed a map with an elongated triangle that curved upward from the bottom. It seemed to sprout from a spinning circle—again moving in a counter-clockwise direction. The anchorwoman was no longer visible, but the highlighted text said it all:

Landfall expected Thursday night somewhere along SE U.S. coast

As if to emphasize this point, the on-screen image zoomed in to show an area of coastline that extended from Jacksonville, Florida up to the Outer Banks of North Carolina.

"I told you, Connor," Danielle said. "That thing's coming this way!"

"Looks like we're in for a bit of a blow," he replied. "Unless it changes course and moves north."

"Weatherman says there's a fifty-fifty chance it'll hit somewhere between Savannah and Myrtle Beach," J'Neece said. She poured the mixture from the shaker into a martini glass and set it in front of Danielle. Then she ran a mug of beer from the tap and placed it on the bar for Connor. "But I don't guess you stopped in just to talk about the weather."

"You guessed right," Connor conceded. The beer was ice cold and it tasted good going down. "Hits the spot."

"So, what's the real reason you're here, Mr. Connor," she said, giving special emphasis to his name.

Connor dug his cell phone out of his pocket, clicked on the photo gallery icon, and showed her the picture he'd taken yesterday. The shot of the smug Carolina redneck slouched behind the wheel of the rusted Econoline van. There was a wide-eyed look of surprise in his eyes, and his mouth was caught in an almost perfect "O."

"You recognize this guy?"

J'Neece didn't seem interested but took a look at the photo anyway. Then she shook her head and said, "Can't say for sure."

"What do you mean, 'for sure'?"

"Dude's your typical cracker. This is kind of a black part of the county, case you didn't notice. But there's still a bunch of white cracker crumbs here and there."

"I heard Mrs. Rollins was being pestered by some punk just a week or so before she died," Connor prodded her. "White punk with long hair."

"I heard that, too," she said. "But I didn't see him, so I don't know."

Connor decided not to press the point. Instead he asked, "What can you tell me about the guy who took a few pot shots here Friday night?"

She shrugged and ran a damp towel across the bar. "That's not him, if that's what you're asking," she answered.

He shook his head, said, "What I'm asking is why some random redneck would want to unload his gun at a funeral reception for a woman like Ruby."

J'Neece stopped her polishing and set her palms flat on the wood counter. She fixed him with hard, dark eyes and said, "Look, Mr. Connor. You mean well, and you're working for a good cause. But you grew up years away from here, and that means you're a babe in the woods when it comes to the way things are."

"You're talking about the whole black-white thing," he replied.

She laughed at that and slowly shook her head. "Let me school you on the whole black-white thing. Let me tell you how an entire race of people was brought over to this country bound in chains, ripped apart from wives and husbands, sons and daughters, and sold off to the highest bidder. They provided the working capital to build the economy of the south, and they were whipped and beaten and killed in the process. Then the war comes because the white masters know their economy's going to fall apart if they don't have unpaid labor to keep prices low. Revisionists and apologists these days get all torn up about states' rights and economic independence, but it all comes down to keeping the tight balance between black and white. Fast forward a hundred fifty years and on the surface you see a lot of tolerance in the land of black and white. On the surface people are polite and cordial. The south is fashioned around a picture of pleasantries, despite the mistrust and hatred that lurks under the surface. It's a very fine line of cultural politics, lies, and deceit. Every once in a while, you get someone—black or white—who ventures over that line, and quite often that journey involves a gun."

"Like the guy who shot the folks in the church in Charleston."

J'Neece picked up her rag and started rubbing again. "Yeah, like him," she said. "But also like my cousin D'Shawan, who we buried last winter after he busted into the wrong home up in Mount Pleasant. See, Mr. Connor: guns don't know from color. They just do what their owner tells 'em to do."

"What does that say about this shithead who shot up Ruby's funeral?" Connor pressed her. "Guy with that much hate in him."

"People aren't born to hate," she said. "They're taught it. And it's a lesson that's been taught for hundreds of years 'round here, Mr. Connor. Old habits die hard."

# Chapter 15

When they arrived back at Connor's place he found a notice that his landlord had taped to the front door. It was a short message that warned about mandatory evacuation of the island if the approaching hurricane looked as if it were going to make landfall in the Lowcountry.

The National Weather Service and NOAA were notoriously imprecise in predicting what path the storm might take, and all the computer models were showing wild discrepancies. Still, Sullivan's Island was a low-lying barrier island that had been all but wiped out during the onslaught of Hurricane Hugo back in eighty-nine. No one in any official capacity was taking any chances this time around.

Connor didn't get around to reading the notice until later, then set it on the nightstand next to the bed.

"Any idea what you'll do?" Danielle asked him, her head snuggled close as if his shoulder were a human pillow.

"I haven't really given it much thought," he said.

"You could come down to Orlando, wait it out there." It was a genuine offer, but she knew he'd resist any suggestion of leaving the area.

"I've never run from anything in my life," he told her. "I'm not going to start now."

"I just want you to be safe—"

"Don't worry," he told her, stroking her hair. "I'm not going to do anything stupid."

"There's going to be thousands of cars on the highway," she pointed out. "You might want to beat the rush, leave a few days early."

"And then what?" he asked. It was a rhetorical question, because they both knew there was no real possibility that he'd hole up in some flea bag motel until the storm blew through. "I've got things to do."

"Everyone has things to do," Danielle pointed out. She propped herself up on one elbow and looked him in the eye. "I just want you to be around to do them, once this thing blows through."

"I know how to take care of myself," he assured her.

"What about your plans with the Camaro?"

"It's going to have to stay where it is," he told her. Then a thought struck him and he added, "I wonder what they do with the inmates out at the jail."

"You're thinking about Lester Rollins—"

Connor nodded as she kissed his cheek. "All those guards and cops and everyone, they've got their own families to look after," he said.

"I'm sure they have a contingency plan."

"Still, the second they lose power that place is going to blow up."

"It's a Hurricane, Connor. Things fall apart." As soon as the words left her mouth another thought struck her, and she said, "Oh my God…the ranch. There's thirty-one horses down there, plus the mules. It's only a few feet above the high tide mark."

Danielle was out of bed in a flash, rummaging through the mound of clothes scattered on the floor. She finally came up with her cell phone and punched in a number from her call log. She wandered over to the open window, wearing only a pair of panties that she'd modestly pulled on when they had finished this latest round of bedroom rodeo, as he had called it. He'd made a comment about lasting more than eight seconds, and she'd though that was hilarious.

Now she was speaking with Mrs. Gregory, at the Second Chance Ranch. She was doing a lot of listening, nodding and going "uh-huh" while the woman talked, then said, "Well, please let me know how I can help." Then Danielle ended the call and slowly turned to face him, as if she knew he was taking in every inch of the view.

"The barns are built on high ground," she said. "If twelve feet can be considered high. Plus, they're four miles upriver from the coast, and they have sand bags. Unless this storm is a record-breaker Mrs. Gregory said they should be okay."

"But you're still on stand-by."

"For afterwards," Danielle said. Her fine curves were backlit by a sky that seemed to be deciding between orange and lavender. "The horses are going to be terrified and the ranch is going to need all the help it can get. And since I have to get up super-early in the morning I'm going to go take my shower now."

Danielle's flight was at six-thirty, which meant she had to be out of the house no later than five. That meant a long day for both of them, which was all right with Connor since it was going to be a crazy week. He had a vague goal to try to spring Lester Rollins before the storm arrived, a fitting tribute to a man whose nickname was Hurricane. Unless Charleston got a reprieve from Mother Nature, however, that objective was looking highly unlikely. Connor had never weathered a storm of this magnitude before, and he had an unsettled feeling that he was misjudging its force.

Still, he'd committed himself to following the Rollins case through to the end, and he wasn't about to let a little weather get in the way. While Danielle was in the shower he mentally mapped out a list of things he needed to tackle over the next seventy-two hours, before the point everything in Charleston ground to stop.

As always during these "things" Connor had a feeling he was missing something. Something that was too close to focus on properly, and almost certainly so close it could get him shot. And not necessarily with the same outcome as the last time.

But first things first. Danielle had just stepped out of the shower, which meant he had a glorious, full view of what God had intended when he pulled that random bone out of Adam's rib cage. If you believed in that sort of thing, which Connor's reptilian side at this very moment most surely did.

Peter Luck was where he said he'd be and was only six minutes late. The place was the Huddle House in North Charleston, on Dorchester Road about a hundred yards from the on-ramp for the 526 loop that ran around Charleston. Luck didn't explain why he'd picked this place nor did Connor ask, but he figured it had something to do with meeting in the absolute, most bland and innocuous place in Charleston he could possibly think of. Which only told Connor that the young man either had spent the night down here for some reason he didn't want to fess up to, or he was going out of his way to be as oblique as possible. Connor didn't really give a shit; all he wanted to do was talk to the guy.

The waitress had tried to seat Connor at the counter, but when he'd said he was meeting someone she showed him to a booth. That's where Connor was sitting when Luck pulled up out front in a totally conspicuous fire red Corvette Z06 with carbon fiber hood and vents finished in Spectra Gray Metallic. Connor knew all this because he'd checked the Chevrolet website just a week ago, figured he was only six PowerBall numbers away from his dream car. And now there it was, with some lucky bastard getting out of it.

A lucky bastard who happened to be the son of the governor of South Carolina.

Peter Luck pushed his way through the glass door and glanced around the restaurant. At seven o'clock on a Monday morning it was busy, mostly local working stiffs cramming down breakfasts way too large for their health. The menu depicted plates of bacon, eggs, biscuits, and chicken fried steak in all their visual glory, and the bellies that pressed against the tables betrayed those who ate here on a regular basis. Then again, this was the heartland of America, where extra notches punched into the belt were standard fashion.

Luck spotted Connor sitting alone in the booth and waved. Either his father had described the tattoos and bald head or he'd deduced it on his own, Connor being the only man in the place sitting by himself with a cup of coffee in front of him. Either way, the governor's kid came over and slid into the seat opposite him.

"Peter Luck," he introduced himself.

"Jack Connor. Thank you for driving down to meet with me."

They shook hands and regarded each other warily, Luck not really wanting to be here and Connor feeling oddly compromised by this young man who seemed to ooze privilege. Peter was of an age where he not only listened to what his father told him, but felt compelled to follow his orders—at least up to a point. That protocol might not last much longer, but Connor figured as long as the old man was the governor, his word still carried weight.

"It's not like I had much of a choice," Peter Luck grumbled. "We gonna be here long enough to eat?"

"Whatever you want," Connor replied. He caught the eye of a waitress, whose nod indicated she'd be right with them. "How's your mother doing, if I might ask?"

"Better. I spoke with Dad on the drive down. The doctors say her vitals are good and she'll pull through. Probably no permanent damage."

His words came out snippy and curt, as if this was one big chore for him. Which Connor figured it was. "Your father says you were the one who found her."

"That's right," the younger Luck said. "She was in the living room, stretched out on the couch and barely making a peep. There was an empty bottle of pills on the table in front of her, along with an empty glass. She was partial to her Old Fashioneds."

Connor had no idea what effect the consumption of alcohol might have on an overdose of Ambien, but he figured it couldn't be anything good.

"Any idea how much she'd had to drink?" he asked.

"What I hear is the doctors pumped out quite a lot of stuff. Look, Jack. There's nothing much I can tell you. I just happened to be walking through the living room and found her there, passed out. At first, I thought she was asleep, but then I saw that her skin was gray and she wasn't breathing. Plus, there was the little brown bottle. So I called Dad."

"Not nine-one-one?"

Peter Luck rolled his eyes, meaning that was one of the dumbest questions he'd heard in a long time. "You really don't know how this works, do you?" he asked.

"How what works?"

The waitress shuffled up to the table and set a mug of coffee in front of Luck. "Special today on chicken fried steak and eggs," she said in a monotone that suggested she'd rather be anywhere but here.

Connor was hungry but not for anything he found on the oversized laminated menu. Luck took a quick glance at the color photos and ordered fried eggs and grits. Once the waitress lumbered away he said, "Power has its privileges, but it's also fraught with pitfalls. One of those pitfalls known as the 'public eye,' and nothing gets you there faster than a frantic call to an underpaid emergency dispatcher."

"I get it," Connor said. He took a sip of coffee, and added, "What did your father do when you told him about her?"

"He was at some sort of meet and greet at the Capitol, lots of media and dignitaries. He slipped out as soon as he could get away and called old Doc Duryea. He's the family physician and an old family friend."

"How much time passed before anyone was able to look at your mother?"

"Twenty, twenty-five minutes," Peter Luck said, his answer more of a guess. "Duryea came to the house himself; even had a black bag with him."

Connor remembered what Howard Luck had told him the day they'd met. "This wasn't at the governor's mansion, right?"

"No. My parents hate that place, moved out before they ever actually moved in. Anyway, when the doctor saw what condition Mother was in he immediately called a private ambulance."

*Mother, not Mom*, Connor thought. *Dad, not Father.*

"And then she went to the hospital?"

"St. Luke's," Peter Luck said. "When she got there, she was admitted under a false name to protect her privacy. HIPPA regs and all that."

Connor had heard of HIPPA but had no idea what the acronym stood for. Only that there were a bunch of regulations that hospitals and medical professionals had to follow. "So, no one knows she's there?"

"Oh, they know, all right. At least the nurses and techs who attend too her. But if anyone says Jack Shit to anyone their asses are grasses. The rules are very clear on that."

"And she's still there?"

"For her own protection, yeah. But she's supposed to go home today."

Peter Luck stopped talking as the waitress approached and set his eggs and grits in front of him. "Watch the plate—it's hot," she said to him. Then she looked at Connor and asked, "You sure I can't get you something?"

"Maybe some more coffee," he told her.

"Be back in a sec, hon."

When she was out of earshot Connor watched as Luck dug into the grits, then leaned forward and said, "So tell me about Ruby Rollins."

The abrupt change of direction in their conversation took the governor's son by surprise. He set his spoon down and placed both palms squarely on the table. "What's your interest in her?" he asked, almost defensively.

"She taught you how to throw that wicked curve."

"Her old man pitched in the old Negro leagues," he said. "And that's not why you're here."

"True," Connor agreed. "I'm here because I believe there's a good chance the wrong man is sitting in a cell about a half mile from here."

"You've been talking to Dad," Peter Luck said. "He's got a bug up his ass that old Hurricane's innocent, and there's nothing can change his mind."

"Do you think he did it?" he asked, clear and direct.

"Cops sure do," Luck replied with a noncommittal shrug. "Nine times out of ten the husband's guilty as sin, and that's good enough for me."

"You don't worry about the other ten percent?"

"That's why you're here, isn't it?"

The waitress topped off Connor's coffee, giving him time to mentally frame his next question. When she wandered off again he said, "Besides her skill as a pitching coach, what do you remember most about Ruby?

"Mostly that she was always there."

"You make it sound as if that wasn't a good thing," Connor observed, catching the edge in Luck's voice.

"When I was a kid it was great," Luck said. "She was there to fix breakfast and pack my sister and me a lunch. She was there when we came home from school. Fixed us snacks and made dinner. Her shrimp and grits were the best I ever tasted, especially when she added her special Gouda cheese sauce." He pronounced it *gow-da*.

"But—" Connor prodded him.

"But later, when I was in high school…well, she was always there. And it wasn't as cool as it used to be."

Connor nodded, remembering his own teenage years. Parental attention turned into oppression almost overnight, and privacy seemed dead. "Your mother took it very hard when Ruby was killed," he said.

"We all did. She was a fixture in our family for as long as I can remember, and even before that. Mother seemed too think she was the greatest creature on God's green earth." He began to scoop a mound of eggs into his mouth, but paused with his fork in mid-air. "It was like they had some sort of special bond, something I could never quite figure out."

"Like they were sisters?"

"That's how Mother always put it," Peter Luck said. "But it seemed to me there was more to it than that."

Connor had figured the same thing when he'd met with Mrs. Luck at the farm last Friday. He didn't know what it was, but somewhere deep in the synapses of his brain something was lurking just out of reach.

"The way your mother tells it, Ruby saved your life when you were born."

"Mother always had a dramatic streak," Luck mumbled through a mouthful of eggs. "She could win an Oscar if she set her mind to it."

Connor considered the young man's lack of appreciation for Ruby's actions that possibly saved his life in those first few minutes after he was born. Maybe he'd heard the story so many times over the years to give it too much thought, or just thought the story was just a bunch of ancient hooey.

"Still, she drove your mother to the hospital when things went wrong—"

"Should've gone to the hospital in the first place," he said with a shrug.

Just then Connor's cell phone rang. He glanced at the screen, saw it was Kat Rattigan. Considering he was having breakfast with the governor's son he thought about letting it ring to voicemail, then decided to answer it.

"Where are you?" she asked in a rushed voice.

"North Charleston," he told her, flashing an apologetic look to Peter Luck. "The Huddle House."

"Well, stay there. I'm just fifteen minutes away."

"Can you tell me what this is about?"

"Not on the phone," she told him, and abruptly hung up.

Connor thought about why Kat was calling, figured she must have a line on his request of the other day. He checked his watch, figured he'd be done with breakfast before she arrived. Still, her call had broken his train of thought, and now he had to concentrate on what he and Peter had been discussing.

"What did your mother do while Ruby was making you all those meals and snacks all those years?" he asked him.

"Practiced her bartending skills," Luck quipped. Then he quickly added, "I shouldn't have said that. It's just that over time booze became her best friend."

Connor could relate. His own mother had grown quite fond of her Mai Tais, especially in the long, dark tunnel of a Michigan winter. Plus, Connor had his own weakness with gin. When he'd come back from Iraq he was putting down close to a bottle a day, eviscerating the memories of his buddies leaving their futures behind in the dusty alleys of hell.

"Did she ever seek any kind of help?" he asked.

"Only the kind an empty bottle could bring," Peter Luck said, a note of despair in his voice. "Booze or pills, take your pick."

"Why do you think she swallowed so much of both?"

"You'll have to ask her."

"What if she doesn't know?" Connor replied. "Or doesn't remember."

"Are you asking me if it was an accident or on purpose?"

"The question must have crossed your mind," Connor pressed.

Peter Luck was scooping up a mound of grits with his fork, but put it down and looked him squarely in the eye. "It's really not that much of a question," he said. "I think she was so messed up in the head that she didn't really give a damn whether she lived or died."

Two minutes after Peter Luck roared off in his new Corvette, Kat Rattigan pulled into the parking lot and stopped alongside Connor's loaner. She was driving her black Porsche Boxster with the 8-ball decal on the hood, and shifted into neutral as she guided the car up to him.

"Where's your Camaro?" she asked him. A scarf was tied over her hair, and her face was most from the August heat.

"In the shop," Connor replied. "They gave me this POS truck to drive while it's being worked on."

"Try to get it back soon," Kat said.

"That's the plan. So, what's so important that you couldn't tell me on the phone?"

"Nothing. I just wanted to see your rippling tattoo-covered biceps again." She waited for a response, but when there was none she continued, "Seriously. I have the summary of that background check, thought I should give it to you in person."

"So, what gives?" he asked.

"What gives is in this." She picked up a manila envelope from the passenger seat and handed it to him. "Everything you want to know about our illustrious governor is in there," she said. "It's pretty thorough. Good reading. I don't know what you're doing, and I don't want to know. But like I said before, be careful. He knows some powerful people."

"I have no doubt," Connor said. "Anything I should know specifically?"

"Not really. Politics is a messy business, and the governor didn't just get ahead by sheer luck."

Connor chuckled ad said, "You worked on that one, didn't you?"

"I thought it was good," she nodded. "Where do I send the bill?"

He thought it ironic that the governor would be paying for his own background check. "Do you have my address on file?" he asked her.

"You still live on Sullivan's Island?"

"So far."

"I'll put it in the mail." She gunned the engine and waggled her fingers at him. "Please listen to what I said. This guy has big friends who don't play nice."

"Yes mother," he replied, but she couldn't hear him as she and her car squealed out of the parking lot.

# Chapter 16

Yemassee is a tiny crossroads town spread across Beaufort and Hampton counties in lower South Carolina, surrounded by fields where soldiers bled out in both the American Revolution and the "War of Northern Aggression."

The railroad station is indelibly etched in the brains of thousands of Marine recruits as the last bastion of civilized life they glimpsed when they filed off their trains and boarded the buses that would carry them to Parris Island. That station now serves as an Amtrak stop for trains heading from New York to Miami, but no one ever gets on or off unless they absolutely must. Other than a few small stores there is absolutely nothing to do in Yemassee, something Connor quickly learned as he made his second pass through town.

He was looking for an address on Bing Street, which he finally found a hundred yards up from the Dollar General store. Caitlin Thomas had located Laysha Rollins' home through local records, and Connor had called her from the parking lot at the Huddle House. Peter Luck had just hauled ass in his red Corvette, not wanting to talk any more about his mother, and Laysha was next on Connor's list. She had told him she'd be home until ten, when she had to leave for her job at Denny's, down near the I-95 interchange.

That didn't give him a whole lot of time, but he'd made good use of the radar detector he'd picked up for the Camaro and had transferred into the loaner truck. The engine barely topped seventy, but the speed traps along Old Savannah Highway were notorious, cops lurking in the trees to avoid detection.

The house that matched the address was small and tidy. The exterior was white clapboard that either had been painted or pressure-washed in recent months. Black shutters framed the front windows and clumps of parched azaleas were trying to survive the Carolina summer. An old tractor tire painted white and lying flat held some withering pansies or petunias; Connor had never been too good with flowers. A third-generation Crown Vic, silver with faded paint on its hood, was parked in the driveway

Laysha was already wearing her waitress uniform when she answered the door. She flashed him a smile full of teeth and said, "C'mon in, Mr. Connor. You made it down here fast."

"I wanted to catch you before you headed out for the day," he told her.

"Well, I've got about fifteen minutes; then I gotta go. I'm late one more time they're gonna fire my sorry ass."

"I'll be quick," he promised her as he followed her inside.

She showed him into a living room that was just as small and tidy as the outside. There was just enough room for a small couch and a Lazy Boy recliner that was about the same age as the Ford in the driveway. Framed photographs were displayed on one wall, each of them perfectly level and spaced, and an older television set—again about the age of the car and the recliner—was set on an old table that looked as if it had been scrounged from the gutter. In fact, everything in the room looked to be recycled street pickings from trash day.

"Please, have a seat," she said, waving him onto the old couch. "Sorry I don't have any coffee or nothin.'"

"No problem," he said as he lowered himself onto the sofa. "I'm all coffeed out."

She nodded at that, as if she knew he'd just spent close to an hour with the governor's son. Then she glanced at the tiny *faux* gold watch on her wrist, as if time was precious.

"You were at the funeral," she told him. "We spoke at the reception afterwards."

"It was a pleasure meeting you and your sister," Connor replied. "And let me say again how sorry I am for your loss."

"Thank you," Laysha said, blinking back a tear. The redness in her eyes suggested there had been a lot of them. "I miss my mom so much. I didn't get to see her a whole lot, not since I moved down here. But I always knew she was close by, in case I needed her. Or just to share stuff with. There's so many times when I say 'I can't wait to tell Mom about that'…and then I realize I can't. Not ever again."

Connor nodded politely at what she was saying, realized this young woman was a lot more talkative than when her older sister was around. At the church and the reception afterwards Jamaicka had dominated the conversation, but this was Laysha's home. Here she was out of her sister's shadow and could enjoy the light. He wondered if Jamaicka had flown right back to L.A. but decided not to bring it up.

"I know you only have a few minutes, so I hope you won't mind if I get right down to why I'm here," he told her.

"Anything I can do to get Poppa out of that horrible place," she said as she perched herself on the arm of the recliner. "I can't stand the thought of him spending one more night in there."

"So, you believe he's innocent?"

She shot him a look that suggested he was crazy for even asking such a stupid question. "He loved my Momma," she said. "There's no way he would ever lift a finger to hurt her."

"The sheriff thinks otherwise."

"Since when did the cops give a fair shake to an old black man?"

"He was holding the murder weapon," Connor pointed out.

The sorrow in her eyes had flashed to a dark fury and her body seemed to tense. "I thought you said you believed my Poppa was innocent!" she snapped at him.

He raised a hand in a gesture of surrender and said, "I'm on your side, Laysha. Everything I've heard about your father tells me he was a decent man. But I need you to help me out here."

She studied him warily, then she let out a troubled sigh. "I get it," she said. "There's only one of you, so you've gotta be the good cop and the bad cop. Go ahead and do your thing."

He shifted his position on the couch and looked her directly in the eyes. "Someone killed your mother," he said. "I aim to find out who it was. And right now, no one seems to know much of anything. So I need you to tell me why someone would want to kill her so violently in the vestry of her own church."

"I don't know why," Laysha said, shaking her head rapidly. "I can't think of anyone who'd want her dead."

"You said you didn't get to see her much," Connor said. "But did the two of you talk?"

"A couple times a week," Laysha sniffed. "I'd call her or she'd call me. Sometimes we just texted, if it was just a little thing."

"In these calls or texts…did she ever sound worried? Maybe distraught?"

Laysha again shook her head, then teased a tissue out of a box on the coffee table and dabbed her nose with it. "She seemed happy and cheerful, just like she always was. Asking me how I was, talking about her day, sharing recipes even though she knew I can't cook worth shit. Said I'd never keep a man if I couldn't put food in his belly."

"Was she right?" he asked her.

"You mean, am I married?" She drew her lips tight stared at the floor a minute, then said, "I was. Ronnie took off coupla months ago, an I ain't heard from him since. Changed my name back and put that snake out of my life for keeps."

"How did he get along with your mother?"

"Like sand and water. Momma warned me, but I was too much in love to listen."

"Did he have a temper?" Connor asked.

"You mean, did he beat me?" She shook her head rapidly, then added, "Poppa woulda pounded the shit outta him if he laid a finger on me, and he knew it."

"What about your mother? Could he have hurt her?"

"No way he killed Momma," she said. "When he up and left he was jus' gone. No coming back."

Connor considered what Laysha was telling him, decided to take a different tack. "Did your mother mention anything that might be troubling her?"

She thought on this just a second, then shook her head. "Nothing. But Momma was really good at hiding her feelings, not talking about things that weren't our business. Like when she worked for the governor's family."

"Tell me about that."

"She spent more time with them than she did with us. And she never said one word about it." The resentment was thick in her voice, after all these years.

"How old were you when she stopped working for them?"

"Twenty-two. I was already out of the house, going to tech school. That's when that snot-ass son of theirs went off to college, and they had no more need for Momma."

"What about your father?" Connor asked. "What was he doing all those years?"

"Anything and everything he could," Laysha said. "He painted houses, mostly. He did some drywall, hung windows. Whatever there was."

"Did you know he was a musician? Before he met your mother?"

"I knew he played a mean sax, but I didn't know anything about his life in Memphis." She took another look at her watch, then stood up from her perch on the arm of the chair. "And I don't see what any of this has to do with getting' him out of jail."

Connor correctly read his cue and pushed himself up from the couch. "He never said anything about why he left Memphis all those years ago?" he asked.

"Nothing."

"He never mentioned that he left town the day after this Al Jackson was killed?"

"My father had nothing to do with that—"

"How could he?" Connor said quickly. "The cops shot the guy who did it."

"All that stuff happened before I was born," Laysha said. "Even before he met Momma."

"That's right," Connor agreed. "Then he moved here, started painting houses, and never picked up his sax again."

"That's not true. He played every weekend at The Nest—"

"A quiet, out of the way joint where no one would ever find him."

"You sayin' someone back in Memphis tracked him down after all these years and killed my Momma? That's crazy talk!"

Connor was expecting this reaction from her, so he said, "What I'm saying is I don't know a single person who doesn't have some secret buried deep in their past. Something they saw, something they did. Maybe something that was done to them. So, what I need you to do is think real hard on your parents, try to remember anything you can they might've told you, or something you might've seen or heard. Anything that might shed some light on what happened to your Momma, and what could get your Poppa out of that jail."

Laysha looked at him doubtfully, then said, "I've got to get to work. They make us punch in, and I have a seven-minute window or I'm late." She walked him to the front door and opened it for him, then hesitated. "There is one thing, but it's probably nothing," she said as she stepped out onto the tiny front porch.

"Anything is more than nothing," he told her, following her out into the thick August heat. "Tell me."

"Well, the week before Momma died she started going all gospel on me, going on about the strength of the Lord and his ability to forgive. Stuff like that. I mean, she was always religious. Made us say our prayers every night and washed out mouths with soap if we used cuss words. But those last few days she was all about sinning and compassion and the mercy of a forgiving Lord."

Connor thought back to Ruby Rollins' encounter with the religious zealot outside the Quick Stop, wondered if there was a connection. "Did she say anything specific, what might've brought this on?"

Laysha shook her head as she locked the deadbolt. "No, and I didn't push her on it. I figured if there was something bothering her she'd let me know."

Connor took a card from his pocket and pressed it into her hand. "You think of anything else, give me a call. Doesn't matter what time it is."

She gave the card half a glance, then slipped it into the pocket of her Denny's uniform. "Whoever did this is creeping around out there, Mr. Connor," she said as she walked with him down the tidy wooden steps. "He killed my Momma, and I want you to nail his ass to the wall."

On the drive back to Charleston, Connor decided to take a small detour.

The Quick Stop convenience store wasn't hard to find. It occupied one of the corners at a three-way intersection on Route 165, with eight gas pumps and a small market that did most of its business selling beer and cigarettes. Some of that beer was evident now as Connor pulled to the edge of the corrugated lot and cut the engine. A half dozen men with nothing better to do on a Monday morning were leaning on the brick wall, sipping from unmarked paper bags and occasionally throwing down a glob of spit that was the by-product of too much chewing dip.

Connor offered a polite nod as he approached, then glanced up at the camera affixed to the underside of the tin roof, positioned so it had a good view of the door. He found two more cameras inside, one aimed at the coolers in back and the other covering the cash registers. He looked around for more, but that seemed to be it.

A young man stood behind the counter, both hands pressed on the flat surface. He seemed about twenty, large and black and squinting at Connor through dark, focused eyes.

"Help you?" he said.

"Is the manager on duty?" Connor asked.

"That's me, least right now," the kid said.

"You're the manager?"

"Assistant's more like it. You lost?"

"Actually, I'm here to see if those cameras work?" Connor replied.

"Who's asking?"

Connor dug a card out of his pocket and handed it to the kid. "Jack Connor," he said.

The kid looked at the card, said, "Citadel Security. You tryin' to sell me stuff?"

Connor knew it was a long shot, since close to a month had passed since Ruby Rollins had been seen arguing with the long-haired scumbag.

"Nope. Just wondering if you might have surveillance video from those cameras."

The kid offered up a wide grin at that, and leaned over the counter. "They're just for show," he said in a whisper. "Cain't afford to keep 'em hooked up."

Connor wrote the monthly check for the security camera and alarm system at the BioClean Plant, so he knew what the kid was talking about. 'I get it," he said in a conspiratorial voice. Then he dug his cell phone out of his pocket and flipped through a file of digital shots. Finally, he found the one he was looking for, held out the camera for the kid to look at.

"You recognize this guy?" he asked.

The kid took a hard look at the photo, then shook his head. "Lots of guys come through those doors. I sells 'em booze and smokes, and none of 'em sticks in my mind."

"I'm the same way," Connor told him. "I'd be horrible picking someone out of a line-up. You know a woman named Ruby Rollins?"

"Course. Everyone 'round here knows—*knew*—Miss Ruby."

"Do you remember her arguing with someone, maybe about a month ago. Skinny white dude, long hair?"

"Sure." The door opened up and two black men of undetermined age walked in and headed straight to the cooler in the back. When they were out of earshot he said, "Saw it myself."

"Is that a fact." A statement, not a question.

"I was right here, and they was right out there, next to the door. Couldn't hear what was going on, but the white guy, he was really laying into her about something."

"Did he follow her into the store?" Connor asked him.

"Neither one of 'em came in. I think Miss Ruby, she was puttin' gas in her car, and that white grease ball jus' came up to her."

"No provocation?"

"Somethin' must've angered him, the way he was goin' on. Then he just jumped in his truck and fishtailed outta here."

"You remember what kind of truck?"

"F150, like everyone else 'round here drives."

"And you don't know what it was about?"

"Nope. Like I said, she didn't come into the store. She paid at the pump an' drove off when she was done."

"This greaseball," Connor said. "Can you describe him?"

The kid behind the counter stared up at the ceiling a minute, then said, "It's been a while. I remember he was thin, long hair, maybe down to his shoulders. Baseball cap on backwards, some kind of logo on it."

"Anything else?"

"Yeah, man. He had tattoos, too, but not quite like yours."

"You remember anything about these tattoos?"

The kid thought on this new question a minute, then said, "Yeah, there was one that stood out, on his neck. It was some kind of snake. Looked like a rattler getting' ready to strike."

Monday mornings usually were quiet for men of the cloth, a day to sleep in after working on the Lord's day of rest. Since Connor had driven all the way down to Yemassee, however, he figured he'd pay Reverend Parker a follow-up visit on his way back. Laysha's words about her mother's recent emphasis on the Lord and forgiveness may have had no bearing on her death at all, but it also could have been an underpinning of why she had been killed. If she had spoken to anyone about this resurgence in faith it would have been her beloved pastor.

Connor found him out back behind the whitewashed church, tending a patch of tomatoes that were baking in the hot sun. He was stooped over, examining them and shaking his head in frustration. He heard Connor approaching and stood up, wiping the sweat from his brow with the crook of his arm.

"Every year it's the same thing," he said, adjusting the soiled Braves cap perched on the crown of his head. "Either the aphids and hornworms get to 'em, or the sun splits the damned things open before they have a chance to ripen."

To emphasize his point, he held one out to Connor, pointing to the crack in the green skin, which had a hole bored right through it.

"Maybe you should switch to squash or pumpkins," Connor suggested.

Reverend Parker hurled the damaged tomato into the woods and brushed the dirt off his faded jeans. "I don't like squash or pumpkins," he said. "But I love me a good juicy red tomato in the summer. And I suspect you're not here to talk about gardening, are you?"

"You suspect right," Connor conceded. "I hate to bother you, but I have a couple things I'd like to ask you about Ruby Rollins."

"Of course," the pastor said. "Let's talk inside, get out of this withering sun."

Connor followed him back into the church. They entered through the side door and the temperature dropped about two degrees. "No AC?" Connor asked as the pastor quickly closed the door behind them.

"Compressor's having fits again," Parker explained. "I crank it up on Sundays, then turn it off the rest of the week, trying to get through the summer. Seems it's another thousand bucks every time I get someone out here to fix it."

The pastor led him into his tiny office, the one that had been fashioned out of an old storage closet. He sat down behind the wooden table that served as a desk and waved Connor into the chair in front of it.

"Any progress?" he asked once they were comfortably seated. "With your investigation, I mean."

"Maybe," Connor said with a shrug. "Hard to know until it all comes together. But there's a couple things that stand out, things I'm following up on."

"And that's why you're here."

"I know I should have given you a call first," Connor told him. "But I was coming back from Yemassee and thought I'd just stop in, see if you were around."

"Yemassee," the pastor said. "You must have been visiting Laysha Rollins."

Connor had dropped the hint and Reverend Parker had taken it. "Exactly," he said. "She's a nice young woman. More open than when we talked at the funeral."

"Laysha does much better when she's by herself," Parker said. "She's always taken a back seat to others, especially when her sister is around."

Connor's eyes roamed the room, settled on a photograph he hadn't noticed the first time he'd been in here. It was a shot of the pastor sandwiched between the former President and the First Lady, solemn faces all around.

"That was taken at the eulogy for the Emanuel Nine," Reverend Parker explained. "Senator Pinckney and I were close friends. So tragic, what happened to him and the others in that church."

"Horrific," Connor agreed. He remembered the eulogy the President had delivered a few days after a deranged gunman had shot and killed nine worshippers at the A.M.E. church in Charleston. Connor and his crew had been finishing a job on Daniel Island that afternoon and he was struck by the sight of Air Force One climbing up from the airport and banking over the marsh, heading north toward Washington. "Humans are capable of unspeakable hatred."

"People aren't born with hatred in their hearts," Reverend Parker pointed out. "They're taught it."

His words were almost word for word what J'Neece had said the day before, and Connor wondered if he had been spending time at The Nest after all. "Someone certainly seems to have had a great deal of hatred for Mrs. Rollins," he said.

"Are you any closer to finding out who?"

"Hard to tell. But it was something Laysha told me this morning that caused me to stop by and talk to you again."

"As I said before, anything I can do to help."

Connor ran an already-damp hand across his brow. The temperature in the tiny office had to be above eighty and seemed to be inching upward. "She told me that the last few times she spoke with her mother she was going on about compassion and mercy and how the Lord has the ultimate ability to forgive your sins."

"Ruby was a very religious woman," Reverend Parker reminded him.

"Laysha made it sound like her mother might have been referring to something specific. Maybe personal."

The pastor put his palms together as if in prayer and rested his chin on them. He appeared to give Connor's words great thought, then straightened in his chair. "You understand there are certain privileges that people come to expect when they discuss personal things with a priest or minister," he said, framing his words as a question.

"Of course," Connor said. "Sort of like attorney-client privilege, except it has to do with confessions and that sort of thing."

"Exactly. When someone comes to me they have a reasonable expectation that I will keep whatever they tell me in the deepest of confidence."

"I understand that. But if Ruby Rollins told you something that could have led to her death, I don't think she'd want you to keep it secret."

Reverend Parker studied Connor intently as he thought this through. Deep worry lines creased his dark face and he picked at the cuticle on his thumb. Finally, he said, "I've given this a great deal of consideration, Mr. Connor. First, let me tell you that Mrs. Rollins confessed nothing to me. She was a very proud and independent woman, and believed herself capable of handling anything life threw at her."

"But she told you something—"

The pastor raised a hand to stop him. "Mrs. Rollins and I spoke of a great number of things over the years. Private things, and not-so-private things. And everything we discussed she expected would remain between the two of us. And I intend to keep it that way. Still—" he let the word dangle there a moment, like bait on a hook "—you are correct. Over the last few weeks of her life Ruby did seem to be worried, even pre-occupied, by something that may have caused her to question the motives of the Lord in ways she had not done before."

"Did she talk to you about this, or was it just something you kind of picked up?" Connor asked him.

"As I believe I told you the last time we spoke, she spent a lot of time here at the church," Reverend Parker explained. "She helped out with Sunday services, and she was involved with a lot of other things we do for the community. When you spend that much time around a person you get to know them. How they think, what makes them tick. That's how it was with Mrs. Rollins."

"How did she seem worried? Pre-occupied, I think you said."

"Her mind....well, it just seemed to be elsewhere. It's hard to put a finger on it, really."

It occurred to Connor that Reverend Parker could have been telling him something he wanted to hear in order to throw him off. Just because Parker was a man of the cloth didn't mean he wasn't capable of causing harm to someone. It wasn't beyond the realm of possibility that the pastor had been involved with Ruby Rollins, or wished he'd been. She had been killed in a burst of passion, and that meant the killer very likely was more than a passing face in a crowd.

"Could she have been having trouble at home?" he asked.

"As I told you before, the Rollins were like rocks. One of the most solid marriages I've ever seen, and believe me—I've seen a lot."

"That's why you're positive Lester is innocent?"

"Completely."

"Laysha told me her mother had doubled down on sin and compassion, really getting into the Lord's forgiveness. That sort of thing. Do you think something she did might've caught up with her and she was trying to atone for it?"

Reverend Parker shook his head quickly—*way* too quickly. "I can't for the life of me think of what that could be," he said. "Ruby—Mrs. Rollins—was always by the book. And when I say book, I mean *The Book*."

"So, if she had stepped off the path of the righteous at some point in her life, she would rely on the word of the Lord to set her straight again? Or at least comfort her?"

"That's not exactly how I would put it, but yes—she was a good Christian. She always turned to the Lord when she needed guidance."

"She also confided in you," Connor pressed. "Look, Reverend: I understand all about the clergy-privilege thing. And your desire to keep quiet about whatever Ruby may have told you. But it's very possible that something she knew— something she confided in you—got her killed. If you truly want to know who took her life—and set her husband free—you should unburden yourself from whatever secret you're sitting on."

Reverend Parker glared at him, then rose from his chair abruptly and planted both palms on his desk. "Look, young man," he said in a voice that boomed as if he were standing in the pulpit on Sunday morning. "I have worked in service to our Lord for close to forty years. I've dedicated my life to His mission of love and goodness, and I do not need *you*—" that last word came out like a thunderclap "—to lecture me on how to deal with the burdens of life. Not mine, and not anyone else's. How I assist my parishioners is strictly between God and me, and I do not need the advice of some impudent cop wannabe who's running all over Creation doing the governor's bidding."

"Please, Reverend Parker—"

But Connor got no further as the pastor raised a hand in a firm gesture to stop him. "I am a very tolerant and compassionate man, but you have tested my patience beyond its limit. The doors to this church are open to those who wish to atone for their sins, and if you ever find yourself in need of doing this, you will be welcomed with open arms. But—" Reverend Parker paused for effect, fixing Connor with his dark eyes that reflected all the fury within them "—until that is the case, I ask you to leave these premises and not return."

His words reminded Connor of the time in middle school when he had been sent to the principal's office because someone had placed a peanut butter sandwich on Karen Loomis' chair. She'd been wearing a brand-new wool dress and had burst into tears, running from the room with a brown stain on her bottom. Connor had been designated the most likely candidate to have committed the deed, and when he finished his slow death march down to the principal's office he was treated to a tirade that seemed to go on for an hour. At the end of it the principal stressed to the thirteen-year-old Connor that if he *ever* saw him in this office again *for any transgression whatsoever*, he would be expelled for the rest of the year.

"Understand?" the principal had pressed him. Just like Reverend Parker pressed him now.

"Who are you protecting?" Connor asked him, calm and collected.

The pastor of the Cavalry A.M.E. church clearly was not accustomed to being challenged in his own house. He stood there, mouth agape, not quite sure what to do beyond physically throwing Connor out.

But Connor made it easy on him, saying, "I apologize for my rudeness, Reverend. Or any trouble I might have caused you. That was not my intent. But an hour from now I'm going to be looking Lester Rollins in the eye and he's going to ask me if I'm any closer to getting him out of there. I was hoping to say 'yes,' but I also was hoping for more cooperation."

This was not entirely true, for at least two reasons: he did not have a scheduled appointment with Hurricane Rollins, although he figured Darryl Powers might be able to help him with that. Also, there was no such thing as looking a prisoner in the eye in the county lock-up because of the closed-circuit video system. But he doubted Reverend Parker knew that.

"I have helped all I can," Reverend Parker told him. The boom in his voice was gone, but his eyes still were as penetrating as ten-penny nails.

"Then I'll leave you to your tomatoes and hornworms," Connor said from the doorway. "And your secrets."

# Chapter 17

Forty-five minutes later Connor snagged a parking space near the visitor's entrance in front of the county jail. He gazed up at the massive façade and thought about the hundreds of men and women languishing inside, either awaiting their bond hearing or—for those who couldn't post bail—a court date set several months down the road. Guilty or innocent, their lives were on hold as the cogs of justice slowly ground out time.

Connor didn't have an appointment, but a couple of twenties pressed into Darryl Powers' palm unlocked the door to this possibility. Twenty minutes later Connor found himself in the same room of video carrels where wives and girlfriends stared at the screens in front of them, gently touching the pixelated faces of their wrongly accused men. Connor was assigned a different viewing station than last time, but all the screens and cameras were covered with the same grime, dust, and fingerprints.

Lester Rollins' face seemed to sag more deeply than the last time Connor was here. Dark folds of skin puffed out under his deep-set eyes that seemed deflated, almost helpless. They kept shifting from right to left, and Connor remembered the man only had a video monitor and a tiny camera lens in front of him. Any vestiges of freedom and dignity had been stripped from him the moment he was penned up inside this ghastly place. He had not shaved in the week since he'd been arrested and his beard was coming in rough, like patches of crabgrass in a poorly tended yard. Mostly he just seemed tired: tired of being in jail, tired of the food, tired of the company he was being forced to keep. And tired of life in general.

"This place is killin' me," he said in a tired voice. "Never in a million years did I think I'd spend the rest of my life in jail."

"And you're not going to," Connor said, as convincingly as he could. "I'm gonna get you out of here."

"Talk is cheap," mumbled the man who once blew his sax like a hurricane.

"You're right," Connor agreed. "Problem is, I can't get anyone to do much talking. Especially Reverend Parker."

Rollins made a noise that sounded like *harrumph*, then screwed up his face as if someone had passed gas next to him. "That man takes self-importance to a whole new level," he said.

"You don't care for him?"

"He's okay, as far as preachers go. They gotta talk like they sound important, being the messenger of God and all that. But Mister Parker—well, he had this way about him sounded like he sat in the lap of the Lord."

Connor knew what Rollins was getting at and gave a slight nod. "I just came from the church," he said. "It's like he has a lock on his mouth when it comes to discussing your wife."

"Did he at least tell you that they'd had a lot of long conversations the last couple of weeks?"

"He didn't want to discuss any of that," Connor replied. "Do you have any idea what they might have discussed?"

Lester Rollins' face tightened a bit and he closed his eyes. He held them that way a minute, either to blink back whatever tears he'd stored up, or just to think things through. When he opened them again, he said, "I could tell Ruby was worried about something, but she refused to talk about it. Whatever it was, she should've known better than to keep it from me. I could read her like a sheet of music, but she insisted she was just preoccupied."

His mind went back to what he had read in Kat Rattigan's report, but he didn't want to give anything away. "Did you ask her what was on her mind?"

"A couple times, but she just said she was busy. The only time she said anything was this one night, sayin' there was somethin' went way back had nothing to do with me. Told me not to set my mind on it. 'Worryin' never fixed a problem the Lord couldn't take care of with enough prayer.' That's what she said, and I didn't ask her about it again."

"Do you have any idea what she was talking about?" Connor asked him.

"Lord knows," he said, managing a slight grin despite the circumstances. "I thought maybe it had to do with Karen; she was always fussing over the Luck family even though they'd been out of her life for years."

"You mean Karen, the daughter?"

"Ruby raised her and her brother Peter."

"Right," Connor said. "But why would Mrs. Rollins be concerned about Karen?"

"It had to do with some medical condition," Lester Rollins explained, massaging his temples wearily. "Kidneys, I think."

"Karen has a kidney problem?"

Connor saw Rollins flex his shoulders in a shrug. "It's what I heard," he said. "Don't know anything more than that."

No one—not the governor, his wife, or his son—had mentioned anything about Karen or her kidneys. There was probably no connection to Mrs. Rollins or her murder, except that Ruby might have been fretting over the health of one of her former charges. Besides, what possible connection would the girl's kidneys—*woman*, since Karen was in her late twenties—have in her death?

Probably nothing.

*But maybe something.*

Never exclude a supposition from the deductive process just because it seems insignificant or immaterial. That was something Connor had learned when the cops arrested the wrong man for the murder of his niece, and the lesson had stuck. The human brain is always looking for shortcuts, but sometimes the long way around is the best way to get from point A to point B.

"Laysha told me her mother had been preoccupied with forgiveness and sin and the Lord the past few weeks," Connor continued.

Lester's face suddenly brightened and a spark briefly flashed in his eyes. "You spoke with her?"

"Just this morning. She said to tell you she loves you more than anything."

The old man's lips tightened and this time Connor did see a tear in the corner of his eye. "I miss that girl so much," he said in a low, raspy voice. "Jamaicka, too, but she's off and running her own race. How's my girl doing?"

"She's holding up, but she wants you home," Connor told him.

Lester Rollins lowered his head in a contemplative nod and did not again raise his eyes to the camera lens. "Tell her I'll be walking with her on the banks of Pelican Creek real soon," he said. "Will you do that for me?"

"Yessir," Connor assured him. He was just about to tell him "goodbye" when a thought struck him and he said, "I heard Ruby had a run-in with some long-haired redneck a couple weeks ago."

Lester Rollins slowly raised his eyes to meet the camera and said, "Yep."

"She mentioned it to you?"

"She said some douche bag came up to her and started calling her nigger and spewing racist hate at her. She brushed him off, told him the Lord doesn't know from color or ignorance. Something like that. Made him even angrier."

*Angry enough to stab her thirteen times?* he wondered. "Did she recognize this creep, or was it just a random act of hatred?"

"There's nothin' random about hatred, Mr. Connor," Rollins said. "It's a religion all its own and its followers wear their own special kind of robe."

"Did she say what this guy looked like?"

"White, dirty, bad skin. Greasy hair stuffed up under a cap. Bad teeth."

Rollins' description didn't match the turd in the Econoline van, but it was similar to what the kid at the Quick Stop had just told him. Walter Hill, too. It didn't give Connor a whole lot more to work with, but there was a possibility that the scumbag may have been targeting Ruby Rollins with his bigoted venom.

"Did she happen to mention a name?" he asked hopefully.

"Nope, and I doubt she knew it," the old bluesman said. "You think maybe he put my sweet Ruby in her grave?"

"Don't know, but I'm going to find out who this redneck bastard was."

Jordan James was already sitting at a high-top table in a dark corner of Dunagan's, an Irish pub two blocks off East Bay Street in downtown Charleston. When Connor had called and said he'd like to buy James a drink, James naturally had suggested one of the half-dozen restaurants in the city that he owned. But Connor wanted to be on neutral ground for this meeting, so he'd chosen this place.

The waitress had just taken James' order when Connor edged onto one of the tall stools. "What can I get you?" she asked him as he placed his cell phone—screen down—on the table.

"I think I'd better just stick with an unsweet tea," Connor said. He'd been the one to call for this meeting, and he knew when James was involved that cocktails were part of the equation. But it was early in the day, too early for it to be wasted on a gin and tonic.

Once the ordering was out of the way James leveled Connor with a long stare. "I know you, Jack. You didn't invite me here just for a pleasant chat."

"I'm not going to beat around the bush, sir. I have a few concerns about the governor."

"I suspected as much," Jordan James said. "What makes you think I can help you?"

"I'm not looking for help, sir. Just advice."

"Advice on what, exactly?"

Connor knew James and Governor Luck were longtime friends. They were of the same political persuasion, and they obviously knew each other well enough for James to have recommended Connor for this job. Their connection had to go well beyond Luck's chain of car dealerships throughout the state, and the Bentley that was parked right now in a choice spot in front of the restaurant.

"I'm just a new arrival here in South Carolina, but it doesn't take a genius to know how things work in this state," he said, choosing his words carefully.

"This state isn't that different from any other," Jordan James said.

"That's my point. I grew up in Michigan, where unions and politics greased the machines."

"South Carolina isn't Michigan, Jack—"

"No, sir. But politicians really aren't that much different no matter where they come from."

Jordan James looked up as the waitress places a double Beefeater martini in front of him, then set a tall glass of tea with a lemon wedge in front of Connor.

James gazed at his martini longingly but did not yet pick it up. "Just what are you getting at?" he asked.

"What I'm getting at is that I did a little digging into the governor's background. Just to get a sense of what kind of person he is."

James narrowed his eyes and stared at Connor a moment without saying anything. Then he picked up his glass and raised it to his lips. Then, after a long sip, he set it down and said, "Howard Luck is a respectable gentleman and an upright citizen of this state."

"So everyone tells me," Connor replied.

"Then what are you worried about?"

"I'm not worried, Mr. James. But I do have a concern."

"What sort of concern?"

"The sort that led Mr. Luck—the governor—to seek me out and hire me."

"He came to you because I suggested you'd be the best man for the job," James explained.

"I know that, sir. And I appreciate it."

"Then why the concern…and the background check?"

"Don't you look into a person before you hire them? Connor asked him.

"Of course. You always want to know you have working for you. It's just the prudent thing to do."

"Exactly," Connor agreed. "And it's also prudent to look into the person who's hiring you."

James fell silent for a moment as he thought about this. Another sip of martini seemed to help the thought process along. Then he said, "Did you check me out when I hired you?"

"Not when you brought me into Palmetto BioClean," Connor said. "I was just out of the Army and I was glad to have a job."

"But—?"

"But over time you hear things," Connor said with a shrug. "And when you asked me to do that thing last year I did a bit of digging."

"Hopefully you found mostly good stuff."

"Of course, sir."

"I sense another 'but' coming here, Jack."

"The thing is, sir, Governor Luck…well, there's a few things that bother me. Not about you, but…well, the governor."

"There's lots of things that bother lots of people about Howard," James replied.

"Yessir. But I'm talking about things most people don't know."

Jordan James had started to take another sip of gin, but Connor's statement caused his hand to stop mid-air. The two men studied each other a moment, and then James set his martini back down.

"Governor Luck is a friend of mine," he said. His words sounded almost like a threat. *Almost*.

"I'm aware of that. Which is why I asked to meet with you."

James finally took that sip of gin, then said, "Okay…tell me what it is you think you know."

Now it was Connor's turn to be silent a minute while he collected his thoughts on what Kat Rattigan had told him. Then he said, "Ruby Rollins was privy to a lot of inner workings of the Luck household."

The governor nodded, but said nothing. This was Connor's story, and he wasn't about to interrupt it. Not now, at least.

"She most likely would have met a man by the name of Warren Drake."

"Drake was Howard's banking partner when he expanded the car dealership," James pointed out. "What does he have to do with anything?"

"Do you know where Mr. Drake is today, sir?" Connor asked.

"Haven't heard or thought of him in years."

"Not surprising, considering he disappeared from public life over twelve years ago."

"He could be dead. And I don't see how he has anything to do with my friend Howard," Jordan James. Again, emphasizing the word *friend*.

"I'm getting to that part, sir," Connor said. "Twelve years ago, the FBI was running a sting operation designed to round up sexual predators in six cities along the east coast. Warren Drake was one of the targets of the operation, but he skipped town the day before the feds hit town. No one has seen him since."

"Could just be a coincidence, Jack."

"Could be. But it also could be that the FBI had him on six airtight charges, including possession of child pornography and solicitation of minors. Child sexual assault."

"How do you know this?" Jordan James wanted to know.

"Same way I know that Howard Luck's house down in Beaufort was where at least two of the child rapes occurred."

"Allegedly occurred," James corrected him.

"Okay," Connor conceded. "But if these incidents allegedly occurred in the Luck house—at the time Ruby Rollins was working there—it's reasonable to assume she had some knowledge of what was going on."

But Jordan James just shook his head slowly, as if he thought Connor was grasping at straws. "Be careful when you make assumptions about people you don't know," he said. "That can get you in a lot of trouble."

"Like it did to Ruby?"

"What—you think Warren Drake came back twelve hours after he disappeared and stabbed this Rollins woman in her church? I hate to say it, but you're reaching here."

"Maybe," Connor said. "But as they say on TV, 'wait—there's more.'"

"What are you talking about?"

"The Drake thing is just one possible scenario I've uncovered," Connor told him. "A couple years before that—right after Katrina—Governor Luck was involved in a scheme to re-title and sell cars that had been flooded in the hurricane. This time his partner—a mobbed-up guy named Tony Moretti—was ferrying them to South Carolina through Memphis. An unnamed witness alerted the feds, and Moretti ended up doing a chunk of time."

"And you think this unnamed source was Mrs. Rollins?"

"I think Howard Luck was himself involved in something but again came out smelling like a rose," Connor replied.

Jordan James took a deep breath, then let it out slowly. Finally, he said, "Is that all?"

"There's more. Tax fraud, insurance fraud, rumors of bribery. But you get the picture."

"And where did you say you got this information?" James asked.

"I didn't. And rest assured: I didn't get it through Citadel Security."

Jordan James grabbed the attention of the waitress and made a check sign in the air. Then he turned to Connor and said, "Be careful where you're going with this, Jack. You don't want to bite the hand that feeds you."

"I'm damned good at feeding myself, sir."

"I know that. But not everyone knows you like I do, and not everyone considers you a friend. Keep that in mind."

"Every minute of every day."

"There's another thing you might want to consider. "

"And that is?"

"Howard Luck hired you to get Lester Rollins out of jail. In order to do that you'd have to find out who really killed his wife. Do you actually think a highly respected governor who has greater political ambitions would do that if he thought any old skeletons had anything to do with it?"

It was a good point, and Connor didn't have a good answer. "I'm just covering all the bases, sir," he said.

"Well, make sure you don't get caught stealing home," Jordan James said.

As Connor was pulling away from the curb down the block from Dunagan's two thoughts kept biting at him: One was obvious: this redneck shit-for-brains either killed Ruby or he didn't. Pure and simple, black or white. Connor had seen hatred turn rational men into violent animals for no reason other than fear that fomented loathing. Could this scumbag have let his hatred for African Americans fester to the point that he could drive a kitchen knife into an elderly woman a dozen times, plus one?

The second question was a bit more complex. Why or how would this sick bastard have singled Ruby Rollins out? Was it a random thing just because she was black and God-fearing, or did he know her from some other time or place? Had they crossed paths before, and maybe he felt she'd insulted him? Could it just have been her color? The shooting at the A.M.E. Emanuel church in Charleston had been a case of racial hatred that festered in a pit of ignorance and fear. Nine people had lost their lives in that incident, memorialized on Reverend Parker's office wall. Was this the same sort of thing, except on a slightly smaller scale?

The more Connor thought about scenario number two the more he realized it didn't hold water. The dirt bag named Dylann Roof who had massacred the nine souls in the A.M.E church in Charleston was a coward. He had sat among them for an hour, screwing up the courage to take their lives. And then when he did he ran, like the chicken shit he was.

By contrast, whoever had killed Ruby Rollins clearly had a vested interest in her death. It was personal, not political. Hatred may have been involved, but this hatred was not of an institutional kind. It was intimate, and Connor doubted the greasy scumbag had enough of a history with her to go to that extreme. More likely he was the sort to exchange racial slurs, then boast to his laughing buddies how he had put the old black woman in her place. All talk and no action, the bravado of cowardice.

The more he thought about it, Connor was increasingly certain that if Reverend Parker revealed just one of the secrets he was sitting on, a cascade of dominoes would follow. Whatever Ruby had been worried about, whatever forgiveness and mercy she was seeking from the Lord, it had led her killer to attack in a most merciless and unforgiving way. The pastor had to know this, yet for some reason he was protecting a colossal truth.

Connor had just pulled into his small driveway when his cell phone rang. It was Caitlin Thomas, and her excited voice squeaked more than usual. "That photo you texted me…it fits," she told him.

"What photo?" Connor asked, just as she expected him to.

"The one you took down near Beaufort. The guy in the van who followed you. His name is Earl Reese."

Connor shoved the truck door closed with his hip and shifted the phone to his other ear. "Does Citadel have access to a facial recognition program?" he asked.

"No…that only works on TV," she told him. "I just happened to be running a search on this Robert E. Lee the fourth."

"Who?" Connor said.

"You know—the guy who owned the white van. I found a photo of him, and guess what?" She actually waited for him to cough up an answer, but when it was clear he wasn't playing along she said, "The guy you caught behind the wheel was with him."

"You're sure it's the same guy?"

"Definitely. It was from the Florence *News Journal*, taken at some rally last summer. The photo's pretty clear, and once I had the name, I Googled him. There's no question it's him."

Connor unlocked his front door and pushed his way inside. "So, what can you tell me about this Earl Reese?" he asked her as he dropped his keys on the kitchen counter.

"This is the part you're gonna love," she said, the excited squeak tightening her voice. "The rally they were at where the *Journal* photo was taken? It was a 'southern pride' thing on the capitol grounds in Columbia."

Following the shooting at the A.M.E. church, the state of South Carolina legislature voted—overwhelmingly but reluctantly—to remove the much-vaunted Confederate flag from the State House grounds. Much ranting and marching had followed that decision, and a number of groups—usually rather small in number—had rallied to force their elected leaders to hoist it back up the pole. The fact that the pole itself also had been removed did not deter them in their efforts.

"You're talking about the flag thing?" Connor asked.

"Yep. This particular photo shows Mr. Lee holding the flag his namesake surrendered to General Grant, while Reese is carrying the one favored by *der fuhrer*."

"He's a Nazi?"

"At least a sympathizer. Oh, and Lee's son is in the picture, too."

"What's his son's name?"

"Virgil. In the picture he's got a flag, too. The Gadsden flag."

"Am I supposed to know what that is?" Connor asked.

"No, but you've probably seen it. It's got a coiled snake on it, with the words 'Don't Tread On Me.' General Gadsden designed it during the American Revolution in protest to the British, but lately it's become a symbol of rebellion."

"So, we've got three flag-waving rednecks," Connor said. "Anything else?"

"Yeah, I almost forgot the best part," Caitlin said. "Standing behind the three musketeers is the one and only Tony Worden."

Connor drew a blank on the name and said, "Who's he?"

There was an audible sigh on the other end, and then Caitlin said, "You're really not from around here, are you?" It was a rhetorical question, and she continued, "He's from upstate, near Spartanburg. About ten years ago he ran for the state senate, and during the campaign it came out that he used to be the head of the South Carolina chapter of the KKK. Rather than denounce the past he bragged about dragging blacks behind his truck and cracking a few skulls with his Louisville Slugger."

"I'm sure that went over well."

"You're forgetting where you are, Tat Man. It got him elected to two terms before he resigned. Some sort of ethics charge finally brought him down. Bribery and racketeering. Anyway, there he is in the picture, standing about ten feet behind Mr. Lee the fourth and his son."

"And Earl Reese."

"You got the picture," Caitlin replied with a giggle. "Literally."

Before Connor even knew what he was doing he'd poured himself a shot of gin over ice. He eased a bit of it down his throat and said, "Any idea what this Tony Worden is up to these days?"

"I knew you'd ask that, so I did a little digging," she replied. "Didn't take much, in fact. Seems about six months after he left the public sector he hooked up with an organization called the Institute for American Heritage. It's based in Atlanta but has chapters all over the south, and He's their director of membership."

"What does that mean?" he asked.

"It means he's in charge of getting people to join up and come to their rallies," Caitlin explained patiently. "That's what he's doing in the flag photo."

"Drumming up membership for the Aryan Brotherhood."

"Actually, the Brotherhood is something completely different," she told him. "Mostly a prison gang with tentacles that reach out across the country. They originally got together for racial purity after the prisons were desegregated, but now they're more into organized crime, drug trafficking, and prostitution. I Googled them. These Heritage guys are a bit more subtle, sort of like weekend warriors. But their message is essentially the same."

"We are the superior race, so don't mess with us."

"Add in a lynch mob mentality and you've got it," she said.

"And this Earl Reese who followed me the other day: he's one of them?"

"There's nothing on his sheet to indicate it, but when you hang with known associates it's pretty cut and dried."

The thought that this Nazi dickwad had followed him for two hours hour—had even waited while he and Danielle ate lunch—totally creeped his skin. Now he wondered if Coach Lee's son was the guy who'd been seen at the Quick Stop, and maybe lurking in the woods after Ruby Rollins' funeral. The guy with the coiled snake tattoo. Because it was dark that night Connor couldn't see him, but the guy could have picked up the plate from Connor's truck as he drove by. Since the truck was a loaner it would have taken some work to track him down, but it was possible.

"What's the four-one-one on this guy?" he asked.

Caitlin burst out laughing, sounding like she was about to bust a gut on the other end. "Don't do that, Tat Man," she told him when she regained her composure.

"What?" he asked her, innocently.

"Some guys can get away sounding street," she told him. "But you, Mr. Painted Soldier —just ask for the address. And no, I don't have an address for Reese, but I do have one for Mr. Lee the Fourth."

"Thank you," he said as he wrote it down.

"You are most welcome," she replied. "But there is something else I found out about Coach Lee. He's been known to hang out a lot at gun shows and pawn shops."

"You think he's stockpiling weapons?"

"I don't think he's buying up old 8-tracks," she told him.

Connor thought a moment while he let the implication of Caitlin's words soak in, then said, "This photo you found. You think you can text it to me?"

"Already did, Tat Man."


Danielle had called while Connor was on the phone with Caitlin, and he rang her back as soon as he'd replenished the gin in his glass. Dr. Pinch would not have been supportive, but the good doctor wasn't there to raise any objections. Connor knew he'd beat himself up tomorrow morning after overindulging tonight, and he knew that sooner or later he was going to have to address the issue. But that could wait for another time.

"How's your baby orangutan?" he asked her after she assured him her flight back was uneventful.

"Infant and momma are doing great," she replied. "You see the latest reports about your hurricane?"

"Looks like we're going to get a spot of rain," he said in a bad British accent.

"You've got to take this storm seriously, Connor," she sighed. "It's going to hit whether you like it or not."

Truth was he hadn't heard one word about the impending storm since Danielle left that morning. For all he knew it could be turning out to sea rather than bearing down directly on the Carolina coast.

"Don't worry," he assured her. "If it comes anywhere near here I'll ride it out at The Plant."

"That's insane," she said. "That place only a few hundred yards from the river."

"It's built solid and the roof is new."

"Turn on the tropical update, smartypants. You might change your mind."

Connor picked up the remote control and aimed it at his TV. He switched the channel to one of the cable stations, which featured a large image of a hurricane taken from a weather satellite. The caption at the bottom read:

Hurricane Eleanor Now Packing 165 MPH Winds

"I'm watching it right now," he told her as he edged closer to the screen. He had to admit it looked much worse than he had anticipated.

"Good. You have plenty of time to load up that rust bucket and get out of town."

Connor promised her he'd be careful and not do anything stupid, then said, "I'll call you back before I go to bed."

"Talk to you then," she said. "I just want you to be level-headed about all this."

There was a click on the other end as the call ended. He set the phone on the kitchen counter and parked his butt on a stool. The image on the TV screen switched from the slowly churning hurricane to the latest "cone" of its projected path. The meteorologist was now explaining how the next thirty-six hours would be critical in determining the landfall and intensity of this storm.

"One thing is certain," he said. "Even if Eleanor weakens as she approaches land, she's going pack quite a punch. All those living in low-lying areas along the Carolina coast should take immediate steps to evacuate or find alternative shelter. This storm is going to be big."

# Chapter 18

After Connor turned off the TV he took a short walk into downtown Sullivan's Island and ordered a plate of enchiladas and a glass of amber beer at the local Mexican restaurant. From the moment he sat down he detected a sense of fatalism in the place, people coming to grips with a reality that was beyond the horizon but fast approaching. This time of year, the TV above the bar would be broadcasting a Braves game, but tonight the channel was fixed on a team of weather geeks chattering about wind speeds, tidal surges, and flood levels.

"When're you leaving?" the bartender asked Connor as she set his plate of food in front of him.

"Hadn't really thought about it," he replied with a shrug.

"Well, you'd better do some serious thinking," the bartender said. She was young, barely old enough to be slinging drinks, with a few excess pounds that he guessed were either lingering baby fat or the byproduct of too much restaurant beer and cheese nachos.

Up on the TV one of the talking heads was commenting on a graphic that showed the impact of the pending storm surge along the entire South Carolina coast. "No matter where this storm makes landfall, people in the low-lying areas should take heed and evacuate now," he said.

"What I think I'm going to do is take heed," Connor said.

"What you need to do is take a look around," the bartender replied. She gazed around the restaurant, a resolute expression locked in her grim eyes. "Three days from now this might all be gone."

"No, I don't see that happening," Connor said, shaking his head. But deep down he knew she probably was right.

After dinner Connor walked down to the beach. The cross streets that ran perpendicular to the main drag were known as "stations," and at the end of each of them were public access paths that led to the sand. Connor regularly came down here early in the morning for a long run, but this evening he simply took his time as he made his way across dunes marked by sweetgrass and sea heather. The hurricane was hundreds of miles away, but the sky seemed lifeless, and dark clouds lumbered in over water that seemed the color of tin foil. Gusts of wind were driving whirls of sand across the beach, and a large flock of gulls was clumped at the water's edge, as if they knew something was lurking just beyond the gray line that defined the horizon. Large breakers pounded the beach, and a lone pelican fought the wind as it skimmed along the surface of the water. Despite the heavy surf, a few godwits darted through the foam, looking for one last meal of sand fleas or whatever else their long beaks could scrounge up.

Like most people who had never experienced the power of a hurricane Connor found it hard to believe that all this could be covered by pounding surf in just a few days. The sand, the wooden walkways, the trees: all could be destroyed by the power of water and wind. The houses perched on stilts might stay put, but anything not nailed or tied down would probably blow away.

Connor had been so focused on Ruby Rollins and his quest to find her killer that he had regarded the hurricane as a simple nuisance. But the note from his landlord and the near-panicked "awfulizing" of the talking heads on TV made it clear that this was not something he could just shrug off. The Carolina lowcountry was about to experience a devastating weather event, and Connor's mission to get Lester Rollins out of jail might just have to be postponed.

When he got back to his tiny apartment Connor pushed open the slider and walked out to his small backyard. The same breeze that had spun up the sand on the beach was rattling the dry fronds in the palmetto trees at the edge of the yard. Somewhere nearby a set of wind chimes was tinkling a frenetic melody.

He studied the view for a moment. At high tide this patch of ground was about three feet above sea level, but during a full moon the water came right to the edge of the grass. He didn't care to think what a massive storm surge might do to this place, but the power of water was immense and would have no mercy for anything in its path. That included Connor's apartment and everything in it.

He sat for a while in one of the cheap plastic Adirondack chairs he'd bought at the supermarket. All around him he could hear people hammering plywood over windows and the roar of chainsaws as neighbors cut down limbs that could come crashing through windows in the high winds. A few folks were already loading belongings and pets into SUVs, the first to get off the island and hopefully make it inland to a relative's house or a motel that still had a vacancy. There was a sense of ordered urgency that reminded Connor of his last days at the F.O.B. outside Kirkuk before his platoon shipped home to the states. The place was like a beehive, all the grunts hustling about, packing up whatever shit they could take with them on the long journey home.

Eventually Connor got up from the chair he figured he would never see again and reluctantly made his way inside. The little patch of grass had been his escape valve for almost two years, ever since he had moved down here to the Lowcountry to work for Palmetto BioClean. He'd stared up at the night sky out here, drunk too much gin out here, and once had even made love to Danielle right there at the edge of the lawn, until the mosquitoes had chased them inside. But if the meteorologists were correct, that chapter of his life was coming to an end, and he approached the change with the stoic fatalism of a dead man walking toward the death chamber at the end of the hall.

After three years in the U.S. Army Connor learned to travel light. He had little need for anything other than the bare necessities of life: a few changes of clothes, a half dozen pair of shoes, one relatively clean sport coat, and a 1967 orange Camaro named Isabella that he hadn't seen in several weeks. His apartment had come fully furnished, right down to the coffee mugs in the kitchen and the TV on the wall, so all his belongings fit in the three canvas duffel bags that he slung into the bed of the truck, along with an old Army-issue bed roll.

Traffic on the causeway leading to the mainland was already heavy. A steady progression of cars and trucks loaded down with suitcases and coolers streamed across the swing bridge. It was a mix of tourists leaving their summer rentals early and year-round residents heading upstate to wait out the storm. Connor followed them onto the 526 spur that looped around the city of Charleston, but while most of them were headed toward I-26 west, Connor took the Long Point Road exit that took him to The Plant.

When Palmetto BioClean opened its doors three years before it had not needed much office space—just enough room for the operations manager to file reports, handle invoices and  submit insurance claims. When Jordan James brought Connor on board he'd taken over the single desk in the small suite, but over the past eighteen months the business had expanded to the point that James had leased the empty garage space next door. That garage was just big enough to hold the BioClean truck and a month's supply of cleaning materials for future jobs.

Connor dragged his duffel bags and bed roll inside and dumped them in the corner of the company's waiting area. At this point he had no idea how this was all going to work, and his mind was occupied by other things. On the drive over from the island he'd begun thinking about the man Caitlin Thomas had identified as Tony Worden, and how he might be connected to Ruby Rollins' death. Caitlin had filled Connor in on Worden's ties to the Klan and a growing movement called the Institute for American Heritage that rallied around the separation of the races.

As if on cue Connor's phone chimed. Caitlin had texted him the photo showing Worden with Coach Lee, his son Virgil, and the kid named Earl Reese. Reese definitely was the douchebag from the van, looking smug and insolent with his arms folded across his chest. The grease ball identified as Virgil was holding a shotgun in his left hand, while his right was raised in a familiar Nazi gesture. No sign of any tattoo. Coach Lee was gripping a rifle with two hands, and a cap with a coiled snake emblem was perched on his head. Worden was standing behind them, a tight smile of defiance on his face as if he knew a storm was looming on the horizon and was anticipating the change that it would bring

Connor sat down at his desk and five minutes later he was scanning several hundred Google listings for Worden. The first one he clicked on was a Wikipedia bio that cited no credible sources but provided a basic thumbnail of the man. Tony Worden, age 56, born in Greenville, studied at the University of South Carolina for a couple years before joining the Marines when he was 20. After two tours and seeing no action he returned home, found a job installing HVAC systems in new homes, and got married. Fast forward ten years and he began dabbling in local politics. As Caitlin had said, he eventually ran for the state legislature, winning handily in a largely white district that didn't seem to mind his overt association with the KKK.

The web entry noted that over the years Worden had been observed stirring the pot at supremacy rallies around the state. His stated message, in quotes, was to "call on men of like mind to instill constant fear in the hearts and minds of blacks through the real threat of old-time lynchings and other torturous methods of maintaining social order." The passage concluded by declaring that it was time for "God-fearing men and women throughout the state to rise as one and defeat the heathens of the Dark Continent."

A few more clicks told Connor what he already suspected: Tony Worden was a self-assured, self-serving, and narcissistic self-promoter. He clearly overestimated his intelligence, was obsessive to the point of fanatical, and had a distorted view of the world that bordered on paranoia. He'd posted numerous essays on the Institute of American Heritage website that echoed his daily rants on Facebook, which generally played along the lines of white supremacy, government conspiracy, the horrors of interracial blending, and anything that had to do with non-heterosexual sex.

An accompanying color photo showed him standing with his feet slightly apart, shoulders square and almost defiant, a rifle clenched tightly across his body. Connor enlarged the photo just enough to see the grim look in Worden's eyes that said, "You tread on me I'll cap your ass good and hard with this here gun." Connor had known a lot of grunts like that in Iraq, young kids barely out of high school who grew up shooting at rats at the dump but never gave a thought to what might happen if the rats had guns, too. They were usually the ones who caved in to their fears first, shitting their pants when they were under fire and quickly getting the picture that when your money ran out in this game you didn't feed it more and keep going.

Connor Googled Earl Reese next. Caitlin had connected him to Coach Lee through the van he'd been driving when he followed Connor and Danielle down to Edisto. There were almost a million hits for the name Earl Reese, but most of them were either random obituaries, profiles of a major league baseball player in the seventies, or stories about a civil rights activist who was murdered back in the fifties. Nothing for a redneck kid from Florence, South Carolina. Connor refined his search parameters by adding the name Robert E. Lee, which produced a few hits from the local Florence newspaper. The newspapers' archives contained several short articles about the high school football team, which Lee apparently had coached for twelve years.

One of the archived stories included a color photograph of a smiling Coach Lee with what appeared to be several members of the varsity football team. They appeared to be celebrating some kind of victory, all smiles and high fives and heads slicked from the routine dousing of Gatorade. Standing next to Lee in a shirt and tie was a young Earl Reese, no more than eighteen. The article was dated seven years ago, which put Reese at around twenty-five today.

Connor sent Caitlin a text thanking her for forwarding the picture and asked her for a couple more pieces of information. He knew it was too late for her to be at work, but he knew she'd handle his request as soon as she got to work in the morning. Whatever her plans for riding out the storm, he assumed she would stick around until the last possible minute before getting out.

Before turning off the computer Connor checked the National Hurricane Center website for the latest update. Not much had changed since earlier in the evening except that the computer models were getting closer in their track of the storm. The cone of probability had narrowed considerably since the last report, and now the graphic showed the city of Charleston almost dead-center in its path. Eleanor had laid waste to the low-lying areas of the southern Bahamas, and a container ship had disappeared in the high wind and waves. Florida's east coast was being pummeled by massive surf, and entire beaches were experiencing serious erosion. Sustained winds were being clocked at 145 miles an hour, and the NHC now was forecasting the Category Five storm to make landfall late Thursday night or early Friday morning.

Eleanor was imminent, she was dangerous, and she would show no mercy.

# Chapter 19

Caitlin's text woke Connor up at 5:47 the next morning. He had laid out his bed roll on the hard linoleum the night before and had fallen into a remarkably deep sleep in seconds. It reminded him of the long treks he and his squad and endured in the Iraqi desert, trudging for hours in the relentless heat and then grabbing a few hours' sleep after the sun went down, only to do it all again the next day. Except this time an ancient AC unit was churning out cool air, and there were no rocks to remind him he was in a foreign land that wanted him and his fellow soldiers gone.

The text read:

Last known address is 545 Noisette Street, Florence. When are you getting out?

Connor rubbed the lingering sleep from his eyes and sent his reply:

Thank you. The roof and walls are solid so I'm staying put.

Ten seconds later he got her reply:

Don't be a hero, Tat Man.

To which he responded:

I'm a big boy, Mother.

Another ten seconds later Caitlin wrote:

Well, if you're going up to Florence, stay there.

Connor thought for a minute, knowing she was probably right. She was just looking out for his well-being, so he replied:

Good advice. I'll take it into consideration.

He didn't, of course.

Two hours later Connor was driving down a quiet, tree-lined street on the outskirts of Florence, a small city of about 35,000 nestled along the I-95 corridor. He had taken highway 41 up through the Francis Marion National Forest, joining a steady stream of cars and SUVs heading for higher ground. State police units were parked at strategic intersections along the way, directing traffic that was only expected to get heavier during the course of the day.

He slowed the old pick-up to a crawl as he looked for number 545. The houses along this street were simple post-war structures, most of them single-story ranches with brick veneer and tidy lawns. It was clearly a working-class neighborhood, most likely home to plumbers and contractors and first responders with kids and dogs and tree houses in the back yard. Almost every driveway had at least one vehicle parked in it, and every other garage had been turned into a storage unit or a man cave.

Connor finally found the house he was looking for. It was only a slight variation on the general theme on Noisette Street: brick with white trim, crepe myrtles lining the weed infested lawn, a silver sedan and a white F-150 parked in the driveway. As Connor pulled to the curb he noticed a Confederate flag decal stuck to the truck's tailgate, surrounded by a gaggle of bumper stickers sure to make any redneck proud:

Straight, White, American Male—And Proud Of It

My Other Auto Is An AK47

Don't Tread On Me

Got Ammo?

He waited a moment while the engine sputtered a slow death, then climbed out and closed the door with a hip nudge. On the way up from Charleston he'd played this scenario out in his head, realized there were many different ways it could go. A quick check of Caitlin's database had given him a phone number, which he had called from a rare pay phone he'd found outside Kingstree. A man had answered on the second ring, and Connor had simply stayed on the line, not saying a thing. After a few seconds the man had said, "Fucking computers," and had hung up.

Unless Robert E. Lee IV had already gone off to work he was probably inside the house. The F-150 reinforced this theory. The sparse info Connor had pieced together told him that the man was divorced, had three grown children, including one named Virgil. He'd been forced to retire from his coaching job several years ago, an incident that involved a reprimand from the local school board as well as a restraining order. Connor had no idea where Lee was employed these days, but the newspaper story made it clear his coaching talents were no longer welcomed by the school district.

Connor made his way up the front walk and mounted the three steps to the front door. He had the distinct feeling that a pair of eyes was watching every move. He hesitated a second, then gave three swift raps on the screen. He thought he heard a shuffle of feet approaching, followed by a sharp voice that barked, "Get your ass off my porch!"

"Mr. Lee?" Connor asked. "Robert E. Lee the fourth?"

"I told you, get the fuck off my property!"

That wasn't exactly what Mr. Lee had said the first time, but Connor figured now wasn't the time to point it out. Instead he replied, "I'd like to talk to you about a white Ford van."

"What part of 'fuck off' don't you understand?" the voice snapped.

Connor said nothing for a minute, deciding how to play this. Robert E. Lee's response was pretty much in line with what he'd expected, but now that he'd gotten to this point there were several ways to go.

"Did Reese follow me on his own, or did you put him up to it?" he asked.

There was no immediate response from inside, just deadly silence as Lee appeared to be thinking this through. Then Connor heard the turning of locks—at least four of them—as Lee made his move. Eventually the door swung open and Lee stepped toward the screen, a large rifle gripped tightly in one hand. Connor wasn't an expert on guns, but he knew this one: a Mossberg pump action shotgun, like the one his uncle Robert used to go turkey shooting with.

"I got a finger just itchin' to use this," he said with a snarl. "Go on and give me a reason."

Connor doubted the guy needed a reason, but again he kept his thoughts to himself. "I'm looking for Earl. I figured maybe you'd know where he was."

"Why the fuck would I know that?"

"'Cuz he was driving your van," Connor told him.

Robert E. Lee IV fixed him with a long, hard stare, but Connor was not about to be intimidated. He figured there might be some kind of South Carolina law that gave the guy the right to shoot first, ask questions later, but Connor didn't think he'd try anything stupid. Not yet, at least.

"What you want with him?" he finally asked.

"Like I said, he followed me the other day," Connor explained. "I want to know why."

"How do you know he followed you?"

"Cut the shit, Mr. Lee. I caught him in the act."

Lee mulled this bit of news over a minute, shifted his weight from one foot to the other. "What makes you think it was my van?"

"You mean, since the license plate had been removed?" Connor asked. "Dumbass should have covered the VIN while he was at it."

There was a flicker of irritation in Lee's eyes, and then he said, "I ain't seen Earl in weeks. He needed wheels for work so I loaned him the van. Nothing illegal about that."

"I didn't say he did anything illegal," Connor told him. "I just want to know why he was following me."

"I don't have a clue."

"Just like you probably don't have a clue where he's living."

"I wouldn't tell you if I did," Lee said, not exactly a denial.

"What's his connection to Tony Worden?"

"Don't know what you're talking about."

"I think you do," Connor said. "I heard Worden has a rally every Tuesday night. I'd like to go to one."

"I don't think you do."

"Last time I looked it's a free country."

"You got that right," Lee snapped. "Everyone in this country's got his hand out, lookin' for free shit. Food stamps, health care, welfare checks."

"Live free or die," Connor countered. "My country, right or wrong."

"My country's been pretty fucking wrong for years," Lee said with a growl. "Totally flushed down the shitter. Niggers, wetbacks, rag heads. faggots, Jews—all of 'em fouling this great nation of ours, from sea to fucking shining sea."

"You come up with that bullshit all on your own, or did you have help?"

"It's the truth, Mr. Connor. Live with it."

"How'd you know my name?"

"Citadel Security isn't the only establishment in this state knows how to locate someone," Lee replied.

This was going nowhere, just as Connor had anticipated it might. "Did you know your son Virgil has taken a liking to hanging around black funerals?" he said, abruptly changing direction.

Connor's question took Lee by complete surprise. He blinked, then made a face as if a cloud of gnats had suddenly engulfed his head. "You leave my boy out of this!" he snapped.

"Your boy is right in the middle, whatever this is. Did you send him down there?"

"I don't know what the fuck you're talking about."

"Ruby Rollins," Connor explained patiently.

"Who the fuck is she?" Coach Lee said, his voice almost a snarl.

"The old black woman whose funeral your boy shot up."

Coach Lee pumped the Mossberg with one hand, like John Wayne in an old movie.

"I suggest you move your ass before I use my constitutional right to squeeze this trigger and eliminate a possible prowler from my front yard."

Connor took this as a cue to make his exit. He raised his palms and backed off a step, then turned to go down the stairs. As he hit the walkway he looked back up at Coach Lee, who wasn't about to relinquish the power the shotgun seemed to bring him.

"Tell Earl Reese I'd like a word with him," he called to him.

"A word about what?"

"I suspect he already knows," Connor told him. "But you can tell him it's in his best interest in the long run."

"How will he find you?"

"He found me once," Connor said. "He can do it again."

Back in the truck another talking head on the radio was going on about the approaching hurricane. The coast was going to be slammed, and the amount of rain that was going to be dumped on the rest of the state would be in Biblical proportions. That ought to scare a lot of God-fearing folks, Connor thought.

"Get to high ground and stay there," was his message for all those who were listening.

Connor suspected the Florence schools had delayed its opening until the storm had washed through, but he did a Google search for the high school anyway and quickly found directions. He knew this was probably a long shot but as long as he was here in town he figured he'd give it a try. He thumbed the address into the GPS in his phone and keyed the engine to life.

The high school was easy to find, and ten minutes later he pulled into a visitor's space outside the front entrance. He was right about the closure: there were no students anywhere in sight, and the parking lot was almost empty. Still, odds were that someone from the administration must be around, getting ready for opening day. The big sign out front mentioned a 'Welcome Dance' scheduled for that Friday night, but a note under it said all new school year events had been postponed.

Even so, there was work to do, and the assistant vice principal was in her office. Her name was Cynthia Noble. She shook Connor's hand warmly as if she welcomed the interruption and invited him to take a seat on the other side of her desk. It was cluttered with papers and worn binders and stray items that had been presented to her over the years. She seemed to have a thing for giraffes, because dozens of them populated almost every flat surface in her office.

"What can I do for you, Mr. Connor?" she asked him after he'd settled into his hard metal chair. She was attractive in a stern, bookish sort of way. Early forties and single, judging from the lack of a ring. Light, wavy hair that was almost the color of champagne, if dishwater had been poured into it. Eyes that seemed too turquoise to be real. Probably contacts.

"I'm actually trying to learn whatever I can about someone who used to be a student here," he told her. He took a business card from the manila folder he was holding and handed it to her, first checking to make sure it was from Citadel Security and not Palmetto BioClean.

She glanced at the card and set it on her desk. "I really can't talk about current or former students," she informed him. "School regulations."

"I wouldn't expect you to," he replied. "But I thought you might have some old school yearbooks around that I could take a peek at."

"This student: is he—or she—in trouble?"

"Not at all, ma'am. I'm doing an employment check for a client that's looking to hire him." Okay, so that was a lie—but it wasn't the first time he hadn't told the whole truth to someone in the principal's office.

She nodded at what he said and seemed to give his request some thought. Then she peered at the full tattoo sleeve on his arm and said, "Did that hurt?" she asked.

It was a question Connor got a lot, and the answer was, "Not that one. But some of them did sting a bit. Depends on who did them and where they are."

Cynthia Noble nodded again and pursed her lips. "This is highly unusual," she told him. "Like I said, we have rules in place about divulging private information about our students."

"I'm not looking for private information," Connor explained patiently. "I'm just trying to track down the parents of this particular individual. I know he attended school here, and I thought I might find some information about him in the yearbook."

The assistant principal thought on this for a moment, then asked, "What is this former student's name?"

"Earl Reese. He probably graduated seven or eight years ago."

"Oh, my…of course I remember Earl. Nice kid. He had developmental issues, but he was so eager to please. Very friendly and likable. His senior class elected him homecoming king."

"I thought you couldn't divulge anything about former students," Connor said.

Cynthia Noble waved his comment aside with a brush of her hand and said, "Earl Reese is a special case. Shoot—his mother works here in the school, over in the kitchen. I'm not sure if she's here today, on account of the weather. But we can go see, if you like."

Connor liked very much. "That would be very helpful," he said.

"You're sure Earl isn't in any trouble?"

"Not that I'm aware of."

"Good. Because he's a very impressionable young man. He has a heart of gold, and he wears it right on his sleeve where everyone can see it."

*I didn't see it the other day when he was stalking me in that van*, Connor thought. "Like I said, I'm just checking an employment thing," he reminded her.

"Well, let's go meet his mother."

Emma Rae Reese was a woman who seemed as if life had snuck up on her and passed her by without even saying "surprise!" She appeared to be in her fifties, with wiry silver hair that Connor thought was way too long for someone her age. Like much of the American public she was overweight, with most of her excess pounds solidly gripping her thighs and hips. She was dressed snugly in mom jeans and a floral blouse that hung from her broad shoulders and ample bosom.

Cynthia Noble introduced the two of them and then said, "Mr. Connor, here, was asking some questions about Earl. I thought maybe he could speak directly to you."

Mrs. Reese eyed him warily and said, "What kind of questions?"

"Don't worry, ma'am," Connor replied. "He's not in any sort of trouble. I work for Citadel Security down in Charleston, and we do employment background checks." Every word he said was true, although none of it had anything to do with why he was there.

"What kind of employment?" Earl's mother asked.

"The file doesn't say, but we do a lot of security checks for local transportation and shipping companies."

"Well, I'm his mother. I've known him since the day he came into this world. A real Yankee Doodle Dandy."

"Ma'am?" Connor said, furrowing his brow.

"Well, he wasn't really a Yankee, of course. Not growing up around these parts. But like the song says, he was born on the Fourth of July."

Connor opened the folder he was carrying and pretended to scribble a note. "When was this?" he asked her.

"He turned twenty-five last month," she said. "He came into this world at the hospital down in Charleston. Me and Henry—that's my late husband—we lived down there at the time. Moved up here when Earl was six or seven."

"Did he do well in school?" Connor asked. He knew it was a dumb question, but he had to keep up the employment ruse, and he knew that educational aptitude was part of the screening process.

Mrs. Reese and the assistant principal exchanged glances, and then Earl's mother let out a long sigh. "I hate to jeopardize my son's job search, Mr. Connor, but you evidently don't know much about him."

"I'm not sure I know what you're talking about."

"Well—the reason I asked what kind of job Earl applied for is that…well, he's really not the sharpest tool in the shed."

Cynthia Noble winced at Mrs. Reese's blunt assessment of her son, but Connor ignored it. "He had a learning disability?" he asked instead.

Emma Rae Reese nodded, then said, "He seemed okay when he was born; the nurse said he had a good Apgar score, although I didn't know what that meant at the time. But after a few months he just showed signs of being…well, slow. The doctor said he wasn't showing the kind of cognitive behaviors that a baby his age should have, so we took him to a specialist. She did some tests and…well, he didn't do so good. I mean, it's not like Henry or me were Einsteins or nothin', but Earl failed just about every kind of test that doctor put in front of him."

Connor knew the score. He had a cousin who was like that up in Michigan, diagnosed as developmentally slow. Little Lucy had been deprived of oxygen at birth and as a result she suffered neurological impairment. That's what the doctors called it. As a child she was amazingly trusting and impressionable, believing in the goodness of everyone around her. She greeted the world with a beautiful smile every day, and never had night terrors when she went to bed. But when she reached puberty she ran into trouble. Other girls shunned her, adults labeled her, and boys found her an easy target.

Connor wondered how Lucy's experiences might have paralleled those of Earl Reese. People were more understanding of the mentally disabled today than they were a generation ago, but a lot of cruelty remained in the world. Bullies always needed an easy mark, and Connor wondered if Earl Reese had grown up with a target painted on his back.

"He still graduated from high school," Connor ventured.

Mrs. Reese tucked a strand of loose hair back under the fishnet and said, "Thanks to a lot of special ed classes. And some very understanding teachers."

"Was Coach Lee one of them?"

"Why do you ask that?" The question came out as a snap, like a rubber band breaking.

"I spoke with him earlier. He had some very encouraging things to say about your son."

Mrs. Reese and Miss Noble exchanged concerned glances, and then the assistant principal said, "Mr. Lee did not exactly part company with this school on the best of terms. And we're not permitted to discuss the circumstances behind his departure."

Connor glanced from one woman to the other, then nodded at the implication behind the message. Lawyers had been involved with Coach Lee's dishonorable retirement, and money very likely had been the bottom line. "That must be why he didn't have much to say to me," he replied.

"That shit bag's already said enough," Mrs. Reese grunted. "Bastard turned Earl into one of his foot soldiers. Along with his own son."

"Virgil?" Connor asked.

"Mrs. Reese, I really don't think we should be discussing this—"

"Hush, Miss Noble," Earl's mother said. "I don't think Mr. Connor here is going to go run and tell the papers that we're discussing that scumbag coach. Are you, Mr. Connor?"

"No ma'am."

"In fact, I don't think this is about a job screening at all, is it?"

Both women looked at Connor, and by the looks of those looks it appeared they would wait however long it took to get an answer.

"Not exactly," Connor reluctantly acknowledged. "The thing is, I actually do work for Citadel Security, but Mr. Lee is the real target of my investigation. I can't say why, other than to say he's a person of interest in a criminal act."

"I'm not surprised," Mrs. Reese said. "But how does that involve my son?"

"Only incidentally," he explained. "Earl was linked to Lee through a vehicle he was driving. We suspect Lee coerced him into doing something. Nothing necessarily illegal, but something that could be misconstrued as accessory after the fact."

He was making this all up on the fly, but as long as Mrs. Reese kept nodding he figured he had her attention.

"Let me tell you something about that sonofabitch," Mrs. Reese said. She glanced at Miss Noble and added, "Do you want me to take this outside, so we're not talking on school prop'ty?"

The assistant principal thought for a moment, then shook her head. "I'm sure Mr. Connor will be discreet about whatever is discussed," she replied. "Even if the governor himself starts asking questions."

Her words caused Connor to freeze for just a fraction of a second. There was no way she could she possibly know about his arrangement with Governor Luck; she had to just be making a point rather than pointing a finger.

"This conversation never happened," he agreed.

"Well, then," Mrs. Reese said. "Let me tell you a little something about Robert E. Lee the fourth."

A little something turned out to be a whole lot of everything. Ten minutes later Connor had the full Monty on the former football coach and social studies teacher, and very little of it was pretty. Coach Lee had been a popular teacher and student confidant almost from day one, counseling students about everything from parents to academics to relationships. His warm, easygoing style helped him establish a high level of trust, and in the early years he treated his students and athletes with dignity and respect. At the same time, he used that trust to identify the weaknesses and uncertainties of adolescence, and to take advantage of them.

At first no one paid any attention to the rumors. Coach Lee was too likable, too respected to be touching students in the equipment room. There was absolutely no way he would change a grade in exchange for a hand job. It was known that he liked to go hunting in November, but the story of him having sex with a sophomore girl in his deer stand down in Danville just wasn't in his character. Neither were the tales of teaching a few select students to fire a gun, using photos of Martin Luther King and President Obama as targets.

Eventually the stories got too numerous and detailed to ignore. While he openly praised every student on his football team, several of his black players accused him of slapping or punching them after a particularly disheartening loss. On another occasion he threatened to drag his star running back behind his truck for failing to rush for two hundred yards in a critical game. There were stories about private locker room hazings that featured broom handles and soda bottles, depending on who was talking. And one time he was seen running from a burning cross that had been placed on the lawn of black teacher who had privately testified against him at a school board hearing.

The last straw was when Robert E. Lee the fourth was caught on surveillance video torching the car of a black lineman who had sacked Lee's Clemson-bound quarterback three times in a divisional playoff game. There was no wriggling out of that incident—digital video doesn't lie—and the following week the school board handed him his walking papers. The player whose car had been destroyed filed a civil suit and won a six-figure out-of-court settlement. Lee sued the school district for wrongful termination, causing a panel of three arbitration judges to utter a collective laugh when they ruled against him.

When Mrs. Reese was finished with her summary there was an uncomfortable silence for a second or two. Then Connor said, "How was your son involved with all this?"

"My son worshipped Coach Lee," she replied. "But that bastard was ordered to stay away from Earl after the car thing."

"So how is it that Earl was driving a van registered to him?" Connor pressed.

"The order was only good until my boy turned eighteen. After that he was legally an adult and could do whatever he wanted."

"Where was his own son during all this?" Connor asked. "Virgil."

"That boy spent most of his senior year in juvie for a string of break-ins," Mrs. Reese said. "Trouble from the git-go."

Connor made a mental note to have Caitlin run a sheet on Virgil Reese. Then he said, "You think Earl continued to hang out with Lee after he turned eighteen?"

"Look, Mr. Connor. Coach Lee didn't rape my boy, if that's what you're thinking. The fact is, he got Earl to buy the gasoline that was used to torch that kid's car. Afterwards they went and drank beer down by the railroad tracks, laughing 'bout what they'd just done."

"Like father and son."

"My husband died when Earl was fifteen. He was looking for a father figure, and that's what Coach Lee provided. He's been tied to that bastard's hip ever since."

# Chapter 20

Connor was stopped twice by state police on the way back down Highway 41 to Mount Pleasant. Both times the officers asked him whether he was aware that a major hurricane was coming, and then demanded to know why he was heading into the storm when people were being urged to evacuate.

"I have to lock down my business," he told them both times. "Soon as everything is secure I'm out of there."

His explanation satisfied the cops and each time they let him continue on his way. All the radio stations were explaining that forecasters now had narrowed the path to an area stretching from Hilton Head to Myrtle Beach. Hurricane Eleanor was expected to hit sometime early Thursday, less than forty-eight hours from now. The winds had weakened a bit but were blowing at a sustained one hundred thirty miles an hour, and the storm surge at the barrier islands was predicted to be fifteen to eighteen feet.

Fact was, Connor had no plans to leave the BioClean shop once he got there. The building was constructed of reinforced cinder block walls and a metal roof affixed to massive steel girders. No hurricane could pack enough wind to blow it off, and he suspected it was high enough above sea level to withstand any sort of tidal surge. He certainly was not going to join the parade of cars pouring out of the coastal area ahead of the storm.

A minute later his phone rang again, and the screen told him it was Kat Rattigan.

"There's one more thing," she said, barely giving him enough time to say "hello."

"What's that?"

"Well, I did a bit more checking and found that Luck has ties to a man named Worden."

"As in Tony Worden?"

"You know him."

"Not personally," Connor said, a shiver tickling his spine. "But I hear he's a real sweetheart."

"Not from what I've found. Anyway, it turns out the governor got to know him when they were both in legislature. Took a couple trips with him to Idaho."

"Famous potatoes?" he said, reciting the slogan on the state license plate.

"And famous supremacists. Seems one of Worden's buddies has a hunting camp up there, and Luck went along for the ride."

"Any idea who else might've been there?"

"Nope. Just thought you'd want to know. Gotta go…traffic is tight."

And with that she was gone.

The wind was already beginning to kick up when Connor arrived at The Plant. He made a quick detour to load up on groceries and water, plus a bottle of gin at the liquor store next door. He took as much cash out of the ATM as it would let him, then filled the truck's tank with gas. By the time he pulled up in front of the BioClean storefront loose palmetto fronds were blowing around the lot. A plastic paint bucket went rolling by like a modern-day tumbleweed as he unlocked the front door. The storm was still several hundred miles away but it was already announcing its arrival. Things were only going to get worse before they got better.

Connor turned the TV to the Weather Channel and left it on in the background as he put away his groceries. All the big-name meteorologists had already descended on Charleston to ride this thing out, but right now they were just standing on various beaches around the lowcountry, instructing their camera people to get shots of the roiling gray surf. The sun was out, although massive clouds were beginning to stream in from the southeast.

Landfall was still many hours away so Connor felt no immediate sense of urgency. Still, he wanted to make sure everything was secure for Eleanor's arrival, so he went outside to inspect Moby Dick, the great white trailer. There was no room for it in the garage, but it was secured to a fence post with a heavy chain and theft-proof lock. It was not about to blow away, but the trailer walls were aluminum sheets riveted to a metal frame, and they could rip out and go flying during a strong gust.

Next, he checked on the company truck in the garage. The fuel gauge was right at "full" and all the fluids looked good. The tank for the back-up generator was full, as well. Electrical power was the first thing to go out during a hurricane—sometimes for days—so the generator could become critical. He checked the roll-up door, which was set firmly in its tracks and seemed as if it could withstand just about anything.

Satisfied that he'd survive whatever Mother Nature threw at him, Connor sat down at his desk and fired up the computer. A thought had struck him on the drive back from Florence, and he wanted to check something he'd overlooked before. Something Lester Rollins had told him the last time he'd visited the old man in jail. He sat in front of the screen a minute, then decided a phone call could be quicker.

"Tat Man," Caitlin Thomas greeted him when she answered the call. "You should be on the road away from here, not hanging out at The Plant."

"If you're in the office, why shouldn't I be?"

"Because Danny is an EMT," she said. "He's first line during the storm, so he's not going anywhere. And neither am I."

Danny was her new boyfriend, and ever since they'd met last spring she'd been like a shadow on a sunny day. "Well, I've decided I'm going to ride this out here at The Plant," he told her.

"Does Mr. James know that?"

"What he doesn't know can't hurt him," Connor replied. "Look, can you track a couple things down for me?"

"I've got nothing else to do," she replied. "All the smart people have already left town. Whatcha need?"

Connor told her what he needed, conceding that what he was looking for probably was a long shot.

"The sheet's easy, but medical records are sealed tighter than Nefertiti's tomb," Caitlin agreed. "Don't get your hopes up."

"Just see what you can find," he said, adding a quick "please."

"Ten-four, Tat Man," she said, and hung up.

Something else Lester Rollins had said continued to pester Connor. He'd ignored the reference at the time, but he knew it was a mistake to latch on to a particular theory at the expense of any others. So, while he waited for Caitlin to do her thing, he brought up Google on his computer and typed in the name "Al Jackson." Connor had run a perfunctory search a couple days ago, but this time he wanted to make sure he hadn't let something critical slide right by him.

As with most things on Google there were several other people also with the same name, but Connor found the Al Jackson he was looking for halfway down the first page. Known as the "human timekeeper" because of his impeccable drumming skills, Jackson was the son of a dance band leader in Memphis who one night tapped his five-year-old boy to play bongos in his jazz combo. Not only did the kid go on to become the drummer for Booker T. and the MGs; he also was backbeat behind many of Memphis's top musicians, including Eddie Floyd, Sam & Dave, Otis Redding, and Albert King. The entry went on to quote Joe Turner, the label's former house bass player, as saying that Jackson was "the embodiment of the rare and unique performing artist. No drummer in Memphis came close to having Al Jackson's precision, timing, and soul, and his death diminished the heartbeat of Memphis music for decades to come."

Connor realized this had to be the same Joe Turner he'd been introduced to at the reception following Ruby's funeral last Friday night at The Nest. Turner had given him a business card and now Connor dug it out of his desk drawer and found two numbers at the bottom. He dialed the cell phone at the bottom and waited to see if fate was smiling on him. It was.

"Hello?" a man answered, a distinct wariness in his voice.

"Good afternoon, sir," Connor said. "Is this Mr. Turner?"

"It is," he replied. "Who's calling?"

Connor introduced himself and reminded him that they had spoken briefly after Mrs. Rollins' funeral last weekend. "You told me to give you a call if I had any questions," he said.

"That's right," Turner said. "I have a call coming up in five minutes, but I'm happy to help in any way I can."

"Thank you, sir. I promise I won't keep you long. I actually want to talk about Al Jackson, if you don't mind."

"You think there's a connection between him and what happened to Mrs. Rollins?"

"That's what I'm trying to find out. What I understand is Al and Lester were close friends, back in the day."

"Brothers to the bone," Turner told him. "No one could play drums like Al, and Lester was the best horn player in all of Memphis, Tennessee."

"After the funeral last Friday, you said Lester disappeared the day after Al Jackson died," Connor said.

"That next morning, if memory serves me after all these years. One day he was there, and the next day he was gone. No one thought much about it at first, not until someone noticed he wasn't around."

"What else do you remember about that day?" Connor asked. "About what happened to Al Jackson."

"It was a long time ago, Mr. Collins. Over forty years. But I remember the whole thing as if it were yesterday."

If Joe Turner had another call coming in Connor never would have known it. For the next fifteen minutes the soul icon filled him in on the racial tension in Memphis during the seventies, the color barrier and mistrust between whites and blacks, and the resentment of many white Memphians to the new class of wealthy blacks associated with Stax Records. Eventually he got around to Al Jackson and what happened that night.

The story was that in late September Al Jackson was supposed to fly to Detroit to produce a music session when he remembered the Joe Frazier–Muhammad Ali fight was happening that night. Jackson called his friends in Detroit to delay the recording session so he could watch the "Thrilla in Manila," and told them he would fly up the next day. Then he attended a closed-circuit broadcast somewhere in town with a couple of friends.

"Could Lester Rollins have been one of these friends?" Connor asked.

"It's possible," Turner said. "He definitely was in town around then, or no one would have realized he suddenly was gone the next day."

Turner then laid it all out for him: After the boxing match Jackson returned home to find people in his house. As his estranged wife Barbara later told police, a burglar told Jackson to get down on his knees, and then shot him five times in the back. Sometime later—after midnight—

Barbara ran out in the street and began yelling for help. She told the police that the burglar had tied her up when he broke into the house, then shot her husband when he returned home.

"Did she say what these burglars took?" Connor asked him.

"That's where it gets problematic," Turner said. "According to police who investigated, there was nothing out of place. Nothing appeared to have been taken, and Jackson's wallet and jewelry were still on him."

"His wife thought he was in Detroit?"

"Apparently so. The interesting thing is, just a few months earlier she had shot Al in the chest because of some sort of dispute. He didn't say what it was, and he decided not to press charges. By the time he was killed he'd already filed for divorce and was planning to move to Atlanta."

"What do you remember about the guy who shot him?" Connor asked.

"I don't remember his name, but it was alleged that he was the boyfriend of one of his wife's friends. It wasn't just some random thing. The cops tracked him from one end of the country to the other, and eventually they gunned him down. That's the story, at least."

"Sounds like more than a burglary," Connor said when Turner was finished.

"I don't like to speculate, not about things like that. All I know is what I remember."

"I think I need to pay another visit to Mr. Rollins," Connor said.

"It's been forty years," Joe Turner said. "Now might be a good time to see what ol' Hurricane remembers about that night."

# Chapter 21

Any conversation with Lester Rollins was going to have to wait. Because of the storm the entire Charleston area was switching into emergency mode, and the county was taking no chances out at the jail. That meant no visitors until the hurricane was history and power and personnel were back at full strength. It also meant that Connor's objective to get Rollins freed before Eleanor hit was a moot point. The old blues man would just have to remain where he was and wait it out.

While Connor waited for Caitlin to get back to him he sketched out two parallel lines of thought about Ruby Rollins' death. One involved Earl Reese and maybe Virgil Lee, and the very possible racial aspect of her murder. Witnesses had seen her arguing with a pale redneck who resembled Virgil outside the convenience store, and he could have been the guy hunched down behind the wheel of the Buick that had been parked in the woods after Ruby's funeral reception at The Nest. Plus, there was no question Earl was the cracker whom Connor had confronted near Edisto last Saturday. His connection to this whole thing was very real, but Connor was at a loss as to what that connection might be.

The second scenario involved Lester Rollins and his life before he moved to South Carolina. Connor wondered if Ruby knew the truth about his past, and whether her husband had witnessed the brutal murder of a close friend. How much had he seen and known? Was it possible someone who had been involved with that incident four decades years ago had tracked the old horn player to the Carolina coast? Some secrets die hard, and Connor guessed there were a lot of secrets surrounding Al Jackson's death. But would any of those secrets been enough for someone to commit another brutal murder, after all these years. And, if so, why would the killer have attacked Ruby instead of her husband?

Connor sketched out the names of the people involved in both of these scenarios, keeping one line of thinking on one side of the page, and the other line on the other side. As hard as he tried he was not able to find any overlap where crossed tracks might have caused a collision. They were two distinct theories, clean and separate from each other. No overlap whatsoever.

Around four o'clock there was a knock on the outer door. Connor considered not answering it, then realized it might be someone who needed assistance battening down the hatches. He had been sitting with his feet propped up on his desk for over an hour, and when he stood up a cramp seized his right leg. He limped out to the lobby area and found a uniformed cop standing squarely in front of the glass door.

"May I help you?" Connor asked as he opened the door.

"Officer Hendrick," the cop said, giving him a glimpse of his badge. "Mount Pleasant Police. There's a mandatory evacuation starting at midnight, and we're making a routine check to make sure you plan on leaving."

"I have relatives up in Florence," Connor lied with ease. "As soon as I finish locking things up I'll be outta here."

"Good to hear," the cop said. "Traffic's getting thick, and at some point, the state police are going to use all lanes of I-26. Same thing with Highway 41. No inbound traffic after that."

"I'll be gone in less than an hour," Connor lied again. "Thanks for stopping by."

"To serve and protect," Officer Hendrick said, and tipped a finger to his hat.

Connor waited for the police cruiser to roll through the parking lot and disappear. As soon as the cop was gone he went out and moved the Toyota around the side of the building, so it wouldn't be so obvious he was there. Even if the cops ran a check of the license plate it would come back as a loaner up in Charlotte, and he doubted the cops would make the effort to find out who was driving it. It was just a POS pick-up that had been left behind to ride out the storm.

The wind had stiffened over the last few hours, and now small branches were being tossed around the parking area. Scraps of trash swirled in small dust devils, and a gust almost snatched the baseball cap off Connor's bald head. The sun was shining through gaps in the clouds, but he could feel the drop in air pressure from just a couple hours ago. The canvas awning over the BioClean door flapped wildly, and somewhere a halyard clanked a steady rhythm against a flag pole.

When he was back inside Connor poured a modest dose of gin into a plastic cup and dropped in a couple of ice cubes from the office fridge. Sure, it was a bit early for that kind of thing, but if he was hunkering down here he was going to take the edge off. Outside something smacked the metal roof and bounced off. A tiny stream of wind screamed in through a slit between the front door and the floor, creating a low, eerie whistle.

Connor returned to his desk and again set his analytic mind in motion. For a husband and wife who were considered pillars of their community, Lester and Ruby Rollins had had a lot of mayhem swirling around them. He was a possible witness to a murder forty years ago and had fled Memphis ostensibly to keep himself alive. What had he seen—or done—that could have led to his wife's death?

On the other hand, Ruby had become entangled in some kind of racial dispute, a quarrel that could have led to her death. But why? She had not been lynched or dragged behind a car; whoever killed her had come into her church and had attacked her face to face. Close enough to plunge a knife into her, repeatedly.

Connor took a sip of gin and rose to his feet. It was hard to concentrate with the wind picking up steam, and the hurricane was at least thirty-six hours off. He turned the TV to a cable channel that ran old game shows, and quickly distracted himself by watching newlyweds saying predictably stupid things about each other.

Eventually the phone rang, snagging him from a dream about a white rhino. It was the desk phone, not his cell, and the read-out told him it was Caitlin Thomas. She had come through for him, at least a bit.

"The first thing was pretty easy," she said. "Virgil Lee has been in and out of jail since he was a kid. His juvie records are sealed, but he's been arrested a half dozen times for a lot of petty stuff. Moistly B-and-E's, and he served thirty days for robbing a convenience store with his finger."

"His finger?"

"Stuck it in his pocket, got the clerk to hand over a couple hundred bucks."

Connor thought on this a moment, then said, "What about the other thing?"

"Well, like I said before, juvie records are untouchable," she explained. "But I made some calls and learned something pretty interesting. Two things, in fact."

"Fill me in," he said. "I'm not going anywhere."

"That's what worries me," Caitlin told him. "It's not too late to get a long stretch of road under your ass."

"I've got everything I need right here," Connor insisted, trying to sound resolute. "So, what did you find out?"

"Gerald Walker."

Connor had almost forgotten about the man Ruby Rollins had married when she had been young and naïve, but Caitlin clearly had not. "What did you find out?" he asked her.

"If you remember, there were eight possibilities that fit the bill. I ran each of them through all the search engines and databased I could find, and eventually cleared seven of them. That left one."

"And you found him?"

"Of course I found him, Tat Man. It's what I do. This particular Gerald Walker's been living in Reidsville, Georgia for the past seventeen years."

"How far is Reidsville from Ravenel?" Connor asked.

"About ninety minutes from Savannah, and then another hour to the church," she told him. "But he's not your guy."

"Why not? He knew the victim, and I'm sure he had plenty of means and motive—"

"But not a whole lot of opportunity. Among a few other totally nondescript things, Reidsville is home to the Georgia State Prison."

Connor said nothing for a moment as her words sank in. "You were playing with me—"

"Just having a little fun, Tat Man. The thing is, he's in there doing life without parole. Killed a state cop during a robbery."

"And they haven't executed him yet?"

"Seems he got a lenient judge, who was swayed by a letter written by his ex-wife."

"Ruby Rollins? You've got to be joking."

"I kid you not. She wrote a heartfelt plea for the state to spare his life, and the judge took it to heart."

He chewed on all this a minute, then slipped Gerald Walker into a small box and pushed it onto a shelf in the back of his mind. "Okay…what else have you got?" he asked her.

"What else I've got is that Lester Rollins was right about Karen Luck. I can't find an address for her, but I did discover that she's suffering from acute renal failure. Caused by a severe bacterial infection."

"Renal failure is kidneys, right?"

"Exactly. Karen apparently spent last summer in Guatemala doing some volunteer work for her church. Somehow, she picked up a bug that gave her sepsis. She got dehydrated and her muscles broke down, releasing too much myoglobin into her bloodstream. She became very ill and had to be flown to a medical center in Houston, where the doctors got her renal functions under control."

"How did you learn all this?" he asked her. "I thought all medical records were sealed."

"They are," Caitlin affirmed. "But church records aren't, and when all this happened her church started a GoFundMe campaign to raise money to assist with bills that her insurance won't pay. The page is still up and has all the info."

Connor scribbled a few notes on his legal pad, then said, "When did all this occur?"

"Last August, just about a year ago. Karen's been in and out of hospitals ever since, and so far, she's flown under the radar. But according to the organizer of the fundraising campaign, her kidneys have all but shut down. She's only twenty-seven but has to undergo dialysis three times a week."

"What about a transplant?" he asked.

"That's why the fundraising page is still up," Caitlin replied. "They've done a good job raising money, but there's been some difficulty finding the perfect donor."

"What about her brother, Peter? He should make a great candidate."

"One would think," Caitlin said. "But there seems to be an issue."

"What kind of issue?" he dutifully asked.

"Maybe you should ask him," she said.

"I think I'll do just that."

After Connor hung up he started to dial Peter Luck, but stopped before he punched in the final digit. He decided to think this through a minute, figure out his best line of questioning. Peter might hold some answers, but the one time they'd met he hadn't been exactly forthcoming with information. Eventually Connor decided to take a different tack and punched a different number into his phone.

"Hello?" a woman on the other end said. She sounded a little frazzled—maybe a touch tired—but otherwise none the worse for what she had recently gone through.

"Mrs. Luck?" Connor said. He'd been hesitant to call her, considering her episode with sleeping pills and booze just a few days ago. "This is Jack Connor. You were so gracious to meet with me for a few minutes last week."

"Yes, Mr. Connor. I remember our conversation. You asked a lot of questions about Ruby. To what do I owe the pleasure today?"

"Well, ma'am, at the end of our meeting last week you gave me your phone number and told me to call if I ever had any questions. I know you've been through…well, a rough patch the last few days, but there was something I wanted to discuss with you." He paused a moment, then added, "And please—call me Jack."

"Of course, Jack," she said. "And you needn't tread so carefully about what you called a rough patch. Truth is, someone put pills in my Scotch and I overdosed."

"Ma'am?" he said.

"You heard me," she told him. "I was drugged. Anything you might have heard to the contrary is a damned lie."

"I've heard a lot of things—"

"Meaning you're not sure whether you can believe me. Listen, Jack: the doctors pumped my stomach. They found absolutely no remnants of pills. None whatsoever. That means the medication was dissolved in my drink."

Connor said nothing for a minute as he absorbed what she was telling him. Finally, he said, "If what you're saying is true—"

"—Someone tried to kill me," Mrs. Luck finished for him.

"But who would've wanted to do that?"

"That's my problem, not yours," she said in short, clipped words. "And that's not why you called me, is it?"

"Well, no," Connor admitted. "I wanted to talk to you about your daughter."

There was a long silence on the other end, and Connor thought he heard the clink of ice in a glass. Whether someone had laced her drink or not, he figured it was a bit soon for her to start in on the booze again.

Mrs. Luck took a long sip and then exhaled an even longer sigh. "My, my, Mr. Connor. Jack," she finally said. "It seems you've chased this one right down the rabbit hole."

Connor had seen both the Disney and Johnny Depp versions of *Alice In Wonderland*, and particularly liked Grace Slick's "White Rabbit." Still, he found the entire story too abstract, and he'd never been good at making sense of vague literary allusions. He preferred direct answers to direct questions, and he sensed now that the governor's wife wanted to tell him something but for some reason couldn't.

"Excuse me?" he said, trying to sound obtuse.

There was another pause, this one shorter than the first. Then she asked, "What is it you think you know?"

There were several ways Connor could answer her question, but Mrs. Luck was too smart for any subterfuge. He sensed she already knew what he was after, so why not just go there and get it over with.

"Your daughter needs a kidney transplant," he said.

"Damn, you're good," she said. "Please don't take offense, but I'm really surprised you got this far so fast."

"No offense taken, ma'am," Connor told her. "And if I may be so bold, I suspect you have a real challenge on your hands. On several levels, in fact."

There was another clink of ice and another long sip. "You know, Jack. I like you. I like your style, I like your manner, and I even like your tattoos. You're brighter than you let on, and I like men who use their brains. Which is why I really can't go any further with this conversation."

"Yes, ma'am," he said. "I just wanted confirmation of my theory."

"And now that you have it, what do you intend to do with it?"

"My job is to find whoever it was who killed Ruby Rollins," Connor told her. "I have no other dog in this hunt."

"Please try to leave my family out of it," she said, her voice almost pleading.

"Your husband hired me, Mrs. Luck," he reminded her.

"His ambition is going to destroy him. And us. I'm asking you: just drop this. Please."

"There's an innocent man sitting in the county jail here, ma'am. Do you really want him to stay there the rest of his life?"

He heard her sigh, but she did not take a sip of her beloved Scotch. "I can't keep you from doing what you think you have to do, Jack. You and my husband and very much alike in that regard. But if you continue down this path, beware the storm that's coming."

When she hung up Connor got up from his desk and paced the floor of his small office. He tried to digest what Mrs. Luck had told him, not just about him leaving her family alone, but also her husband's ambition. There had been rumors that the governor had his sights set on the White House; was it possible he was so focused on power and career that he bwas foregoing his wife and kids? Could he be so crass and calculating to think that freeing an old black man from prison might help him garner votes among the state's African American population? Was Connor just a pawn in a backroom game to seek higher office?

He knew politics was an addiction for people who craved power, recognition, and affirmation in a life that often was lacking all three. Connor's father had been friends with a big wig in the Autoworkers Union, a short balding man with three kids, a wife, and a stiff mortgage. Louis Amici had worked the Ford line for twenty-six years before he rose to power during a time of intense contract negotiations, and he'd loved the attention and power. The union gave him a purpose in life that bolting axles to chassis had never provided, and after a deal was struck he never went back to the assembly line. Last Connor had heard, Louis was the elected chairperson on some sort of executive board within the union, dealing with pensions.

There was another thing gnawing at Connor, however. Mrs. Luck had made a point of telling Connor that someone had slipped the overdose of Ambien into her Scotch. She'd been adamant about it. That meant someone had tried to turn her lights out, someone who had access to both her booze and her pills. Had she been trying to tell Connor something without actually pointing a finger?

Eventually he sat back down at his computer and pulled up Google. He typed "kidney transplants" into the search window and scrolled through the results. He didn't have to look far.

According to the National Kidney Foundation, more than 100,000 Americans are on the kidney donor list at any given time. Unfortunately, just seventeen percent of them receive an organ in time to save their lives. In fact, every day twelve people in America die while waiting for a kidney. One of the reasons so few patients receive a kidney is because of the small pool of donors, both living or dead. Because most people are born with two kidneys, one of them can be donated, but because of the risk of rejection, a suitable donor kidney is often very difficult to find.

Another article—this one from the Renal Resource Center—identified three tests that are conducted to evaluate donors. These tests—blood type, crossmatch, and HLA testing—are used to determine if a donor kidney is compatible to the intended recipient. The article went on to explain that transplant results are best when the donor and the recipient are identical on the white blood cell HLA antigen series:

Because of inherited genes, a perfect match can only happen between brothers and sisters, where there is a 1 in 4 chance of a perfect match. Parents and children have only a 50% match because only half of the genes in a child come from each parent. Although this is usually acceptable, occasionally there are problems with red cell (ordinary blood group) typing. Transplants with living related donors more likely to be successful than with unrelated, or recently deceased donors because the tissues are more likely to be closely matched.

Connor pushed back from his computer and stared at the wall beyond the screen. It was all starting to make sense, while not really making sense to him at all. He eyed the cup of gin on his desk, but all this material about kidneys and HLA antigens and renal failure made him think twice about taking another sip.

He picked up his phone and started to dial Governor Luck's number, but just then something made a loud crash outside in the parking lot. Connor had been so intent on his web search that he hadn't noticed the wind picking up, but the sudden crack jolted him back to the present. He hesitated for only a second, then rose to his feet to go see what had come down.

He unlocked the front door and stepped out into a light rain. The first outer bands of the hurricane were starting to sweep in from the east, just as the Weather Channel had predicted. A small oak branch tumbled through the lot, propelled by a stiff gust of wind that hurled it against the chain link fence. That's when he noticed that the top of a pine tree had snapped off and fallen right on top of Moby Dick.

"Oh shit," Connor said. He braced himself of against the wind and crossed the parking lot to where he had secured the large white trailer just a few hours ago.

The downed tree had caused a serious dent in the trailer roof. The aluminum skin had warped, and a gap had opened between two of the side panels. Connor could tell that any serious gust would probably cause the whole trailer to rip apart and scatter to the wind.

There was nothing he could do, not right now. The trailer's fate lay at the mercy of Hurricane Eleanor, the eye of which now was a couple hundred miles offshore. For the first time Connor wondered if maybe it was a mistake to stay put and wait this thing out. *Too late*, an inner voice told him. He took one last look at the trailer, figuring he'd deal with it once this was all over, then turned to head back inside. Maybe he'd have that sip of gin after all.

That's when something hard came down on the side of his head, turning his world dark as his legs folded beneath him and he crumpled to the ground.

# Chapter 22

Forty-three days after arriving in Iraq Connor had sustained an injury to the head.

It was a concussive blow just below the right temple, and he had spent forty-eight hours in the FOB's combat support hospital recovering from his injury. It had not been a bullet that struck him; rather, he had been hit by a brick that had been hurled off the roof of the building he and his squad were attempting to enter. Connor's helmet had lessened the impact much the same way a Kevlar vest stops a bullet: no fatal injury, but it hurt like hell.

Whatever had struck him this time had the same impact. He blacked out instantly and when he finally regained consciousness his skull was throbbing like a sonofabitch. This time the injury was greatest at the base of his skull, and the agony pulsed outward, engulfing his entire brain. In fact, the agony was so excruciating that he thought he might black out again, something he almost welcomed as an escape from all this torture.

But he did not black out again. Eventually the intense throbbing subsided to just a dull cranial roar that felt as if his head had been run over by a bus. Whatever had knocked him out had caused his eyes to stop functioning, and for a second, he was stuck with the very reality that he might have gone blind. He quickly forced that idea from his mind, telling himself that he would have time for panic later. Right now, he needed to know where he was.

It was when he tried to push himself up that he began to understand the full impact of his situation. His hands were just as useless as his eyes, for the very real reason that they were tied behind his back. Tightly bound with what felt like duct tape wrapped several times around his wrists. Same thing with his feet, except the tape had been applied directly over his socks.

And now as his brain began to clear just a bit he realized there was a piece of tape across his mouth, as well.

Connor had no idea where he was, nor how long he had been unconscious. He tried to move his body without the use of his hands, but there was no room to shift around. He was lying on his right side, knees drawn up toward his chest, and the surface beneath him was hard. Something rigid was pressing into his back, and for some reason his brain screamed "tire jack." Which told him he probably was in the trunk of a car. And since there didn't seem to be any motion or engine noise, he figured the car must be parked.

He also figured since the engine wasn't running it was going to stay put, at least for a while.

Connor battled every instinct that told him to be scared. When this sort of thing happened to a soldier in Iraq it always came to a bad end. He shuddered when he thought about the agonizing hell prisoners had gone through during those last few hours before they lost their heads and other body parts. Iraqi insurgents could be very inventive when it came to inflicting pain, and he had no idea what his own captors—presumably Americans and probably rednecks—might be capable of.

He knew struggling would only twist the material and make it tighter, so he just lay where he was and tried to steady his breath. The air already smelled stale and with his mouth covered he needed to be able to regulate his intake through his nose. Breathe in, exhale slowly. Repeat. He tuned his ears to any ambient noise that might be coming from outside the dark trunk, but the rush of wind from the looming storm drowned out the rest of the world.

Connor slowly inched his body toward the rear of the compartment. If this was the trunk of a car he figured it must be a large one, since there seemed to be more room than most new cars had. Plus there was an aroma of age, the kind of odor that came with a car that had a history of dust, cigarette smoke, dogs, and whatever else had come and gone over the years. It was a comforting smell, sort of like his father's old Toronado before it got T-boned by a delivery van.

His mind immediately went to the old Buick that had been backed into the trees the night of Ruby Rollins' funeral. If he was right about how this was all coming together, it would make a certain kind of sense. Of course, clipping Connor at the base of his skull and stuffing him into the trunk of a car didn't make much sense at all, so scratch that. Whoever had snatched him out of his own parking lot hadn't used much brain power at all.

Connor tried to remember what he knew about old Buicks. Or any old GM car with a boat-sized trunk. The lid was solid and designed long before the days of safety locks. There was no miracle rip cord he could pull to free himself—even if he'd had partial use of his hands, which he didn't. He knew there was a full-sized spare tire located in a bin beneath the trunk floor, along with the standard Detroit issue jack that still seemed to be pressed against his spine.

The back seat was another matter altogether. The rear wall separating the trunk from the passenger compartment was fabricated with steel frames that provided solid support for the upright rear seatback. In most cases there was enough space between them that a child could crawl through if the seat was removed. Connor was not a child, nor did he have the ability to crawl. Still, despite the ringing pain in his head, he was not about to just lie where he was and wait for someone to come for him.

At first Connor had thought he'd been hogtied, but this wasn't the case. He managed to wriggle around so he could plant the soles of his shoes against the fiberboard backing of the rear seat. His ankles were still bound by the tape, but there was enough strength in his legs to give a solid shove. Old GM cars were built tough, so at first nothing gave. He tried again, and then again, then one more time.

Finally, he felt movement. Just a bit at first, but he also thought he heard the fiberboard begin to crack where it probably was held in place by self-tapping screws. He lashed out with another shove and felt more movement. Connor had no idea where his abductor might be, but he couldn't have been anywhere near the old car.

A dozen more well-placed kicks and the seat finally gave way. Not enough for Connor to slide through, but enough to allow some fresh air to rush in through the opening. He lay there a minute, again listening for any sounds that might tell him where he was, and this time he thought he heard voices. Distant voices, or possibly just one. The growing wind made it difficult to tell.

Connor took a deep breath, then inched closer to the opening he had created. His eyes picked up a glint of light somewhere, and then he began to see shapes in the darkness. He had not gone blind, nor had his kidnapper made any effort to blindfold him.

A couple more quick thrusts with his feet moved the old seat enough for Connor to poke his bound feet through the opening. He wriggled closer until his knees were through, and that's when he ran into a problem. He was lying in the wrong position to snake through any further, plus the duct tape was holding his ankles together at an impossible angle. That's when he realized—again—that his captor had applied he tape directly over Connor's socks, rather than his skin.

He brought his legs back through the opening, then used the flattened edge of the pressed metal post to catch the back of one shoe and pull it off. He repeated the process with the other shoe, and then repeated it all with his socks. They were tight and stiff—his abductor had used lots of tape—but eventually he got them both off.

Now at least his feet were free.

Again, he inched his legs back through the opening into the rear passenger compartment. It was easier this time because of his increased mobility, and within a few seconds he had made it up to his hips. This was going to be the problem point, but he managed to twist around to just the right angle so he could fold himself through the gap. From there it was just a matter of seconds before he slid through up to his shoulders, and then he repeated the twisting motion until he was completely out of the trunk.

Connor managed to sit up on the bench part of the rear seat. He glanced through the window and found that the car was parked in a lot jammed with other vehicles. He twisted around and used his bound hands to pull up the door lock. Then he found the handle and opened the door with a *clunk* that seemed louder than it had to be. He leaned his weight against the door panel and gave it a shove, and a second later found himself on the damp gravel of the parking lot. He quickly pulled himself to his feet and inched the door closed, then zig-zagged his way through the parked cars.

While he had been working his way out of the car he'd also been working on the piece of tape fastened across his mouth. He'd used his tongue to keep it moist, and eventually it became so wet that some of the glue began to separate from his skin. Over time it continued to loosen so that now he just needed to brush up against the side view mirror of a parked F-150 to tear it away completely.

All he needed to do now was free his hands.

That proved to be more a more difficult task, but he managed to find the solution in the cab of another truck. Connor peered through a window and found a large survival knife with a serrated blade lying on the front seat. It was an odd but not uncommon place to stash a weapon, but at the moment he wasn't about to question motives.

Thirty seconds later he was free. He tucked the knife into the waistband of his jeans, then quickly crept back to the car that had been his cage. It was, indeed, a Buick—the same one he had seen the other night in the woods. He slipped his shoes and socks back on, then crouch-ran to the edge of the parking lot.

Despite the growing wind, Connor could hear the words of a man speaking inside the building. The amplified voice was muffled by the cinder block walls, so he couldn't make out what was being said. A sudden jolt spiked through Connor's head, and he blinked back the pain. In the movies the throbbing always seems to go away within seconds, but not so in real life. He closed his eyes and waited for a wave of dizziness to pass, then inched toward the building while making sure he stayed out of the glare of the flood lamp. He made his way toward the front door, then stopped when he noticed a man seated just inside.

He was one large tub of redneck lard, about the size of an ox and probably about as bright. He was sitting in a folding metal chair, tipping back against the wall and chewing on his nails. If he was supposed to keep watch on comings and goings out in the parking lot he was the wrong man for the job.

Not wanting to tangle with this example of poor human genetics Connor slipped around the corner of the building and into the shadows. The weeds were thick and overgrown along the side of the structure, and the dumpster smelled like rotten fish. Fortunately, the wind in the trees and the amplified noise inside the warehouse kept the sound of footfalls to a minimum. The wind also was damping what otherwise would have been a serious mosquito problem, but Connor now found himself swatting at phantom pests.

When he came around the corner of the building he was surprised to find a large motor home parked in the weeds out back. It was a Fleetwood Bounder with a pop-out room that extended from the driver's side. An electrical cord had been plugged into a metal box at the base of the warehouse wall. The inside of the vehicle was lit up, but curtains had been drawn across the windows so no one could see in.

Or out, which was good news for Connor.

He stayed close to the thick pine woods as he made his way toward the camper. No guard had been posted outside, but he strongly suspected that someone was inside the vehicle, keeping an eye on things. Connor stealthily slipped around the front of the camper and cupped his hands as he peered through the windshield. There was no one in either the driver's or shotgun seat, but beyond that a full-length curtain blocked his view. He edged around to the passenger side and found the door ajar, a sliver of light slicing out onto the ground. He touched his hand to the knife in his waistband, then straightened out of his half-crouch and grabbed the door handle.

"Freeze," he yelled as he yanked it open.

"What the fuck!" snapped a man who was sitting directly inside the door, just to the right. A light was on further back in the camper's living quarters, but it was too dim for Connor to make out the guy's features. Except for his hair, which reached down to his shoulders. His eyes traveled to the floor, where a gun was lying at his feet.

"Don't you move a goddamned inch," Connor snarled, thrusting the knife toward him. "Do what I say and you keep your ears."

"How the fuck did you get out of the car?" the man said, blinking his eyes in disbelief.

Connor didn't answer; instead he said, "Kick the gun over here," he said. "Slowly. No funny shit."

The man hesitated, thinking this through. Then he did as he was told, anger and hate etched deeply in his eyes. He'd had one job to do here, and he had fucked it up.

Connor carefully bent down and picked up the gun. It was a Glock, with what he guessed was an 11-round magazine. "Let me guess: this camper belongs to Tony Worden," he said, once he had the weapon in his hand.

"Fuck you," the guy snarled at him. His breath smelled of onions and pepperoni.

"Cool it with the big words," Connor said as he ejected the magazine. It was full, and he assumed there was one in the chamber.

"You are in one heap of shit—"

"Yet I have a gun and you do not," Connor reminded him as he slid his knife back into his waistband. "On your feet."

The guy was slow to get up, just itching to get a chance to surprise Connor and overpower him. That wasn't going to happen again, so in one quick motion Connor whipped the gun around and slammed it into his jaw. The man's head flew back, then recoiled off the fake wood wall.

"That's for earlier," Connor snapped at him. "Now you have two seconds to move or I shoot your knee out."

The guy barely knew what hit him, but he wasn't as stupid as he looked. He shook off the blow from the Glock, then struggled to his feet and moved a few feet further into the RV.

"Worden's gonna kill you when he gets back," he seethed through brown picket-fence teeth. "If I don't get to you first."

"No one's killing anyone," Connor countered. He hefted the gun in his hand and added, "Unless you try something really stupid."

The guy said nothing, and for the first time Connor was able to see his pasty white face and corn-fed jowls. He was wearing a black wife-beater and tufts of hair were poking out from under his arms. A coiled snake was inked into his neck, along with the words "Don't Tread On Me." American exceptionalism at its best.

"Virgil Reese," Connor said. "I knew you'd show up, sooner or later."

"How you know my name?"

"Word gets around. Did Worden put you up to this, or was it your old man?"

"Don't know what you're talking about."

"Where're your keys?"

Again, the guy said nothing, but another flick of his eyes pointed Connor to where he'd dumped them on a table next to where he'd been sitting. Virgil Reese had to be a disaster at poker. Connor grabbed the keys and slipped them into his pocket.

"Nice set of wheels," he said. "Should get me home just fine."

"Fuck you."

Outside the wind took a break and Connor could hear Tony Worden whipping his followers into a frenzy: "It is time for us to take control from the forces of evil and purge this once-great nation of its human garbage," his voice boomed. "America is sinking into a cesspool of racial, religious, and social impurity. Jews are in control of the banks and the media. The rag-heads are on a *jee-had* to invade this country like a swarm of African killer bees. Faggots and rug-munchers are destroying our Constitution and our Christian beliefs."

"You believe this shit?" Connor said to the guy.

"It's pussies like you's fucking this country," he replied.

Connor could have whipped the butt of the Glock across the man's nose, but instead he said, "I fought for this country, douchebag. But I'll bet you've never done more than stroke your guns and cower from the bogeymen crawling around in your weak little mind."

"Go to hell."

Inside the warehouse Worden's words were growing louder and more impassioned. "Goddamned wetbacks are crawling over, around, through and under our borders night after night," he was yelling. "They're taking our jobs and raping our wives and daughters." There was a pause, punctuated by cheers and jeers. Then he started in again: "Then there's the niggers. Shit, they've lied and cheated and stole until they got one of their own living in the White House. I'm telling you, this country needs one giant flush to get rid of this nation's waste. We need to clean it out. Clean 'em out. Clean 'em *all* out."

His words inspired his followers to yell "clean 'em out—clean 'em out." The calls built into a rhythmic chant that intensified to a furious crescendo inside the warehouse, segueing into a rousing rendition of "God Bless America." Then the wind shifted again, all but drowning out the voices inside the warehouse as the rally came to an end.

"That's your future?" Connor asked the guy at the dinette.

"You'll see—Worden's gonna take this country back," he snarled.

"Yeah—at least a hundred years," Connor replied. He shifted his position so he could keep an eye on both his captive and the entrance to the RV. "Will he be coming right here, or does *der Fuhrer* usually linger with his brown shirts a while?"

The sound of a steel door slamming answered the question. The guy's eyes flicked to the doorway, prompting Connor to level the Glock at him again.

"Don't even think about it," he said.

"Worden's got a gun. He's gonna shoot you dead."

"Maybe. But you'll be dead first."

That's when the door to the motor coach slammed open and Tony Worden burst inside.

# Chapter 23

"Jesus Fucking Christ, is there no one but me around here smarter than dog shit?"

The entire RV rocked as Tony Worden stormed inside. He yanked the door closed, then yelled, "Virgil—get me a beer." Getting no response, he called out again, "Virgil!"

Again, there was no answer, so Worden pushed his way into the area where Connor was waiting for him. Connor had to suppress both a laugh and a touch of pity at the sight of Worden, dressed as he was in a Confederate general's uniform, a Civil War re-enactment costume that appeared genuine, right down to the brass buttons, braided epaulets, and broad-brimmed hat. All that was missing was the horse.

A grim frown crossed Worden's face when he saw Virgil sitting at the dinette. He was about to bark something at him when he noticed Connor standing there, gun in hand, a determined look on his face. The frown shifted to a genuine scowl as his mind appeared to race through several scenarios.

Then he said, "Who the fuck are you?"

"I'm the guy this douchebag stuffed into the trunk of his car and brought up here to this dumb-fuck neck of the woods," Connor said. "And you're going to tell me why."

It was clearly not the response Worden was expecting. He studied Connor a minute, then shifted his gaze to the guy named Virgil. "He telling the truth?" he asked.

Virgil's eyes dropped and he said, "It was my dad's idea."

"You're still taking orders from your old man?"

"He said it was for Earl. To protect him."

Worden shook his head and stared up at the ceiling of the motor home. "Dear God, why have you surrounded me with such idiots," he said.

*Maybe because they're the only ones who'll listen to your bullshit,* Connor wanted to say.

"Do you mind getting back to the point, sir?" Connor said. Showing this repugnant sonofabitch any kind of respect caused his stomach to churn, but he could play the game for a while.

"And what point would that be?"

"This is Jack Connor, Mr. Worden," Virgil blurted out.

"I see." Worden turned to Connor and said, "I heard you were asking around about that poor kid. Might I ask you why?"

"That kid's involved in something big and nasty," Connor said. "I think he's in over his head and Virgil, here, knows why."

"I don't know nothing—"

"That's for sure." Connor used his gun to wave Worden toward the dinette where Virgil was seated. "Sit down, sir. Please."

Worden shrugged and slid in next to his human lapdog. "Do you mind getting me a beer out of the fridge, there," he asked. "My throat is parched."

"With all that fire and brimstone, I would think so." Connor kept the gun leveled at them both as he opened a small refrigerator and grabbed a couple beers. He tossed a bottle to each of them, forcing them to expose their hands to catch them. It was an old Army trick.

"So—you've got the gun," Worden said as he twisted off the cap. "What is it you want?"

"Sounds like you really know how to get a crowd riled up," Connor replied, cocking his toward the warehouse.

"You probably don't agree with my point of view. A lot of people drink the mainstream media Kool Aid and don't know shit. No matter—we live in a free country, where we're free to say what we want."

"And that makes you one very popular man."

"It's not me; it's the message," Worden told him. His eyes looked like deep wells of hate boring out from the cesspool of hell. "There are a lot of angry people in this country today. Auto workers from Detroit, home builders from Queens, plumbers and painters and postal workers from just about everywhere."

"Angry white men."

"Mostly, yeah. And they all want to be heard."

"What about angry white women?"

"This isn't the place for them. Those men in there are good, hard-working Americans. They're tired of hearing from women and about women. And men trying to *be* women. Women have been giving men shit from the womb to the tomb, and we're damned tired of it. If we didn't have so many women in the workforce there'd be more jobs. Women are one reason this country is so fucked up, and we aim on taking it back."

"You think they'll all just passively wander back into the kitchen and strap aprons around their waists?" Connor asked him.

"From the beginning of time men have done the hunting and women have done the tending. Time to get back to the basics."

"Actually, it's time to get back to why I'm here." Connor then turned back to Virgil and said, "Why did your pop think it was such a great idea to put out my lights and stuff me in a trunk?"

Virgil shrugged and said, "He didn't tell me."

"Do you do everything he says?"

"Not always. But usually, yeah."

"Meaning?"

"Meaning I trust him."

"That doesn't answer the question," Connor said.

"I'm not planning on answering nothing."

Connor could tell he wasn't going to get anywhere with the guy, but he had to make one last try. "I've met your old man, and you know what I think? I think he's a coward."

"Dad ain't no coward—" Virgil grunted.

"Sure he is. Guy sneaks around, torching kids' cars and busting heads in the dark. That tells me he's a coward *and* a pussy."

Virgil started to rise from where he was sitting, a raging fire blazing in his eyes. But Tony Worden put a hand on his shoulder and pushed him back into his seat. "Now's not the time," he told him. Then he turned to Connor and said, "No one's looking for any trouble here, Mr. Connor."

"Trouble's all you serve in this place, Mr. Worden," he replied. "Whip your angry white brain stems into a fever and turn 'em loose."

"I tell them the truth. What they choose to do with it is their business."

"You mean like Ruby Rollins?"

If the name meant anything to Worden he didn't show it. "Never heard of her," he said.

"Earl Reese never mentioned anything?"

"It's not like that kid and I talk a lot," Worden replied. "Like I said, I don't know any Ruby Rollins."

"But *you* do," Connor said, turning his attention back to Virgil.

"I never heard of her neither."

"Bullshit—you're the worst bluffer in the world. Did Earl Reese have a beef with her?"

"I don't know what you're talking about," Virgil insisted.

"So tell me something you do know."

Virgil hesitated, his eyes shifting to Worden in an obvious cry for help. He wasn't going to get any. "What I know is Earl Reese was a good kid, got hit with the stupid stick the day he was born. My dad took a shine to him, helped him out."

"Helped him out in what way?" Connor pressed.

"Taught him to be tough. To survive and endure."

"By setting fire to a black kid's car?"

Virgil fixed him with the eyes of a cobra that had been cornered and was just waiting for a chance to strike. "Nigger had it coming to him," he grumbled.

"For winning a football game?"

"Look, Mr. Connor," Worden interrupted, taking a long pull from his bottle of beer. "We're through here. Virgil made a mistake bringing you to this place, so you're free to go. And I suggest you do it quickly. And quietly."

"Or what?" Connor wanted to know.

Worden calmly cocked his head in the direction of the warehouse. "There's a couple hundred very angry men out there, Mr. Connor. They've been pounding whiskey and beer all night and right about now they're itchin' to let off a little steam. Trust me—you really don't want to be in the middle of that."

Connor gave some thought to what Worden was saying. He'd seen the power of a mob mentality, especially a mob comprised of men who collectively wanted to beat the shit out of someone. He also had a strong feeling that, while Virgil was somehow connected Ruby Rollins' death, his involvement was only indirect. He looked from one man to the other, then nodded in agreement

"I think I'll take your advice and be on my way," he said. Then to Virgil he added, "I'm keeping this gun and taking your car for a ride."

"The hell you are—"

But Connor didn't wait around to hear any more. He rushed to the front of the RV and slipped out the door, then ran down the length of the camper toward the side of the building. He heard yelling behind him, and a couple of men who had attended the rally watched him race past. They were slow to catch on that Connor was trying to make a run for it, so they just watched as he bolted for the parking lot.

Connor had a bit of a head start, but he knew he had to move fast in order to get the old Buick on the road before Virgil sent up a call to arms. He yanked open the door, jumped inside, and jammed the key into the ignition all in one continuous move. The engine started right up and the rear wheels dug into sizzling gravel. The rear end fishtailed through the parking lot and onto the state highway, disappearing into the night.

Connor wasn't sure where Virgil had taken him, but about two miles down the road Connor found a sign that announced, "Charleston 32." An arrow pointed left and he turned in that direction, going against bumper-to-bumper traffic that was inching along at ten miles per hour. Evidently a lot of folks had figured it was best to evacuate in the dead of night in an attempt to avoid the daylight jam, but this thinking clearly was flawed. No time of day or night was sacred when a quarter-million people were trying to head inland from the coast.

A few miles later Connor saw a sign and realized he was on Route 521 for the second time that day. He decided to head down to Andrews and then take Highway 41 back through the national forest. Rain was now coming down in sheets and pooling on the road, so Connor eased his foot off the gas and let the old Buick Electra tell him what it wanted to do. It was like driving his old Camaro, which seemed to have a mind of its own if he gave it a little free will.

The outbound traffic remained steady but so far, the police weren't stopping incoming cars. Connor knew it was only a matter of time before all lanes would be turned over to the stream of evacuees, so he drove steadily through the rain to make it home before it was too late. Wind was whipping through the pines and cypress on both sides of the highway, and the traffic almost came to a dead stop where an old oak had fallen across the road. A work crew was cutting it up and cars were inching around it, and Connor was able to make it past by pulling well over onto the shoulder. The earth was already soggy, but the Buick's tires bit into the mud and a few seconds later he was on his way again.

A few miles south of the town of Huger—pronounced *hew-jee*—the outbound traffic slowed again. Connor was doing around thirty-five when all of a sudden, a large animal appeared in front of the car. He jammed on the brakes and came to a stop, not knowing what he had seen or where the creature had gone. The headlights of oncoming cars made it difficult for him to see much of anything in the hard rain, and he started inching forward again.

That's when he saw the animal again. It was a dog, soggy and limping down the center of the road. The poor thing obviously was soaked to the bone, dazed and confused. He turned his head and looked up as Connor edged past, his eyes reflecting a very real fear and panic. Connor had seen that look before in the streets of Iraq, the eyes of children staring out the windows of bombed-out houses, frozen in the horror of what was happening to their lives.

All Connor wanted was to get home, back to The Plant, and hunker down for the looming storm. But the look in the dog's eyes—terrified and almost pleading with him—stayed with him after he had driven past, and he touched his foot to the brakes. He opened the door and looked back at the drenched dog, who now was eyeing him with just a faint glimmer of hope that someone actually cared.

"Come here, boy," Connor called out, not sure whether this dog was a boy or a girl, and not giving a damn.

The dog hesitated only a second, then started limping toward the car. Its back leg obviously was injured, and for a second Connor wondered just how bright it was to let a stray animal into his car. But the look in its eyes when he'd driven past yanked at his heart, and when the dog came up to the open door Connor got out and helped it onto the wide bench seat. Then he slid back behind the wheel and closed the door against the storm.

"What's your name, big fella?" Connor asked him. When the dog had jumped in he'd noticed that he was, indeed, a male. "What're you doing out here?"

He ran a hand across the dog's head, and he responded with a lap of a large pink tongue. Connor then ruffed up the fur on his neck, where he found a collar with a tag on it. Because of the dark and the crowded highway, he wasn't able to read the tag, but a half mile up ahead he found a place to pull the car off the pavement.

Connor set the brake, then turned on the dome light to get a better look at the dog. He was a chocolate lab, soaked from the rain and shivering as if it were below freezing. He had a small abrasion on the side of his head that seemed bloody but not life-threatening, and blood was caked on his left leg. The dog gave

Connor another swipe of his tongue just as Connor turned the tag around so he could read it:

My Name Is Clooney

No phone number, no address, no license number.

Then Connor felt something else stuck to the collar. It was a wad of paper that had been hastily applied with tape. He scraped it loose and unfolded what turned out to be a hurriedly scrawled note:

Please watch over me. No room in car. I'm housebroken and full of love.

The dog whose name was Clooney stared at Connor with a renewed sense of hope. He was shaking from the rain and the fear, but somehow he knew this man in this car on this dark and stormy night would keep him warm and dry, and for that he seemed grateful.

Connor looked into Clooney's deep brown eyes and couldn't help but grin. He ruffed the soggy dog behind his ears, then turned off the dome light. "You ready to go home, Clooney?" he said as he shifted into gear.

Out came the tongue again, this time with a vengeance.

# Chapter 24

Connor arrived back at The Plant a little before three in the morning.

He left the old Electra in an empty parking lot behind a garden store and walked up the road in the horizontal rain with his new canine friend. By now the rain was falling in steady sheets and the wind was howling through the trees. Occasional gusts hurled branches and trash—anything that wasn't tied down—through the streets, and several times Connor had to deflect flying debris more than once. The car radio had said the hurricane was a good eighteen hours away from making landfall, but the outer bands were ripping the coastline.

Things were only going to get worse.

When they finally got inside Connor bolted the door and flicked on a light. After drying Clooney off with a towel from the work truck Connor gave him a closer inspection, beginning with the small wound on the side of his snout. It had been bleeding when he had jumped into the car, but now it appeared to have closed up. Good news.

He ran a hand down both sides of Clooney's body, inviting more tongue strokes. When he got to the left leg the dog gave a little yelp, indicating a soreness that was causing the limp. Connor figured he might have been injured when he had been pushed out of the car, and that image caused a flash of anger: what sort of person could possibly abandon his or her dog on a dark highway in the middle of a storm? That would be like abandoning a squad member in the desert just because the troop carrier was a little crowded. You don't leave your fellow soldier behind—*not ever*—and you sure as hell don't dump your dog and run.

He folded the towel up and placed it on the floor in the corner of his office. Clooney seemed to know what it was for and padded over to it. He gave it a sniff, then curled up with his back against the wall. He tucked his chin over one paw and stared at Connor with eyes that just wouldn't quit. He had no idea who this man was, or where he had brought him, but right now Connor was the only person on earth who cared about him. He'd saved him, and that was all that mattered.

That's when Connor wondered if Clooney might be hungry. Palmetto BioClean was located nowhere near a grocery store, and at that hour every market would have been closed. He wasn't even sure if markets would be open in the morning and, if they were, there would probably be a run on essentials. Then Connor remembered the time a few weeks back when D-Dub had brought his German Shepherd in for a couple days because there was no one at home to watch him. He'd brought a big bag of kibble, and now he found it tucked away in a corner of the garage bay.

Connor poured some onto the lid of a plastic pail and brought it back into the office. He set it down in front of Clooney, who devoured it within seconds. No telling when he had last eaten, and when he was done he looked gratefully at Connor for giving him a meal.

It was close to four when Connor rolled out his sleeping bag and stretched out. Despite the hour the air was warm and the rain pumped the humidity close to one hundred percent. Still, he fell asleep in seconds, the roar of the wind and the sheets of rain on the roof drawing him into the depths of a deep sleep. Sometime during the night Clooney got up and came over to where he was sleeping, then curled up against his feet in order to stay in physical contact.

They both slept a good deep sleep for six hours. Then a loud crash yanked Connor awake, and the first thing that hit his brain was "bomb!" It was mental shrapnel from Iraq, and over time Dr. Pinch had helped him push it from his mind. The memories of his buddies being blown apart—and his own brush with an IED—would linger forever, but time was beginning to form scar tissue. Sleep would never be the same again, but he was learning to live with those terrors that came to him in the dark of night. And in the light of day.

This crash was not a bomb, of course. It was the top of a light pole that had snapped off and plummeted to the ground at the far end of the parking lot. Wires had come down with the pole and had landed in a puddle, causing the electricity to flicker and then die. Connor studied the damage from the safety of his doorway, realized there was nothing he could do to fix it. He suspected the utility crews would ignore power outages until after the storm had blown through and they began to grasp what they were dealing with. No one would be coming for a couple days, at least.

"Looks like we're riding this out in the dark," he said to Clooney, who had followed him to the door.

Even though the wind was howling the rain had let up a bit, and the dog gazed longingly at the patch of grass across the lot. He gave Connor a pleading glance that in dog-speak meant *please...now!*

"Do you want to go out, big fella?"

Clooney wagged his tail like a hummingbird beating its wings, so Connor opened the door and let him out. For a moment he was worried the dog might run up to where the wires had fallen, but the dog really did have to go. He shot across the parking lot to the grass and lifted his leg for what seemed like five minutes. When he was finished doing his business he trotted back to where Connor was waiting.

"Good boy," he said as he ruffled the fur on Clooney's neck. He let the dog back inside, then bolted the door tight against the wind. Clooney kept wagging his tail, so they both retreated back to the office, where Connor hit the power button on the TV.

Nothing happened, of course: the electricity was out.

Connor's laptop worked—the battery was almost fully charged—but there was no Internet. Fortunately, he didn't have his phone on him when Virgil Reese hijacked him, and when he'd returned to The Plant he plugged it into the charger. Now he had to use it mindfully, since there was no telling when he might be able to plug it in again. There was a generator in the truck, but it only had a ten-gallon tank and would be needed for more critical things once the storm blew through.

That left the battery-powered radio that Jordan James kept as an emergency back-up, just in case. "Palmetto BioClean essentially is an emergency responder," he'd explained the day he hired Connor. "The hard truth is that any situation can cause blood to be spilled, and we need to be prepared for all things, at all times."

"Yessir," Connor had replied, a little dubiously. At the time he did not see what kind of emergency might require the services of a blood clean-up crew, but in the coming days he would change his mind.

Now the radio was saying Hurricane Eleanor had weakened slightly to a category four, packing winds of about one hundred thirty miles an hour. That was the good news. The bad news was that the computer models were predicting the eye probably would strike the Charleston area just north of Mount Pleasant. Since the eye was about twenty miles in diameter, the most ferocious winds were expected to come ashore right over Sullivan's Island and the Isle of Palms. Anything in the storm's path would be hit with ultimate fury: whatever the wind didn't blow out, the storm surge would wash away.

"State police and local authorities are ordering everyone who lives in low-lying areas to move inland immediately," the radio announcer was saying. "A mandatory evacuation is in effect, and anyone who ignores this order does so at his or her own peril."

Connor looked at Clooney, who was staring at him with those trusting eyes. "I guess that means us," he said. "Are you sure you want to put your eggs in my basket?"

The dog lowered his nose and touched it to his paw, a move that said, *Wherever you go, I go, pal.*

"The National Hurricane Center also has issued a warning about the destructive force of the eye wall," the radio kept going. "This is the area located at the edge of the eye where the most damaging winds and intense rainfall is found. The eye itself often is totally calm, and many people are tricked into believing the hurricane has passed. Not so. When the eye wall hits it is easy to be caught off guard, as the winds can go from zero to over a hundred in just seconds."

For the first time of many to come over the next twelve hours, Connor wondered if he had made a poor decision to stay put. He could load the dog in the cab of his truck and hit the road, but by now all lanes would be clogged with other people who had waited until the last minute. Besides, he had no place to go once he was on the road, so now he figured it was best just to ride it out. Besides, if he'd done any of those things yesterday he wouldn't be sitting there right now with Clooney at his side.

He picked up his cell phone and used the speed dial function to make a call.

"I hope you're on the other side of I-95, Tat Man," Caitlin said when she answered.

"I'm holed up in an undisclosed location," Connor replied, going for humor. "And I just have one quick question."

"Seriously…you're still working on this thing?"

"No time like the present. Listen—do you have access to the county's birth records?"

"It's all computerized. You just need the access code and a User I.D., which I just happen to have."

"Are you anywhere near your computer?" he asked.

"No, but I can do it from my tablet," she said. "If the system is up and running I'll see what I can do."

He spelled it out for her, then said, "Thanks, Caitlin. I owe you big time."

"Just stay safe, you big idiot," she said.

"I'll be just fine with Clooney by my side," he told her.

"Clooney?"

"Later," he said, and ended the call.

Next, he dialed the cell number on the card Reverend Parker had given him that first day when the team had cleaned the vestry of his church. Hard to believe it was just a little over a week ago.

"Seriously?" the pastor said, an incredulous tone in his voice when Connor told him what he was looking for. "You're calling me in the middle of a hurricane?"

"Lester Rollins is still in jail, and he needs your help," Connor reminded him. "It's just a simple question."

"I'm in a car right now," the reverend said. "It's not a good time."

"All I need is a 'yes' or 'no' answer."

There was a pause on the other end while the reverend thought this through. Then he said, "Go ahead—ask your question. But I can't guarantee I can answer it."

It was not an immediate "fuck off," and that was something. "Does Ruby's murder have something to do with the fourth of July many years ago?"

"I don't know what you're talking about," Parker said.

"I think you do," Connor countered. "I'm running a records check now, so I'll have the answer no matter what you say."

There was another long pause, and Connor heard other voices in the car Parker was riding in. Probably family or friends heading inland to escape the storm. Then the pastor uttered a deep sigh and said, "It was twenty-five years ago, Mr. Connor. The past is past and cannot be changed. Focus on the present instead."

"The present springs from the loin of history," Connor told him. "Otherwise you wouldn't be preaching from that book of yours."

"Good-bye, sir," Reverend Parker said. "And I mean that with all my heart. Please do not call me again."

Next on Connor's brief list was Emma Rae Reese, Earl's mother. Something she had said yesterday morning continued to bother him, and he hadn't known why until now.

"I'm not sure I should speak with you, Mr. Connor," the woman said when he told her who was calling. "I believe I may have said way too much last time we spoke."

"Not at all, Mr. Reese," he said. "In fact, you were very helpful in putting a lot of things in perspective. I wanted to thank you for your help."

"No one calls someone in the middle of a hurricane to say 'thanks.' I can tell—you have something on your mind."

"Just one more question, and then I'll leave you alone."

She sighed a minute, then said, "I've got a lot of company right now," she said. "My brother and his family just got here from McClellanville. They got slammed real hard by Hugo and aren't taking chances this time."

"I understand, ma'am," Connor replied. "There's just this one thing. Please."

"Go on, then," she said.

"Did your son have a friend in high school, name of Virgil?"

"He sure as hell did. Virgil Lee. Coach's son. Nothing but trouble, Drugs and break-ins. Why do you ask?"

"Nothing, ma'am. His name just came up and I was just wondering. I know I said one question, but do you mind if I ask you something else?"

"In for a dime, in for a dollar," Mrs. Reese said.

"Well, when we spoke yesterday you mentioned something about the governor asking questions," he reminded her.

"It's just something I said. Doesn't mean anything."

"But what if it does mean something?" he asked her.

"What is it you want to know?" she replied, her voice a demanding whisper.

"Did someone from the governor's office call you? Or maybe someone from his family?"

"I don't know what you think you know, Mr. Connor. But I'm going to ask you to leave me and my boy alone."

He ignored her words and instead said, "Do you know where Earl is now?"

"Like I told you before, probably somewhere doing Coach Lee's bidding. Good-bye, Mr. Connor."

He started to frame another question, but the click and dead air told him she had ended the call.

Connor looked over at Clooney, who was eyeing him with those big pools of love. "Looks like we're getting somewhere, big fella," he said.

He checked his phone, saw it was just over ninety percent charged. Not bad for now, but by this time tomorrow it would be less than half that, and there was no telling when he might be able to plug it in again. Or if there would even be an operating cell phone tower nearby. He decided he'd better make one last call and then turn it off for the duration of the storm, unless there was a dire emergency.

Danielle beat him to it.

"Hopefully you've found a place to hole up for the night and you're safe and dry," she said when he answered her call.

"In a manner of speaking," he told her.

"I don't like the sound of that," she replied. "Where are you—and tell me the truth."

"Somewhere safe and dry."

"Connor—"

"A few things came up and I was a little…delayed getting out of here."

"By 'here' you're telling me you're still there?" she pressed him.

He knew she was going to have a fit whenever he told her that he'd decided to stay put. Might as well get it over with now. "Wherever you go, there you are," he told her.

"Jack Connor—have you lost your mind?" she snapped at him. "Haven't you been watching the TV at all?"

"There is no TV," he told her. "The power's out."

"Please tell me you at least evacuated your place on the island."

"Of course I did," he said. "Do you think I'm stupid?"

"I'm going to withhold comment on that, you dumbass."

"Just remember to tell me when this is all over?"

"As long as you promise you'll be alive."

"Me and Clooney," he told her. "Cross my heart."

She hesitated a second, then said, "Clooney, as in George?"

"As in my new best friend," he told her, then quickly added, "Second best, after you."

"What are you talking about?"

"It's a long story. I'll tell you everything next time we talk."

"And when will that be?" Danielle asked him.

"Good question," he said. "I have to save my battery."

They both said their "I-love-you's," and then hung. Connor started to turn the power off, but then his phone rang one more time. At first, he thought it might be Danielle calling back, but then he recognized Caitlin's private cell number on the screen.

"Tat Man," he said. Something large crashed right outside The Plant, probably one of the spindly pines that grew in a tight cluster across the parking lot. "You have something for me?"

"A few choice words for being so stupid," she said. "But you don't want to hear that, and it's not why I called."

"So, what's up?"

"What's up is you were right. Same date, same year."

"Bingo," Connor told her.

"You want to tell me what you're thinking?" she asked.

"Not yet. I need to fit the pieces together, see how it all works."

"Well, you're going to have plenty of time to do that," Caitlin informed him. "The roads are closed, the beaches are flooded, and trees are down everywhere. And the main event hasn't even taken the stage. All the smart people have left town."

"Thanks for the support," Connor said. "Just so you know, I'm going to turn my phone off to conserve power."

"Stay safe," she said.

"So far so good," he told her.

Connor ended the call and powered the unit down. He set it on his desk, then went over to where Clooney was lying on his folded towel. He rubbed the dog behind his ears and endured a couple of strokes from his eager tongue.

"It's just you and me, kid," he said just as something bounced off the side of the building.

Clooney gave him a look that said that was just fine with him.

# Chapter 25

Hurricane Eleanor hit with a vengeance about ninety minutes later. The radio gave a blow by blow description of her approach, including current wind speed and wave height. Most of the broadcasts featured reports from various first line emergency personnel as they encountered flooded roads, fallen trees, and downed phone lines. The bridge across the Cooper River had been closed hours ago, and thousands of cars were trapped on I-26 headed west.

The National Weather Service reported the eye came ashore around Seabrook Island, just to the south of Charleston. That was bad news for the city of Charleston, which now fell just inside the right front quadrant. The guy on the radio dutifully explained that the right front quadrant was where a hurricane packed most of its punch, although anywhere near the eye of the storm was treacherous and extremely dangerous.

Out at The Plant the wind steadily increased and more and more things began to be hurled around outside. Wind poured through the small spaces around the front door, causing an eerie scream that set Clooney on edge. Branches and stray pieces of trash periodically scraped across the metal roof before launching into the air, and several battery-back-up security alarms had started screaming throughout the business complex.

Connor managed about an hour of sleep before he was awakened by the sound of a wrenching, ripping sound unlike anything he had ever heard before. Not in Michigan, and not in Iraq. At first, he didn't have a clue what was happening, but suddenly a bright gap opened in the roof overhead. Dozens of ceiling tiles flew away in an instant, and a torrent of water poured into the office. Connor squinted through the rain and saw that the metal roof had been peeled away like a sardine can.

He sprang to his feet and gathered up his sleeping bag and a few other things. "Shit," he cursed as he grabbed a clump of Clooney's neck fur. "We've got to move."

Connor guided him toward the back of the office suite, then pushed his way into the garage area where the BioClean truck was parked. The roof and ceiling were clattering wildly, and he suspected it was only be a matter of time before the wind reached in under the rest of the metal and began to peel it back. He edged around to the back of the truck and opened the rear door just as another section of the roof tore off.

"Load up, boy," he said.

Clooney didn't need to be told twice. He jumped inside and made room for Connor, who threw in his sleeping bag and then climbed up inside. He yanked the door closed, then moved forward toward the bench seat positioned up against the front of the compartment. Clooney watched him warily; he'd already been left behind in all that rain and wind out there and wanted to make sure this man was going to keep him safe and warm and dry.

"Over here, big fella," Connor said. Again, the dog did as he was told and squeezed over to where he was sitting. Clooney studied him with those big eyes that said, "You're the boss," and curled up at his feet.

There was another loud ripping sound as a large section of the roof flew off, followed by the hammering of rain on the top of the truck. The howling was almost deafening, but Connor flicked on the radio he'd stuffed into his sleeping bag as they'd fled into the garage. He only got static from the small speaker, and figured the station's transmitter must have blown off whatever tower it was bolted to. He turned the dial, found another voice providing the play-by-play of the storm.

"...No updates coming out of Charleston at the moment," the announcer was saying. "The city is flooded, and there's widespread damage throughout the low-lying areas—especially the barrier islands. Our prayers are with those who were unable to get out in time."

"That's us," Connor told Clooney above the din.

Clooney replied with a massive swipe of his tongue.

Several hours later the wind died and the rain stopped pounding the roof of the truck. The change seemed to happen within the space of seconds, the noise going from a deathly roar to eerie silence. It was as if someone were playing a trick on them both, trying to lure them out of the truck just to hit them with a pie in the face.

Or something much worse.

Clooney eyed him with a look of anticipation, and Connor remembered enough dog-speak from his childhood to know what it meant. "You need to go outside, bud?"

The dog's tail began thumping vigorously, so Connor cautiously opened the truck door and peered out. He was instantly struck by the sheer destruction around him, beginning with the gaping hole overhead. The roof was completely gone; just a few jagged sheets of metal dangled from the overhead steel rafters where they had been fastened down. Wet clumps of trash were scattered everywhere, and boxes of cleaning supplies that had been stored along the garage walls had been ripped to shreds, their contents scattered everywhere.

Clooney looked anxious to jump out and do his stuff, but Connor stopped him. The garage floor was covered with an inch or two of water, and even though the electricity had gone out hours ago he wanted to make sure it was safe for them both to get out. He tossed out an old towel, then a plastic bucket, but neither seemed to cause a spark.

"Me first," he said as he climbed out and touched a foot to the water.

Nothing happened, so he allowed Clooney to jump out, as well.

Connor hadn't seen such destruction since his days in Iraq. Hurricane Eleanor had leveled just about everything she touched. The damage to the BioClean garage was extensive, and the office suite was almost completely destroyed. Nothing had been left intact. His computer was on the floor, a shard of sheet metal protruding from the flat screen monitor. His desk was a tangle of wood and shredded fiberboard, and the contents of his file cabinets had been blown throughout the room.

The gentle whimper beside him reminded him there was a dog in dire need of a grassy patch, so he made his way toward the front door and unlocked it. Clooney shot out and raced across the pavement to a clump of bushes that had been stripped of its leaves.

Connor stepped outside into the false calm. Unbelievably the clouds overhead were parting and for a moment the wet parking lot seemed to sparkle in the sun. Branches and garbage were piled everywhere, and he was struck by the fact that every tree was completely bare. A massive limb had fallen across Moby Dick, the great white trailer, almost carving it in half. Windows had been shattered by the force of the wind and chunks of debris that had been hurled about. The brick walls had held tight, but everything that wasn't held in place by mortar or bolts was a victim of the storm.

A sudden gust hit Connor from behind him at the same time the sky seemed to darken. A blast of rain hit him on the face, and he realized the eye wall was upon them.

"C'mon, Clooney," he said. "Back in the truck."

The dog remained where he was, answering nature's long-anticipated call. When he was finished he trotted back over to where Connor was holding the shattered door open for him. Clooney stared at him with a look that said, "I'm not going back in there."

The crack of a falling tree changed his mind and he trotted inside. Connor locked the door even though it wasn't holding anything out, then led Clooney back into the garage. Another torrent of rain began to pour down from the darkening heavens, and both dog and man were happy to get back inside the truck. Connor grabbed some food for both of them, as well as a jug of water before pulling the door closed.

"The National Hurricane Center says Eleanor has begun to lose some of its punch," a different announcer was saying when Connor flicked the radio on. This one was a woman with a British accent, and she explained that the storm now was a strong Category Two. "The tidal surge is causing widespread flooding up and down the South Carolina coast," she said. "There are reports of bridges being out in some areas, and a number of pleasure boats have either capsized or washed ashore."

She went on to say that the brunt of the hurricane came at near-low tide, which meant the streets of Charleston so far had not flooded as much as predicted. "Still, we won't know the full extent of Eleanor's effect until the storm is well inland and emergency crews are able to assess the damage."

Connor turned the radio off to save the batteries, then turned on his cell phone. He waited for it to power up, then pressed Danielle's number from speed dial. There was a silence, then a click followed by the words, "We're sorry…we cannot complete your call at this time."

He tried again, then a third time, but it was clear that either a tower was down or circuits were busy with emergencies. Either way, Danielle was going to have to wait.

"Just a few more hours, Clooney," he said as he massaged the dog's ears. He checked his watch, saw that it was almost five in the afternoon. "How 'bout a little dinner?"

Clooney thumped out his answer with his tail.

The hurricane wrung out the last of its wrath just before midnight. Wind rattled the trees and belts of rain continued to pummel the roof of the truck. But Eleanor's ferocity had burned out, and Connor knew the worst of it was over. He and Clooney had survived.

Even though it was dark he opened the rear of the truck. Clooney jumped out first and began nosing around what was left of the garage. Connor worked his way around to the cab of the truck and turned on the headlights, which bathed the space in an eerie glow. Piles of leaves and scraps of trash had mounded just about everywhere, and one section of drenched drywall had fallen away. The entire roof was gone, as were all the ceiling tiles and air conditioning ductwork. The damage to the Palmetto BioClean plant was vast, and complete.

There was no point in unlocking the shattered front door. Connor kicked out the rest of the panel and stepped through it. Tempered chunks of glass crunched like diamonds under his feet. Clooney followed right behind, but Connor led him away from the sharp fragments so he wouldn't cut the pads on his paws. Again, the dog shot over to the soaked patch of grass and took care of business while Connor stared at all the damage.

In the distance he heard the wail of a siren. It was the first of many that would define the next few weeks, but at the moment it told him he wasn't alone here in the aftermath of the storm. Somewhere another tree fell, toppled by the wind and drenched earth. The air was filled with the odor of pluff mud and raw sewage, and even this far up the Wando River he could smell the salt surge from the ocean. Looking around at all the desolation made him feel as if he were a bit player in Stephen King's *The Stand*. Or Stanley Kramer's *On The Beach*, one of his dad's favorites.

Then a voice behind him said, "Hey mister—what are you doing here?" and he just about jumped out of his skin.

# Chapter 26

The voice was that of a cop on patrol, searching for the injured and keeping an eye open for vandals. Connor didn't fit either description, but the officer still wanted to know what he was up to.

"I'm checking out the damage," he replied.

"This your business?" the police officer asked.

"It was. The storm wiped everything out."

"Didn't you evacuate?"

"My truck wouldn't start." Connor threw a glance over his shoulder at the closed garage door. "I tried calling a couple friends, but they'd already bugged out."

It wasn't far from the truth, and the cop seemed to be buying it. "Where did you ride it out?" he asked.

"In the truck. It's in the garage."

"My God, man—you could've been killed."

"Yeah…the thought did cross my mind. How's it look out there?"

"If you mean the rest of Charleston, it's pretty bad," the cop told him. "Trees and power lines down everywhere, roofs blown off, like yours there. Lots of flooding near the marshes and beaches. You have anywhere to go?"

Connor shook his head as Clooney wandered up and nuzzled his leg. "I had a little place over on Sullivan's," he replied. "I doubt it's there anymore."

"Don't count on it," the cop said. "They're setting up shelters, mostly at local schools. You should try to get to one, cuz you can't stay here."

"Soon as I get the truck started."

The cop had walked in from the street, where he'd parked his Ford Explorer. He wished Connor well, patted Clooney's head, and went on his way. Connor kept an eye on him until he disappeared around the corner of the low-slung building, then poked his way back through the shattered door and into the garage. There was little Connor could do until daybreak, so he climbed back into the work truck and dozed for the next few hours, until Clooney started to get restless.

At first light he could tell it was going to be impossible to move the truck out of the garage. The roll-up door had been hammered by the wind for twenty-four hours and had come off the track in several places. Shards of metal jammed the path of the rollers, and after a few hard tugs of the rope that ran over the pulley at the roofline it was clear the door wasn't going to budge.

That's when Connor remembered the POS pick-up he'd parked at the back of the complex before the storm hit. He'd left it there so the cops wouldn't know there was anyone inside the place. Anyone dumb enough to try to ride out the storm.

He poured Clooney a couple scoops of kibble, then grabbed his keys and wallet out of the work truck. "C'mon boy," he said when the dog had finished devouring his breakfast.

Man and dog exited through the crumpled door and made their way around fallen branches and debris to the far end of the building. The old Toyota was covered with pine needles and a branch had fallen across the bed. Aside from a hairline crack in the windshield, however, it seemed unscathed, and the door creaked open when Connor pulled on the handle.

The engine started on the second try. Connor had filled the gas tank before driving it back to The Plant, so the needle was on "full." He let the engine run for a couple minutes while he went back to the demolished office and gathered up a few personal things. Clooney didn't let him out of his sight for a second, determined not to let anyone abandon him ever again. He tried Danielle's number one more time, got the same result as before.

"Load up, boy," Connor told him when he'd stashed everything in the cab of the pick-up.

Clooney didn't need to be asked twice, and a few seconds later Connor backed the truck around and pointed it toward the road. He had no idea what he might find out there, but at the moment anywhere was better than here.

He didn't get far. A half mile up the street he came to a road block, where a large tree had fallen from one side of the road to the other. A cop car was on the scene, blue lights flashing, while a man with a chain saw patiently sliced through the trunk. Connor pulled up behind the cop car and shifted into park.

"Stay here," he told Clooney, and then stepped out of the truck.

"Back in your vehicle, sir," a voice called over a P.A. speaker. "This is an emergency situation. You are not permitted out on the street."

Connor considered the situation, then walked up to the window of the police unit. It rolled down and a young cop—really no more than a boy—looked out at him.

"I'm here to help," Connor said. "Jack Connor, U.S. Army. Strong, willing, and able to do anything that needs doing." He hadn't played the Army card since he'd been discharged from Fort Drum, but he figured this was as good a time as any to start.

This clearly wasn't what the young officer was expecting. "Where did you come from?" he asked. "There was a mandatory evac in place. Governor's orders."

"I got trapped before I could leave," Connor said.

"I could arrest you," the cop said.

"That would waste your time and mine. Meantime there's a huge mess to clean up, and I'm volunteering to help."

The officer drummed his fingers on the steering wheel while he thought this through. Then he said, "Where's your home?"

"Sullivan's Island. At least it was. We rode out the storm at my business, just up the street."

"We?"

"Me and my dog. In the truck, there."

The officer didn't seem to care about any dog just then. Instead he said, "Well, you need to go home and stay off the roads until further notice."

"I don't have a home," Connor pointed out. "The hurricane blew the roof off."

"Look, Mr. Connor. We have an emergency situation going on. The governor just declared the entire South Carolina coast a disaster area. So unless you have a note from him, go back to your plant, or whatever you call it. Understand?"

"That phone there…does it work?" Connor asked.

"It's an emergency band, so yeah, I have signal. But don't get any ideas."

"No ideas, not from me," Connor replied. "But if you can make just one call—"

"I told you…it's reserved for emergencies only. And top-level state business."

"Would a call to the governor count as top-level?"

The cop glanced at Connor's tattoos and battered truck, said, "You gotta be shittin' me."

"I'm working on something for him, and I need to get in touch." Connor really wanted to talk to Danielle, but he could tell the officer took his job seriously. Instead he scrolled through his contacts until he found the number for Howard Luck's cell. "It's important."

The officer gave him a hard cop stare borne out of suspicion and doubt. "If this is a prank I'm slapping cuffs on you and hauling you up to Leeds," he warned him. "And since there's no bond judge going to hear any cases for at least a week, you won't be going anywhere."

Connor was willing to take the chance, and said, "Tell him Jack Connor wants to talk to him."

The cop dialed the number as Connor read it to him, then waited for it to ring. The governor finally answered on the fifth ring, and the cop seemed genuinely impressed—and more than a bit dismayed—that Connor had been telling the truth. The two men exchanged a few words, the cop keeping his side of the conversation to things like "yes, sir" and "of course sir." Eventually he handed the phone to Connor and said, "You can stay and help, long as you don't get in the way."

Connor nodded in agreement, then said into the cell, "Thank you, sir. I owe you."

"No, I'm the one who owes you," Howard Luck replied. "Just find whoever killed Ruby."

"Well, about that, sir," Connor said. "I'm getting close."

That seemed to pique the governor's interest. "How close?" he asked, anticipation in his tired voice.

"Top of the ninth," Connor told him. "I know you're busy, but I need to explain a couple things to you."

"What kind of things?" The anticipation seemed to click over to wariness.

"The kind that shouldn't be discussed on the phone."

"I see. Well, right now I'm up to my ass in alligators. The entire nation is looking to see how South Carolina responds to this storm, if you know what I mean."

"Loud and clear," Connor said, thinking, *You mean your political ass is on the line.*

"Where are you?"

"Charleston," Connor said. "Actually, Mount Pleasant. I wasn't able to get out before the hurricane hit.

"Dammit, Connor—I didn't hire you to be a hero!"

"I don't feel like a hero, sir. I'm wet, tired, hungry, and homeless."

Governor Luck thought for a second, then said, "Look. I'm going to be down there later this morning. I have a stop at the Custom House, then a church, and then there's a media thing at the Yorktown. If you can get yourself there at noon I can give you five minutes."

"I'll find you, sir," Connor replied.

He stuffed the phone back in his pocket and looked at the cop, who did not seem too pleased to be contracted by the Big Man up in Columbia.

"Stay out of the way and you'll do just fine," he growled.

Connor helped the man with the chainsaw carry chunks of tree to the side of the road, and thirty minutes later he was on his way again. The cop made it clear he didn't want to run into him again, so Connor took the entrance to the I-526 loop and headed toward Highway 17. Traffic was almost nonexistent, just a few emergency vehicles rushing from one incident to another. The radio confirmed that the governor had declared most of the state a disaster area, and the president had promised federal funds for those people and agencies in need.

Wherever Connor drove he found houses with roofs torn off or sliced in half by toppled trees. Cars were crushed by branches, entire porches were missing from homes, and fences and street signs were flattened. Every few hundred yards there was another tree that needed to be cleared or more debris to be dragged to the side of the road.

It took Connor two hours to drive the four miles to the area known as Patriots Point, where the USS Yorktown aircraft carrier was moored. He arrived early, so he took Clooney for a walk and watched the media vehicles as they began to pull into an area specially cordoned off for them. Normally an appearance by the governor would bring a large crowd, but most of the locals were miles inland, snaking their way back to the Lowcountry. The media outlets had assigned skeleton crews to stick around to record the mayhem, and that's who was starting to show up now.

At a quarter to noon a chime alerted Connor to a text. He felt a jolt of excitement, knowing that service was starting to come back online. The message was from Danielle, inquiring about his whereabouts and safety:

Hope my private dick made it through and survived unscathed. Your phone is probably low on power so we can talk later when you have time to charge it. Love you.

Connor started to type a suitable reply but realized anything he wrote would either be a lie or would invoke her wrath. He had not told her he was going to ride out the hurricane at The Plant, and she wouldn't be pleased to hear the reality now. Still, he figured it was better to get the fury behind him now, however, rather than postpone the inevitable.

He punched in her number from speed dial and waited with abject fear for her to answer.

"Connor…you made it! Where are you?"

There were several ways he could answer that question. He could either go with the complete truth, or shoot for total obfuscation. "I'm waiting here for the governor," he told her, going for total cowardice.

Danielle hesitated only a second and then said, "Where is here?" Evidently, she was wise to his methods.

"He's getting ready to address the national media on the deck of the Yorktown."

"Isn't that the ship you can see from the bridge?" she asked.

"That's right."

"Right there in Mount Pleasant."

Here it comes, he thought. "Right again." *Five, four, three, two…*

"Connor, you moron!" she shouted. Except she used a different noun instead of moron. "You lied to me. You said you were going to get out of there—"

"I tried to, Danielle," he said quickly. "Really, I did. But then someone attacked me, and I woke up in the trunk of a car with my hands tied behind my back. I managed to get loose and found the guy who grabbed me, and I took his gun and got away. But then I found a dog on the side of the road, and by the time I got back to The Plant it was too late, so we rode it out in the back of the work truck in the garage." It all came out so quickly there was no space between the words, and when he finished he just let his explanation hang there.

There was a sigh of exasperation on the other end, and then she said, "You're not lying, are you?" It was a statement, not a question.

"No, ma'am," he said.

Another silence, and then she said, "What did you say about a dog?"

So, he told her about Clooney, how he'd found him wandering on the side of the road with a note taped to him.

"You mean someone just pushed him out of the car and left him to die?" she gasped. "A dog with *a name*?"

"Looks like," Connor said. "He's really very sweet. He's sitting here with me."

"Dammit, Connor—you could have died. The TV says at least thirty-two people didn't make it."

Connor hadn't been watching the TV, and the radio wasn't getting into numbers. "It was pretty bad," he admitted. "I think my place on the island is gone, and The Plant is almost leveled. No roof, nothing."

"My god," she said. "It sounds like a war zone up there."

"Just about," Connor said, speaking from personal experience.

"So why are you waiting—" she started to ask, but then her voice clicked off and he lost her.

He tried calling her back, but once again there was no signal. Just an automated operator apologizing for no signal, inviting him to try again later.

# Chapter 27

Governor Luck arrived by helicopter ten minutes later. Connor wasn't sure where he was going to land or how they were going to meet up, but the media folks solved the first problem and Luck himself solved the second. Connor just followed the people with the cameras and microphones, and then in a whirlwind of dust the chopper touched down on a stretch of soggy grass just a few yards from the near-empty parking lot.

A minute later Governor Luck stepped out and greeted the small crowd with a wave and a salute. This was, after all, a war memorial, and South Carolina voters did like their wars. One war in particular, but anything that rang freedom's bell drew them in like skeeters.

As soon as Luck stepped away from the churning rotors he was bombarded with questions, idiotic stuff like "How bad is it?" to "Has the death toll gone up?" He waved them off, and a woman whom Connor presumed was some sort of PR flack told them a news conference would be held in ten minutes.

"Governor Luck has a private matter to attend to first," she said.

That's when a security official tapped Connor on the shoulder. "Come with me," he whispered in his ear.

Connor followed him to a waiting SUV, a black Chevy Tahoe with heavily tinted windows and a state government plate. The security guy opened the door and said, "Get in—the governor will be with you shortly."

"Shortly" turned out to be ninety seconds, and when Howard Luck climbed in the back the first thing he did was pull a flask from an inner pocket of his seersucker jacket. He unscrewed the cap and took a small hit, then handed it to Connor.

"Gentleman Jack, Jack?" he asked.

"No thank you," Connor replied. "I don't want to get pulled over later."

The governor couldn't tell whether Connor was serious or sarcastic. No matter—that just left more for him. To emphasize this point he took another swig, then stuffed the flask back in his pocket. Then he squared himself in his seat to face Connor, and said, "I don't have much time—this whole fucking place really is a disaster, and people are looking to me for leadership. What have you got?"

Connor stared him in the eyes, which already were a little glassy from the booze. He wondered what time the governor had started nipping this morning, or every morning. "What can you tell me about the night your son was born?" he finally asked.

"Peter? What does he have to do with this?"

"Just humor me here, sir. As I recall it was the fourth of July."

The governor glanced out the tinted glass, watched for a moment as the media folk looked for something to do. There was no driver in the front seat, so there was no reason not to talk. "Linda's water actually broke late on the night of the third," he said. "I was away at some lousy meeting or something and wasn't there for her. My wife was a very headstrong woman back then, and she'd decided she wanted to have our children at home. No hospitals."

"That's why Ruby was there," Connor filled in for him. "She was a nurse."

"Among many other things, yes," Howard Luck said.

"But there were complications," Connor pushed him. "Ruby ended up taking your wife to the Medical Hospital in Charleston."

"If you already know all this why am I here?" the governor asked. His brow was creased in confusion—or was it worry?

"Because I have a very important question to ask you, sir. I need you to answer it very, very carefully."

"I don't think I like the sound of that, Jack—"

"You hired me to find the person who killed Ruby Rollins," Connor explained. "In order to do that we need to be very clear on something. Something very important."

It was clear the governor didn't like the sound of this, but he dropped his head in a slight nod and said, "What do you need to know?"

"Have you ever heard of Emma and Henry Reese?"

The governor screwed up his face as if someone had just passed gas. Then he regained his composure and asked, "Who the fuck are they?" he asked.

Connor was no expert at reading faces, but something told him the governor was hiding something. "Neither name rings a bell?"

Governor Luck shook his head with certainty and said, "Never heard of 'em. But I hope they voted for me." Going for levity in the midst of confusion.

"I'm sure they did, sir," Connor assured him. "How 'bout Earl Reese?"

The name drew another shake of the head, and then the governor glanced at his watch. "I'm running out of time, Jack—"

"So is Lester Rollins," Connor reminded him. "No telling how things went down in that jail during the storm."

"I already checked on him. He did just fine." Governor Luck reached into his pocket and pulled out the flask again. He took a sip and said, "So who are all these people named Reese, and why should I care?"

"You should care, sir, because I think Earl Reese was responsible for Ruby Rollins' death." All of a sudden Connor wanted a sip from the governor's flask, but decided not to ask.

Howard Luck checked his watch again, then seemed not to care about the cameras or the microphones out there waiting for him. "Go ahead and tell me what you think you've got, Jack," he said. "But please—try to keep it to just the facts."

Connor did his best to do just that, but even the facts took a good ten minutes. Several times the governor's aide rapped on the window, but Governor Luck just ignored her. Instead he sat and listened intently while Connor filled him in on everything he'd uncovered over the past nine days. He explained about Ruby's altercation with a young redneck named Virgil Lee outside the Quick Stop, Reverend Parker's reluctance to betray a pastoral confidence, Mrs. Luck's alcoholism and depression, her alleged suicide attempt, and a white power movement that gave Earl Reese motive, opportunity and, probably, means.

When he had finished, the governor studied Connor for a full ten seconds that grew more uncomfortable with each passing tick of his Rolex. Then he said, "It's a fantastic story, Jack, but I just don't see how it all ties together."

Connor figured he wouldn't see the links, at least not right away. "It ties together through your daughter," he explained.

"My daughter? What does Karen have to do with all this?" Luck said, annoyance building in his voice.

"I know she's ill, sir. Something she picked up last summer that caused her kidneys to shut down. She needs a transplant."

"That's…how did you find out?" The annoyance in his voice had risen to the point of anger. "Medical records are sealed!"

"But church fundraising web pages are open to the public, sir."

Governor Luck closed his eyes and sat back in his seat. He studied the flask in his hand but did not drink from it. Finally, he said, "You're right, Connor. Karen is sick. Very sick. Her doctors are looking for a suitable donor, but they're having trouble finding one."

"From what I've learned, siblings usually are the best match."

Luck pulled out the flask one more time, drained the contents, and said. "You're talking about Peter—"

"Exactly, sir," Connor said. "I think you know why. And so did Ruby."

# Chapter 28

Half an hour later Connor was sitting at a roadblock on Ben Sawyer Boulevard. Three cop cars were parked lengthwise across the causeway leading out to Sullivan's Island, and several officers were explaining to angry drivers why they could not return to their houses. Some of the discussions apparently turned heated, causing the cops to produce handcuffs and threaten to use them.

Clooney sat patiently on the seat beside him, tongue drooping from the side of his mouth. The air conditioning hadn't worked since Connor had picked up the truck, so he'd rolled the windows down to let in some fresh air. Air that was expected to hit ninety-eight degrees by mid-afternoon, with humidity to match.

One by one the cars ahead of Connor's turned around and retreated to points unknown. Eventually it was his turn to be rejected, and a weary officer explained in no uncertain terms that he could not go out to the island.

"The bridge is stuck," he explained. "No through traffic."

"I figured," Connor said. "I was just wondering how the island fared."

"Lots of destruction and flooding, but fortunately no fatalities," the cop explained. "At least not that we know of. What's your interest, anyway?"

"I live out there," Connor said. "Me and Clooney, here."

The cop looked at the dog sitting in the passenger seat, then said, "I hate to break it to you, but a lot of places out there washed out."

"Yeah…that's what the radio said. Any word on when residents will be allowed out to check on things?"

"When the bridge is inspected we'll be letting small convoys through. That's gonna take a couple days. Until then you're going to have to be patient."

"Guess I don't have a choice," Connor replied.

The officer gave him a sympathetic shrug. "You can turn around over there," he said, cocking his head toward the gravel patch where everyone else had turned around.

Thirty minutes later he was back at The Plant, or what was left of it. Everywhere Connor went he had to dodge tree trunks, mailboxes, garbage cans, and law furniture that had taken flight in the wind. At one point he detoured to the supermarket to get a few jugs of water, but it was closed until further notice. So were most of the gas stations, and those that weren't closed had signs that read something like:

No Gas – No Water – No Shit

Connor parked the truck in front of The Plant and cut the engine. The late summer sun baked through the cloud cover like a steam iron, and a dense curtain of moisture rose from the pavement in thick ripples. Connor's shirt was soaked through to the skin, and Clooney was panting and drooling like a rabid dog. Fortunately, the outside hose still worked, and Connor held it while the parched dog lapped at the steady stream. He then held it over his head and let the cool water run down the length of his body. Clooney gave a vigorous shake and eagerly looked up at Connor, as if asking for more.

He spent the next hours making some sort of order from the mess. He dragged the twisted lengths of metal and broken furniture across the lot and dumped them in a pile. Tree limbs went in a separate heap, and mounds of trash were stuffed into plastic haz-mat bags from the service truck. The job took most of the afternoon, but Connor had nothing else to do. Clooney watched him from the shade of the damaged roof next door, occasionally drinking from the bowl of water Connor had set near him.

Eventually he gave up for the night. He fed Clooney, then ate two Hot Pockets he'd found in the office fridge. Without power he had no way to heat them, which didn't matter because the damaged microwave was now part of the heap. He found a chair that survived the falling limbs and carried it outside to the parking lot, where he poured himself a small dose of gin. He sipped it warm as he watched the sun glide through bands of clouds. The sky shifted from orange to violet to crimson and finally to black, as the first day after Hurricane Eleanor became part of history.

Two cups of gin into the evening a cell phone tower came back on line and Connor finally had a signal. A string of chimes told him he had three text messages and one missed call, and he decided to quickly check them before calling Danielle to update her on the rest of his day.

The first text message was from Jordan James, who had written:

I hear you stayed in C-Town. Dumb bastard.

Connor could have ignored the text, but until further notice Jordan James was his boss. And maybe he was a dumb-ass for staying put, but at least James had boots on the ground to assess things for him. So he typed a reply that read:

This dumb bastard is fine. Weathered the storm at The Plant, which is mostly gone. See you when you get back.

The next text message was from Mrs. Luck. Her words were brief and to the point:

You son of a bitch. What have you done?

Connor stared at the message on the screen, thought of all sorts of rejoinders.

There were so many ways he could reply to her accusations and allegations, but none of that would serve any purpose. He'd already guessed that Linda Luck had no complicity in this deal until it was far too late to do anything except go along with everything. Ruby Rollins had set her own fate in motion the night she'd whisked mother and child to the hospital in Charleston, and for a quarter of a century Linda probably had no idea what had happened. Not until her daughter's kidneys failed and she was hit with a stark dose of reality.

Connor decided not to engage Mrs. Luck in a battle of words, so he moved on to the third text, which was from Caitlin:

When you get this—and I know you will—I just want to say I'm glad you made it. Oh, and you were right about the HLA test. Now what?

It was too late to call her, but Connor wanted Caitlin to know he'd survived the storm and had received her text. So he replied:

Made it through the storm. The Plant is gone, but we can rebuild. Thanks for the word on HLA. Hope you're safe.

The missed call was from Danielle, but she either hadn't left a message or the system wasn't accepting them. Connor hit Danielle's speed-dial number and just about melted when he heard her voice again.

"I just want you to know I still think you're an idiot, Jack Connor," she told him.

"Every village needs one," he quipped.

She couldn't help but giggle at that and said, "Well, you can tell any village that makes an offer that you're already spoken for."

"I'll keep that in mind," he assured her.

"So…is it as bad as it looks on TV?"

"There's no TV. No power, either, and as you can see, cell service is spotty. Half the roads are flooded, and there's no way to get out to the island."

"So where are you staying?" Danielle asked.

"Well, this idiot is sleeping in the back of his truck until further notice."

The chit-chat continued a few more minutes, Connor describing conditions on the ground and Danielle explaining what she'd seen on the Weather Channel. Their combined reports painted a bleak picture of widespread damage that would take weeks to sort through. People who had evacuated were trying to get back to their homes, but state police were being cautious to only allow *bona fide* residents through the road blocks. So far there was no serious looting, and the authorities wanted to keep it that way. FEMA had already responded and both the governor and the feds were initiating disaster relief programs. And the news media were awfulizing the storm to catastrophic proportions, as only the media can do.

"Any word on your horses?" Connor eventually asked her.

"My what?"

"The horses at the sanctuary," he explained. "Did they survive?"

Danielle was quiet for a moment, and Connor started to expect the worst. Then she said, "Well, I was going to save this for when I come up there, but…well,

I just got a call from Mrs. Gregory. She told me the full force of the storm hit at low tide, so flooding was less severe at the farm than it could have been. All the horses made it."

"Excellent," he said. He'd never thought much about aging horses before, but he felt a very real chill of relief hearing Danielle's words. "So when are you coming up here?"

"Well, that's the other thing," she said. "The real reason Mrs. Gregory—Elena—called was because she and her husband had a lot of time to talk about things while they hunkered down with the horses. Anyway, she offered me the job."

"What?! You waited all this time to tell me?"

"I just found out myself. They need me up there as soon as possible, but I have to give at least two week's notice here. Right now, I'm looking at the Monday after Labor Day."

"Seriously? That's only—" he did some quick mental math "—seventeen days."

"You're awfully smart for a village idiot," she said.

"Smart enough to love you," he replied, going for triple points.

They chatted a bit more, and eventually Connor said he had to hang up to save power. No telling how long until he would be around a reliable power source. She said she understood, and they both tried to keep their "good night" banter to a minimum. Eventually they agreed to hang up on the count of three, but Connor killed the call at two-and-a-half.

It was too hot and humid to sleep in the back of the truck with the door closed, and Connor didn't want to run the engine all night to keep the AC going. He thought about rolling out his sleeping bag in what used to be his office, but the storm was producing bands of rain that came through in spurts. Eventually he and Clooney stretched out on the truck floor with the door propped open, hoping to catch an occasional puff of wind drawn through by Eleanor's trailing fingers.

All went well for the next few hours. At one point, Clooney jumped down from the truck to go find a bush, but he came right back and hopped inside. He lay down with a heavy sigh, and within two minutes Connor heard him ease into sleep. Connor drifted off not long afterwards, and likely would have slept until dawn if it hadn't been for a sharp metallic clang followed by the words "Oh, fuck."

Connor's eyes shot open at the sudden sound. He felt Clooney go rigid, then a low growl started to come up from his throat. Connor was sure that whoever was out there in the garage heard it, too.

"Just so you know, I've got a gun," Connor called out. This wasn't true; the Glock he'd taken off Danielle's now-ex-husband more than a year ago was sitting in an FBI locker somewhere. And the shotgun he'd lifted from a meth head up near Myrtle Beach was at the bottom of the Intracoastal Waterway.

But whoever was out there—and Connor was sure there *was* somebody—didn't know that.

"Either state your business, or get the hell out," he added.

But the person behind the noise did neither. Judging from the sound that had awakened them, the intruder was somewhere near the front of the truck, close to the driver's door. Right on the other side of the wall from where Connor was slowly and silently edging upright.

"You have ten seconds to get out. I spent two years in Iraq and I'm pretty good with a gun." Connor's actual time in-country was sixteen months, but in fact he did have a pretty good aim, especially in tight quarters. He didn't like to talk about it, but the result of that aim was why he continued to meet with Dr. Pinch once a week.

It also was why there always seemed to be a gin bottle close at hand.

"I'm not going to count it down like they do in the movies," Connor said. He realized now that he had committed himself, gun or no gun, and he had to follow through.

Another second or two passed, and then he heard the mad shuffle of feet. Whoever it was banged into something else hard and metallic, which brought another yelp of pain.

"Fuck me," the voice cussed.

Connor inched toward the rear door of the truck, whispering in Clooney's ear, "You stay here, boy."

But Clooney didn't speak English and had no interest in staying neutral in this fight. He followed Connor out of the truck with another growl, ready to sink his teeth into anyone or anything that threatened this man who had saved him from the side of the road.

Connor edged along the side of the garage wall and found a length of steel track he'd removed from the roll-up door earlier that afternoon. Weapon in hand he called out, "Keep moving and get out!"

There was a grunt on the other side of the garage wall, where the office once had been. Whoever had broken in seemed to be taking Connor's advice and was retreating. Connor hoped he would keep going, because he really didn't want to get into a hands-on fight with this guy. It was possible he was armed himself, and Connor didn't want to find out the hard way.

That's when Connor thought he heard the guy stumble over something in the dark. He searched his brain but couldn't figure out what it could be; he'd emptied the room of its contents and piled it all on the trash heap out in the parking lot. Maybe the intruder had tripped over his own feet as he'd tried to climb through the broken door, which was still in its frame. Either way, there was a loud thud and a yelp of pain as the guy went down.

The gunshot came a fraction of a second later, and Connor froze. He heard a grunt of pain, then nothing.

A micro-second after that he was back in that burned-out corner store in Iraq, the kid he'd just shot gasping his last breaths.

# Chapter 29

A single officer arrived seven minutes after Connor dialed 911. That cop took one look at the victim and realized he was still alive, but just barely. Connor had done his best to try to keep the guy breathing, stuffing a pillow under his head and talking to him in the dark, encouraging him to hang in there.

Occasional flashes of moon through the open roof provided enough light to show that the guy had shot himself in the chest, very close to his heart, and he was bleeding profusely. His lungs were gurgling, and a dark pool was forming under his body. At one point there was enough moonlight for Connor to get a glimpse of his pallid face, and that's when he recognized the guy from the white van backed into the trees down near the horse farm in Edisto.

Earl Reese.

By the time the ambulance arrived, Reese's lungs were struggling to keep working. His face was as white as the moonlit clouds above, looking almost unearthly. When the cop arrived, he'd told Connor to back off, but Connor kept his fingers on Earl Reese's wrist, monitoring his pulse.

The EMTs worked hard to get Reese stabilized, but it quickly became evident that he needed to get to a hospital, stat. The slug had punctured a lung and also may have nicked an artery near the heart. The guy was bleeding out, and there was only so much they could do there in the dark. The glare from their headlights was inadequate for what they needed to do, so they loaded Reese onto a stretcher and slid him into the back of the ambulance.

Connor watched it drive away, figuring there was no way Earl Reese was going to survive the trip. Too much of his blood had drained from his body, and Clooney was beginning to show an interest in where it had pooled on the floor. "Get away," Connor told him, pulling the dog back by the scruff of his neck.

By that time two other police officers had arrived on the scene. That made three total, and their job was to isolate the crime scene—if that's what it was—and conduct a preliminary investigation before a detective could be found to come out and take over. One of the new cops on the scene busied herself by taking photos of the blood and the gun, which was lying next to where Earl Reese had gone down.

"Tell us what happened," the other cop said. He was what would be described as an average white male: a little under six feet, mid-thirties, no remarkable features. close-cropped hair. He looked oddly familiar, but Connor couldn't immediately place him. The badge on his uniform said his name was Martin.

"All I know is what I heard," Connor told him. "Clooney—he's my dog—he and I were sleeping in the back of the truck, in the garage. All of a sudden there was a noise, and I got out to investigate. We both did."

"What came next?"

"What came next was it sounded like the guy stumbled over something, probably the broken door. I remember him swearing, and then the gun went off."

"What do you think he was doing out here?" Officer Martin asked. "Doesn't look like there's a whole lot to loot."

"That's what I can't figure out," Connor replied. "Anything of any value was ruined in the storm."

What he really couldn't figure out was why Earl Reese had come to see him, in the middle of the night. Unannounced and uninvited. With a loaded gun.

"Do you recognize the victim?"

This was where things could get dicey. The cops had already searched for a wallet and had found no identification, but Connor knew from experience that denying he recognized Reese could backfire on him. More than a few people knew he had been asking questions about the guy, and to lie about any connection now could be problematic in the future.

So he said, "It's possible I've seen him somewhere, but I can't say exactly who. Or where."

"You knew him?"

Connor knew what the cop was trying to do, so he patiently explained, "You asked me if I recognized him. It's possible I've met him, but I can't say for sure."

Officer Martin made a note of this in his notebook, then said, "The guy had a gun. What do you think he was after?"

Connor had been pondering this question from the moment he'd called 9-1-1, and still hadn't come up with a good answer. "That's what I'd like to know," he replied.

Martin asked him a lot of other questions after that, starting with why he was sleeping in the back of his truck in the first place. Did he have permission to be on the premises? Where did he live? Why didn't he evacuate like everyone else? Didn't he realize he was in violation of an official order? And why would the victim have been lurking around the place if he and Connor didn't know each other?

"What I'm wondering is how he got here in the first place," Connor said. "I mean, he must have had a car—so where is it?"

"Did you hear a car?"

"No. Which tells me someone either dropped him off or he parked it somewhere else and walked the rest of the way."

The cop who had been busy with the camera now came over and said, "He's right—go take a look."

There seemed to be a pecking order here, because Officer Martin did what she said. A little begrudgingly, probably because she was a woman, and misogyny was alive and well.

After they were gone the woman cop—she introduced herself as Sergeant Campbell—said, "I heard what you were saying, and I think you know more than you're letting on."

Again, there were several ways Connor could respond, and any of those responses could lead to future blowback. If anyone could connect Earl Reese back to his investigation there would be questions about why he hadn't been more helpful to the cops. But he'd learned the benefits of obfuscation while serving under one particularly obtuse Major in the Army, and that experience came to mind now.

"I'm not sure I know what you're thinking," he told Sergeant Campbell.

She gave him a look that said *give me a fucking break*, then said, "What I'm thinking is you know this guy, and you're shocked that he showed up here. With a gun. A gun that probably killed him."

"Any word on his condition?" Connor asked.

"Not yet," she replied. "And don't try to change the subject. I think you know who he is, even if you don't know why he came to see you."

Sergeant Campbell clearly was smart. Attractive, too, in an overweight sort of way that told Connor that she had been in better physical shape when she had joined the force. Job stress and bad diet that no doubt included lots of Krispy Kremes had been less than kind over the years.

"Look," Connor said, trying to buy himself a few valuable seconds of thought. "The guy looked familiar. I can't say for sure, but I think I saw him a couple days ago. I have a good eye for faces, and that one kind of stayed with me. But I don't want to say for certain."

He wasn't sure that she bought his explanation, and he got the impression she wasn't sure, either. But she lifted a shoulder in a shrug that said she'd let him run with his story, truthful or not, at least for the time being.

Earl Reese died later that day. According to the official report, a single bullet had traveled upward through his rib cage, ripped through the left circumflex artery, and punctured his lung. The EMTs had managed to keep him alive on the mad race to the hospital, and the on-call surgeon tried to patch things up as best he could. Reese was placed on a life support machine, but at two-twenty-three p.m. his heart gave out and he was pronounced dead.

Twenty-eight minutes later several of his organs, including both kidneys, were harvested for transplant. Connor did not learn any of this for several more days, but when he did he was not the least bit surprised.

According to the ballistics report, gunshot residue on Reese's wife-beater

T-shirt suggested he had been shot at close range. The medical examiner determined that the gun had been fired no more than six inches from his torso, and patches of GSR on Reese's hands was "not inconsistent" with the notion that he had stumbled and had shot himself. Sergeant Campbell had tested Connor's hands for GSR just as a matter of course, but the result was negative. Connor was not a suspect, and SLED—the State Law Enforcement Division—officially determined Reese's death was "accidental, per autopsy." The autopsy showed nothing to indicate otherwise, so the Reese case was officially closed.

But the story didn't end there. Reese's van—actually the same white van that belonged to coach Robert E. Lee the fourth—was parked several hundred yards down the road from Palmetto BioClean. He'd parked it in a weed-strewn lot behind a shipping container, and a forensics team discovered an old Guns and Roses T-shirt with dried blood caked on it. DNA tests were conducted on the blood and on several profuse sweat stains under the sleeves, and two conclusive matches were found. The armpit perspiration belonged to Earl Reese, and the dried blood matched that of Ruby Rollins.

Not only was it clear that Earl Reese had wielded the blade that killed her; the dumbass had either been too proud or stupid—or both—to dispose of the evidence.

The county solicitor pored over the evidence for forty-eight hours and grudgingly decided that he and his deputies had been a bit hasty in arresting Lester Rollins for the murder of his wife. Yes, Hurricane Rollins had been found with the murder weapon next to him, but copious amounts of his wife's blood were found on one of Reese's favorite shirts. The next morning Lester Rollins walked out of the Charleston County Jail a free man.

His daughter Laysha drove up from Yemassee to get him, and she then escorted him back to the house he had shared with his late wife. News crews from the local TV stations and two newspapers peppered them with questions as they drove off, but Reverend Parker shielded them from the incessant harassment.

"The Lord always knew Mr. Rollins was innocent of the crimes of which he was accused," Parker said to the cameras as they were getting into Laysha's car. "I prayed that he would deliver the truth upon us, and that truth set an innocent man free."

*Bullshit,* Connor had said to himself, then asked the bartender if he could switch the TV to a Braves game.

The next day Connor was allowed to go back to Sullivan's Island. The swing bridge across the Intracoastal had been repaired, and the police were letting small groups of residents through the roadblock. Connor showed them his license and was waved on through.

The island was a disaster. Virtually every building had sustained damage of some kind, either missing roofs or deck rails or stairs. Streets were flooded and pieces of lumber, fencing, window shutters, and tree branches lay scattered where the wind tossed them. Authorities had erected detours to prevent residents from going anywhere except to their own homes, and when Connor got to his little apartment on the marsh he just sat behind the wheel and stared.

It was gone. The storm surge had washed across the island and had taken out everything at ground level. His place had been constructed beneath a house that was erected on concrete pilings, and the power of the waves had ripped right through Connor's living room and pushed everything in its way out to the marsh beyond.

Connor got out of his truck and made his way around a mound of debris to where his front door had been. There was nothing left except the concrete pad and a few floor tiles. The deck from the house above had collapsed when its support posts washed away, and the grassy patch out back where he had watched hundreds of sunsets and consumed too much gin was just a slop of mud. Parts of his kitchen counter, his bed, and what was left of his furniture were a hundred yards out in the sweetgrass, where they were quickly becoming one with nature.

There was nothing left to indicate that anyone had ever lived here. Almost two years of his life had washed away, a grim reminder of the power of nature and the constancy of change. Here today, gone tomorrow, so don't get too comfortable. *We do not own this world*, Connor thought as he climbed back into the truck. *We're just passing through, enjoying the scenery.*

Jordan James' home had fared better, despite the fact that it was just across the street from the Ashley River in downtown Charleston. So had his first ex-wife's McMansion on Isle of Palms, where she lived with their son Eddie James. Both buildings sustained damage of some kind—everything in the lowcountry did—but it had been largely of the aesthetic kind. Palmettos were toppled, roof shingles had blown off, and the gazebo in Mr. James garden had been crushed by a falling branch. But both places were habitable, and ten days after the storm had passed through, life was getting back to normal.

Business at Palmetto BioClean also was in full swing. The official death toll in the Charleston area was put at twenty-seven, and several of those deaths involved residents who had stubbornly not evacuated their homes and ultimately suffered the consequences. Four of them had not been discovered until more than a week had passed, and by that time decomposition had become a serious issue. As a result, Connor and his crew were in high demand to clean up decay and putrefaction across the lowcountry.

About a week after the hurricane Connor got a call from Caitlin Thomas. He didn't have her working on anything at the time, so he was surprised when her name came up on the screen.

He went through their typical Tat Man routine, then asked her, "To what do I owe the pleasure?"

"Actually, I have a piece of information I thought might interest you," she told him. "I just got word that a body was found floating in the Black River, up near Kingstree."

"And just why am I supposed to be interested in this dead body?" he said, feeding into her flair for the dramatic.

"Because it was identified as Virgil Lee."

"Coach Lee's son?"

"The one and the same," she said.

"Holy shit. Any idea how long he'd been in the water?"

"A few days, at least," Caitlin told him. "And from what I understand he may have had a run-in with a chainsaw. He was found tangled in the limbs of a fallen oak tree, missing a few of his extremities, about a mile downriver from a highway bridge. SLED thinks he may have entered the water from there."

"On his own, you think, or maybe with a little help from his friends?"

"The case remains under investigation," Caitlin told him. "I just thought you'd like to know."

*Sonofabitch*, Connor thought as he hung up the phone.

Eight days after the storm Jordan James moved The Plant from its old location to another facility he owned in an industrial area further up the Wando River. The space was larger than the company needed but it had been vacant for months, and the warehouse provided ample room for all the supplies required for the post-hurricane clean-up jobs. It also had a shower and a small kitchen, so Connor was able to move in with an inflatable mattress and a dog bed for Clooney. The area was zoned against residential living, but Mr. James didn't mind and both the county and state governments had their hands full worrying about other things.

It was at this new location—dubbed The New Plant—that Connor awoke one morning a few days after moving in to the sound of someone pounding on the glass door. Clooney jolted upright, too, and immediately started woofing.

"Settle down, boy," Connor said as he dragged on a pair of cut-offs and a T-shirt. "I'll go see who it is."

But Clooney wasn't going to let him out of his sight and followed Connor to the door. A man was standing out there, peering through cupped hands to see what was going on inside. He was wearing old black jeans and a thin T-shirt from the Darlington 500, and a baseball cap was perched on his head backwards. His lower lip bulged from a massive wad of dip, and it looked as if he hadn't shaved in close to a week.

Connor recognized him as Coach Robert E. Lee the fourth, and he didn't look very good.

"Coach Lee," he said through the glass.

"I wanna talk to you, Connor."

"Well, here I am."

"Open the fucking door."

"Tell me why I should think that's a good idea."

"Cuz you look like the kinda man who likes to hear the truth."

Connor eyed Coach Lee through the glass. He had stepped back from the door and had crossed his arms across his chest in a move he probably thought was defiant, but actually was defensive. Still, as long as both hands were in plain view they couldn't be holding a gun.

He turned the dead bolt and pulled the door inward. Coach Lee took a step forward but Connor stopped him, saying, "Whatever this discussion is, we're having it out there."

Lee seemed okay with that and took a step backward to let Connor come out. He unfolded his arms and started to put his hands in his pockets, but Connor stopped him.

"Hands where I can see 'em."

Coach Lee looked genuinely surprised. "You think I've got a gun?"

"This is South Carolina," Connor replied. "Everyone's got a gun."

Lee raised his hands, palm outward. "Not me," he said. "Not today, anyways."

"Long as we keep it that way we'll both be fine. And for what it's worth, I'm sorry about your boy."

"What do you know about that?"

"Just what I heard on the news, sir. That's got to hurt a ton."

"Virgil had a good side, but it was the other side took hold when he was young and eventually got the better of him. Way it is."

"But that's not why you're here," Connor ventured.

"No, it ain't," Coach Lee said. "Earl Reese didn't have to die."

"He tripped and fell."

"You're not stupid, Mr. Connor. You don't really believe that."

"You think I shot him?"

"In fact, I do not think that. But Earl…that boy was afraid of guns. Virgil and me, we both tried to teach him to shoot, but he was scared. Sure, that gun was his. I know, because I gave it to him. But he was terrified of it. I suspect it had to do with something that happened when he was growing up. Something his father did, maybe."

"His hands were covered with GSR," Connor explained. "That's gunshot residue."

"I know what it is. And I call it bullshit."

"Facts don't lie, Mr. Lee."

"Maybe not, but they can be misinterpreted."

"What's that supposed to mean?" Connor asked him. "You think the evidence was tampered with?"

"You tell me," Coach Lee said. "You were there. What did you see?"

"It was dark, so I didn't see anything. But I heard someone prowling around the place, and then there was a shot. One shot. And when I got a flashlight I found Earl Reese on the floor, with a hole in him. The gun was near his hand."

"Which hand?" Lee asked.

Connor thought for a minute, then said, "His right."

"There you go," the coach said. "Earl Reese had almost no use of his right hand. Some neurological thing he had from when he was born. Kid couldn't have picked up a gun with his right, much less pulled the trigger."

Connor absorbed what Lee was saying but decided to put it through the mental processor later. "If he couldn't use his arm how did he get a license?"

Coach Lee blinked, then said, "What are you talking about?"

"A driver's license. He followed me all the way from my home down to Edisto. In a van that belonged to you."

"Just like God, the state of South Carolina works in mysterious ways."

"Doesn't answer the question why he was following me."

"You'd have to ask him," Coach Lee said as he turned to go. "Except the poor kid's not talking no more. Just like Virgil, and no one gives a shit."

# Chapter 30

The "grand reveal" had to be postponed until two weeks after the storm. The original plan was to hold the event on the street in front of Mrs. James' beach house on Isle of Palms, but the post-storm recovery effort was keeping all but residents' cars and emergency vehicles off the island. Plus, Eddie and his mother were living in a short-term rental on Daniel Island until the private elevator was functional again.

Instead, Jordan James had volunteered the use of a bowling alley out in Summerville, about twenty miles west of Charleston. It was one of several dozen businesses he owned throughout the lowcountry, and since this event was in honor of his son he was more than happy to loan it out for a few hours. The place had survived the storm unscathed, and the parking lot was large enough to accommodate all the camera trucks and satellite vans. Not to mention the hundreds of fans who were expected to show up for the festivities.

Everything was timed down to the last second to coincide with the taping of a popular talk show out in Hollywood. Because of the three-hour time difference everything had to be set to go right at four o'clock, on a day where the mercury had teased the hundred-degree mark. At three-forty-seven the second unit director announced that the taping was right on schedule. The car transport that had driven down from Charlotte had been parked a hundred yards down the street, and when the director gave her cue it started rolling. So did Eddie James, who had been in the bowling alley enjoying a game for the first time since his accident in Iraq. Despite the fact that he only had one arm and his brain was never going to recover fully from the impact of the blast, he managed to score a sixty-eight, without using the bumpers. Not quite the same kind of game he bowled when he was in a league, but it was probably his greatest victory ever.

That's when an assistant director from the TV show gave Eddie's mother and father the cue to come outside. Connor was already standing on a blue "X" that had been taped to the pavement, and he was perspiring from the fierce sun overhead. A make-up person had dabbed his forehead before the camera started rolling, and now another assistant director from the talk show was holding a microphone up to his face.

"Whatever gave you the idea to do this?" she asked him as another river of sweat trickled down the side of his head.

"Eddie James is a hero," Connor heard himself saying. "He and other brave men and women sacrificed so much in the name of freedom, and when they came home a lot of people forgot about them. Eddie almost lost his life out there in the desert that day. I was there and I saw what happened. When that bomb on wheels T-boned us we all could have been killed. We did lose one brave soldier in that explosion, but Eddie hung in there. He went through hell and back, but it was not his time to die."

Connor wasn't sure it was okay to say "hell" on television, but the assistant director with the microphone didn't flinch. Maybe they could edit it out later.

At that point Eddie rolled out the front door of the bowling alley. He was riding his electric scooter and was flanked by both parents while a camera operator was in front of them, backing up while taping their movement. Eddie's face was etched with a look of utter confusion, not comprehending what was going on or why the parking lot was a sea of humanity. Men and women of all ages and colors were screaming and waving at whatever cameras they could find, and Eddie whipped his head from left to right, trying to make some sense of what he was seeing.

As if on cue the massive crowd began to part. Then, at the far end of the lot, came a flash of brilliant orange. There was a throaty rumble as the 1967 Camaro inched through the parting sea, accompanied by an enthusiastic roar of approval. Another camera operator wearing what Connor recognized as a Steadicam was walking alongside the classic muscle car as it inched forward toward Eddie James.

"Oh mah got," Eddie said in his clipped speech pattern. He'd been working with a therapist over the past year and he was beginning to form full sentences. "Is at really ooh, Is-bell?"

He leaned forward and stared at the brilliant orange metallic paint job and the scooped hood, then glanced around anxiously. Connor realized instantly the panic that was building in his head and moved over to be by his side.

He clamped a hand on his buddy's shoulder and said, "What do you think, Eddie?"

"Whuh is zis?" Eddie asked him.

"We gave Isabella a facelift," Connor explained. "Come take a look."

He accompanied Eddie over to the car, which had come to a halt about ten yards away. The driver door opened and a man slid out from behind the wheel, leaving plenty of room for Eddie—and the accompanying camera operator—to get a good look inside. At that point another man emerged from the crowd and said, "Welcome to your new car, Eddie James."

Mild mayhem erupted after that. The man from the crowd was named David Topper, and he explained to the camera that he ran an organized called Vehicles For Vets. The goal of the group was to retrofit classic cars so wounded veterans could get behind the wheel again and go for a spin. Not necessarily on the highway at seventy miles per hour, but at least on a closed course where they could take their time and remain safe.

"Your friend here, Jack Connor, contacted us about six months ago and asked if we could retrofit your classic car so you could drive it again," Topper explained. "He explained your abilities, we came down from Charlotte and looked at the car, and then we adapted the mechanics to fit your needs."

Eddie James' mouth was hanging wide open as he soaked in what he was hearing. He stared at the car, then glanced up at Connor. "You did zis fer meh?"

"Isabella's your girl," Connor explained. "It's time you got her back."

"No, Jack...I gafe her to you."

Connor shook his head and said, "She's yours, dude. I just had the privilege of taking care of her for a couple years."

That's when the TV people cut away to the talk show host who was taping her program out in Hollywood. Connor couldn't hear what she was saying, but there evidently was a studio audience out in California that was cheering wildly at the story that was unfolding. Then the woman with the microphone who had interviewed Connor earlier said, "Mr. James...maybe you'd like to get in and see how the new controls fit."

Eddie didn't know quite what to do, so Connor lent a hand and helped him move from the scooter to the bucket seat. It was engineered to pivot to the left so he could slide in easily. Eddie still had good use of his left leg and arm, and he was able to position himself comfortably behind the steering wheel. Then he noticed the hand-controlled accelerator and brake grips and said, "Whuhs zis do?"

David Topper explained how he and his crew had modified the car so Eddie could drive it. "As long as you can turn the wheel and squeeze the grips you can do everything you need to drive again," he said.

"Hole shid!" Eddie said, another thing the director would have to bleep out of the show in the final version. Then he draped his wrist over the wheel, just as he had done a thousand times before he'd gone off to war. "Hop id, Jack. We gowan go fuh rite."

It turned out to be a slow ride, topping ten miles an hour along a fifty-yard straightaway between orange cones set up in the parking lot, but the beaming smile on Eddie's face made it all worthwhile. He quickly learned how to manipulate the hand brake and accelerator, and to shift and clutch with the new extension mechanism that operated the manual transmission. He knocked over a few cones on his circuit of the lot, and once or twice a couple fans had to jump out of the way as the car lurched through. But eventually Eddie brought the car back to where he had started, more or less, and brought it to a stop.

He sat there in the driver's seat, good hand on the wheel, staring through the windshield a moment as the past few minutes of his life sank in. Then he did something Connor had never seen him do, not even when the bomb had exploded and his arm had been ripped from his body and tossed him into the air.

He cried.

Connor had no idea that the car had been fitted with a camera, and the studio audience out in Hollywood was going nuts. All he knew right then was that Eddie James was the happiest man alive, tucked in behind the wheel of his car that a bunch of guys with big hearts had up-fitted for this wounded warrior out of the kindness of their hearts.

Out in Hollywood the talk show host was saying "Enjoy your beautiful new car, Eddie James," but neither he nor Connor could hear her. Nor did it matter, because Eddie was finally home from the war.

There was a small party after that, private, inside the bowling alley. The '67 Camaro had been carefully tucked back into its transport trailer and was on its way down to the James' house on Isle of Palms. The TV crew closed up shop and went back to wherever they had come from, and the remaining cheering fans were treated to free chicken sandwiches courtesy of a national fast food chain. The local dignitaries who had been invited lingered until the photo ops dried up, and then they disappeared as well.

Eddie and Connor were the focus of the party, something neither of them were very good at. Especially Connor, who had never felt the car was really his and had thought of as his "blood prize." Isabella was Eddie's and she deserved to go back to her rightful owner, plain and simple. He had never intended to be become a media hero for doing what he felt was right, but now it seemed everyone thought he had found the cure for cancer. All he wanted to do was slip out the back door and go home.

That was not to be. Jordan James must have read his mind, because he squeezed his shoulder with one hand and handed him a martini with the other.

"To the man of the hour," he said. "I can't tell you how much this means to my son. And to me."

"It was the right thing to do," Connor told him.

"He'll never be able to drive it legally—"

"He knows that. It doesn't matter. He'll be able to go on a slow drive around the block as long as someone is with him."

Mr. James had set down his own martini when he had gripped Connor's shoulder. Now he picked it up and touched it to Connor's. "Not too many people would have done what you did, Jack."

"Not too many people would have done what your son did, sir," he replied. "Here's to never sending kids in to fight a stupid war again."

"I'll drink to that," Jordan James said, and washed the rest of his gin down his throat.


Later that night Connor was slouched on his new sofa bed out at the New Plant. Mr. James had sprung for a television and Connor was stretched out with his feet up on a crate of cleaning solvent, watching nothing memorable. He hadn't sat in Dr. Pinch's office since before the storm, but now as he surveyed his new digs—missing the island and the marsh and the waterway beyond—a flurry of questions raced through his mind. At the top of the list: What had he really gained by riding out the hurricane when everyone else succumbed to common sense and evacuated upstate? He'd done a good job convincing himself it was because he'd been close to solving Ruby Rollins' murder, but that was a weak excuse when a catastrophic storm was bearing down on the lowcountry.

Second, and just as important: what drove his need to dive head-first into a murder investigation that had no direct bearing on his life? Sure, the governor had promised him a big payout if he was successful, but money had never been a big motivator in Connor's life. That was especially true when he was in the Army, putting his life on the line for a monthly paycheck of thirteen-twenty-four, after taxes. The concept of patriotism and serving one's country was one thing, but Pinch had caused him to wonder why he took unnecessary risks when other guys were attracted to less perilous pursuits, things like fishing or camping or NASCAR.

Try as he did, Connor was unable to come up with a convincing explanation. At the good doctor's urging he'd done a little research on risky behavior and cavalier attitudes, but had come up empty. Sure, he could have been repressing his guilt from Lily's death, but he'd come to believe that was more of an excuse than an answer. Ditto the tremors of PTSD that regularly invaded his dreams, the responsibility he felt for ending the lives of a couple young men who had never invited shock and awe into their country. He knew that a common response to the death of a loved one, or even one's buddies from war, contributed to risky behavior. People do things they would never do under normal circumstances, whether it's topping a hundred miles per hour on a winding country road or jumping out of an airplane with a parachute strapped to your back. Or wandering into a fire ant mound while searching for the truth about the murder of an elderly black woman.

He took a sip of gin, barely giving any thought to a commercial for a cut-rate insurance company on the TV when there was a knock on the front door. Clooney had been squeezed in on the couch against Connor's legs and now he bolted upright and uttered a low woof. "Who's that?" Connor said to the dog as he sat up.

Clooney let out a low growl and looked at his new master for clues about what he should do.

"Let's go take a look," Connor told him.

There was another knock on the door, but Connor didn't respond. Not immediately, at least. After what had happened to Earl Reese, Jordan James had installed a 24/7 surveillance camera under the eaves, pointing down at the door. The video system was tied into the TV, and Connor hit a button on the remote control to view what was going on outside. The image was somewhat grainy, but because the outside light was on he could easily identify his visitor.

Governor Luck.

"Good evening, sir," Connor said when he opened the door. "I sure didn't expect to see you tonight."

The governor stood there a moment, then reached out to shake his hand. "I saw on TV what you did for your friend. Not a lot of guys would do that."

"Not a lot of guys went through hell like Eddie did," Connor told him.

"So it seems."

The governor stood there in the doorway a moment, holding a black leather bag in his left hand. It took Connor a minute to realize he wanted to be asked inside, which meant this was more than just a quick visit.

"You look like a man with something on his mind," he said. "C'mon in and get out of the heat."

"Thank you," Governor Luck said. "I brought you something. Two things, in fact."

He stepped inside, and when the door swung shut he opened the bag and pulled out a bottle of Russell's Reserve ten-year old Kentucky bourbon. After that came two crystal tumblers, which the governor set down on the reception desk.

"You celebrating something?" Connor asked him.

Governor Luck pulled the cork out of the bottle and dribbled a little amber liquid into each of the glasses. "I like to drink with a man who gets things done," he said as he handed one of them to Connor. "That would be you, Jack."

"I appreciate the sentiment, sir. But I'm not sure I know what you're referring to."

"What I'm referring to is my daughter Karen is resting peacefully at the Medical Hospital," Luck said. "Her new kidney is functioning fine and she looks healthier than she has in months."

Connor nodded at what he was saying, then took a small sip of the bourbon. Damn, if it didn't taste smooth as satin going down. "That's what this was all about in the end, wasn't it, sir?"

"Excuse me?" Governor Luck said.

"The search for Ruby's killer. All along you really were looking for a donor who had similar DNA and would be a good HLA match."

Luck nodded almost imperceptibly and said nothing for a second. Then he took another sip and said, "I hired you to find a murderer. That's what you did."

"And it was just a coincidence that he happened to have the kidney that your daughter needed to stay alive."

"That was never a part of this," the governor said.

Over the years Connor had heard numerous times how you can tell when a politician is lying: their lips are moving. That was true now, but to call the governor on his subterfuge would be like exposing the world for all of Oz to see.

"How's the first lady doing?" he asked instead.

"She's recovering beautifully," Luck replied. "The entire family is doing well, in fact. Thank you for asking."

Connor got the feeling Luck wasn't there just to drink fine bourbon with him. He had something on his mind, and he wasn't going to leave until he shared whatever it was. He decided to let the guy get to it in his own time.

Eventually he did. He swirled the remaining liquid in his glass and stared at it a minute, then said, "Do you know why I got into politics, Jack?"

"I don't have a clue, sir," Connor replied. "Just seems like a big power trip to me."

"That's it for a lot of folks, for sure. But not for me, especially when I started out. I believed people and businesses were getting a stale deal. They paid taxes through their asses and what did they get? To quote the old song, 'another day older and deeper in debt.'"

"'Sixteen Tons,'" Connor said. "My dad loved the Johnny Cash version."

"Probably the best. But what I'm saying is I got into politics because every time you turned around in this state there was some sort of political scandal. Bribes, affairs, kickbacks, campaign sweeteners. A cesspool of good ol' boys and smoke-filled rooms. Still is, in many ways."

"Yes, sir," Connor said, simply because the governor stopped talking and he figured he should say something.

"I thought I could change things, bring some honesty and transparency to Columbia. And maybe I've done that, just a little bit. But there are times when it's necessary to be discreet and keep private things private."

"Like when family is involved."

Governor Luck nodded, apparently encouraged that Connor was getting this. "Especially when family is involved."

"If you're asking me not to talk about Earl Reese and his link to your family, don't worry. That's your business, not mine. You hired me to do a job and I did it. Discreetly."

"Yes, you did. And I know I sound imprudent even bringing it up. I just wanted to make sure we still had an understanding."

"My word is my bond, sir." Connor finished the bourbon in his glass and handed it back to the governor. *Please go home*, he was thinking.

"I appreciate that, Jack," Luck said as he tucked the glass inside the black leather bag. "Just like I appreciate all you've done for my family."

"What I did, I did for Lester Rollins," Connor reminded him.

"Of course." The governor polished off his glass and slipped both it and the bottle back into the bag. "Well, time for me to go. Best of luck to you, son."

"And to you, sir."

"Thank you." Luck picked up his bag and turned to go, then stopped and said, "Oh…I almost forgot."

"Forgot what?" Connor said.

The governor didn't answer, just reached into the pocket of his seersucker jacket and then pressed something into his hand. It was a set of keys.

"What's this?" Connor asked.

"Compensation for your time, son. If you don't like it, or prefer a different color, there's a three-day exchange guarantee. Just bring it by and we'll change it out for you, or you can have the cash price on the sticker."

"Sir?"

"Like I said, you did a fine job," Governor Luck told him. "That is payment in full. I'd prefer this not go on the books, so no receipt."

And with that he was gone.

Connor stood in the small office a moment, looking at the keys with the familiar Chevrolet logo on it. He heard an engine start outside and tires chewing through the gravel lot. Then, when the governor clearly was gone, he opened the door and stepped outside to see what this was all about.

What he found was a brand-new Chevrolet Camaro. Brilliant orange, with a scooped hood and rally stripes, convertible top, and twenty-inch chrome rims.

# The Eye Wall

The following evening Connor and Danielle were invited to Lester Rollins' welcome home party. Fact was, next to Rollins himself, Connor was the guest of honor. Everyone in the joint knew that without his persistence, old Hurricane Rollins would still be locked up on Leeds Avenue.

The celebration was held—naturally—at The Nest on the bank of Pelican Creek. The roof had been ripped off in the storm and the old wood deck was gone, but J'Neece Taylor had been wise enough to buy an insurance policy that covered a full replacement of both. The roof work had not been completed yet so the rafters were open to the moon and stars above, but on that hot summer evening in early September a good breeze was blowing in from across the marsh. The lack of cover was welcome.

J'Neece had set up some picnic tables at the edge of the creek to make up for the lost deck. That's where Connor and Danielle were seated now, nursing martinis served in jelly jars. A serious spread of oysters, shrimp, beans, okra, crab, and gumbo had disappeared quickly, and the crowd inside now was dancing to the groove of Blacks and Blues, with Walter Hill on bass and Lester Rollins wailing on the sax. They were well into the Muddy Waters classic "Hoochie Coochie Man," and Connor found himself nodding gently to the beat. Far in the distance a skiff was slowly drifting down the crooked creek, a lone light on the bow looking like a firefly in the marsh. The moon through the pines caused him to know why so many folks who grew up down here never had a mind to leave.

Clooney had joined them for the party, and now was lying on the grass at Connor's feet. He had one paw tucked under the other and was staring out at the creek, lost in a place where dogs go when they don't have a care in the world. Occasionally he would glance up just to make sure Connor was still there, and then he would drop his head again and exhale a heavy dog-sigh.

Connor glanced over at Danielle. At that moment he thought she had never looked lovelier, even with those worry lines creasing her brow. One of the horses at the farm had developed a bad infection after the storm, and even though he was on the mend there remained the risk of a downturn. She had explained it all to Connor when he'd picked her up in his new car. He had made good on Luck's three-day guarantee and traded it in for the cash equivalent, then went down to Savannah Highway and bought the sixty-nine Plymouth Fury he had seen through the window of the governor's limousine. The yellow one with the black racing stripe and the 383 V8 under the hood.

Danielle was wearing a black skirt, cut well above the knee, with a white top that hugged every curve. Her hair was pulled away from her face in a tight French braid, and despite being a minimalist she had applied a fresh dusting of eye shadow.

"I suppose now is as good a time as any to say I'm sorry," she told him as she cradled her jelly jar in both hands.

He glanced over at her, found a streak of moonlight lighting her deep blue eyes. "Sorry for what?" he asked.

"For giving you so much grief about this job," she said. "If it weren't for you, that poor man would still be locked up."

"All's well that ends well," he assured her.

He was reminded again of why he loved this woman so much. Over the past year they had had built a rhythm in their lives, a perfect fit that at times seemed almost too perfect. Connor had never been one to believe in soul mates, and Danielle's divorce had diminished any illusions she'd once had about grand passion. But tonight, he figured that if he did believe in such things, the woman sitting next to him gazing out at the moon glimmering on the creek would have to be his.

He fingered the small box in his pocket, just as he had done almost a month ago at the restaurant on Shem Creek. If he was ever going to find the right time and the right place, this was it. He started to take out the box when he heard the familiar refrain from a song in Disney's *The Lion King*. "The Circle of Life," which also happened to be the ring tone for Danielle's cell phone. Ever the workaholic, she'd forgotten to turn the damned thing off.

Clooney looked up at her, almost flashing her a look that said *really?*

Danielle sneaked a guilty peek at the screen to see who was calling her. She did an honest double-take, then said, "I'm sorry, Connor—this'll only take a minute."

"No problem," he told her. "Life goes on."

She gave him her best apologetic look: wide eyes, innocent face, letting him know this wasn't her fault. "It's a work thing. Sixty seconds, max."

"Do what you have to do," Connor said. "I'll just sit here and commune with the moon and the stars."

Danielle hit the answer button, and Connor couldn't help but hear her side of the conversation. It was mostly things like "Really? That's encouraging. No, let's hold off on increasing the dose. He should improve by morning. I'll check on him when I get home. Okay, you too."

Then she hung up and made a show of turning off the ringer. Then she leaned over and kissed him, saying, "Buster's getting better."

"Hope so," he said. Buster had been Danielle's first test the day she showed up for her new job, and she had shared her concerns with Connor. "He's come too far not to pull through."

"Thank you for being who you are," she said as she reached out and squeezed his hand.

While Danielle had been on the phone Connor had actually opened the box while it was in his pocket. Now he fingered the marquis-cut diamond, knew without question this was the right thing to do. He and Danielle had talked around the edges of spending the rest of their lives together, and they both had known it would not be easy while she was down in Orlando and he was up here in Charleston. But she had surprised him by making the big leap

Connor gently took her hand and subtly turned it over, slipping the ring into her palm. He knew enough not to put it on her finger, not just yet. With Danielle things had to be done in baby steps.

She had not sensed the ring in his hand before, had not known he was even holding something until she felt the faceted stone pressing against her skin. She shot him a suspicious look as she released her grip on his hand, and saw the diamond.

The expression on her face was a mix of excitement, love, fear, and worry. It was accompanied by an audible gasp as she stared at the ring, then at him, then back at the ring. It lay there in her palm, the light from the moon reflecting off it.

"Connor—what is this?"

Connor thought it was pretty clear what it was, so he did what he'd spent the last four weeks planning to do. He picked up the ring, turned it over in his fingers, and held it in front of her. Then he shifted his position on the picnic table and gazed into her eyes. He could see the wheels spinning in her head, moving just as fast as the cogs that were whirring in his own brain, the ones that were yelling at him, *Dammit, Jack—just do it. Ask the damned question.*

But his jaw muscles chose that moment to jam and his lips froze with a goofy look that made him look like a politician caught with his hand in some lobbyist's shorts. Maybe he'd been spending too much time with Governor Luck. At any rate, Danielle stopped staring at the ring, raised her eyes until they were fixed on Connor's and said, "If this is what I think it is, isn't there usually a question involved?"

He nodded, momentarily at a loss for any words at all, let alone a question. He'd had this all worked out well in advance, thought of all the right words to string together not to sound like an imbecile. But at that very moment, with that spectacular moonscape and the most incredible woman he'd ever met, his brain got the hives.

"You're right," he eventually agreed. "A question is, indeed, in order."

So, he took her hand in his, looked right back into those deep eyes of hers and conjured up the words he'd rehearsed in his mind ever since he'd walked out of the jewelry store on King Street. He exhaled a breath he hadn't realized he'd been holding in his lungs, leaned over and kissed her as he slipped the ring on her finger.

"Danielle Simmons, will you marry me?" he asked her, suddenly terrified by what he would do if she turned him down. A man's worst fear—that and dying a virgin. But now, as she again stared at the diamond, the corners of her mouth lifted in a smile, and those fears immediately vanished in the moonlight.

That's when she said, "What the hell do you think, you moron? Of course I will."

Like most men when placed in the same situation, Connor had not thought of what to say next. He'd expected—at least hoped—that Danielle would say "yes," but he had not considered that this answer would require a response on his part. So he just looked at her again, the same imbecilic look on his face, and said, "That's great."

Then it hit him all at once. What he had asked, what she had said, and the fact that the two of them were now engaged. So he leaned over and gently took her face in his hands and kissed her. Hard and long.

"This is so...totally unexpected," she said when he finished. She was shaking her head and studying the ring on her finger.

"I believe that was the point."

He looked at her, remembering instantly what had attracted him to her the moment he first saw her. Well, not the first moment, because that was when she had unloaded a painful dose of pepper spray in his face. But when she had come back to apologize he found himself instantly attracted to her self-assurance, the distinct sense that she was comfortable in her own skin.

They talked then, mostly about family and friends and when to tell them. They discussed whether they should have a big wedding or just a small, private ceremony with cocktails and munchies on the beach. Considering this was the second time around for both of them they opted for Plan B. Should they have it somewhere in or around Charleston, or in Michigan or Georgia where they had grown up. Then Connor asked her where she might like to go for their honeymoon, if she could go anywhere in the world.

"The islands," she answered without hesitation. "Somewhere in the Caribbean where the water is warm and I can skinny-dip with the turtles."

Connor pictured this in his mind and grinned: *lucky turtles*.

"Works for me," he said, thinking he would travel to Antarctica in July as long as he had Danielle beside him.

A few minutes before midnight they decided to leave. Neither wanted to spoil the moment but Danielle had to be up early with her horses and Connor had a clean-up job in North Charleston. The party was going full-bore inside and probably would continue until dawn. The band was going more up-tempo and contemporary now, blasting out a high-octane version of "Proud Mary." Even outside at the edge of the creek the ground was trembling from the force of the music and the bodies moving to the beat inside.

Connor had parked the Plymouth Fury about a hundred yards up the unpaved road. He'd pulled it as far as he could onto the shoulder without sliding into the drainage ditch, which was filled with run-off from the storm. Parking had been scarce, so he'd had to wedge it in between an oversized sedan from the eighties and an old Ford pick-up slathered with mud.

Now he slipped his arm around Danielle's waist and they strolled through the moonlight up the dusty lane. He caught her sneaking an occasional peek at her ring, but neither of them said much of anything as they slowly strolled along. As they got to the car he clicked the key fob to unlock the doors.

"Your place or mine?" he asked her.

"Mine is closer," she said. Part of her arrangement with the Second Chance Ranch was a small apartment down near the stables, complete with kitchen and a patio overlooking one of the fenced pastures. "And I have to be up at dawn."

"Are dogs allowed?"

"The Gregorys have four of them," she said. "I don't think they'll mind."

Connor opened the door for her, but Clooney edged in front of her and jumped in first.

"Back seat," Connor ordered him.

Clooney knew what that meant and leaped into the back, while Connor took Danielle's hand and gently helped her into the car.

"You're still the last gentleman in Charleston," she told him as she slid in. It was a joke that went back to their first real date together, the first night they kissed and very likely would have done more had he not suggested they take their time.

Connor glanced around at the forest and the glimpse of moon overhead. "I don't think we're in Charleston anymore," he said, as he leaned over and kissed her.

Just then a shadow eased out of the night from behind a car parked on the other side of the road. Because it was dark Connor only sensed the presence of something—*someone*—moving swiftly up behind him. It was a heightened sense of awareness that had been with him ever since he'd come back from Iraq, and Dr. Pinch had been working on with him to take control of the moment. Usually it turned out to be nothing, but tonight he definitely sensed it was something.

Clooney let out a loud *woof* just as Connor felt the hard barrel of a gun press against his spine. Then a voice said, "Don't you fucking move!"

"You really don't want to do this," Connor heard himself say.

"Keep your fucking mouth shut, no one gets hurt," the voice said. It was more of a snarl, but Connor picked up something familiar about it just as one last tumbler in his mind went *click*.

In the backseat Clooney wasn't sure what he was supposed to do. He let out another *woof*, but he wasn't in a position to do anything more. And he somehow sensed that whatever he did could get his people killed.

"Get your dog to shut up or I'll shoot him," the man with the gun said.

"Put the gun down, Peter," Connor told him. "This isn't going to work."

"You're a smart man," Peter Luck said. "Just not smart enough."

"Jack—do whatever the man says." Danielle said. *Jack,* not *Connor.*

"Listen to your lady friend, asshole—"

"Give him your wallet," she added. "Whatever he wants."

"He doesn't want my wallet," Connor said. "Do you, Peter?"

"I told you—"

"I know—shut the fuck up. But think this through. Whatever you're planning to do, it's not going to go well for you."

There was an instant of hesitation, and in that moment, Connor knew Peter Luck was harboring doubt. Doubt over what he was doing here, and doubt about what he should do next.

Then he said, "Move away from the car, Connor. Slow and easy."

Connor did what Luck told him. He backed up several steps but made sure he remained between the gun and Danielle. Then he turned and faced Peter in the darkness.

"It was all going so well for you," he said. "Now you've messed it all up."

"Shut up!" Peter Luck said, a thread of panic in his voice. That was not good.

"Just walk away," Connor told him. "I promised your father I was done with all this."

"Too late. He already knows."

"Your father loves you, Peter. Your mother, too."

There was a moment of silence, and then Luck said, "But he's not my father. And she's not my mother."

Connor knew there were a lot of things he could say right now, but none of them would make a bit of difference. Peter Luck was consumed by an idea that no amount of reason or empathy would cure, and his blistering resentment had festered ever since he'd learned the truth. He and Earl Reese had been born the same day, and after Ruby Rollins had rushed Mrs. Luck and her newborn son to the hospital she had quietly switched them. Since she had been a pediatric nurse on that very unit she knew her way around, and looked for the opportunity to trade them out. Ruby Rollins had put it upon herself to make sure Mrs. Luck went home with a healthy baby boy, and nothing could reverse that reality now.

"You don't have to do this—"

Luck stared down at his feet for a second, not nearly long enough for Connor to make a move. He had no doubt the gun was loaded, and this scene could easily go downhill in a fraction of a second.

"It was that nigga bitch did this," Luck said when he glanced up again.

"And you killed her because of it."

"She fucked my life up."

"Because of her you got to be the governor's son," Connor reminded him.

"Damn straight. But then when Karen got sick that nigga started to see God. She heard His words in her head and all that shit. He told her she had to right her past wrongs, and at the top of the list was me."

"C'mon, Peter. Put the gun down—"

"She took away everything I had," Luck continued. "Overnight my life turned to shit."

"How did you find out?" Connor asked, trying to distract him. "About Earl Reese?"

"How do you think? Ruby told me. Part of her atonement tour, I guess."

"And you confronted him?"

"Dumbass was just on the plus side of retard," Luck said with a shrug. "By that time my father had hired you to get Lester out of jail, so I told Earl you were trouble. I figured he'd take it from there, dumb as he was."

"You planted that bloody shirt in Earl's car."

"Like I said, the bastard was a fucking retard."

"That bastard was the real Peter Luck. You led him to me. Not once, but twice. And then you shot him to make it look like an accident."

"Doesn't matter, dick-head. None of it matters."

"What about the GSR?" Connor pressed him. "What I want to know is how you got it on Reese's hands?"

"You can pull a lot of strings when you're the governor," Luck said. "Or his son."

Then another thought struck Connor, something that didn't make sense. "You poisoned your mother," he said.

"She wasn't my mother," Peter said with a snarl.

"Still, you spiked her drink. So why did you then try to save her?"

"Her heart wasn't beating and she wasn't breathing. Her skin was blue. I thought she was dead."

"So, you called your father and made like you were a hero trying to rescue her."

"A minor mistake."

"Desperate thinking leads to desperate deeds," Connor told him.

"Yeah? You want to know what I'm thinking now?"

"I hope you're thinking about giving this up—"

"Too late for that," Luck said. "Actually, what I'm thinking is which one of you I'm going to shoot first. You, your girl, or your dog, there."

It was then that Connor realized this was going to end badly if he didn't do something. Anything. Right now.

He moved forward and planted himself squarely between Peter Luck and the car. His body was blocking Danielle and Clooney, so any first shot Peter took would have to be at him.

Luck clearly had not expected this move, and he lunged at Connor. Connor braced himself for the blow as their bodies collided. He felt something hard in his abdomen, figured it was the barrel of the gun. Figuring he had only a second or two left in his life, he brought his head forward as hard as he could, cracking Peter Luck's skull with the sound of a snapping tree branch.

Luck let out a scream and threw all his weight into Connor, pushing him backward toward the old Plymouth.

Until now Clooney had not recognized the danger of the gun, or the harsh words that were being exchanged. But he knew when someone was physically attacking his master, and that was his trigger point. So to speak. He flew out of the back seat and caught Luck's arm in his teeth before he even touched the ground.

Peter Luck screamed and the gun fired. At the same instant Connor smacked his own head on the windowsill in an explosion of stars that bounced around inside his skull. Then he saw another white flame erupted from the barrel of Luck's gun, and he heard Danielle let out a muffled groan.

Now Clooney went for Luck's throat. Luck tried to pry the sharp canine teeth loose, but Clooney had clamped on tight and was not about to let go.

"Sonofabitch," Luck snarled as he staggered backwards. "You are *so* going to die."

Luck got off another shot that smacked into the passenger door just inches from Connor's head. At the same time, he managed to wrestle his arm from Clooney's jaws, then spun away as Connor launched himself off the car and again charged at him. The collision of bodies pushed them both backwards into the road, as one more muffled shot rang out.

Connor sensed Luck's body shudder as they both collapsed to the ground. Luck hit the dirt with the back of his head and did not move, the gun still gripped in his outstretched hand. In the light of the moon Connor saw the look of shock and pain in his eyes, then grabbed the pistol and scrambled away. He felt something wet and rough on his face, realized Clooney was licking him. Either to make sure his master was okay, or because he had a feral taste for blood.

That's when Connor heard Danielle, her voice barely a whisper.

"I think I'm hit," she said.

He heard her gasp for air, two short breaths, and then her voice choked off. She was slouched to one side in the passenger seat, blood oozing from the open wound where the slug had torn into her.

"No!" he cried out as he ripped off his shirt and pressed it to her chest.

"It...burns—"

"Stay with me, Danielle," he pleaded with her. "Just—stay with me."

In the distance he heard the band playing something that sounded like John Lee Hooker. Lester Rollins was still wailing away on his sax, and people were singing and dancing to the music. Clooney had inched close and was whimpering; he could tell something bad was going on and cocked his head in confusion.

"Danielle...please," Connor said to her, his voice no more than a whisper.

"Jack...I love you," she said.

That's when he felt something vibrate against his leg. At first, he thought maybe he'd been shot in the hip, and just didn't know it. He reached down just as he felt the vibration again.

It was his phone, which he had set on vibrate earlier, when Danielle had taken her call from the horse ranch. Just before he'd given Danielle the ring. Now he pulled it out of his pocket, saw the familiar number on the screen.

"Caitlin!" he screamed.

"Connor—it was Peter Luck all the time," she almost yelled at him, her voice filled with fear. "He killed Ruby Rollins."

"I know—"

"He just shot his mother and fiancé," she barked. "Get out of there now! He mentioned something about knowing you were going to Rollins' party at that old roadhouse—"

"Too late," Connor said. "I need an ambulance!"

"I'm on it," she said. "I called the cops as soon as I heard what he'd done."

That's when he heard the siren, followed almost immediately by a glimmer of bright blue shadows flashing through the tall Carolina pines. The siren grew nearer, but it still seemed an ocean away.

Connor dropped his phone and touched a finger to Danielle's neck. Her pulse was erratic, little more than a quiver.

"Jack," she whispered.

"Shhh," he told her, forcing the panic from his voice. "Stay with me."

"I see a light—"

"No—" Connor warned her, a lump rising in his throat. "Turn away from it."

"It's so…blue. And flashing."

He started to reply, but his mind momentarily slipped back to Iraq and he was wrapping a length of his torn shirt around Eddie James' arm. Or what was left of it. Blood was everywhere and guys were screaming. Connor's own head had throbbed like a sonofabitch, but he'd hung in there, keeping Eddie alive just long enough for a chopper to show up and whisk him back to the surgical team at the F.O.B.'s medical hospital. But there were no helicopters tonight, here on the edge of Pelican Creek, just a lonely moon casting its solemn glow on this desolate stretch of unpaved road winding through the tall Carolina pines.

At that instant a county sheriff's car rounded the final bend in the road and skidded to a stop. The high beams from the headlights lit up the woods like a flood lamp, and seconds later a uniformed deputy was crouched beside Connor on the ground.

"What's going on?" he wanted to know.

"She's been shot," Connor replied, his breath ragged. "You've got to save her."

"Who's that?" the cop demanded, looking at Peter Luck.

"The bastard who shot her," Connor said. "Please…don't let her die."

"Why I'm here," the deputy said as he motioned for Connor to back up. He felt Danielle's neck for a pulse, then listened to her breathing. This brought a look that Connor interpreted as cautious optimism, but the cop said nothing as he gently pulled the fabric away from the wound above Danielle's left breast. The entry wound was about the size of a nickel and there was a lot of blood, but it was oozing rather than gushing. Another positive sign.

So was the ambulance that appeared thirty seconds later, its high beams sweeping through the woods like a searchlight. Just moments after that, two paramedics were kneeling over Danielle and the deputy was saying to them, "Two gunshot victims. That one appears to be dead, this one's walking the line."

"Please save her," Connor said.

"We'll do our best sir," one of the paramedics said. To Connor he was just a voice on a warm summer night, one that offered a slim chance of hope.

"I'm thinking the bullet nicked the subclavian artery," said the other one, another anonymous voice in the moonlight. "Probably punctured a lung."

"Is she going to be okay?"

"We'll do our best," the first one told him.

Things happened fast after that. The two EMTs worked feverishly to stabilize Danielle, then hustled her into the back of the ambulance. Connor was encouraged by the rise and fall of her chest, slow as it was, and a tiny flicker of an eyelid. He started to ask if he could ride with her, but then two more sheriff's vehicles came plunging down the dirt road and sizzled to a halt on the dry dirt.

Connor immediately recognized the man who got out. It was the sheriff himself, the glum-faced man who just days before had been forced to concede that he'd gotten it all wrong. This was just before he'd set Lester Rollins free, reading a prepared statement to every reporter and news crew from across the Lowcountry.

"Don't even think of going anywhere," he said in a booming voice.

"But that's my fiancé—"

The sheriff glanced at the driver, said "Get her out of here," then looked back at Connor.

The ambulance sped off in a storm of dust as the sheriff walked over to where a yellow sheet now covered a mound in the dirt. He pulled it back a bit, stared at Peter Luck's face, then covered it up again.

"That's the governor's son," he announced, as if a gaggle of reporters were hanging around. "What happened here?"

"He came out of the woods and started shooting," Connor explained, figuring the fewer words he spoke, the better. All he could think about was Danielle, and what was going on in the back of that ambulance as it raced against time to get to the hospital in Charleston.

That's when the first deputy on the scene whispered something in the sheriff's ear. The county's top cop apparently didn't like what he'd heard, because he spun on his heels without saying a word and marched back to his car. In the glare of the headlights Connor saw him bark something into his radio, but he was too far away to hear what was being said.

A lot of confusion followed. Peter Luck was dead, Danielle was on her way to the hospital, and the sheriff intended to get to the bottom of what had just gone down. Still, the county's top cop wanted to avoid any rush to judgment as had happened in the Ruby Rollins case, so he took his time until the SLED investigators arrived and started doing their thing. Curious revelers began to drift out of The Nest to see what all the commotion was about, the presence of so many cop cars causing an uneasy stir. Time crawled, and with each passing minute Connor felt every beat of his heart as he sent out a silent plea of hope for the woman he loved. The woman who had rescued his heart from all the scars of the past.

After what seemed like a century, but may have only been twenty minutes, he felt his phone vibrate. *Caitlin again.* He was hesitant to answer, afraid to know why she was calling, and instantly sensed the worst. She always seemed to know everything, and that wasn't always good. Still, he hit the icon an answered.

"Tat Man from Katmandu," she said, her mousy voice squeaking in his ear.

"Please…not now," he told her in a terse voice.

"Sorry…my bad. I just thought you'd want to know."

"Know what?" he demanded, a sudden fear gripping his heart.

"Details are sketchy, HIPPA laws being what they are," she said. "But word is, she made it to the hospital and they're prepping a room for surgery."

"Surgery for what?"

They refuse to say, and not even Mr. James has that kind of pull. All I know is she's critical but stable."

"I need to see her—"

"I know. Mr. James called the governor, who sent a car. It should be there any second."

Right on cue, a very long and very black car came careening around the bend. It was the same stretch limo the governor had ridden in that very first evening in front of the church. *The night all this had begun.* It lurched to a stop just inches from a second ambulance that was waiting to transport Peter Luck's body to the morgue. Half a second later the front door flew open and Deputy Stroble jumped out.

"Get in," he yelled to Connor.

"This asshole's not going anywhere—" the sheriff barked at the deputy. "No one's going anywhere until we figure out what the fuck happened here."

"Check your phone," the deputy said.

The sheriff looked ready to rip this impudent state cop a new one, said, "Who the fuck do you think you are?"

"The governor just sent you a text," Stroble told him. Then to Connor he said, "Get in the car."

The sheriff's lips moved as he read the message that had just arrived on his cell. "That could be from anyone," he snarled when he was finished.

"Go ahead and call him—you have his number. Meanwhile, we're out of here."

"Where we going?" Connor asked, his heart thumping with adrenaline.

"Hospital," Stroble said. "Orders from the big guy."

"I can't leave my dog," Connor told him. Clooney had remained quiet throughout all the chaos, but now he had an anxious look of abandonment in his eyes.

"He can ride in back," the deputy said, opening the rear door for him.

"How fast can this thing go?" Connor asked.

"No one's outrun me yet," Stroble said. "Which means you'd better buckle up tight. When your girl wakes up you want to be the first person she sets her eyes on."

# About the Author

Reed Bunzel is a mystery writer, biographer, "media anthropologist," and president of Bunzel Creative Services, LLC.

The former President/CEO of an online music company (TheRadio.com), Bunzel also served as Executive V.P. of Al Bell Presents LLC. Previously, he was editor-in-chief for United News and Media's San Francisco publishing operations; earlier in his career he was editor-in-chief of Streamline Publishing's *Radio Ink* and *Streaming* magazines, as well as an editor at Radio & Records and Broadcasting magazine. Additionally, he served in an executive capacity at both the National Association of Broadcasters and the Radio Advertising Bureau.

A graduate of Bowdoin College in Brunswick, Maine, Bunzel holds a Bachelor of Science degree in Anthropology, *cum laude*. A native of the San Francisco Bay Area, he currently resides with his wife Diana in Charleston, South Carolina.